8-10-1598

8-19-1598

8-31-1598

10-2-1598

10-6-1598

3-24-1600

4-24-1600

3-14-1600

12-16-1598

11-2-1598

1-22-1599

1-31-1599

D0855753

Outgoing fleet
Faith
Fidelity
The Gospel
Hope
Love

PARS JAPONICA

Also by William de Lange

A History of Japanese Journalism (1998)

Iaidō (2002)

A Dictionary of Japanese Idioms (2005)

PARS JAPONICA

THE FIRST DUTCH EXPEDITION
TO REACH THE SHORES OF JAPAN

OR

How a Seafaring Raid on the Coast of South
America Met with Disaster and How, Against
All Odds, One Ship Was Eventually Brought
to the Shores of Japan by the English Pilot
Will Adams, the Hero of *Shōgun*

WILLIAM DE LANGE

FLOATING WORLD EDITIONS

First published in 2006 by
Floating World Editions
26 Jack Corner Road,
Warren, CT 06777
www.floatingworldeditions.com

Floating World Editions publishes books that contribute to a
deeper understanding of Asian cultures. Editorial supervision: Ray Furse.
Charts: John de Lange. Book and cover design: William de Lange.
Proofreading: Mike Ashby. Production supervision: Bill Rose.
Printing and binding: Oceanic Graphics Printing, Inc.
The typefaces used are BernhardMod BT and Old English Text.

Front and back endpapers show the routes of the
Dutch fleet and its ships imposed on sea charts drawn by
Cornelis Doetszoon and carried aboard the *Love*:
Outgoing fleet ———— *Faith* ·····-·· *Fidelity* —·—
The Gospel ----- *Hope* ——— *Love* ··········

Library of Congress Cataloging-in-Publication Data

De Lange, William.
Pars Japonica : the first Dutch expedition to reach Japan or how a seafaring
raid on the coast of South America met with disaster and how, against all odds,
one ship was eventually brought to the shores of Japan by the English pilot
Will Adams, the hero of Shogun / William de Lange.
p. cm.
Includes bibliographical references and index.
ISBN 1-891640-23-2
1. Japan—Relations—Netherlands. 2. Netherlands—Relations—Japan. I. Title.
DS849.N4D45 2006
952'.024—dc22   2006041742

Printed in China

For Teruo and Taeko Takayanagi

CONTENTS

ILLUSTRATIONS

CHARTS

And now abideth faith, hope, love,
these three; but the greatest of these is love.

—— I Corinthians 13:13

PREFACE

When at the first I took my pen in hand,
Thus for to write, I did not understand
That I at all should make a little book
In such a mode; nay, I had undertook
To make another, which when almost done,
Before I was aware, I this begun.

So wrote John Bunyan toward the middle of the seventeenth century. In more than one way it seems apt to start this book and its chapters with lines from his timeless work, *The Pilgrim's Progress*.

Life imitates art. And even though this story's protagonists set out on their fateful journey centuries before that phrase was ever coined and decades even before Bunyan was to put pen to paper, yet there is an uncanny similarity between their vicissitudes and those of Bunyan's hero. Like his pilgrim, Christian, the men that populate the following pages leave the comfort of home behind to seek their Celestial City. And though that city was a far cry from that envisaged by Bunyan, it was with the selfsame singular, almost religious devotion that they pursued their worldly goals. Thus the terrible hardships endured amongst the desolate shores and shallows of the Strait of Magellan are grimly in keeping with those that Christian is made to endure in the Valley of the Shadow of Death, and the depth of despair as winter descended must have been as acute as the "darkness and horror" that fell on Christian when he feared that he would not "see the land that flows with milk and honey."

The belief that life, however insignificant, is a journey with a divinely ordained purpose—a pilgrimage in search of meaning—not only inspired Bunyan to write his book; it was deeply held by most of his contemporaries. Time and time again it is demonstrated in the words and deeds of the men who shaped this particular episode in Dutch maritime history. Yet it is expressed perhaps most forcefully in the words of this story's hero, the English pilot William Adams, when, after almost twelve years of enforced exile following his arrival in Japan, he has finally found an opportunity to write home to his "unknown friends and countrymen." Though desperate that they should learn about his fate, the long-lost pilot draws undiminished hope from his deep-seated and unshaken conviction "that compassion and mercy is so, that my friends and kindred shall have news, that I do as yet live in this vale of my sorrowfull pilgrimage."

INTRODUCTION

This book tells the story of a most remarkable expedition in the history of Dutch overseas exploration. In view of what it set out to achieve, however, it is remarkable for all the wrong reasons. For the expedition under the command of Jacques Mahu and Simon de Cordes that set sail from Rotterdam on June 27, 1598, was by almost all accounts a resounding failure. Of the five ships that sailed under the talismanic names of *Ghelooue* (*Faith*), *Trouwe* (*Fidelity*), *Blijde Bootschap* (*The Gospel*), *Hoope* (*Hope*), and *Liefde* (*Love*), only the first ever entered a Dutch port again.

For one, the expedition did not live up to the high expectations of those who had invested time and money in it. A total capital of close to fl. 500,000 had been registered under the names of Johan van der Veken and Pieter van der Haegen, the shipowners and the principal shareholders in the venture. Only a fraction of that money was ever recovered. Even though the ships had been insured (at a premium of 30 percent), the costly equipment and cargo they had carried had not, and only with the help of the authorities, who exonerated him from liability, did the main investor, Van der Veken, escape bankruptcy. None of the cargo ever made it to any market; most of it was lost with the four unfortunate ships that did not return. The cargo of the one ship that did return (trunks filled with trinkets for bartering and some woolen cloth) was of little value in Holland and did not go very far to satisfy the creditors.

Neither in scientific terms did the expedition attain any major success. Inevitably, the main contribution it did make lay in the field of geographic exploration, in particular concerning the Strait of Magellan. During the sixteenth century Spanish navigators had collected a considerable amount of information about the region in the form of their *deroteros* (nautical descriptions), but given the relationship between the Netherlands and Spain, not much of this information was available to the Dutch. The limited data on the strait that was in Dutch possession—some poorly graduated English charts—was therefore considerably complemented by the work of Jan Outgherszoon, the chief pilot on the *Ghelooue*, who had been instructed by De Cordes to redraw the coastlines of the strait. Originally trained as a carpenter, Outgherszoon lacked the proper skills and his drawings are somewhat crude, but his findings were valuable enough to be published on his return in 1600. Titled the *New Complete Description of the Treacherous Strate Magellani*, the work charts the geographical characteristics of the strait in written, rather general descriptions. The text is interspersed with sketches of coastal profiles and nautical charts of sections of the passage in which are recorded various data such as soundings, distances, and the magnetic north. In 1606, Outgherszoon's sketches were used for a chart of the strait that appeared in the first Amsterdam edition of an atlas by the Flemish cartographer Gerhardus Mercator. Though the name of the author is not given, the chart clearly draws on Outgherszoon's sketches and descriptions, and was the first detailed chart of the strait to appear in print in the Netherlands. A modest contribution to botanical science was made by Outgherszoon's captain, Sebald de Weert, who brought back plant specimens from coastal Guinea and the strait. They were donated to the collection of the famous Leiden botanist Carolus Clusius, who incorporated them in his seminal work *Exoticorum Libri Decem*, published in 1605. Nevertheless, both Outgherszoon's and De Weert's contributions remained marginal and, due to the *Ghelooue*'s premature return, limited in scope, while much of the data gathered by the rest of the expedition was lost with the less fortunate ships.[1]

Nor did the survivors' account of their indisputable hardships establish itself in the Dutch popular imagination as readily as other disaster epics such as, for instance, the *Memorable Account of the*

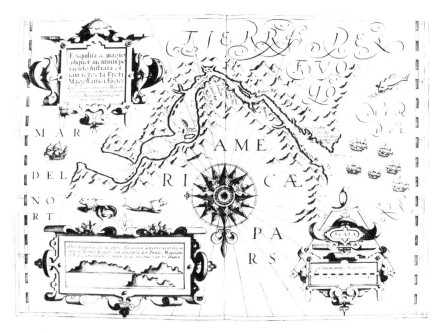

Outgherszoon's topsy-turvy representation of the Strait of Magellan as used in the 1606 edition of Mercator's atlas. The cartouche in the bottom-left corner gives the coastal profile of the Sebald Islands, encountered by the *Ghelooue* on her return voyage.

Eight-year and Very Adventurous Voyage of Willem Ysbrantsz. Bontekoe from Hoorn, to East India, Containing Many Marvellous and Dangerous Matters Encountered on the Said Journey, which upon its publication in 1646, appeared in a dozen pirated copies throughout the Netherlands and, by the end of the seventeenth century, had been reprinted some seventy times. Even though the *Exhaustive Account of That Encountered by the Five Ships through the Strait of Magellan* was published soon after the events it relates and was hardly less adventurous, it did not enjoy anywhere near the same popularity as Bontekoe's account and was reprinted only a number of times. There are several reasons why this should be so. Whilst unmistakably in the moral vein of its genre, the *Exhaustive Account* is written in the third person rather than the more direct first person narrative that characterizes the more popular works.

Though the original account is that of Barent Potgieter, the ship's surgeon on the *Ghelooue*, who kept a journal throughout her voyage and illustrated its main events in a number of fairly accomplished drawings, the published work was written by Zacharias Heyns, a linguist from Amsterdam who had made a name for himself by translating into lofty Renaissance prose the work of his much admired hero, the French Huguenot poet Guillaume de Salluste du Bartas. Consequently, the *Exhaustive Account* lacks the vivid descriptions and emotional involvement of works in the uncensored words of those who had lived their ordeals.[2] More to the point, perhaps, Potgieter's story failed to fit the mold in which the majority of the Dutch disaster epics of his time were cast. This required the protagonists to overcome their tribulations and recognize in their delivery the very hand of God. Regrettably, in this endeavor, most of the protagonists simply failed to survive. Of the 491 men who sailed on the five ships, 405 perished, more often than not in the most wretched of circumstances; whilst for the few who eventually did reach a destination of sorts, deliverance not so much depended on divine intervention but rather on the more secular offices of an English pilot.

By all accounts then, the first Dutch expedition through the Strait of Magellan under the command of Jacques Mahu and Simon de Cordes would still be little to write home about—had it not been for that English pilot. For it was Pilot-Major William Adams, who, not only safely delivered the *Liefde* and her twenty-five remaining crew to Japanese shores, but also obtained from the Japanese ruler a license for the Dutch to trade with his country, and in doing so, helped lay the foundation for a mutually profitable relationship that would last for centuries. And thus, in spite of all its immediate economic, scientific, and stylistic shortcomings, the account of one of the most disastrous expeditions in Dutch maritime history does, with the benefit of hindsight, thankfully meet some sense of reward—if not a purely Dutch one.

PART I

DREAMS & ASPIRATIONS

The Iland of Japan is many Ilands one by the other, and are seperated and devided only by certaine small Créekes and rivers, it is a great land, although as yet the size thereof is not knowne, because as yet it is not wholly discovered and knowne, nor by the Portingalles communicated. It beginneth at 30 degrées, and runneth till you come to 38. It lyeth East from the main land of China by about 80 miles, and from Maccau by the waye that the Portingalles travaile n.e. warde, is about 300 miles, and the Haven where commonly the Portingals use to traffique, is called Nangasache. They have like-wise other places where they traffique and have their intercourse. It is a cold land, and of much raine, snow and ice too. It hath some corne land, but their common sustenance and food is ryce. In some places the land is hillie and unfruitfull. They eate no flesh but the flesh of wild beasts and such as is hunted, wherewith they nourish themselves wonderfully well, although there are Oxen, Cowes, Shéepe, and such like Cattel good store, yet they use them to other thinges and labours; because it is tame flesh, which they cannot brooke, and refuse it as we do horse flesh; they do likewise refuse to eate Milke, as we do blood; saying that it is blood of beast, although it is white. They have much Fish, whereof they are very desirous, as also all kindes of fruites, as in China. Their houses are commonly of wood covered with wood or straw; they are fine and artfully wrought, specially the rich mens houses, they have their Chambers adorned with handsome Mattes, which is their greatest treasure. The Japens are not so curious nor so cleanly as the Chinos, but are contente with a meane, yet for the most part they goe very well apparelled in Silke, almost like the Chinos. The countrie hath some mines of silver, which from thence is by the Portingals yearely brought unto China in exchange for Silke and other Chinese wares that the Japeans have néede of.

—Jan Huyghen van Linschoten, *Itinerario*, 1596

The Netherlands at the turn of the sixteenth century was still a country in the very infancy of nationhood. Yet already this tiny collection of provinces straddling the North Sea, resisting Spanish rule so tenaciously, held within its grasp all the ingredients for the fantastic successes of the Golden Century that was to follow. Nevertheless, the road to nationhood was long and painful, and it was to take until 1648 before the Dutch Republic was finally recognized by those whose harsh rule had led to its conception.

Ever since 1555, when governance of the Netherlands was passed from Charles V to his son, Philip II, Dutch popular discontent with the Spanish sovereign had grown. The qualities that had been esteemed in the father, who spoke the Dutch language and who, though foreign, was deemed to be an understanding ruler, were not recognized in the son, who did not speak the language, let alone seem to understand Dutch ways. Thus the climate was set for hitherto subdued resentments over tax levies and new efforts toward centralized control to surface. Rational though the voiced objections were, they were always fired by a strong national sentiment and a need for the religious and political structures that would be in keeping with their traditions. It was almost inevitable, then, that sooner or later passive acceptance of a rule that had seemed benign would give way to active resistance against one that seemed intrusive.

Within two years of Philip's succession, the same nobles who had dutifully served the father censured the son's war with France on the grounds that it was not waged with Dutch interests in mind. When peace came, the States General, the body that had represented the shared interests of the Dutch provinces since the middle of the fifteenth century, insisted that the notorious Spanish garrisons be withdrawn from Dutch soil. This was done, but within a decade Spanish troops were marching back into the lowlands, this time under the command of the able yet ruthless Duke of Alva. His task it was to punish the unruly subjects after they had vented their hatred of religious persecution in an iconoclastic rage that had swept throughout the Netherlands. Alva went about his task with such grim determination that within weeks the court installed for the purpose became known as the Blood Council. Terror and intimidation were the instruments by which the Iron Duke sought to bring the recalcitrant subjects back into the Iberian fold. Wherever Spanish troops descended to restore order, torture, rape, and murder were in habitual attendance. Many of the noblemen who had earlier petitioned the king of Spain to abolish the Inquisition now came to their end on the scaffolds erected in the town centers. The remainder submitted. Some made it into exile. And it was under one of them, William of Nassau, that the first, feeble attempts were made to expel the duke and his evil forces.

Relying on the eagerness of the Dutch populace to throw off the Spanish yoke, William crossed the Maas on October 6, 1568, to confront his enemy. The shrewd duke, confident that the systematically intimidated townspeople dare not stir, avoided direct engagement and simply looked on from afar as the vast but unruly army of largely German mercenaries blundered through the Dutch landscape. Deeply dejected by the reluctance of his fellow countrymen to rise to the occasion, the hapless prince led his army on to France where, hopelessly short of funds, he saw himself forced to escape by stealth, back to the safety of his ancestral home at Dillenburg. His countrymen were rewarded for their inaction with the introduction of the Tenth Penny, requiring them to remit 10 percent of the proceeds of every transaction to their oppressors.

The sensational capture of the port of Den Briel by the Sea Beggars (Dutch pirates) in the name of the Prince of Orange, on April 1, 1572, followed by the revolt of Flushing, Enkhuizen, and most of the other towns in the provinces of

Holland and Zeeland, changed the fortunes of the to all intents and purposes chosen liberator. Spanish troops duly marched back into Holland to lay siege of Haarlem. On their way they callously sacked Naarden; except for a handful of citizens who had escaped across the snow at night, every man, woman, and child in the town was killed. Haarlem, too, eventually fell, but it was clear that the tide had turned in William's favor when first Alkmaar and then Leiden withstood the siege, relieved over flooded fields by the indispensable Sea Beggars. Alva in the meantime had returned home, and the feeble attempts at a negotiated truce by his successor, Don Luis de Requesens, only emphasized the clear unity of interests that now existed between the rebellious northern and submissive southern provinces. When he died in 1576, a number of the former hastily convened a sitting of the States General, inviting the latter to send their deputies so that a rapprochement might be effected in time before the new governor would arrive. Thus the first step toward a unified front against Spain was taken.

Yet it was the notorious Spanish troops that galvanized the process; chronically underpaid, they had mutinied repeatedly during the long campaigns against troops retreating behind water and towns sustained over yet more water. After the siege of Zierikzee had drawn on for nine months and with their pay twenty-two months in arrears they packed up on the very day the town fell and set off toward Brabant, where they made Aalst their base amidst general mayhem. When they subsequently fell on Antwerp to submit its citizens to yet more unspeakable atrocities for days on end, the northern and southern provinces took the second step and ratified the Pacification of Atrecht. The largely independent town of Amsterdam followed on May 26, 1578, when a band of Protestants took possession of the city hall, thus bringing about the town's so-called Alteration. Wary of the Protestant spirit of the revolt, the Catholic southern provinces of Brabant and Flanders cowered and sued for peace with Spain. Thus it was left to the northern provinces to take the final step toward independence. This was done on January 23, 1579, when, at the Union of Utrecht, Holland, Zeeland, Utrecht, Friesland, Groningen, Gelderland, and Overijssel signed a pact and created the Republic of the United Netherlands.

The United Netherlands was to suffer many a blow and setback before it was to achieve true independence, and nothing hit the Dutch and their cause harder than the assassination, on July 10, 1584, of their beloved prince at the hands of a Catholic fanatic. William of Nassau, the Prince of Orange, had personified the revolt. He had been a reluctant rebel, and had alienated the Calvinist clergy by refusing to abandon the ideal of true religious freedom. Yet his last words, uttered as he lay dying on the steps of the Prinsenhof in Delft, reaffirmed beyond doubt where his allegiance lay: *"Mon Dieu, Mon Dieu, ayez pitié de moy et de ce pauvre peuple."*

Without a leader to encourage and guide them in their struggle, the Dutch people faced one of their darkest moments yet. In an attempt to stave off a crisis, the powerful States of Holland hurriedly instated a Council of State to pursue the war with Spain and lead the army and navy. Unable to bear the heavy burden of leadership, within a year, the council saw itself forced to turn to France and offer the French king sovereignty over the Netherlands. Henri III, tolerant of Protestants but fearful of militant French Catholics, declined. Meanwhile the new Spanish governor, Alexander Farnese Parma, had beleaguered Antwerp. In April 1585, after a long and cruel winter, the town fell. This time the town was spared retribution, but nevertheless some 38,000 of its citizens left for the north. As a last recourse the Dutch turned their gaze across the North Sea, to England. This time help was at hand, and that autumn both countries ratified the

Treaty of Nonsuch, the first treaty between the Dutch Republic and another European nation. The next year Robert Dudley, the Earl of Leicester, was installed as head of the Council of State under a protectorship of Queen Elizabeth I. But the Englishman's colorful personality sat uneasy with the staid Calvinist mentality of the Dutch oligarchy, in particular the leading Dutch statesman Johan van Oldenbarneveldt. Many were the points of contention between the two men, but none perhaps more so than Leicester's insistence on a total embargo on trade with Spain and those countries under her control. The measure caused most indignation among the powerful provinces of Holland and Zeeland. They were the military and economic seat of Dutch resistance, and they rightly stressed that in their struggle for survival, trade, even with the enemy, was of paramount importance. In 1587, after a spell of only two years in which practically each and every of his initiatives had been frustrated, Leicester took his leave with a lengthy letter to the States General, who he deemed "so careless of her Majesty, and of such as love them."

Now the United Netherlands had to go it alone. And it did so in a most miraculous fashion. Under the military command of William's son, Prince Maurits of Nassau, and guided by Oldenbarneveldt's steady statesmanship, a small and beleaguered republic rose to become one of Europe's principal military and naval powers—a feat only achieved on the financial strength of its seaborne trade.

At the outset that trade had largely hinged on the traffic between the Baltic countries and France, Portugal, and Spain, but when, with the union of the Portuguese and Spanish crowns in 1580, Lisbon became Spanish territory, the Dutch merchantmen were compelled to seek their commodities farther afield. Within a decade Dutch ships had entered the Mediterranean, and only a little later the first Dutch traders landed on the South American coast. Such was the explosion of Dutch maritime activity during the last decade of the sixteenth century that already by the turn of the century they had explored most of the trade routes of the later East and West Indian Companies. By then, Dutch ships were carrying cereals from the Baltic ports of Kopenhagen and Dantzig; wood from Norway; precious metals, wine, and semitropical fruit from Italy and Spain; sugar from Brazil; tobacco from the Caribbean; and salt from Cape Verde. Most exotic of all were the spices: the cloves, nutmeg, and pepper from the Far East. Stimulated by trade overseas, industry and commerce at home began to flourish as never before. Thousands of craftsmen found employment in the burgeoning shipyards of the Zaan region near Amsterdam. In that town, as well as in Rotterdam and Middelburg, huge *trafieken* (refineries) were built to process the vast quantities of salt, sugar, and tobacco that entered their ports, while the influx of Flemish weavers helped revive the linen and wool industries around Leiden and Haarlem. An inestimably important role in Dutch economic expansion was played by the thousands of refugees from Antwerp. Dispersed across Europe's major trading towns, they wove a vast network of trade connections with Amsterdam firmly at its center. Yet the key element in all Dutch endeavors, whether they were a success or failure, was the sea. It was the sea that had given them their land; it was the sea that had helped them in their struggle for independence; and it was the sea that now gave them unlimited access to all the riches of the earth.

I

THE OUTSET

This Hill, though high, I covet to ascend,
The difficulty will not me offend,
For I perceive the way to life lies here;
Come, pluck up, heart; let's neither faint nor fear:
Better, though difficult, the right way to go,
Than wrong, though easy, where the end is woe.

Dutch maritime exploration toward the end of the sixteenth century reached its climax in the seven years between 1594 and 1602. In that short and exhilarating period some sixty-five ships sailed from Dutch ports on voyages of discovery and trade. New worlds with unknown peoples, strange cultures, and rare commodities opened themselves to the Dutch as their ships set off in the directions of the four winds. Yet in whatever direction they sailed, whether it be north to seek the mythical Strait of Ainan, south round the Cape of Good Hope, or west through the treacherous Strait of Magellan, to the late sixteenth century Dutchman it seemed that all roads must inevitably lead to one goal: the fabulous riches of the East.

Given the Iberian threat, it was only logical that the first Dutch initiative to reach the East sought to do so by way of a northern passage. But even though the organizers were in agreement on the purpose of the expedition—to reconnoiter the northern region—they were less sure of the route that it should follow, since it was not yet known whether Novaya Zemlya was part of a larger, Arctic continent. A compromise was found, and on June 5, 1594, three ships under the command of Cornelis Nay sailed north from the Texel.[1] To satisfy all parties, the ships were initially to sail in convoy along the Norwegian coast. Having passed the Lofoten, one of the ships,

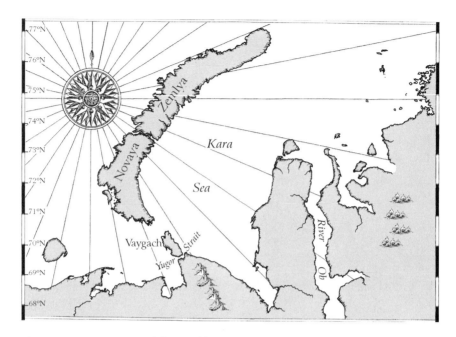

the '*t Boot*, captained by Willem Barents, was to sail north-north-east and thus find a passage between the two continents. The *De Swaen* and *Mercurius* were to try and reach the passage by way of the Yugor Strait, south of Vaygach, a small island locked between Novaya Zemlya and the West Siberian mainland. The '*t Boot* managed to penetrate as far north as a latitude of 77°, off Novaya Zemlya, but when she ran into thick ice, Barents decided to return and join the other two ships. These had meanwhile passed the Yugor Strait, advancing more than a hundred miles into the Kara Sea without encountering any ice. It was concluded that this was the best route to take, and having accomplished its mission, the expedition returned to Holland on September 16 of the same year.

Encouraged by the positive results of the first expedition, preparations were soon under way for a second, larger expedition, again under the command of Nay, but this time with the aim of reaching the East. The expedition consisted of three tall ships, the *Griffioen*, *De Hoop*, and *Windhond*, and four pinnaces of 80 tons each. These lighter vessels drew far less water than the tall ships and were ideally suited to explore the narrow waters of the strait. The fleet sailed on July 2, 1595, quickly putting the first leg of the journey behind it, but when it reached Vaygach on August 19 heavy pack-ice blocked the strait. A company of fifty-four men went ashore to try and look for open water. They found none, but in an encounter with a group of indigenous nomads, the Nenets, they learned that they had nine more weeks before the winter would set in. Over the following weeks several attempts were made to break through the ice, but all efforts proved futile. Then, on September 15, heavy pack-ice drifted into the strait, and after some vehement altercations between Nay and his chief pilot, Willem Barents, the commander decided to abandon the expedition. On October 26 of the same year in which they had set sail, the seven ships returned home.

The negative results of the second expedition did little to reduce hopes of finding the northern passage. No lives had been lost on the first two attempts and the only thing that seemed to stand in their way could be overcome with a spell of warm weather. And when, early in 1596, the States General awarded a premium of fl. 25,000 for the first expedition to successfully negotiate the Northeast Passage, plans were soon drawn up for a third attempt. As the Yugor Strait had turned out to be a bottleneck, this time course was set along the great circle, from the Lofoten, over the polar sea in a latitude of 82°N., toward the Strait of Ainan, which was believed to connect the Atlantic and Pacific oceans.

The expedition, which had now been placed under the command of Willem Barents, did not make an auspicious start. Soon after they had set sail, on May 16, 1596, the two ships were forced to turn back by strong northerly winds.[2] The second start proved more fruitful and on June 4, both ships reached a latitude of 70°N. without any incidents. Keeping a north-northeast course, the expedition made its first major discovery when, on June 8, it chanced upon a small island that, after an encounter with one of its inhabitants, was named Bear Island. On June 13, the voyage was resumed amidst increasingly dense pack-ice. Six days later land was sighted once more, this time toward the east. Barents named it Spitsbergen (Peak Mountains), assuming it to be part of Greenland. The bird-infested promontory where Barents and his men first set foot on land was aptly named Vogelzang (Birdsong). For five days they sojourned on the windswept island, after which the initial course was resumed, but before long heavy headwinds blew the ships back, this time to Foreland Sound. After lengthy and acrimonious deliberations it was decided to sail south, but when, on July 1, they once more encountered Bear Island, the growing discord between Barents and his second in command, Jan Corneliszoon Rijp, came to a head. Rijp, keen to keep to the instructions, wanted to continue heading north; Barents, who had met with the Arctic pack-ice during the first expedition, preferred the coastal route. Eventually, after another heated debate, both parties decided to go their separate ways. As it turned out, Barents proved to be right; in a latitude of 81°N., heavy pack-ice forced Rijp to relinquish his plan and when his attempt to join Barents was also thwarted, the young captain conceded defeat and returned home. Barents meanwhile had sailed eastwards, toward the meridian of Cape Kanin, where to his amazement he found wide-open water where four decades earlier Willoughby and Chancellor claimed to have found land. He continued eastwards until, on July 17, in a latitude of 74°N., he sighted the rugged features of Novaya Zemlya.

It was midsummer when Barents and his men cast anchor on the western shore of Novaya Zemlya. Yet in spite of the promise of the season, dense pack-ice rapidly crowded in upon their ship, and by July 20 she was fully wedged in by the ice. Only by increasing her ballast with heavy rocks from the shore did they manage to break through the ice and reach the peninsula's most northern cape, which they christened IJskaap. Here a small landing party went ashore to find out whether any open water could be seen toward the southeast. This proved to be the case, and with renewed energy the journey was resumed. On August 18, the cape was rounded with great difficulty, but after only four miles vast plates of ice forced them to seek shelter in one of the many fjords on the island's east coast. Over the next days conditions failed to improve, and on August 24 the drifting ice plates threatened to crush the ship. The rudder was split under the massive pressure, but the sturdily built vessel miraculously remained intact, leading her crew to spend another week in frantic efforts to cut a passage to open waters. Then, on the first day of September, massive ice shoals lifted her out of the water, and all hopes of an escape over water were irrevocably dashed. Taking with them as many victuals as possible the men abandoned ship to build a shelter of salvaged timber on the barren shore.

The men now had to spend the winter in one of the coldest regions of the world. Ironically, the little progress for which they had fought hardest had only worsened their prospects in that it left them stranded on the most inhospitable part of the island. Here, cut off from the tempering influence of the Gulf Stream and isolated by an extension of the Ural Mountains, temperatures dropped as low as -40°C. Yet after almost a year of constant privation, much of which spent in total darkness, the emaciated and scurvy-crippled men emerged from their *Behouden Huis* (*Safe House*) to embark on a voyage of twelve hundred nautical miles to safety. And finally, on September 2, 1597, having spent close to three months in two open boats with few rations and only the crudest of instruments, all but five of Barents' men reached the port of Kola (Murmansk) to be met by none other than Jan Corneliszoon Rijp. Barents himself, though he had made it through the winter, did not live to tell the tale. The strain of leadership and incessant cold had tapped his strength beyond repair. He died on the return voyage and, on June 30, 1597, was given a burial on the ice of the sea that was to bear his name.

Until 1624 the Dutch persevered in their search for a northern passage. They searched in vain; it would take up until 1879, when the Swedish explorer Otto Nordenskiöld first managed to accomplish the feat and (equally in vain) sought to claim the reward put up by the Dutch authorities almost three centuries before. In the interim the data gathered by the three Dutch missions represented the limit of scientific knowledge about the region. And whilst of little use to the spice trade, Barents' discoveries were to benefit a wholly different, and far more sinister industry. For over the following decades Spitsbergen became the backdrop to the vast try-houses where the Dutch and the English extracted the coveted trainoil from thousands upon thousands of whales.

Not the kind to bet all their stake on one card, the Dutch did not wait for Nordenskiöld to make his discovery. In the same year in which Barents first sailed north, another expedition, that of Cornelis de Houtman, set sail in the opposite direction. Two years earlier De Houtman had been sent to Lisbon with instructions to insinuate himself into the world of the local spice merchants and extract as much information as possible. A fastidious and, even by Dutch standards pathologically frugal man, De Houtman acquitted himself well. On his return to Holland, early in 1594, he presented his employers with *A Short Treatise by Cornelis de Houtman of the East-Indian Countries or the Conquests of Portugal and a Discourse on the Trade in East-India*, in which he stressed the damage that English raiders were causing to deep-sea Portuguese trade. As a direct result of De Houtman's findings, the expedition that left Holland on April 2, 1594, sailed with explicit instructions to pursue its goal by peaceful means but with sufficient arms to fend off any assailants; the fleet of four ships—the *Mauritius*, *Hollandia*, *Amsterdam*, and *Het Duyfken*—with a total capacity for cargo of 600 tons, carried well over a hundred cannon.[3]

Satisfied with his findings but aware of his questionable talents as a leader, the shipowners stopped short of giving De Houtman overall command of the expedition. On the strength of his expertise in Southeast Asian commerce, he was appointed chief merchant on the *Mauritius*. Day-to-day command of the expedition was to be exercised through the *scheeps-raad*, or ships' council, consisting of the captain and chief merchant from each ship—an organ that, under normal conditions, would only concern itself with matters of broad policy. The serious drawback of this solution became apparent already at the outset of the voyage, when De Houtman and the chief merchant of the *Hollandia*, a certain Gerrit van Beuningen, felt compelled to draw knives on each other. All semblances between the two men ended with their profession. De Houtman, an uneducated man with a rough-hewn, churlish personality, loathed the gregarious ease with which Van Beuningen was able to win the devotion of the young and impressionable midshipmen. Van Beuningen, urbane and sophisticated, but afflicted with an impulsive trait, detested De Houtman's narrow-minded miserliness. Almost from day one, the fleet sailed amidst an atmosphere of backbiting animosity and mistrust, with no absolute authority to pull the ranks together; the whole enterprise had become a veritable powder keg, requiring no more than a fuse—a fuse that was to present itself when, several months into the voyage, the captain of the *Hollandia* was felled by scurvy.

The first casualty of scurvy was claimed when the convoy passed the equator on June 4. Soon more followed. By July 18, when they had reached Martin Vaz, the island group from where the prevailing Westerlies would carry them toward the Indian Ocean, most of the men were suffering from the appalling symptoms to some degree or other. During the long haul east toward the Cape of Good Hope that followed, conditions rapidly grew worse until, on August 2, when the cape was sighted, as many as twelve men had succumbed to the disease whilst a hundred more were in a very poor state. At the cape a shore party managed to barter chisels and other steel implements against some sheep and oxen from the local Hottentots, but the meat seemed to have little effect on the sick so that the ships' council decided to sail on to Madagascar in the hope of finding fresh victuals. Progress was slow and when, on September 3, they finally reached the island, the death toll had risen to two dozen, while many of the sick were tottering on the brink of death. Sailing westwards along the coast, they intercepted a canoe with three natives with whose help safe anchorage was found in Ampalaza Bay.

Here the sick were accommodated on a small island situated in the mouth of the bay; and while they were tended to and the ships cleaned, a party was sent ashore in search of fresh fruit and other victuals. But with the exception of some confused encounters with natives, the landing party produced no results. *Het Duyfken*, which had meanwhile explored the west coast of the island, had more success. After three days sailing she had run into a large bay (St. Augustine Bay), flanked by lush green valleys with trees that carried the wholesome tamarind fruit. For many of the sick, however, these refreshments came too late. In the three weeks that had passed since their arrival in Ampalaza Bay, thirty-one of the sick had died. They were buried where they had died, on the small island, which was given the sobriquet of Hollands Kerkhof (Holland Cemetery). Amongst the dead was also Jan van Quadijk, the captain of the *Hollandia*—and it was with his death that trouble really began.

Given the seriously weakened state of the men, the ships' council proposed to postpone the appointment of a new captain until they had reached the newly found bay. Van Beuningen, who was now the *Hollandia*'s chief (and most popular) officer, blatantly ignored the council's decision; acting against Van Quadijk's last wishes, he independently appointed his fellow townsman and protégé, the chief pilot, Pieter Keyser, as captain of the *Hollandia*. The ships' council, unable to reach a unanimous decision, decided to consult the company's instructions. To De Houtman's utter dismay, these too put forward Keyser as Van Quadijk's successor, even though it turned out that the seal on the instructions had been broken by Van Beuningen. With the ships' council in two minds the fleet sailed on for the bay of St. Augustine, where a place near the beach, shaded by trees, was designated as a sick bay. Again Van Beuningen acted against common consent; he instead had the sick men from the *Hollandia* evacuated to a place farther inland, although he failed to put any men on watch. Presently, a band of hostile natives chanced upon the encampment and proceeded to molest the invalids. Alarm was only raised after some of the hapless men had managed to escape and crawl back to the other camp. Incensed with Van Beuningen's recalcitrance and his callous treatment of the sick, the ships' council had him removed from his post and transferred to the *Mauritius*. This, in turn, caused an outcry amongst the merchant's many followers on the *Hollandia*. To avert a mutiny, the ships' council had the men distributed over the remaining ships, while De Houtman took command of the *Hollandia* to restore order. Yet the ships' council stopped short of restricting Van Beuningen in his movements and the latter was bent on revenge.

Van Beuningen's chance came on Christmas day. A week earlier the fleet had left its anchorage in the bay of St. Augustine to sail for the East Indian archipelago. The ships were now making good headway; they had rounded the southern end of the island, and to celebrate the occasion, a banquet was held on *Het Duyfken*. It was toward the end of the day, when boats were launched to carry the officers from the four ships to the pinnace, that Van Beuningen spotted De Houtman's boat on its return leg and quickly hauled it over to let himself be carried back to the *Hollandia*, where the

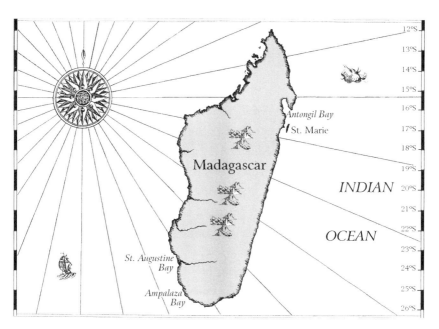

remainder of his followers and De Houtman's unpopularity ensured him of a warm welcome. Painfully aware of his unpopularity amongst the crew of the *Hollandia* and fearful of a mutiny, De Houtman saw no other way out than to resign himself to his old quarters on the *Mauritius*. His position on the ships' council was further undermined when Van Beuningen, back in control on the *Hollandia*, discovered De Houtman's journal, in which the latter fulminated in no uncertain terms against the spineless vacillation of his fellow officers. As if to confirm De Houtman in his verdict, the council issued a general pardon, although, on his insistence, it did refrain from extending it to Van Beuningen.

Again, however, the worsening physical condition of the men had to take precedence over the moral infirmity of their leaders. The success of finding food on the western shores of Madagascar had been limited, and within weeks of their departure scurvy was again crippling the already weakened limbs of the sailors. To make things worse, they had now reached a time of year in which fierce hurricanes swept over the Indian Ocean. It was clear that to continue the voyage would be the death sentence for many a man, and it was decided to set course for St. Marie, a small island in the mouth of the Antongil River on the northwest coast of Madagascar, in the hope of finding the food that would reinvigorate the men. It was a well-advised decision, for when the expedition reached the bay, it was met by natives in canoes carrying the victuals it so desperately needed: lemons and limes, as well as rice, fish, and poultry.[4]

Shortly after their arrival, De Houtman and the other members of the ships' council were invited ashore, where the chiefs led them to their village, situated on the banks of the Antongil River. Built on stilts, their dwellings were enclosed within a palisade of sharpened poles, which led the visitors to call it Spakenburgh. Here De Houtman and his hosts passed the night, feasting on a rich local brew from rice and honey. Over the next days water supplies were replenished while the sick were greatly helped by the "very healthy fruits, by which the scurvy of the fleet has wholly vanished."

Having enjoyed their warm welcome the Dutch set about to get in store sufficient victuals for the long journey ahead, and at the going rates (four beads for a pound of rice) the holds were filling up fast. After almost a year at sea the ships had to be caulked anew, while much of the rigging, too, was in bad repair. Preparations progressed with such speed that within only three weeks all ships were ready to sail. But on February 3, on the eve of their planned departure, another vicious storm hit the island, causing the *Amsterdam* and the *Hollandia* to collide and lose their boats. The next day, after a long search, the boats were found along the beach, wholly wrecked but not by the waves. The natives had dismantled the vessels in order to extract, down to every nail, the metal reinforcements that had held them together. A vexed ships' council now demanded to be compensated with two of the small barges by which the natives ferried their dignitaries about, but when some men were sent ashore to claim the indemnity, they were met upon landing with a hail of stones. In revenge the Dutch raided the village shortly before they departed and left it burning. The sad contrast between their reception and the manner of their departure was not lost on midshipman Jeronimus Maryen, who ruefully observed that "such was the gratitude to the people who had nourished us."

The passage across the Indian Ocean, where the combined tug of the South Equatorial Current and the Southeast Trades reduced progress to a minimum, was long and uneventful. With little to distract them from the monotony of their daily chores, the recovered men were soon driven to boredom and discipline was in constant danger of being undermined by trouble—such as on *Het Duyfken*, where boatswain Jacob Pruijs drew a knife on his captain. Found guilty of insubordination he was executed by a firing squad. This was two days before land was sighted, but already the first seagulls and jetsam heralded landfall. As they were sailing into the unknown waters of the East Indian archipelago, Pruijs' execution conveniently served to tighten discipline amongst a crew that grew more excited with the prospect of foreign ports and what they entailed. The boatswain's execution also enabled the ships' council to address another and far more serious problem—that of Van Beuningen's unlawful resumption of command on the *Hollandia*. The council had not forgotten the commotion Van Beuningen's transfer had caused only a few months earlier, and by exercising its authority now, it was able to test the prevailing mood among the crew. The execution had the envisioned effect, and on June 9, the council felt emboldened enough to move against Van Beuningen. He was summoned aboard the *Mauritius* and accused by De Houtman of inciting her crew to mutiny so as to have them sail the vessel to Malindi. Van Beuningen's protestations to the contrary carried little weight with the council, which on the following day decreed that he "be imprisoned on the *Mauritius* in such quarters as deemed fit by the ships' council, without having converse with any man on this or any other ship outside the wish of the council."

With discipline restored the expedition reached its destination on June 23, 1596. This was the bustling port of Bantam on Java's west end. Ruled since the early sixteenth century by a Muslim merchant

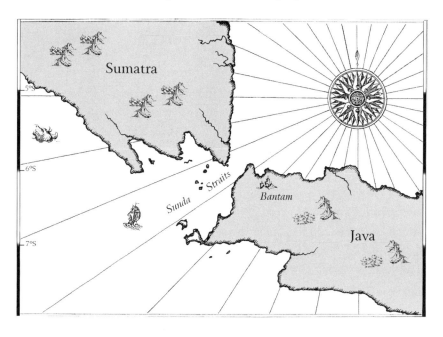

oligarchy and strategically positioned at the mouth of the Sunda Strait, the city-state of Bantam had become a focal point of East and Southeast Asian commerce. From here Chinese and Japanese junks set sail for the Chinese provinces of Fujian, Guandong, and Zhejiang, and to Cambodia, Vietnam, Luzon, the Philippines, and Japan; from here Indian *baghlas* sailed to Gujarat, Coromandel, and Bengal; and it was from here too that the Portuguese carracks carried pepper, cinnamon, clove, nutmeg, and mace to Goa, Malacca, and Macao. On the *pasar*, the bustling local markets that enlivened Bantam's outskirts, Chinese, Japanese, Indians, Turks, Arabs, Gujaratis, and Portuguese thronged to ply their trade. On display was all the produce of the Far East: silk, porcelain, and gold from China; precious stones and medicine from Persia; linen and cotton from India; silver, swords, fans, and other paraphernalia from Japan; and slaves and elephants from Burma. Yet the main commodities on offer on the *pasar* were the harvests from the plantations farther inland, and from Sumatra and the Moluccas. Vast quantities of spices exchanged hands for equally vast sums of the local currency, the punctured Chinese *caixa*, strung together for convenience in lots of hundreds or thousands. Some two thousand tons of pepper alone were annually shipped from Bantam. And it was in this lucrative trade that the Dutch newcomers sought to gain a foothold amongst jealous competitors.

To the delight of the Dutch merchants, initial contacts with the local authorities were more than promising. One day after the fleet had arrived in the Bay of Bantam, it was visited by the port's harbormaster with gifts of fresh fruit, poultry, and goats. He informed the Hollanders that they had chosen a good year to visit Bantam, as the year's pepper crop was expected to double the normal harvest and prices would be low. On June 29, his visit was followed by that of Hi Patih, guardian of the infant prince and *de facto* ruler of Bantam. The regent, who was received with much ceremony and presented with several gifts, assured the Dutch that they would have the first choice when the harvest came in and invited De Houtman to visit him at his residency.

21

De Houtman knew how to impress his host. On June 1, he had the longboat launched and set out in the company of nine midshipmen and twelve sailors, all dressed in colorful uniforms. Ashore, he had them lined up in two columns and, to the tune of a trumpet to "enliven the occasion," set off toward the regent's court, where he introduced himself by the Portuguese title of *capitão-mór*. Having been ushered in, he presented the regent with a letter from the Dutch prince, which was read out in both Portuguese and Arabic. Not a man to cut corners, De Houtman had already drafted a pact under which both countries would commit themselves to mutual trade, promising to form a united front against their common foes. The pomp and circumstance seemed to have the envisioned effect, for within two days De Houtman became the proud owner of a mutually ratified treaty of "peace and confederation."

Yet where trade relations were fostered by De Houtman's bent for ostentation, trade itself was crippled by his inability to compromise. The main stumbling block for the merchant was the local exchange rate for the Spanish bullion they had brought with them to trade. On the *pasar* of Bantam the exchange rate for the Spanish *real* lay at twelve thousand *caixa*, but De Houtman, who knew that the rate was far from fixed, refused to buy any spices unless he was offered fifteen thousand *caixa*. The regent, however, refused to give in to De Houtman's demands, although he did grant the Dutchman a concession to establish a factory in Bantam's Chinese quarters. But the factory, too, became a bone of contention. To blame were the local merchants, who bought great quantities of merchandise on credit, to be payed off in kind with the first harvest. Being the man he was, De Houtman took issue with the regent over the matter, and weeks went by as both parties persisted in their exchange of mutual recriminations, while not one pepper corn changed hands. Then, in a stroke of particular diplomatic genius, De Houtman accused the regent of breach of contract. The latter, who had thus far suffered his guest's supercilious tantrums with stoic resignation, sent De Houtman on his way by reiterating his refusal to interfere in either commercial or monetary issues. But when, five days later, he was subjected to yet another round of verbal abuse by the Dutchman (who had now noticed how Portuguese junks were already loading spices) his patience ran out and he imposed a ban on all sales to the Dutch.

Matters now began to escalate out of control in rapid succession. Challenged by the regent's decree, the Dutch began to demonstratively patrol the harbor with their pinnace. This caused great consternation amongst the population on the local junks, who expected the worst and cut their anchor ropes to let their vessels drift ashore. While all this was taking place, De Houtman had a missive delivered to the regent's court, demanding immediate payment of outstanding accounts. On August 28 he visited the regent in person and threatened to impound the Portuguese junks by force if payments were not made by the end of the next day. Then he set off toward the Dutch factory, but no sooner had he arrived than the factory was occupied by the regent's men and he and his men were held hostage. An envoy dispatched to the fleet by the regent to negotiate a settlement was received with similar hospitality. Then the regent threatened to kill all the hostages unless his man was released forthwith. A flurry of letters ensued between the factory and the fleet in which a reticent De Houtman pleaded with the ships' council to release their prisoner lest he and the others meet an untimely end. When the man was set free, the regent released De Houtman's men but kept the merchant in custody to enforce his offer for a resumption of normal relations. The offer was eagerly endorsed by De Houtman himself, but turned down by the ships' council, which to his great distress bluntly repeated his own original ultimatum. This, however, failed to achieve the desired effect and, on September 5, the Dutch fleet sailed up the bay, impounded the Portuguese junks, and opened fire on Bantam's outskirts. Two days later they again took the town under fire, killing fourteen of its citizens. More casualties followed when *Het Duyfken* tried to intercept a hastily departing Portuguese junk. With a deeper draught than the junk, she got lodged on a coral reef, and by the time her crew had got her afloat again she was besieged by a dozen *kora-kora*, the indigenous rowing vessels. Faced with the threat of being boarded, the captain of *Het Duyfken* ordered his men to fire. The broadside that followed wreaked terrible havoc amongst the assailants; a large number of the fragile vessels was sunk while near to a hundred of the regent's men were lost in the melee.

In spite of his losses at the hands of his guests the regent had not lifted a finger against his prisoner. He was even willing to negotiate a truce, although he put a large price on De Houtman's head. This brought out the best in the merchant, who, having spent a week in terror, now began to beat the regent down over his own ransom. This haggling took up so much time that the fleet, which was running low on drinking water, was forced to sail to Sumatra to replenish supplies. When they returned on October 2, they learned to their amazement that De Houtman had made considerable headway in his negotiations with the regent. Eventually, on October 13, a settlement was reached under which De Houtman was released and the Dutch were able to purchase their prized pepper for the fixed exchange rate of fifteen thousand *caixa* a *real*. Two thousand of those *real*, however, could not be spent on pepper; they had to be used to pay off De Houtman's ransom.

De Houtman's venture was far from a commercial success. The sale of the Eastern commodities following the return of the fleet, on August 14, 1597, only served to recoup fl. 80,000 of the original investment of fl. 290,000. In human lives, too, the expedition had taken its toll. Of the 240 men who had sailed from the Texel three years earlier, only eighty-seven returned. But in the same way in which the rich luster of the West's golden nugget was to attract the nineteenth century American gold digger, so did the exotic fragrance of the Eastern spice attract the sixteenth century Dutch maritime merchant; in the year following De Houtman's return, no fewer than twenty-two Dutch ships set sail from Dutch ports, all of them destined for the East Indies.[5]

II

THE CONTEXT

Let Ignorance a little while now muse
On what is said, and let him not refuse
Good councel to embrace, lest he remain
Still ignorant of what's the chiefest gain.
God saith those that no understanding have,
(Although he made them) them he will not save.

The early Dutch maritime expeditions were far from being the ill-prepared ventures their hurried departure suggested. Each of them was the culmination of an on the whole carefully executed plan (De Houtman's expedition alone had taken several years to prepare). Yet none of these expeditions would have been possible had not their organizers been able to build on the knowledge and experience acquired over the previous centuries. This was true for the material and the men, as well as the financial means with which these expeditions were realized. The ships that left the Dutch ports in such numbers during the last years of the sixteenth century were the accomplished products of a shipbuilding industry that went back for centuries. Their crews were recruited from a vast workforce that had learned the ropes on the Baltic trade or on one of the three thousand *haringbuizen* (fishing vessels) that plied the North Sea's fishing grounds. Their owners drew on the capital resources accumulated in the fisheries, the Baltic trade, and the even older river trades. The *wilde vaerten* (wild voyages), then, as they were commonly but unaptly called, were a natural expansion of an industry that had been established when the first Dutch vessels chose open sea.

Natural though it was, the push toward the East nevertheless posed a whole new gamut of requirements. For in order to reach these new and distant destinations, the navigators required accurate instruments and maps, whilst the commercial success of the venture relied heavily on knowledge of the regions, and reliable information about their markets. When the Dutch had first turned their gaze toward the East, such knowledge was still in the proud possession of the Portuguese. So jealously did the Portuguese guard the sea routes by which they reached their Indian empire that up until the middle of the sixteenth century not one Portuguese map or book on the subject ever found its way into foreign possession. And yet, even though the Netherlands and Portugal were technically at war, given the countless Dutch sailors that sailed on Portuguese vessels, it was inevitable that knowledge of that empire and the sea routes by which it could be reached would sooner or later end up in Dutch hands.

The almost inadvertent transfer of knowledge between these two hostile nations was most vividly illustrated by the exploits of Jan Huygen van Linschoten. Born in The Hague around 1562, Van Linschoten grew up in Enkhuizen, a port on the Zuiderzee, spending much of his youth playing in and around the port's bustling harbor. From an early age Van Linschoten had been "inclined to the reading of strange things, countries and histories," and with an imagination fired by the ships that returned from far and exotic ports, the young Van Linschoten became consumed with a "desire to see strange and unknown countries." That desire was satisfied when, at the age of sixteen, he obtained permission from his Catholic father to go and join his two elder brothers, who had found employment in Spain and Portugal. Joining a fleet of some eighty merchant vessels bound for Sanlúcar de Barrameda, the young Van Linschoten sailed from the Texel in December 1579. He first stayed with his brother in Seville and, endowed with a natural talent for languages, soon made himself useful. Following the death of his brother in September 1580, he left Spain to join his brother in Lisbon, arriving just in time to witness the entry of Philip II as the new king of Portugal. Van Linschoten entered the service of a maritime merchant and remained in the Portuguese capital for two years. Driven by a "natural curiosity and interest in things strange," he began to make notes and sketches of anything he "deemed peculiar" or anything that "differed from our national character, customs and habits." His real chance to travel came in 1583, when, through the offices of his brother, he entered the service of a Dominican friar by the name of Dom Frey Vincente da Vonseca, who had just been appointed archbishop of Goa.

Following his arrival in Goa, and already five years abroad, Van Linschoten began to see how auspicious his decision to leave home had been. Writing to his parents, the young globe-trotter observed that "no time is worse spent as when a young man remains in his mother's kitchen, like a simpleton, and knows neither wealth nor poverty, nor what the world contains, the which oftwhile is the cause of his undoing." Now, with plenty of free time on his hands, he was in the perfect position to expand on the work he had begun in Lisbon. Whenever he accompanied the archbishop on his travels around the Indian continent, the young scribe recorded his observations. Little escaped his attention. Of each area he visited he charted rivers and mountains, described the local climate. He listed the minerals, the prominent cash crops, and animals he had seen. In his description of coasts and harbors he noted strategic aspects, such as the presence of Portuguese strongholds and the strength of their forces. He also paid attention to local trade, its products, currencies, weights, units, and values. To enliven his accounts, he added observations on politics, social customs, moral codes, language, local tales, art, dress, and folklore. What he had not seen himself or heard from others, he read in accounts by Iberian expatriates, such as the physician of the Indian viceroy, García da Orta, the poet-soldier Luis de Camões, and the Augustine monk Gonçalez de Mendoça.

Van Linschoten also made friends during his stay in Goa. His most enduring friendship was that with another Dutch adventurer, Dirck Gerritszoon Pomp, alias Dirck China. Like Van Linschoten, Pomp, too, had been raised in the port of Enkhuizen and had sailed for Lisbon as a young man to make his fortune. Eighteen years Van Linschoten's senior, by the time the two met, Pomp had already visited China and Japan. He had been the first Dutchman to do so, and the feat had earned him his byname. When Van Linschoten wrote his letter home, Pomp had again departed for the Far East, this time on the *Santa Cruz*, leaving his young friend to muse:

> I would be much inclined to go to China and Japan, which is once as far as from here to Portugal, and one is three years on the way. Had I a hundred ducats: two or three would make six or seven. This year a Dutchman, a good friend of mine, has sailed there as petty officer on a ship, who would well have wanted to see me travel with him; but to start the such with empty hands, seems folly to me: since one must be well off to start with in order to make a profit. The said petty officer has been there once before, and is well off. He is by birth from Enkhuizen and has lived in this country for [sixteen] years, and is married to a Dutch woman. His name is Dirck Gerritsz. and [he] intends to undertake this voyage once more and then go home.

Van Linschoten's disappointment at having to remain behind was somewhat ameliorated when Pomp, on his return to Goa in 1588, presented his friend with the logbooks he had kept on his voyage. Van Linschoten's wish to join Pomp on his next voyage also materialized, although it was not to the Far East. During his long absence Pomp's wife had died, and not long after his return to Goa, the forty-three-year-old sailor resolved to sail home. Meanwhile, the archbishop's death had left Van Linschoten unemployed, and when it was followed by news of the death of his second brother, he too decided to sail home. The opportunity to do so came when the *Santa Cruz* joined the annual spice fleet to Lisbon and, through the offices of his friend, Van Linschoten was enabled to work his passage home as her supercargo. Departing from Goa on November 28, 1588, the fleet safely reached the Azores on July 24 of the following year, having narrowly escaped an English squadron. Here the inquisitive Van Linschoten decided to stay. Pomp sailed on to Lisbon and arrived in Holland in the late summer of 1590.

When Van Linschoten eventually returned home on September 3, 1592, he arrived just in time to witness the publication of a new work by his fellow townsman Lucas Janszoon Waghenaer. Seven years earlier, Waghenaer had made international furor with his *Spieghel der Zeevaerdt* (Mariners Mirrour), a general seaman's guide with sailing instructions and various maps. But whilst that work had dealt only with navigation in European waters, his latest work, the *Thresoor der Zeevaerdt* (Treasory of Navigation), had significantly widened in scope to include Mediterranean navigation. It also contained a lengthy account of the voyages of Drake and Cavendish, and, to Van Linschoten's considerable surprise, a lengthy article "Of All the trade in Merchandise that occurs in India, and the adventures that are to be had in these lands: written down from the mouth of Dirck Gerritsz." Not only his friend's experiences had found their way into Waghenaer's work. Without Van Linschoten's knowledge, his father had handed part of his letter from Goa to Waghenaer, who incorporated it in his work under the title "Description of all the Merchandise, which are brought to India from divers countries and Islands, and from there on to Portugal and other countries."

Although Van Linschoten had already played with the thought of publishing his travel accounts under his own name, he felt he was still "in need of more acumen and training to satisfy the intellectual." But the people around him read them with such "extraordinary amazement, pleasure, and satisfaction" that he decided to approach the famous Amsterdam publisher Cornelis Claeszoon. The publisher, who specialized in maps, nautical treaties, and travel descriptions, instantly recognized the value of Van Linschoten's "glorious work," but also its shortcomings. There was hardly any mention of Africa's west coast and none at all of the American continent. On Claeszoon's initiative, therefore, the author approached yet another fellow townsman, the renowned scholar Bernardus Paludanus, with whose help he wrote an additional volume of eighty-one and a half folio pages, sixteen on the African west coast, the rest on the American continent. It was appended to the main work with an independent pagination and titled *Beschrijvinghe* (Descriptions). Spurred on by his publisher, Van Linschoten next set about creating a third work, in which the many sailing directions he had collected were "all faithfully compiled with the greatest accuracy and diligence" into an all-encompassing sailor's manual. This work also received its own pagination, and was appended under the title *Reysgheschrift* (Sea Directory).

For the Dutch navigator of the time the *Reysgheschrift* was by far the most important of Van Linschoten's works, for the first thirty of its sixty-seven chapters guided the sailor along the major trade routes that connect Europe and the East. They drew heavily on the works of experienced Portuguese and Spanish pilots such as Diego Afonso, Vicente Rodríguez, and Francisco Gualle. So did most of the next twelve chapters, which dealt with the voyage from Goa to Japan, although a number were lifted from Dirck Pomp's logbooks. Then there followed some chapters on topics such as sea currents, tides, regional seasons, and their accompanying weather patterns. Chapter fifty and onwards dealt with the sea routes to the New World, while the last four, unnumbered chapters gave the latitudes of important ports and their mutual distances.

So important was the *Reysgheschrift* considered to be that, even though it was written last, it was printed first; no time was spared by Claeszoon and Van Linschoten to get it ready, and in the spring of 1594, after half a year of frantic work, it was rushed to the press, just in time for De Houtman's expedition. On Claeszoon's initiative and account the *Reysgheschrift* was enhanced with a set of "neat and perfect" charts of the west and east coasts of Africa, the western and eastern regions of Asia, and part of the Americas, engraved by the brothers Arnoldus and Henricus Florentii van Langren. Finally, in the spring of 1596, all three works were compiled into one single volume of 389 folio pages, lavishly illustrated with thirty-six drawings from the author's hand, all engraved by Joannes and Baptista à Doetechum. Complementing the whole was a world map

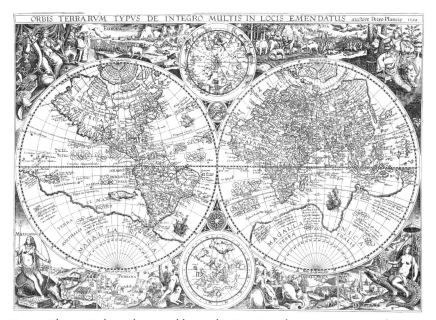

ORBIS TERRARVM TYPVS DE INTEGRO MULTIS IN LOCIS EMENDATVS auctore Petro Plancio 1594

Petrus Plancius' planisphere world map for Van Linschoten's *Itinerario*. The map clearly illustrates the scholar's varying degree of knowledge on the Northeast, Southeast, and Southwest passages at the time of publication.

from the hand of a certain "Petro Plancio," also published by Claeszoon in 1594. The *Itinerario*, as the collective work was titled, was an instant success. It was reprinted many times and translated into Latin, English, French, and German.

Where Van Linschoten showed the navigators of the early expeditions the sea routes by which to reach their destination, it was the geographer Petrus Plancius who taught them how to sail them, although by training Plancius was a theologian. In 1576, following an education in Germany and England, Plancius was ordained as a member of the Calvinist clergy at the age of twenty-four. Over the following years he preached in Mechelen, Brussels, and Leuven. He built a number of churches and gathered a large following that, in the face of fierce Catholic antagonism, was "willing to wage goods and blood for the confession of the Evangelical faith."[1]

It was only after 1585 that the first products of Plancius' extensive reading in mathematics, astrology, and geography emerged. In that year Brussels surrendered to the Spanish forces and the theologian was forced to flee to Amsterdam, and it was there that he contributed a small world map, as well as a "geographical description of paradise" and other biblical places, to a Bible issued in 1590 by Laurens Jacobszoon. Two more years it took before Plancius completed his first major cartographical work, which appeared under the title *Nova et exacta terrarum orbis tabula geographica ac hydrographica* and was dedicated to the States General.[2] In this large world map, the patent claimed "all lands, towns, places and seas are presented with their proper latitudes and longitudes," while a "short description of the characteristics of landscapes and peoples" was given in sixteen footnotes. Measuring 146 cm by 233 cm, the map drew heavily on a private collection of fourteen maps Plancius had acquired from Bartholomeo de Lasso, the star pupil of the cosmographer to the Spanish crown, Pedro Nunes. It was patented for a period of twelve years to Cornelis Claeszoon, who had it engraved in eighteen separate charts by Joannes à Doetechum and published in 1592 at a price of fl. 4.10. Plancius' atlas sold well and widely. A special edition for the southern provinces was issued by Johannes Baptista Vrient, an Antwerp publisher. Two years later it appeared in an English edition, along with "a plaine and full description" by Thomas Blundeville.

Despite their great popularity, Plancius' charts—like most other charts of the time—had serious shortcomings when it came to accurate navigation. The traditional methods of projection by which these charts were made caused such a distortion in their representation of direction that it was impossible for the mariner to plot a line of constant bearing (or rhumb line) as a straight line without incurring errors. It had been another Flemish cartographer, Gerhardus Mercator, who in his famous 1569 sea chart *Nova et aucta orbis terrae descriptio ad usum navigantium emendate accommodata* had first managed to correct the dramatic errors in conventional sea charts. It was Mercator's genius to step away from the method of projection

and construct, by way of the revolutionary principle of waxing latitudes, a map that preserved the correct relationship of angles and
thereby preserved true bearing. Plancius' maps, by contrast, had
thus far either been made by means of azimuthal projection, such as
his Bible map and contribution to Van Linschoten's *Itinerario*, or,
more often so, by means of cylindrical projection, such as his plane
maps in the Portuguese tradition.

This changed when on September 12, 1594, Plancius obtained
from the States General a patent to "print and sell a sea chart…in
which he, with great and constant toil, has brought all the coasts of
Europe, Asia and Africa…under their true latitudes and longitudes." What had made the effort so significant was that he had
"practiced a new form of nautical charting in which the three sides
of a triangle are right and true, in that the latitudes are in natural
proportion to the longitudes." In doing so Plancius had become the
first Dutch cartographer to construct a sea chart with waxing latitudes in Mercator's image.

Revolutionary though they were, Mercator's and Plancius' true
sea charts were not received with much enthusiasm by the sailing
profession of the time. The charts failed to give an explanation concerning the mathematical principle by which they were constructed,
whilst their legends were in Latin. More perplexing, though the scale
was the same in all directions for any small area, the scale from latitude to latitude differed, increasing progressively with every degree.
To compensate for this distortion and thereby enable the navigator
to calculate his distances, it was necessary to apply trigonometrical
tables—tables that only first became widely available in 1599, when
Edward Wright published his *Certaine Errors in Navigation*. The
cumulative result of all these complexities was that the average sailor
could not make much of sea charts with waxing latitudes. Even the
Cambridge scholar Thomas Hood professed as much in 1592 when
he took up the post of teacher of navigation in London and told his
pupils that he had just completed a work "concerning the use of
Mercator's card" but had not the leisure to explain it to them. Eight

years later, the Dutch cartographer Albert Haeyen still failed to comprehend that in Mercator's representation true scale had to give way to true bearing, when in his *Short Treatise Concerning the Art of Navigation* he (inexplicably) complained that "the 1,400 mile gap by which China and Hamburg are divided in longitude has been obscured by some 1,000 miles." More unforgivably, he misconstrued Plancius' laudable objective by accusing him of "conjuring up before the eyes of the inexperienced navigators a shorter way," so that, thus emboldened, they might "sail that terribly harsh and unexplored Ice Sea with greater devotion."

For all its wrongheadedness Haeyen's suspicion was not altogether without foundation. In all three attempts to find a Northeast Passage Plancius played a leading role, even though his knowledge of the region was as poor as that of the next geographer. Thus, whilst he knew that Novaya Zemlya curved eastward, toward the Siberian mainland, he at the same time believed that it joined the continent, reducing the Kara Sea to a vast inland sea. It was this mistaken belief that drove him to encourage Barents to sail round the peninsula and "in doing so attempt by all possible and feasible means to reach the East." Barents' failure and Nay's success set the tone for the second expedition, through the Yugor Strait. The failure of that attempt eventually led Plancius back to his original plan and Willem Barents to his doom.[3]

Where Plancius had to adjust his view of the Northeast Passage with each new expedition, with respect to the Southeast Passage he was charting more familiar waters. Already prior to De Houtman's return from Lisbon, Plancius had written a memorandum for the "education of those in command of the fleets destined for India," gleaned from English, French, and Iberian sources. In it, Plancius cautions the navigator who has just passed the Canary Islands not to approach the Guinean mainland within more than sixty miles. There, coastal calms threaten to delay the voyage. Equally, a course at more than seventy miles from the mainland will make a ship susceptible to the Northeast Trades and the North Equatorial Current, which will carry her toward the West Indies. Once the Line (equator) is reached, any progress east, beyond the meridian of Cape Palmas, will bring the ship within reach of the Guinean Current, resulting in a delay of up to two months. At the same time, the Southeast Trades threaten to carry her west, toward the Abrolhos Archipelago, off the Brazilian coast. For a successful crossing, therefore, one is to continue southwest from the meridian of Cape Palmas until one has reached Martin Vaz, at 20°S., 30°W. From there the Westerlies will carry one past the Cape of Good Hope and into the Indian Ocean. Inevitably, Plancius' knowledge of navigation beyond the Cape of Good Hope is increasingly sparse and his instructions are limited to far more general statements concerning distances and directions of winds and currents. New information obtained on De Houtman's return from Lisbon was incorporated into the memorandum *Concerning the East-Indian Navigation and her Characteristics and Remarks*, shortly followed by a *Further Explanation of the East-Indian Navigation*.

The seasoned minister knew well that for his teachings to truly take root scriptural study ought to be complemented by oral instruction, and thus, in between sermons, Plancius would invite the navigators of the early expeditions to congregate around the pulpit of the Oudezijds chapel. There his motley congregation, armed with crossstaff and astrolabe, became the recipients of a scientific and rather more secular exposition of the universe. During these seminars Plancius primed his students in the basic principles of navigation: how to determine one's latitude by means of celestial observations and one's longitude by means of dead reckoning. These activities were anything but exercises in charity. For his instruction of the navigators of the second expedition for the East Indies, under the command of Jacob van Neck, alone, the scholar was remunerated with the generous sum of fl. 3,000, a hundred times the monthly wage of any of his students. Nor did Plancius' financial involvement stop there. Already in the first and most speculative of the southeast expeditions, he had been a principal shareholder. Of the total capital of fl. 768,466 that was raised for the second expedition, he had held a share of fl. 51,333, and by the time the fourth fleet sailed, the amount of his investment had grown to fl. 99,833.[4]

Yet more than worldly gains, it was his desire for progress that drove this early forerunner of the Scientific Revolution. And that this man of strict religious principle, who never accepted any payments for his pastoral activities, had no qualms to resort to such worldly means to achieve that scientific furtherance is evinced by the fact that it was Plancius who, following the second expedition's failure, persuaded the States General to grant the reward of fl. 25,000 to keep entrepreneurial interest for the northern expeditions alive.

Well prepared though they were, the late sixteenth century Dutch maritime expeditions were far from being a concerted effort. Whereas

Petrus Plancius instructing the navigators of the *wilde vaerten* from the pulpit of the Oudezijds chapel. The shining column at the center of the illustration refers to the title of the atlas on the cover of which it appeared: *The Great Shining Collumn*.

in Spain all overseas trade and maritime activities fell directly under the authority of the crown through the all-powerful Casa de la Contratación, in the Netherlands, traffic to the East Indies was fiercely contested by a growing number of independent companies. By the turn of the century, no less than eight different companies, based in Amsterdam, Rotterdam, Middelburg, Hoorn, and Enkhuizen, were all competing for the largest stake in the spice trade. And since they were organized on either a regional or munic-ipal basis, the only form of central control was exercised indirectly by the States General when it ratified the grants and licenses awarded earlier in the day by the States of Holland, Zeeland, or the powerful government of Amsterdam. One thing, however, these first compa-nies involved in the so-called Rich Trades did have in common. They were all run by men with a mission, a brand of men who had the experience, the vision, and the entrepreneurial courage to embark on a venture the dimensions of which had not been seen before.

One man to fit that description was Balthazar de Moucheron, scion of the Lords of Boulaye, a Norman aristocratic family of Huguenots. In 1530 his father had emigrated to Middelburg, mar-ried the daughter of another Huguenot, and made his fortune in commerce. The economic decline of that town toward the middle of the century had forced the émigré to move again. This time he moved to Antwerp, and it was here that Balthazar was born and raised, learning his father's trade on the Antwerp bourse. The young De Moucheron remained in Antwerp until 1585. In that year the town surrendered, and he and his family fled, as his father had done, to Middelburg. Thousands had done likewise, and on the wave of economic revival that followed, the young merchant was soon pro-pelled to the head of a prosperous trading firm.

In keeping with De Moucheron's flamboyant and restless nature, his trade ranged far and wide. He made a successful start carrying wine from the Canary Islands, but soon his ships were sailing as far afield as the west coast of Africa and the West Indies—France, Spain, Senegal, Cape Verde, Guinea, Costa de la Mina, Terre

Neuve, and the island of Principe were the destinations that made up the nodes of his impressive trade network.

It was not only southward that the instinctive entrepreneur had turned his eye. For years his ships had been plying the Baltic trade route to Narva, and already before he left Antwerp, news of Frobisher's northern expeditions, and Pet and Jackman's penetration of the Kara Sea, had inspired him to undertake a similar adventure. In 1584, whilst Antwerp was under siege, he launched his first northern expedition. It was led by Olivier Brunel, an adventurer who had accumulated extensive travel experience in Russia in the service of the illustrious merchant house of the Stroganovs and had been the west European to sail farthest east when, in 1576, he sailed up the River Ob on board a Russian coaster. De Moucheron's expedition, however, ended in tragedy. Having reached the mouth of the Pechora River, a boat sent ashore with merchandise capsized and several men, including Brunel, drowned.[5]

De Moucheron's move to Middelburg put a hold on his northern ambitions, but not for long. In 1593 he presented to the States of Zeeland detailed plans for a renewed attempt to find a Northeast Passage. When the merchant entered into negotiations with Prince Maurits, Oldenbarneveldt, and the other heads of state, the project received such publicity that the States of Holland insisted on participating. Eventually, all parties agreed to make the venture into an *affaire d'Etat* for which De Moucheron would be "recompensed fairly and liberally." Next, he approached Van Linschoten and Plancius. Eager to widen the scope of his work, Van Linschoten agreed to join the expedition in the capacity of merchant. Plancius, too, agreed but soon realized that his proposed route was irreconcilable with that of De Moucheron, who insisted that they sail through the Yugor Strait, as Brunel had done. Plancius therefore persuaded the government of Amsterdam to finance one ship (the *'t Boot*, captained by Willem Barents) that would sail with its own instructions. And thus it was that the first Dutch expedition in search of a Northeast Passage sought to do so by two separate routes.

Far more extensive was Plancius' involvement in the southern expeditions. Only his clerical position induced him to play his invaluable role behind the scenes, away from the limelight. And thus, on many a frosty evening early in 1594, the preacher could be observed furtively entering an establishment in the Warmoesstraat belonging to the wine merchant Martin Spil. This was the place where, under the scholar's guidance, a small group of Amsterdam merchants first formed the bold plan to organize an expedition to the East Indies and decided to dispatch Cornelis de Houtman to Lisbon to seek the necessary information. Three of these directors, or *bewindhebbers*—Hendrik Arentzoon Hudde, Reinier Pauw, and Pieter Dirkszoon Hasselaer—were Protestants who had risen to prominence within Amsterdam's magistracy with the town's Alteration in 1578. There were other, less eminent figures, such as Jan Poppen, a German trader in cereals from Stör on the Elbe, and Dirck van Oss, an émigré from Antwerp. Upon their arrival in the capital the two men had joined forces and made their fortune in the Baltic trade. Then there were men like the stock merchant Hendrick Corneliszoon Buyck, whose moderate Catholic stance had helped him survive the turbulent days of the Alteration, in which his great-uncle, former mayor and fervent Catholic Joost Sybrandszoon Buyck, had been expelled from the town.

Another party to join in the race for the East was the partnership of the Rotterdam shipowners Johan van der Veken and Pieter van der Haegen. A refugee from Antwerp, Van der Haegen had moved to Amsterdam and found a niche for himself in the burgeoning Dutch market by trading in cloth. In 1595, he moved again, this time to Rotterdam, where he became involved in a number of business ventures. The first saw him sign a contract with Nicolaes Seys, on March 19, 1596, to freight a vessel belonging to Jacob Claeszoon van Monnikendam. On the ship's return, however, a dispute arose amongst the three men, which was only resolved after the matter was entrusted to a group of Amsterdam merchants, acting as referees. In his next business venture Van der Haegen consorted with Hendrick Anthoniszoon Wissel, a shady yet brilliant financier. Together they fitted out four ships that were to sail for Santa Domingo and Portorico under the command of the former Sea Beggar Melchior van den Kerckhove. In view of the fleet's Latin destination a request was put to the States General to have it manned with mainly Spanish and Portuguese sailors—a request that was only reluctantly granted. The outcome was not a success, but already prior to the fleet's return, Van der Haegen had drafted plans for yet another expedition, this time to the East Indies. And since Wissel had meanwhile landed in jail, he now turned to a fellow émigré and merchant, Johan van der Veken.

Van der Veken was a man of altogether different pedigree. Born into a respected family of mercantile patricians from the Flemish town of Mechelen, Van der Veken had moved to Antwerp as a young man, earning his living with the manufacture of baskets, and becoming a freeman of the town in 1575. Anticipating the town's fall, he began to sell off his possessions in 1581 and two years later moved to Rotterdam. There he set himself up in the herring trade, gradually expanding his activities to include the transport of cereals from the Baltic to Portugal, Spain, and Italy. By carefully nurturing his relations with men of influence Van der Veken eventually created sufficient credit to establish his own bank, whose clientele included no lesser men than Oldenbarneveldt. It was this aspect of Van der Veken's business activities that made Van der Haegen turn to his former fellow citizen. For, though rich in ideas, of credit he was always short. Yet, in spite of their differences, their common background and shared vision helped forge a partnership between the two émigré entrepreneurs—a partnership that must have been rooted in deep conviction, for the plan for which Van der Haegen finally obtained the support (and the considerable financial clout) of Van der Veken was a bold one. It was to try and reach the East by way of a third and far less explored southwest route, right through the treacherous Strait of Magellan.

III

The Outfit

Well, Ignorance, wilt thou yet foolish be?
To slight good counsel ten times given thee?
And if thou yet refuse it, thou shalt know
Ere long the evil of thy doing so:
Remember man in time, stoop, do not fear,
Good counsel taken well, saves; therefore hear:
But if thou yet shalt slight it, thou wilt be
The loser, Ignorance, I'll warrant thee.

The first indications that things were afoot in Rotterdam came in the autumn of 1597, when, not long after De Houtman's return, Van der Haegen and Van der Veken submitted a request to the States of Holland and the States General in which they sought permission to:

> undertake, with three or four large ships and a yacht or pinnace, a voyage from the [River] Maas to the East Indies; so as to bring from there and to the lands of Holland, all sorts of spices and other costly wares, by which the residents of the said lands shall be greatly enriched and bettered. And to carry hence and exchange other merchandise through which this republic shall be, not weakened or harmed but, on the contrary, enriched and furthered in profit and trade.

Further requests were made: for material assistance in the form of eight 24-pounders, for the permission to purchase the *Oraingien* from the Admiralty of Rotterdam, and for toll-free passage of incoming and outgoing convoys for the first five voyages. To most of these the States of Holland gave its stamp of approval. In its resolution of December 23, 1597, it granted the expedition free passage, furnished it with four of the 24-pounders, and provided an additional

41

loan of fl. 8,000 toward the financing of the remaining four. Within the same day the resolution was approved by the States General, although it limited the exemption of taxes to only two passages.

To raise the required capital, Van der Haegen and Van der Veken approached a large number of merchants, the five chief investors of whom were eventually appointed to share in the directorship. These *bewindhebbers* were Jasper Quignet, Van der Veken's brother-in-law; Hans Broers and Nicolaes Seys, both wealthy Amsterdam merchants; Jacques Mahu, a merchant from Cologne; and Simon de Cordes, a merchant who had spent several years in Lisbon. Together they raised a total capital of fl. 500,000, of which just over half (fl. 267,000) was registered under the name of Van der Veken.[1]

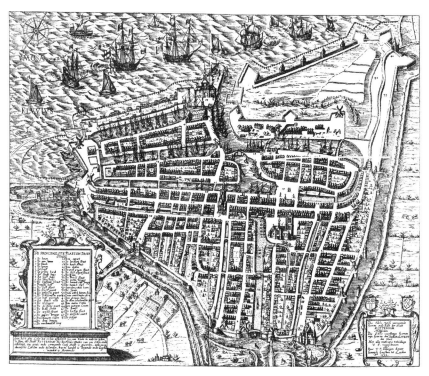

A 1599 plan of the port of Rotterdam by Henrijck Haestens. The five ships at anchor on the Maas in the background are almost certainly those of the expedition under the command of Jacques Mahu and Simon de Cordes.

The *bewindhebbers* suffered a considerable setback when their acquisition of the *Oraingien* fell through. The Rotterdam Admiralty had vetoed its sale, as it did not want to part with what it considered to be one of its best ships. Five ships were eventually acquired. Of these, the *Hoope* (*Hope*), with a displacement of 500 tons, was the largest. Being the only vessel in the fleet with three mast tops she was designated as flagship. The coat of arms on her flag featured an anchor accompanied by a female figure. It was repeated on her stern, where, in keeping with Dutch shipbuilding traditions, it was framed in the elaborate baroque ornamentations of friezes, convolutes, and other whorls, and supported by lions, cupids, and caryatids. Second in line was the *Liefde* (*Love*). She had formerly sailed under the name *Erasmus*, after the famous sixteenth century Dutch humanist. Even after her rechristening his image continued to feature prominently, not only on her stern, on which he was depicted holding a Bible, but also on her bow, which carried a figurehead in his image. With 300 tons the *Love* was slightly smaller than the third ship in the line, the *Ghelooue* (*Faith*), which could carry twenty tons more. The *Faith*'s coat of arms contained two stone tablets with the Ten Commandments. Fourth in line was the *Trouwe* (*Fidelity*), a ship of 220 tons. Her coat of arms depicted two hands folded as if in prayer. The last ship in the line was a pinnace of 150 tons. This vessel was originally called *Vliegend Hert* (*Flying Deer*), but was renamed *Blijde Bootschap* (*The Gospel*) to tie in with the biblical names of the other ships, although, pressed for time, here too the depiction of a deer on her escutcheon was left untouched.

Given the great number of ships that were leaving for the East in 1598, it was not an easy task for the *bewindhebbers* to man the fleet. By the time the five ships were ready and their crews could be recruited, no less than three expeditions, consisting of a total of thirteen ships, had already sailed. It was with some difficulty, then, that they were able to recruit 491 men for the expedition: 130 on the *Hope*, 110 on the *Love*, 109 on the *Faith*, 86 on the *Fidelity*, and 56 on *The Gospel*.[2]

Command over the ships and their crews was entrusted to a small core of officers: the captain, the ship's master (or skipper), two pilots, a boatswain, a quartermaster, and a gunner. A special position was occupied by the merchants, on whose shoulders fell the responsibility for the cargo and thus the financial success of the enterprise. Officers and merchants were assisted by a scribe. To take care of the physical and spiritual health of the crew, each ship had on board a surgeon, a physician, a cook, and a preacher, whilst a carpenter, a sailmaker, and a *schieman* (boatswain's mate), each assisted by an apprentice, ensured that the woodwork, the sails, and the rigging were kept in good shape. Then there was a large number of youths, the *putgers*, or cabin boys, whose duty it was to wait on the officers and the other senior members of the crew. The great majority of the crew were, of course, ordinary seamen. Most were Dutch, but there were also Germans, Portuguese, Spaniards, Scandinavians, Frenchmen, and Englishmen. All had sailed extensively on the west coasts of Europe and farther north, to Norway and the Baltic—Yarmouth, Harwich, Rouen, La Rochelle, Bilbao, Lisbon, Setúbal, Ayamonte, Sanlúcar de Barrameda, Cádiz, Genoa, Venice, Terceira, and Las Palmas were the ports between which they had led their harsh and often squalid lives, but they all knew the ropes.

The same could not be said of those under whose command they sailed. Command of the expedition was entrusted to one of the *bewindhebbers*, Jacques Mahu, a thirty-four-year-old, unmarried, and wealthy merchant from Cologne, who was appointed admiral of the fleet on the *Hope*. By all accounts an "experienced and reasonable," even "renowned" merchant, Mahu was still a deeply questionable choice, considering he had hardly ever set foot on a ship before and never held command over one, let alone a fleet of five. Appointed as vice admiral on the *Love* was another *bewindhebber*, Simon de Cordes. He too had proven his mettle in the field of commerce, both at home and abroad, but had no experience whatsoever when it came to leading hundreds of men in an enterprise certain to tax even the most experienced to and beyond the very limits of their abilities.

Hardly more experienced were those appointed as captain on the remaining three ships, although the *bewindhebbers* did manage to take on board a man who had played a remarkable, albeit questionable role in De Houtman's expedition. This was none other than Gerrit van Beuningen. Upon the return of De Houtman's fleet he had been incarcerated in Amsterdam, but after two months had passed the public prosecutor had seen no reason to hold him any longer. On his release he was approached by Van der Haegen, and with no prospect of a *repêchage* in De Houtman's second expedition, he had gratefully accepted the captaincy of the *Faith*. With his thirty years, the captain of the *Fidelity*, Jeurian van Bockholt, was the youngest and least experienced amongst the captains. One year Van Bockholt's senior, Sebald de Weert, who was appointed captain of *The Gospel*, had little more experience. He was a graduate of the Antwerp gymnasium, who had filled much of his early days composing patriotic poetry in Latin. In 1592, at the age of twenty-five, he had joined the Company of Trade on Barbary, a company his father, Hans de Weert, had run with two partners. When the birth of an illegitimate child threatened to bring his career to a premature end, an offer by his father's former partner, Hans Broers, to join the expedition enabled De Weert to escape public censure.

The *bewindhebbers* were hardly ignorant of the lack of seagoing experience in the commanders. Even the qualifications of a man like Van Beuningen, who had visited the East Indies, lost much of their luster when one realized that he had done so in shackles below decks. It was with some relief, then, that they were able to hire a man who had spent most of his young life on deck, albeit of Portuguese vessels, sailing between India, China, and even Japan. This was, of course, Dirck Gerritszoon Pomp, who was hired at the handsome salary of fl. 50 a month, and appointed chief pilot on the *Love*. Another old hand was Jan Outgherszoon, like Pomp a native of Enkhuizen. He had started out as a ship's carpenter but had taught himself the rudiments of navigation, which earned him the rank of chief pilot on the *Faith*.

Pomp and Outgherszoon, however, were the only Dutch officers with any experience on long-distance voyages the *bewindhebbers* were able to enlist. And thus they recruited nationals of the only other European nation outside Portugal and Spain that had launched long-distance expeditions; English pilots were hired to navigate the expedition through and to the seas that English ships had explored during the previous decades. Men such as the thirty-five-year-old Timothy Shatton, who had navigated the Strait of Magellan under Cavendish, an experience that earned him the position of chief pilot on the fleet's flagship, the *Hope*. Appointed as second pilot under Shatton was another Englishman, William Adams, whose brother, Thomas Adams, was made second pilot under Pomp on the *Love*. Of the two brothers, William was by far the most experienced and all-round sailor. Though trained as a shipbuilder, he had begun sailing at the age of twenty-four. In 1588, he had held command over a small supply ship of 120 tons, the *Richard Dyffylde*, carrying victuals to Drake's fleet as it was fending off the Armada. Over the following twelve years he had been employed by the Company of Barbary Merchants, whose ships plied between the British Isles and Morocco, occasionally raiding Iberian vessels homeward bound from the East Indies or the New World. It was through the Moroccan connection that Adams had come into contact with the *bewindhebbers* of the Dutch rival company, and that, through the offices of Hans Broers, he and his brother were recruited as pilots for the expedition.[3] One more Englishman was appointed as pilot. This was John Richart, who was placed on the *Fidelity*.

In view of the route by which the expedition was expected to reach its destination, there were serious limitations to the degree in which it could prepare itself scientifically. Reliable data on the western route to the East was exceedingly scarce. As far as recorded voyages went, the bottleneck in that route, the Strait of Magellan, had only been navigated by Europeans eleven times before, most notably by Ferdinand Magellan, Francis Drake, and Thomas Cavendish.

Ferdinand Magellan, the Portuguese navigator who lent his name to the strait, had sailed from Seville on the *San Antonio* in 1519, discovered the mouth of the strait on October 21 of the following year, and passed through it in just over a month. The first Iberian to follow was the Spanish explorer García Jofre de Loaysa, who reached the strait on April 8, 1526, and sailed into the Pacific on May 26 of the same year. Half a century later the feat was repeated by the first Englishman, when, toward the end of August 1578, Francis Drake completed the passage under favorable conditions in just over a fortnight. Drake was followed by Pedro Sarmiento de Gambóa, the eminent Spanish scientist who between 1579 and 1580 explored the Chilean archipelago for the king of Spain and successfully navigated the strait in the opposite direction in less than a month. The second Englishman to pass through the strait was Thomas Cavendish. He found his way through the strait using charts drawn up by Drake some ten years before. Yet despite the considerable profile the strait had acquired by the end of the sixteenth century, detailed geographical data on the peninsula remained sparse. Except for De Gambóa's *deroteros* of the northwest part of the Patagonian archipelago, no systematic survey of the region had been undertaken, whilst of the strait itself, there were hardly any reliable maps at all.

Ironically, as these expeditions were undertaken by different nations and at intervals that in some cases spanned several decades, none of the seafaring nations were able to fully benefit from the accumulated data. This situation was exacerbated by the state of animosity that existed throughout the sixteenth and seventeenth centuries between the Iberians on the one hand and the English and Dutch on the other. The exchange of information between the English and Dutch also frequently suffered from a reluctance to mutually divulge information that was considered to be of strategic importance to their territorial interests. At times, these concerns were allowed to take on such importance that men like Drake were willing to mislead even their fellow countrymen by misinforming them about the exact route of their expeditions. By the end of the

The Strait of Magellan as it appears on one of the plain sea charts carried onboard the *Love*. Drawn by Cornelis Doetszoon, the chart largely draws on the work of Plancius, although there are also traces of Drake's and Cavendish's findings.

sixteenth century, therefore, a situation prevailed where, even though most of the strait had been explored at some stage by one nation or other, comprehensive knowledge of the strait remained an elusive ideal for any single nation. Inevitably, any widening of Dutch knowledge about the Southwest Passage—or any other route, for that matter—suffered from these impediments as much as that of the English, Spanish, and Portuguese.

Here again it was Van Linschoten's work that helped the Dutch to shed light on this distant region. For the fifty-fifth chapter of the *Reysgheschrift* was the journal of none other than Nuno de Silva, the Portuguese commander whose vessel, the *Santa María*, had been raided by Drake off the Cape Verde Islands, and had been forced to serve as pilot on Drake's fleet, only to be dropped some 4500 miles westward on the coast of Mexico. According to De Silva:

This Streight may bee about an hundred and tenne leagues long, and in bredth a league. About the entry of the Streight, and halfe way into it, it runneth right foorth without any windings or turnings: and from thence about eight or tenne leagues toward the ende, it hath some boutes and windings, among the which there is one so great a hooke or headland, that it seemed to runneth straight out againe. And although you finde some crookings, yet they are nothing to speake of. The issue of the Streight lieth Westward, and about eight or tenne leagues before you come to the ende, then the Streight beginneth to bee broader, and it is all high land to the end thereof, after you are eight leagues within the Streight, for the first eight leagues after you enter is low flat land, as I sayd before: and in the entrie of the Streight you find the streame to runne from the South sea to the North sea.

In nautical terms, however, De Silva's descriptions are crude, and little of true value to a prospective navigator is recorded by the pilot. But it was not for its nautical data that his account was valued by the *bewindhebbers*. It was the vivid descriptions of the spectacular losses the Portuguese and Spanish had suffered at the hands of the queen's pirate and the apparent ease with which they were inflicted that fired the imagination of the Dutch entrepreneurs. It was the military aspect of Drake's and Cavendish's expeditions that Van der Haegen and Van der Veken sought to emulate and thus shaped the true nature of the venture. The unstated objective of Van der Haegen and Van der Veken's expedition was to thwart the Iberian overseas effort wherever possible.

For a nation at war, the furthering of national interests and the frustration of those of the enemy had to be one and the same thing. This principle, if not always explicitly stated, was implicitly understood by all. None more so than by the States General, which, in one breath, pronounced the expedition to be of "great service to the country" and "to the detriment of the enemy."

What had been discreetly left unstated in the *bewindhebbers'* request to the States General was expressed with evident eloquence by the fleet's weaponry. The *Hope* carried thirty-four cannon. Eight of these were heavy bronze cannon, which could fire rounds ranging from 4 up to 25 pounds. The lighter, cast-iron pieces could fire up to 9-pound rounds. The *Love* carried eighteen cannon, including six bronze and a number of lighter pieces, as well as 300 rounds of chain shot, 50 quintals (pieces of 100 kg), and 350 rounds of fire ammunition. The *Faith* carried twenty cannon, of which six were bronze. The *Fidelity* carried sixteen pieces, four of which were bronze. Even the pinnace, *The Gospel*, was armed with nineteen cannon, eleven front-loaders and eight rear-loaders. All in all the fleet carried over one hundred cannon. For each large cannon, eighty cannonballs were shipped, whilst each ship carried 500 one-and-a-half pound rounds to feed the lighter pieces. To propel all this weight, some 20,000 pounds of gunpowder were shipped.

Such armament was by no means exceptional. Most of the other expeditions that left for the East Indies were armed just as well, if not better. What did make this expedition stand out were the far-reaching provisions for military operations on land. Of the total number of 507 men, well over 200 were sufficiently trained to act as troops. As support, the *bewindhebbers* had also signed on a band of thirty English trumpeters and other musicians—an indispensable item in sixteenth century warfare. A group of Frenchmen had been especially hired for the maintenance of the hundreds of harquebuses, muskets, and pistols. Complete suits of armor were shipped, all neatly sealed and marked. Even the construction of fortifications featured in the plans of the *bewindhebbers*, for among the cargo were large quantities of raw ingredients for the manufacture of mortar, as well as bricks, ironware, and other building material.

As such, the expedition of Van der Haegen and Van der Veken bore a remarkable resemblance to that under the command of the Rotterdam taverner Olivier van Noort. The four ships that sailed from Rotterdam under command of this former naval officer roughly three months later were also bound for the Strait of Magellan, their holds equally filled with the implements of warfare. But in sharp contrast with Van der Haegen and Van der Veken, Van Noort made no secret of his ambitions. His boastings to the guests of his tavern, De Dubbele Witte Sleutels, were the talk of the day, sufficiently so to alarm one of them, who happened to be a Spanish informant, to dispatch a report about Van Noort's plans to the governor of Andalucía, Alonso Pérez de Guzmán, the Duke of Medina-Sidonia and onetime Admiral of the Armada.

Whatever it was that featured in the plans of Van der Haegen and Van der Veken, none of it was ever communicated to the lower ranks. And while it was clear enough to all that the East Indies must be the expedition's ultimate destination, no one knew about its immediate objectives, let alone its ulterior aims. Even the route by which the *bewindhebbers* expected the fleet to reach its destination was shrouded in secrecy. This was just as well, perhaps, since in order to ship the large quantities of military hardware in addition to the commodities of trade, far-reaching concessions had been made on the storage of provisions. Consequently, the successful completion of the enterprise relied heavily on the opportunity for victualing along the way. The crew was blissfully ignorant of these impediments and their serious repercussions on the viability of the enterprise. Had they known of the double-barreled purpose of the expedition, had they known that the provisions were not sufficient to last for the duration of the voyage, and had they known that its itinerary was to lead them, not round the Cape of Good Hope, but through the treacherous Strait of Magellan, they would certainly have thought twice before they signed on.

PART 2

TRIALS & TRIBULATIONS

rom Goa only one ship sailes every year to bringe the aforesaid goods to the Iland of Iapan: yet first they call at China with Reals of eight, Oil and Wine, and buye therewith Gold, silke, and all kinde of costly wares, the wich they bring to the Iland of Iapan; where there is much Silver, the which they againe barter against the foresaid goods from China. Then they travel againe with Silver from Iapan to China, and barter it in turne for Gold, Silke and divers costly wares, and arrive therewith againe in Goa: yet they have to lie waiting at each of the aforesaid places as much as six monthes. So that such voyages will take three years in going. But every year shippes saile with all this costlinesse from Goa, to the Cape of Bone Esperance, and from there to Lisbone.

The people of the Iland of Iapan are a friendly people: but they are Idolaters alike unto those of China. They also have images in their churches. But in the towne of Nagesacke, and more others which have subject of the King of Portugal in them, are the Iesuites, which they have driven out over certaine yeares by reason that all of them desired to be merchants. This Iland is as great as England. From there onwards, those from India or from Goa saile no farther. The countriemen of China and Iapan are a fat people, broad in coun-tenance, and mostly white men. There are those among their own nation who are black: but all are of like appearance and body.

——Dirck Gerritszoon Pomp, *Thresoor der Zeevaerdt*, 1592

The sea at the turn of the sixteenth century was not a place for the timid or the faint-hearted. Those who went to sea faced a life of malnutrition, poor pay, and physical hardship, only rarely punctuated by moments of splendor; generally, it was Spartan and insecure, and few sailors had the dubious fortune of reaching old age. More often a sailor's career was cut short by a brawl, a fall, or by the gangrenous consequences of crude surgery. For the average sailor, then, professional life, if not life itself, was short-lived.

This was all the more true for the deep-sea sailor; in comparison to those who sailed in European waters, the sailor who boarded ships bound for the East and West Indies faced added dangers, brought on by the protracted periods spent at sea, for on the long hauls across the Atlantic and the Indian oceans, ships could spend anywhere from several weeks up to half a year at sea without ever making landfall.

Expeditions that sailed under such conditions required a large number of additional preparations to ensure the well-being of those who sailed in them. It required clothing suitable for weather conditions that could change dramatically in the course of several hours. It required provisions that could endure humidity and heat and still somehow meet nutritional requirements. Most important, perhaps, it required strict supervision of hygienic standards. Sadly, it was in each of these areas that the Dutch, English, French, Spanish, and Portuguese alike fell short, albeit in varying degrees; and throughout the early voyages, the great care that was given to the material aspects of the expeditions stood in stark contrast with the almost callous disregard for those on whose health their success so obviously depended. No eyebrows were raised when crews embarked with no more than the clothes they wore. The same, blithe attitude was taken toward victuals. And even if care had been taken to ship sufficient provisions, many a captain was known to economize on rations, only to sell on arrival the surplus accumulated at the cost of his men. Few were the captains who maintained basic hygienic standards. The notoriously appalling conditions on board the Spanish and Portuguese ships in the Carreira da India were already proverbial; and even though the Dutch East Indiamen had a markedly better reputation than their Iberian, French, and even English counterparts, still their relative spruceness was insufficient to ward off the onset of disease.

When disease struck, it did so with devastating effect; on the long hauls it was not uncommon for crews to be halved. Circumstance dictated that those quartered before the mast, the common sailors, were hit hardest. Living in exceedingly cramped conditions, with nothing more than their hammocks to guard them from the ever present vermin, the men before the mast were the first to suffer the onset of transmitted disease. Officers, who had their own, albeit small and poorly ventilated cabins, ran less risk of exposure. They also received double rations, while hardly any restrictions at all were imposed on those who dined at the captain's table. Different it was for the common sailor, who had to rely on the mess kit for his grog and rations and thus, unwittingly, exposed himself directly to the afflictions of his mates. Those who were struck down by scurvy, typhoid fever, pleurisy, dysentery, malaria, beriberi, or any combination that ill fortune cared to inflict, had little hope of recovery. Carried belowdecks, they were left to the primitive care of the ship's surgeon. Only few of those who felt the maggots gnawing at their wounds or watched their limbs contort and blacken with scurvy ever regained the strength to rise above the hatch and feel the fresh sea breeze in their nostrils. The majority pined away in the sweltering heat of the lower decks, amid the stench of putrefied provisions, festering sores, and the waste of incontinent stupor that gathered in the hold.

Those on deck faced their own hardships, for no matter how weak or few in number, still they had to climb the yardarms, "day and night, in storm and tempest." It was at moments far into the voyage, therefore, that the endurance of the weary, weather-beaten, and hungry men finally wore thin and onboard discipline was put to the ultimate test. At such moments the survival of the expedition came to rely wholly on the competence of those in command. At best an able commander would see the expedition through, lifting the spirit of his men through example and the display of sound leadership. At worst an unfortunate combination of setbacks, missed opportunities, and senseless loss of life sufficed to strain the existing cords of dissent. And it was especially then, when authority sought to reassert itself through the imposition of an unduly harsh regime, that initial intransigence tended to spill over into full-blown mutiny. Not every mutiny was the act of desperation. Many simply sprang from greed, revenge, or plain villainy. But even in those instances, the plea that the men "had been starved like dogs" and the sick had been "left to die most wretchedly" rang true in spite of the seriousness of the offenses committed.

Whether by choice or by default, the chief instrument for onboard discipline was punishment. Blasphemy, theft, failure to attend religious service, and insolence were generally punished by the imposition of fines. As an alternative or complementary punishment a sailor could be flogged. For this he was tied down to the capstan or the mast to receive ten to two hundred lashes of a rope end to the exposed buttocks. This form of punishment often followed that of keelhauling. Or ducking from the yardarm, in which an offender was weighed down with lead and hurled into the sea from the yardarm, to be hauled up again by his arms tied behind his back. Like keelhauling, ducking from the yardarm was normally repeated three or four times—enough for the subject to pass out at least once. Both treatments were the preferred penalty for those who had stolen rations, failed to perform their daily chores, or drawn a knife in anger. If blood had been spilled, the assailant was nailed to the main mast with his own weapon; if life had been taken, he was thrown overboard, tied to his victim. Short shrift was made with those found guilty of mutiny. Hardly any consideration was given to mitigating circumstances, and the ringleaders invariably faced the death penalty. Ashore it was usually exacted by hanging; on board, where a more creative approach was taken, the condemned could face anything ranging from the firing squad, being hanged from the yards, being thrown overboard with hands tied, or being left behind on some distant and forgotten shore.

When adding the dangers of sailing in unknown waters, the rudimentary instruments of navigation, and the unpredictable ferocity of the elements—not to mention the raiders that loomed in the offing—it was close to a miracle that any of these ships ever reached their destinations. Yet they did. And getting there was only half the job; homeward bound, with heavily laden yet seriously impaired ships, a fleet was twice as vulnerable, whilst the happy few who did eventually make it back home alive often failed to return from their second or third voyage. And herein lay the true mystery: that having gone through the eye of the needle these simple and superstitious men were still willing to put their lives on the line. Yet they did. For each sailor knew only too well that on the other side of hardship opportunity beckoned, and in the small universe of the lowly sailor it beckoned with grander gestures than any other vocation open to them. To these men the yarns the old salts spun as they squandered their modest fortunes in the countless taverns and brothels that lined the quays of Dutch ports seemed to define their existence. For it was the sea that offered an escape from the oppressive squalor of the rundown doss-houses; it was the sea that gave them a chance to rise above their ranks; and it was the sea that promised to bring them all the exotic delights of the East.

IV

THE CROSSING

Behold ye how these crystal streams do glide
(To comfort pilgrims) by the highway side;
The meadows green besides their fragrant smell,
Yield dainties for them; and he that can tell
What pleasant fruit, yea leaves, these trees do yield,
Will soon sell all, that he may buy this field.

The expedition sailed from the mouth of the Maas on June 27, 1598. A fresh offshore breeze soon set the five ships across the North Sea, but with the English coast in sight the wind shifted south, and they were forced to join the many other ships riding at anchor in the Downs and wait for a fair wind to carry them through the Strait of Dover. Aware of the limited reach of the provisions, Admiral Mahu was anxious that the fleet should victual at every opportunity, and thus the two weeks that passed before they set sail from the Downs, on July 15, saw a constant flurry of toing and froing between the Dutch fleet and the port of Dover.

Several uneventful weeks followed, but on August 10, shortly before sunset, four sails were sighted, creeping north along the horizon. They were now in the latitude of Cape de S. Vincente, well into Spanish territory, and they had good cause to suspect that they had intercepted an enemy flotilla. These suspicions seemed confirmed when one of the ships was identified as a Spanish carrack and presently the flotilla split into two, adding sail in an attempt to shake off their waylayers. Keen to make their first kill and emboldened by the enemy's evasive maneuver, the Dutch gave chase as they cleared their ships for action. Being the fastest sailer in the fleet, the *Hope* was the first to close with and fire in anger at the largest of the four vessels. She returned fire, and the exchange continued, even when the *Faith* had overtaken her and fired several shots into her windward side. Finally, at dawn, after the *Love* and *Fidelity* had caught up with the others, the as yet unidentified alien flagship struck her colors and the chase was over. The whole event had taken place under moonlight and no one on board any of the Dutch ships was too sure at whom they had been firing; but now, in the gray twilight of morning, it dawned on them that two of the ships they had been pursuing were English. The third vessel was indeed a Spanish carrack, while the fourth, to their surprise, turned out to be a Dutch merchantman. Boats were launched and the English commander was invited to the *Hope*, where an embarrassed exchange of mutual apologies followed. It turned out that the English ships had been taking part in the blockade of Spanish ports. The only conquest they had made on the enemy was the carrack, which had been bound for the Canary Islands. A better prize was the Dutch merchantman. She had been intercepted outside the Strait of Gibraltar, bound for San Lucar. She had come from Livorno carrying silk, a large amount of local merchandise, as well as grain and rice. It had been the cereals that had rendered the Dutch vessel prey to the English raiders, for under the Treaty of Nonsuch Dutch or English vessels carrying weapons, ammunition, or victuals to enemy ports were technically smugglers, liable to be seized by either party. Not willing to act in contravention of a pact with his country's sole ally, but equally concerned about his fleet's provisions, Mahu offered to purchase some of the rice in the Dutch vessel against a bill of exchange. The offer was accepted, and after three Dutchmen—a bosun, a bosun's mate, and a cabin boy—were taken over from the Dutch merchantman, both parties went their separate ways.[1]

No other sails were seen following their encounter with the English; by August 19 the fleet had passed the Strait of Gibraltar and was being carried rapidly south by a steady northeasterly wind. That night, however, disaster almost struck when the lookout sighted land straight ahead. When soundings were taken, the lead went down no more than twelve fathoms—a few more miles and they would have irretrievably foundered on the Barbary Coast. The strong wind made it impossible to tack back to deeper waters, and all five ships had to anchor on the lee shore with less than four fathoms below their keels. At dawn, to everyone's relief, all of the ships were able to make it back to open sea, but not before two men had taken to the water in order to extricate an anchor cable that had been entangled in an underwater reef. Back safe at sea, all pilots were called over to the flagship, where they were severely rebuked by a greatly distempered Mahu and ordered to compare their dead reckonings twice a week so as to avoid a repetition of such a shameful blunder.[2]

There were other, equally pressing problems that required Mahu's attention. His fleet had been at sea for less than two months, but already the number of men suffering from scurvy and other diseases was increasing with the day. To make matters worse, many of the ships were short of water, while perishable foods such as fish, fruit, and meat had run out altogether. All in all, conditions were deteriorating at such a pace that by the time the islands of Cape Verde were sighted on the last day of August, on the flagship alone half the crew were too ill or weak to perform their normal duty. On the same day Mahu called together the ships' council in order to deal with the emergency. The council unanimously decided to call at the port of Ribeira Grande on the island of São Tiago, which, although a Portuguese colony, was known to be an important victualing station for transatlantic shipping.[3]

The fleet arrived off Ribeira Grande late at night. In the dim moonlight a number of carracks could be seen riding at anchor in the port's roadstead, and a plan was hatched to board some of them under cover of the dark. If the operation went unnoticed on land, they would then try to land a shore party. But by the time all the boats had been launched and manned, the onshore wind had developed into a small gale; and when fire signals on the shore suggested that they had been seen, the operation was called off reluctantly.

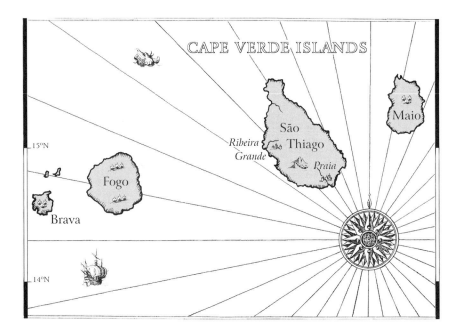

The fleet now sailed on to the nearby island of Maio, where they anchored on the following morning. Gerrit van Beuningen was sent ashore with a small party. He remained on the island until the next day but all he encountered was an old man herding a few emaciated goats. The old man, who spoke the Portuguese language, came from Praia, a small town on the south side of São Tiago. Its harbor, according to the herdsman, was formed by a small bay, lined with a narrow beach and flanked by low-lying land to port and a high promontory to starboard. The town itself was situated on the prominence and well fortified toward the sea. Its garrison, in the old man's estimation, consisted of five hundred Portuguese soldiers and some fifteen hundred armed conscripts, while its cannon were usually trained on the entrance to the harbor below.

That evening Mahu again called together his officers. Judging by what Van Beuningen had learned from the goatherd, Praia promised to be a tough nut to crack, but with few other options open the ships' council unanimously decided to again sail for São Tiago and try their luck at the island's most southern settlement.

The old man's assessment of Praia's defenses had been true enough; when on September 2, the Dutch fleet rounded the promontory, they were fired on from the town's defenses. Down below in the harbor, three ships, a large merchantman and two smaller vessels, were riding at anchor. Braving the enemy fire, boats were launched to inspect the ships. The two smaller vessels, both Portuguese caravels, were unmanned and all but empty; the five cases of biscuit and a few casks of wine and oil that were found on them were ferried back to the flagship. The merchantman was German. Obviously she was not on hostile terms with the Portuguese, for when the boats drew near to her the fire from the town ceased. Her captain, a man by the name of Herman Webbe, was invited over to the *Love*, where he was prevailed upon by Vice Admiral De Cordes to go up to the town and negotiate with its occupants on his behalf. Having seen the serious plight the Dutch were in, the German consented and, accompanied by De Cordes' scribe, went ashore toward evening. The two men returned at midnight but not with good news; the commander of the town's garrison had—with some justification—failed to be convinced of the good intentions of the Dutch; he had accused them of sacking his ships and had refused to enter into any further negotiations until he had received instructions from the governor of the islands, who resided in Ribeira Grande.

Mahu, equally suspicious of the commander's intentions, convened a meeting of the ships' council. All agreed that the Portuguese were simply trying to win time and had probably already sent for reinforcements from Ribeira Grande, and to preempt the arrival of more troops, they unanimously decided to storm the town at daybreak. Overall command of the operation was given to Gerrit van Beuningen, who was to be assisted by Sergeant Major Rombout Hooghstoel. Under cover of the night, 150 troops were put ashore. At dawn they were filed into ranks and, to the roll of drums and under flying banners, marched off toward the town.

The town could only be reached from the harbor along a long flight of steps, which were steep and narrow, with room only for two men to proceed simultaneously. They led straight up to a small opening in the town's outer defenses, which, too, was only four feet wide. Bracing themselves for heavy casualties, Van Beuningen and his men ascended the steps as fast as they could, intermittently firing their harquebuses and keeping close formation. To their surprise hardly any fire was returned and the action was over almost as soon as it had started. When they reached the bulwarks, it appeared that the town had been evacuated; they had been held up by no more than a rear guard making a last stand. These surrendered, and during the rest of the day the Dutch, who had suffered only eight casualties, prepared the town for a possible counteroffensive. This proved to be more difficult than anticipated. The town's walls had been built only to withstand attacks from the shore; landwards, they simply terminated, giving way to a flat, open landscape. Expecting a

Barent Janszoon Potgieter's depiction of the raid on Praia. Using a contemporary convention, Potgieter has contracted time to show both the Dutch attack on, and their later defense, of the Portuguese settlement.

counterattack from this direction, Van Beuningen had the town's three cannon positioned at the north side of the town.

Though the immediate objective had been achieved with surprising ease, to Mahu, the situation was far from satisfactory. Already three days had passed since they had first sighted São Tiago, and each day had passed without an opportunity for victualing, so that water supplies on most ships had almost run out. Victuals, too, were running low, and to make things worse, the number of sick men was still on the increase. In none of these respects did the capture of Praia promise relief. The town had a well, but its elevated situation made it exceedingly difficult to transport water to the ships, whilst its defense imposed an additional strain on the men's reserves and their tight rations. Any further bloodshed would pose an additional threat to the viability of the expedition, and though the anticipated counterattack on the next day failed to materialize, the admiral was well aware that the seizure of Praia had done little to warm the Portuguese to a more peaceful conclusion of their mutual affairs. This seemed to be confirmed when, after several Dutch attempts at reconciliation, the Portuguese commander reiterated his earlier position that such matters could only be dealt with by the governor. And thus Mahu decided to turn directly to the governor.

That same day, Dirck Gerritszoon Pomp, who had a good command of the Portuguese language, was dispatched to Ribeira Grande with a letter in which Mahu explained that "being in great need, and short of fresh water" he had been forced to "resort to any means to obtain the aforesaid" but that if his demands were met, he would forthwith return the governor's ships and "whatever the crew might have plundered." Should the governor, however, fail to furnish him with the required goods, he had resolved to "sail for Ribeira Grande so as to acquire by force what cannot be obtained by trade."

Pending Pomp's return, the admiral returned to the fleet toward the evening, still ill at ease amid growing concerns that at night or at dawn the Portuguese might yet launch an attack. Van Beuningen, too, had returned to his ship, exhausted by the events of the previous day. He had been replaced by De Weert, who now held the fort with some three hundred troops. But the night passed without incident and the following day, September 4, began peacefully. At noon Pomp returned from Ribeira Grande with a letter in which the governor expressed his deep disappointment at the "unfriendly" way his people had been approached, taking particular offense at the sacking of the town's church, but that, in return for the stolen goods, he agreed to furnish them with what they required. For this he also urged them to sail to Ribeira Grande, the only port in the colony that had the facilities for victualing. Again Pomp was dispatched with a letter from Mahu, who now argued that it was inexpedient for him to abandon the fort, but that he would send one of the caravels round to Ribeira Grande to collect water and victuals, along with hostages who could later be exchanged against the governor's ships. In conclusion, he urged the governor to make haste with his reply; rather than dispatch his messenger again he would prefer to resort to the forceful means set out in his previous letter.

Mahu's request for a swift reply was met, for late that evening a delegation of four Portuguese arrived at Praia. They were ferried over to the *Hope*, where they were received by the admiral and his captains. The delegates, one of whom was a Jesuit priest, assured their hosts that the governor was willing to provide them with the required victuals but that he was unable to do so at their current anchorage. Not wanting to procrastinate any longer, nor willing to use force in spite of his earlier threats, Mahu agreed to sail for Ribeira Grande. The next day, whilst Praia was evacuated, Mahu and his guests worked out the details of their mutual agreement.

Not all was to go as planned, however, for that evening sudden winds sprang up from the Atlantic and developed into a fierce gale toward midnight. With little natural protection, one by one the ships in the bay began to drag on their anchors, and were forced to sail out to sea, away from the lee shore. At daybreak, the only ships left in the bay were the *Faith* and *Fidelity*. From the town, two masts could be seen toward the east, close under the shore of Maio.

They were the two caravels; the night before, they had lost their sails and tackle and both had been given up for lost.

Though blown out to sea, the *Hope*, *Love*, and *The Gospel* had remained together and, unable to make it back, all three had sailed for Ribeira Grande. Beating against the wind, they reached the port toward evening, but unabated onshore winds made it impossible for the ships to anchor on the port's roadstead. Simon de Cordes Jr., the vice admiral's son, and twelve strong oarsmen were sent ashore in the longboat. He was to inform the governor that the storm made it impossible for them to victual at Ribeira Grande and that they would return to Praia, where they intended to honor the agreement arrived at two days before. But as soon as the men in the boat had braved the violent surf and slid onto the beach they saw their mistake. The governor's troops had been deployed in full force along the beach,

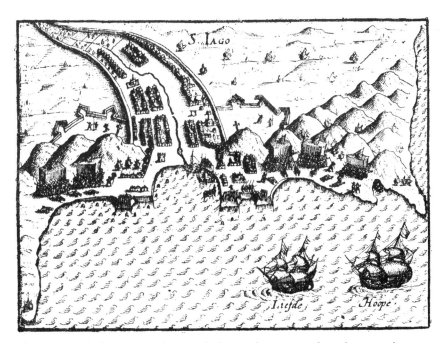

The arrival of the *Love* and *Hope* before Ribeira Grande (*The Gospel* is not depicted). At the center Simon de Cordes Jr. and his men are about to land and be arrested. To the left and right are the governor's cannon and troops.

where cannon had been placed on improvised platforms overlooking the port's approaches. As his men were marched off to prison, De Cordes was led before a "greatly distempered" governor, who, in spite of the raging gale, again accused the Dutch of having deliberately scuttled his vessels on Maio's shores, and, having vented his anger, had De Cordes, too, thrown in prison. By the next day the storm had abated. So, apparently, had the distemper of the governor, who now set all of his prisoners free, but not without the injunction that they had better not return, since the only victuals that awaited them in Ribeira Grande were "powder and lead."

With no appetite for a bloody conflict, Mahu decided to return to Praia and rejoin the *Faith* and *Fidelity*. The two ships had apparently also been blown out to sea, for the bay was found empty, so that, in anticipation of their return, the admiral decided to reoccupy the town. Once again its inhabitants fled as soon as Captain De Cordes and a few dozen of armed men began to ascend the steps leading up to the town. He nevertheless posted guards around the town and entrusted its defense to a small group of men under the command of Rombout Hooghstoel, and to meet the by now acute demand for water, put the remainder of the men to work filling the ships' water barrels at the town's well.

It was now September 7; they had spent more than a week in the Cape Verde Islands, but those suffering from scurvy fared no better than when they had first arrived, whilst the island's "unwholesome air" had claimed many new victims, including the admiral, who had retired to his cabin, plagued by recurrent bouts of fever. To most it was becoming tantalizingly clear that any prolongation of Praia's occupation held no merit, especially now that the only thing it had to offer had been replenished. The growing frustration over their predicament led to disagreement among the fleet's senior officers and before long the ships' council was paralyzed by deep-running divisions. Largely to blame were the pilots, who, given their experience in long distance voyages, had good reason to criticize Mahu's endless dallying in their urge to press on so as not to arrive in the

Southern Hemisphere out of season. One of them, the *Hope*'s second pilot, William Adams, recalled how the simmering conflict came to a crashing head when:

> I and all the pilots of the fleet were called to a councel; in which we all shewed our judgements of disliking the place; which [was] by all the captaines taken so ill, that afterward it was agreed by them all, that the pilots should be no more in the council, the which was executed.

The pilots' misgivings seem to have been taken to heart nonetheless, for when the next day the *Faith* and *Fidelity* were spotted out at sea, tacking to and fro but unable to make for the bay, the remaining members of the ships' council decided to re-embark the troops and join the two ships. Praia was torched and left to burn.

Not yet, however, were the Dutch ready to leave the Cape Verde Islands behind; the *Faith* and the *Fidelity* had missed the opportunity to replenish their water supplies, and given the continuing shortage of victuals, a continuation of the journey was considered too hazardous. Fortunately, the fleet's next stop, at the island of Brava, a few miles to the west of São Tiago, proved more fruitful. On September 12 Sebald de Weert, whose ship drew least water and was able to draw close under the shore, found a freshwater stream leading down into a small bay. The bay was too shallow for the *Faith* or *Fidelity* to anchor, and their crews spent much of the day in the boats, ferrying the large water barrels to the shore and back to the ships, an exhausting and precarious operation that lasted till midnight. Hoping to find at least some fresh food before the journey was resumed Sebald de Weert used the interlude to search farther inland. Not long after they had set off, they happened on a clearing with several huts, one of which turned out to be filled to the roof with corn. Fearing the dwellers' return De Weert immediately set his men to work, carrying the corn back to the shore. He had brought along only seven men, who, in the absence of bags or any means of transport, had to make do by tying up their trousers around their ankles and carry the corn in the trunks of their trousers. As if to reward them for their efforts, on the beach, the hungry men found two giant turtles that had just laid some six hundred eggs.

Meanwhile, the admiral's cabin on board the *Hope* had become the scene of far more solemn undertakings. Since their departure from Praia, Mahu's health had failed to rally. On September 15, perceiving his end to be imminent, he had the captains gather on the flagship. When all had gathered around his bed, the gaunt and feeble admiral transferred the general command of the expedition to Vice Admiral Simon de Cordes. During the next few days Mahu's health rapidly deteriorated, and in the night of September 23, with De Cordes and Van Beuningen at his bedside, the thirty-four-year-old admiral drew his last breath. As they had already sailed from Brava, it was decided to give the admiral a burial in the naval tradition. This was done two days later, when the admiral's coffin, weighed down with stones and draped with a mourning veil, was carried from the officer' quarters on the rear deck to before the mast, where, to the ruffle of dampened drums and the roar of a broadside salvo, the mortal remains of "our good and prudent" commander were committed to the deep.

Succession in case of the premature death of a commander was formally laid down in the fleet's sailing instructions. And that same day the ships' council gathered on the flagship, where with due ceremony and in the presence of all officers the sealed instructions were opened. These stipulated that "in case Admiral Iacomo Mahu happens to die on the voyage, Vice Admiral Simon de Cordes is to step in his place." Though anticipated, the outcome was met by all with "joyful hearts," and having received the oath of obedience and loyalty from all his senior officers, De Cordes immediately proceeded to reappoint his captains. Command over the *Love* as vice admiral was given to Van Beuningen, who marked the occasion with an uplifting speech by which "the earlier sadness was greatly reduced." Command over the *Faith* was given to Sebald de Weert, while Dirck Gerritszoon Pomp was made captain of *The Gospel*. To replace

Pomp, William Adams was transferred from the flagship to the *Love*, to serve as pilot major, above his brother, Thomas Adams. The only captain whose station was not affected by the death of the admiral was Jeurian van Bockholt, who remained in command of the *Fidelity*.

The time-consuming formalities brought about by Mahu's death almost plunged the fleet into yet more misery, when shortly after his burial the lead climbed to twenty-six fathoms. The fleet had drifted east toward the mainland and was now in serious danger of foundering on the Guinean coast. To get away from the land, course was set southwest. Over the next days calm winds continued to blow them southwest, until October 6, when course was set east-southeast and several days of calm sailing gave De Cordes time for reflection.

The events thus far did not provide the newly installed admiral with much material from which to draw strength; though they had not met any disasters, neither had they booked any successes. Their stay at the Cape Verde Islands had been particularly disappointing, especially when one considered that the expedition's chief aim was to annoy the enemy in Drake and Cavendish's image.[4] Most worryingly, the stay had done next to nothing to improve the condition of the sick—the chief reason for their visit in the first place. On September 12, five days after the admiral had taken to his bed with fever, his physician, Jan Eldricks, died, having been plagued for several days by similar symptoms. Daniel Resteau, chief merchant on the *Hope*, died in the same night as the admiral. And though, following their departure from Brava, the reported deaths from fever had somewhat abated, the scorbutic symptoms had returned with a vengeance. The affliction was spreading with such ferocity that within only one month the flagship had hardly enough men to handle her sails. With over seventy sick lingering belowdecks, conditions on the *Faith* were hardly any better. The other ships were hit hard too, each carrying between thirty and forty gravely ill men, so that, by the time the Line was crossed, on November 2, death from disease had become a daily occurrence.

On that day De Cordes presided over the ships' council for the first time. It unanimously decided to try and reach Annobon, an island in the Gulf of Guinea and well known for its abundance of fresh victuals. Assuming their position to be roughly southwest of Annobon, course was set northeast in the hope of thus reaching the island. That same night a signal shot rang from the flagship sailing at the head of the convoy signalling that its lookout had sighted land—it was not Annobon but the African coast. They had failed to heed Plancius' warning and crossed the meridian of Cape Palmas. From there the Guinean current had rapidly carried them east so that even as the council had met, the fleet had already passed Annobon by more than a hundred miles. Worse still, during the night they had lost sight of one of the Portuguese caravels, which had carried the corn found on Brava. Some reported they had seen her bearing up to the wind, raising suspicions amongst others that the eleven men who had sailed in her had deliberately broken rank with the convoy. This was not confirmed, since neither the vessel nor any of the men was seen again.[5]

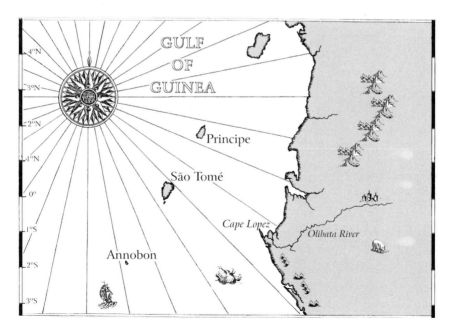

In the morning of November 4, some scouts were put ashore to look for edibles. They spent the rest of that day and the following day ranging up and down the coast in search of a clearing through which they could move further inland, but the dense vegetation that lined the shore proved wholly impenetrable. A continuation of the search was interrupted by strong southerly winds that, combined with a northerly coastal current, caused the ships to drag so hard at their anchors that the *Faith* lost the stock on one of hers. On November 6, therefore, anchors were weighed and, having traced the coast northward for three days, the fleet found a good anchorage in the mouth of a small river that joined the sea just north of Cape Lopez, and on the shores of which an encampment was erected to nurse the sick.

The next two weeks were spent in a continued search for victuals. Vice Admiral Van Beuningen set out with a boat upriver, taking with him trinkets and ironware to barter with the natives, who had been sighted on the beach from the ships as they had followed the coast. Only with the greatest of difficulty did Van Beuningen manage to approach a number of them, but the latter remained wary of the aliens. When he returned two days later, he had little more to show than a few fowl and some bananas. A more substantial addition to the men's limited rations was the fresh fish that was caught in "quantities that exceeded the men's appetite," as well as watercress and edible seaweeds that grew in the riverbed and proved astoundingly wholesome to those suffering from scurvy.

The arrival, on November 23, of another Dutch merchantman promised unexpected relief. Her captain, Barent Erickszoon, had sailed on the coast of Guinea since 1593. His pilot, a Frenchman, even claimed to have lived among the local tribesmen, mastered their language, and to be still on friendly terms with their chieftain. Their village, according to the pilot, was situated along the river about two days upstream, and that same day Captain De Weert and the pilot embarked in two boats to seek out the chieftain. After two days' rowing they reached the village, where both men were received with great ceremony. They were led into the presence of the chieftain, who sat on a kind of shoemaker's stool and was dressed in the full regalia of his office. He wore a scarlet robe, embroidered with artificial gold, and on his head "a cap of yellow, red and blue Oriental cloth"; around his neck hung, "as Kingly ornament, a Paternoster of Muscovite," whilst the white ashes with which his face had been painted made De Weert wonder "in what aid all this blanching was done." In a wide circle behind the chieftain sat his village elders, their heads adorned with hens' feathers and "their black skin painted very red." A stool next to the chieftain, placed on a small rug, had been reserved for the captain, who, having greeted the chieftain according to the local custom, sat down to explain through the pilot the purpose of his visit. Trade relations were soon established but the purchasing power of the merchandise De Weert had brought along was disappointing. So was the meal with which he was presented. After what seemed an eternity, a servant brought in a wooden tray. On it were some fried bananas and smoked hippopotamus, of which the chieftain "ate with great modesty." Not as modestly as De Weert, who only managed to partake in some of the meat by washing it down with large quantities of what the pilot identified as Vin de Palma. In a remarkably generous but, under the circumstances, understandable gesture, De Weert proffered a sample of his own spare provisions, some biscuit, smoked fish, cheese, and a bottle of Spanish wine. Especially the wine seemed to agree with the chieftain, so much so that he was forced to leave his guests to sleep off its intoxicating effect. The next morning, having spent a restless night in the chieftain's quarters, the Dutch set off downriver again, their boats laden with the proceeds of their inland trade: two goats, some poultry, and "a good deal of bananas."

On the first day of December, another party was dispatched upriver. This time the proceeds were even more paltry. Yet the daily diet of fresh fish and greens, complemented by the meat of wild birds, wild boars, and two buffalo, shot by De Weert's men on one of their forays into the bush, did not miss their wholesome effect on

The meeting with the chieftain of the upstream village. The chieftain is depicted sitting on a stool, in front of his men on the left. De Weert sits on the right, flanked by the French pilot and a number of the English trumpeters.

the sick. On the admiral's orders, they were the first to receive the best of what was on offer. All were nevertheless in one degree or other afflicted by fevers, and sixteen had already died. On December 4, the depletion in numbers was temporarily stalled by the arrival of another Dutch ship, the *Moriaen*, one of De Moucheron's merchantmen; she had come from the island of Principe, and was bound for the West Indies. Thirteen of her sailors joined the expedition and, on December 8, the reinforced crews were ordered to re-embark and set sail for the island of Annobon.

The five ships cast anchor on Annobon's shore in the afternoon of December 16, 1598. A landing party under the command of Captain Pomp was sent ashore, where they were met by a group of islanders. These seemed unhappy with their guests but grew more cordial when

Pomp addressed them in Portuguese, and told him to come back the next day when they would bring him the required victuals. Wary, but hopeful that he had won the friendship of the islanders, Pomp returned to the fleet, but his fears were confirmed when the next morning he and his men were met by a large contingent of armed Portuguese soldiers and told to leave.

Vexed by their cold reception, that same day, the ships' council decided to sack the settlement. All able men were armed, distributed over the fourteen available boats, and divided into two landing parties. The largest, consisting of ten boats, was placed under the command of Sergeant Major Rombout Hooghstoel; the remainder under the command of Captain Bockholt. They met with hardly any resistance; the settlement's inhabitants had taken the same course of action as those of Praia, and had evacuated the settlement dur-

The raid on Annobon. On the left, Captain Jeurian van Bockholt's men have just landed and opened the offense. They are about to be joined by those of Sergeant Major Rombout Hooghstoel. The orchard is depicted on the right.

ing the night, leaving behind only a small force to win time. After some desultory firing, in which a Dutch trumpeter was injured, this rear party, too, retreated into the nearby mountains and the Dutch proceeded to occupy the settlement.

Like Praia, Annobon's settlement consisted only of a few dozen simple dwellings, built of sun-dried brick. Though primitive and partly destroyed by a fire that had erupted during the skirmish, the protection it offered was welcomed, for shortly after the Portuguese had been evicted they began to resort to guerrilla tactics. From the surrounding bush they shot at anyone who dared to venture beyond the settlement's walls to collect the wholesome fruit that grew in a nearby orchard. Their first victim was Wouter Wouterszoon, who was found lying amongst the orchard's fruit trees on December 19. He had been beaten to death and left lying in his own blood to serve as an example. To avoid further casualties, De Cordes imposed a curfew, but the lure of the forbidden fruit continued to get the better of his men; they kept returning from their secretive errands with sniper wounds until De Cordes had a gallows built on the settlement's outskirts to serve as a reminder of the punishment that awaited the more persistent trespassers. To deal with the snipers, a punitive expedition of 150 well-armed men was sent inland on December 24. One of its scouts discoverd that the Portuguese had withdrawn to a small stronghold, situated on a mountain, not far from the settlement. Two paths led up the mountain from different directions, and after some deliberation, it was decided to divide the forces in two and storm the stronghold from two sides. The plan worked, though this time round, the Dutch suffered a number of casualties, mostly men who were injured by the large rocks that were cast down by the stronghold's defenders. One man had been shot. It was Captain De Weert's scribe, the young Jan Kloeck, who had carried the banner and had been the first to storm the stronghold. He was hit straight in the heart.

Again the same problems that had plagued the men during their stay at the Cape Verde Islands and Cape Lopez returned to haunt them. While the fresh tropical fruit had quickly dispelled the scorbutic symptoms, within days tropical disease began to take its toll, so that "as the one bettered, the other fell ill," causing another thirty men to find their grave on Annobon. Yet in spite of the losses the island enabled the fleet to continue its journey, for it was found to be "very fertile," offering fruit and livestock in great quantities. A group of men, sent out on December 20, came back with twenty-seven cows. They had also managed to salvage some provisions from the mountain stronghold, including a barrel of ship's biscuit, some canisters with Spanish wine, and, to the men's general merriment, even some Dutch cheeses.[6]

There were no further encounters with the Portuguese or the islanders, and the rest of the time spent on Annobon was used to careen and clean the ships, before their storerooms were filled with the island's fresh produce. On the eve of their departure, amidst a generally cheerful spirit, the crews of the five ships celebrated New Year's Eve, 1598. It had been six months since they had sailed from Rotterdam; during the two months they had spent in the Gulf of Guinea alone, they had lost one man with nearly every day.

Finally, on January 3, 1599, encouraged by a brisk south-southeasterly wind, all five ships raised anchor and set sail to embark on their long transatlantic haul. No further landings were anticipated and course was set southwest, directly for the Strait of Magellan. But after only six days' sailing the main mast of the *Faith* broke into three and was lost overboard. Its core had been eaten away by mold to such an extent that the carpenters who were ferried over from the other ships to assemble a makeshift mast from the main yard thought it "a miracle" that the old one had held for so long.

By January 22, they had reached Ascension, 8°30' south of the Line, and by the last day of the month they were in a latitude of 20°20'S. It was now midsummer in the Southern Hemisphere and, as they drew close to the tropic of Capricorn, the sun was right overhead so that the men were "unable to tell their own shadows."

That day the lookout sighted the Abrolhos Archipelago, signaling the fleet's arrival under the coast of the Brazilian mainland. Blown along by a moderate northeasterly wind, the fleet followed the coast southward, reaching a latitude of 41°30'S. on March 9.

It was on that day that a sailor on the *Hope* was sentenced to death for stealing food from the storeroom; he was the first to face such a penalty since the fleet's departure. The sentence was exacted on the following day when he was hanged from the bowsprit. Toward evening his remains were taken down and thrown overboard, to be dragged along on the same line from which he had been hanged, so as to serve as "a Mirror to those who might contemplate to undertake the same." The sickly sight of the man's limp remains, bobbing and turning in the ship's wake, rather reminded his fellow men of their empty stomachs. On the admiral's instructions, rations had been brought down to an absolute minimum; each man now received only one pound of biscuit every four days and "the like proportion of Wine and Water." The effects of these austere measures were recorded by the physician on the *Faith*, Barent Potgieter, who noted that "when the fellows were given mess-food, sentries had to be posted to look on, so that they would eat with manners, for they guzzled with such greed, that some burnt their mouths to such a degree that the pieces would fall out." On the *Love*, Adams observed how "others fell into so great weaknesse and sicknesse for hunger, that they did eate the Calves skinnes, wherewith our Ropes were covered." The hardships suffered on board the ships seemed to be underscored by an ominous change in the color of the sea, which in a latitude of 42°42'S., not far from Río de la Plata, turned bloodred. When water was drawn, it was found to be "full of little red worms, which, when taken in the hand, sprang away like fleas."

With disease and hunger rampant, death was not far behind. On March 7, one of the six English trumpeters on the *Fidelity* was struck by "a rare illness." Sitting at his mess, the musician suddenly fell over backwards, vehemently foaming from the mouth but without uttering a word. He died at noon on the next day. Two days later a young man, coming from the quarterdeck, "grew very loud." When approached by some of his fellow men, he flew into such a violent rage that he had to be tied down in his bunk. There he languished without food or drink for four days, after which he began to ramble deliriously (a proffered ship's biscuit was at first "beheld with much terror" and then "consumed as if by a savage"). Remaining very poorly, the man eventually died of gangrene, "since, in his stupor, he was unable to clean himself, so that his feet, having frozen with the damp cold, had to be amputated."

On March 23, the ships were enveloped in a dense fog that dispersed again toward the evening. The same happened three days later, when again the fog lifted toward evening, and all ships were able to reunite. When soundings were taken, the lead recorded sixty fathoms. Meanwhile weather was deteriorating rapidly and that night a "tremendous storm" broke the flagship's bowsprit. It was dragged under the hull with much of the rigging, causing the ship to take so much water that her three pumps had to be manned round the clock. On the morning of April 1, the lead climbed to thirty-six fathoms, and that same afternoon, sailing west-northwest before a southwesterly wind, high land was sighted toward the northwest; by the evening they were less than five miles away from the mainland. Keeping close to the land, they continued due south for the next three days, down to a latitude of 50°46'S., where the lead went down to only thirty fathoms. Then, on April 5, in a latitude of 52°S., Captain De Weert recorded in his log how the whole fleet "sailed for 2 miles along the land, being high like Dover"—they had reached Cape Virgin, marking the entrance to the Strait of Magellan. Once more they were blown back to sea, but finally, on April 6, 1599, all five ships rounded the cape and "fell into the mouth of the Strait with a southwesterly wind." Yet the time at which they did so could hardly have been worse, for in the seasonal cycle of the Southern Hemisphere it was already mid-autumn and winter was approaching fast.

V
THE PASSAGE

The trials that those men do meet withal
That are obedient to the heavenly call,
Are manifold and suited to the flesh,
And come, and come, and come again afresh;
That now, or sometime else, we by them may
Be taken, overcome, and cast away.
O let the pilgrims, let the pilgrims then
Be vigilant, and quit themselves like men.

The fleet's first stop in the Strait of Magellan was at Zealous Anchorage, behind Cape Dungeness. The weather was calm, the sky overhead clear, and the night passed without incident. The next morning, April 7, 1599, anchors were weighed, and sailing before a southeasterly wind, the ships slowly moved up the strait, closely following the northern shore. Toward the evening they reached the First Narrows, where the ships again dropped anchor. Aboard the *Faith*, however, the exercize went awry. During the three-months' crossing of the Atlantic, constant exposure to the elements had weakened the thick manila anchor cable. Because of the calm weather during the first night in the strait the flaw had gone unnoticed, but when winds picked up, and the anchor began to bite, the weakened hawser snapped. Having spent the night on a spare anchor, much of the next day was spent in trying to locate the missing anchor, but it had dragged the anchor buoy under water and there was no trace of either.

As a result of the delay and the onset of mist, it was already late in the day before the five ships reached the Second Narrows. Here again the fleet ran into difficulties. The *Faith*'s chief pilot, Jan Outgherszoon, who had been commissioned by De Cordes to make

81

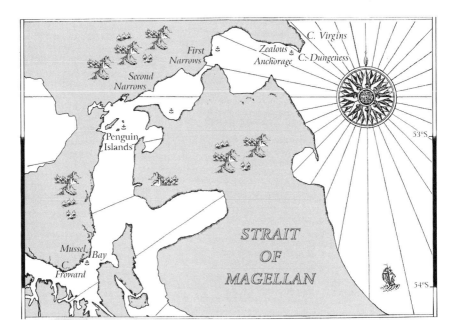

a detailed survey of the strait, recorded how in the narrows "there ran such a strong ebb and flow, that, carry as much sail as we might, we could not outsail it, but were set back as if we had carried no sail at all." Unable to pass the narrows, the fleet anchored on the south side of the strait in thirteen fathoms, a mile away from the shore, at a point from where the northern extremity of the First Narrows was still faintly visible toward the northeast. The following day, with the tide on their side, the fleet passed the Second Narrows without trouble, but during the day the wind turned due south, interrupting any further progress and forcing the fleet to anchor off the Penguin Islands, just south of the narrows.

The islands, which had earned their collective name by the vast colonies of penguins by which they were inhabited, had been visited by both Drake and Cavendish for victualing. Following the example of the English expeditions, on April 10, a group of men landed on Elizabeth Island, the largest of the three islands, and killed some fourteen hundred of the birds, which the men jocularly called "divers (as they dive to collect their food from the seabed)." The *Fidelity* had

82

anchored just off St. Magdalena, the second-largest island. Here, too, men went ashore; they found only a few of the birds, but returned with five seals. Van Beuningen and De Weert used the interlude to bury the remains of merchant Jan Dirckszoon van Dort on St. Martha, the smallest of the three islands. He was the first Dutchman to die in the strait.

By noon the wind had shifted to the northeast again, when shots from the flagship signaled the resumption of the fleet's passage. Victualed with penguin meat "sufficient to nourish the whole fleet," and "having much wind, which was good for us to go through," to Pilot Major William Adams and the other pilots the opportunity for a quick passage seemed to beckon. Not so to the admiral, however, who on the contrary thought it a good moment for the "refreshing of our men" and "watering and taking in of wood." And thus, late in the evening, having advanced no more than twenty miles south of the Penguin Islands, anchors were dropped once again, this time close under the western shore.

The next day, fifty men went ashore to search for "signs of life or ships that might have passed"; they followed the strait's wuthering shore for three miles but found nothing. A second excursion, on April 13, fifty miles farther south, proved equally fruitless, although fire-wood was found in abundance. In the meantime water supplies were replenished from a small freshwater river that ran into the bay where the ships had anchored. The bay was christened Mussel Bay (San Nicolaes Bay), for its shallows and a small island at the center of the bay were covered with mussels. During the next days, the wind being contrary, much time was spent in collecting the wholesome shellfish until, on April 17, when, before an easterly wind, the fleet resumed its passage, first southwest, then west-southwest, and then northwest, all the while "sailing between the high land, through which," to pilot Outgherszoon, "it seemed we would not have found a passage, given the height of the mountains, which seem to run into each other."

They had now rounded Cape Froward; already two-thirds of the strait lay behind them. From here onwards the Strait of Magellan ran due northwest, terminating in the Pacific Ocean in roughly the same latitude as its eastern entrance. But on April 18 their passage up the strait came to an abrupt end when the wind turned northwest and failed to leave its quarter, so that, having reached a latitude of 54°S., the fleet was forced to take shelter in a "green bay" (Fortesque Bay) on the north side of the strait.

As far as safe havens in the Strait of Magellan went, the bay in which the fleet had taken refuge was, according to Potgieter, "the best bay." Its depth ranged from twelve to forty-five fathoms, offering ample opportunity to anchor without the danger of being driven aground. In the center of the bay lay a small island, which dissolved into three islets when the tide was high. The island was largely covered with sand on which the water rose sufficiently high to careen the ships. As in Mussel Bay, a freshwater river poured into the bay,

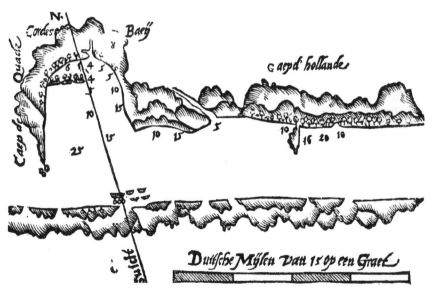

On Outgherszoon's chart of the bay, which already carries the name it was to receive later, the three tree-covered islets are clearly visible. The cape on the west side of the bay has apparently been named after Jacob Quaeckernaeck, skipper of the *Love*. The character R (printed upside down) marks the men's common burial site.

and apart from some ducks and geese, here too, there was "a multi-tude of Mussels," some of them "as much as a span in length, so that the flesh, cooked out of the shell, weighed as much as a pound." It was the green laurel-like trees that lined the bay and covered the bay's islands that led the Dutch to call it Green Bay.[1]

The first few weeks in Green Bay were passed in good spirits. Nourished by the fresh shellfish and water, the crews looked out expectantly for improvement in the weather. At first the occasional calms did seem to hold out hope for a quick passage before winter would set in, but weeks passed as winds remained contrary and merely increased in intensity. When autumn began to draw to its end and the awareness began to take hold among the commanders that a wintering in the bay might be inevitable, they began to prepare their men and ships for a protracted stay as best they could.

As the days grew shorter and shorter, it became painfully clear that the men's clothing was hopelessly inadequate for the harsh climate. The leaders' belated concerns were shared by Potgieter, who observed that most of the men "had no clothes, headgear, or working toggery, as they believed that they would come to a hot country where they might go half-naked." As a result, the physician found that "the majority suffered greatly through cold and discomfort." On Potgieter's advice, De Cordes ordered several cases of woolen cloth to be taken from the cargo. Their contents were distributed among the men to fashion the thick cloth into winter garments. To further ward off the cold and keep the many immobile and sick from freezing, fires were kept going on all ships, day and night.

As one storm followed on the heels of the other, the crews had to man the windswept decks in a perpetual toil of backbreaking chores: weighing anchors, putting them out, and weighing them again. In spite of their constant efforts, the ships would often collide, or drift toward land from their moorings, so that whole days were spent in frantic efforts to get them moored again. Meanwhile, others had to row ashore in rain, wind, and cold to gather wood, water, or food, "through which constant toil the men became very wornout."

Food, or rather the lack of it, was a constant concern. During the crossing, rations had been brought down to six pounds of biscuit, some dried fish, a little oil per man in every eight days, and two draughts of wine, meted out in the morning. It added up to a subsistence diet at best—enough to stave off a quick death; too little to sustain the weakening men through the long winter months that lay ahead. For those whose health permitted physical effort, the scramble for food became a daily preoccupation. The fish that were caught (few in number and small in size) were reserved for the officers. For the common sailor the only way to supplement his meager rations was to wade through the cold and nebulous shallows of the bay in search of seafood, or comb through the poor vegetation of the surrounding landscape for hours in search of some edible roots or herbs of sustenance. Back on board and inspired by the imagination of an empty stomach, they would try to cook up a palatable meal from the scant ingredients they had gathered. One commonly served dish consisted of the roots of a plant found not far from the bay, chopped fine and stewed with ship's biscuit. The staple ingredient in all of these dishes, whether steamed, roasted, or fried, was the mussels, of which there was no dearth throughout their stay. The ubiquitous shellfish presented an additional burden for the officers, who again had to take watch during messtime, since many a man was tempted to sell his small rations for great sums of money, which led to "such dropsy that many a man died with a sound heart."

Those whose hunger got the better of them and sought to take what they were not given faced severe punishment. The first such case since the fleet's arrival in Green Bay occurred on the night of April 21, when two men were caught red-handed in the storeroom of *The Gospel*. The next day they were led before the ships' council, and being found guilty of stealing oil, both were sentenced to death. That same day they were rowed out to the bay's island to be hanged on a scaffold that had been erected there for the purpose. The first to be hanged was Jacob Willemszoon. The other culprit, who was made to watch his mate's execution, was pardoned after he had broken down and begged for mercy, even though he was "heartily flogged," together with another culprit who had owned up to having shared in the crime's proceeds.

The attrition in the men's numbers at each leg of the journey was now beginning to show. Already before the fleet's arrival at the entrance of the strait more than one hundred men had been lost, either in combat, through disease, or by law. By the end of April the complement of each ship had shrunk to roughly eighty. On May 5, in an effort to try and halt the spiraling death rate, the ships' council decided to increase rations to half a pound of biscuit a man a day, but the measure had only limited effect. At first, shots were fired to mark the loss of yet another man. But as the death toll climbed, and conditions worsened, the ceremony was silently dropped so as not to distress the crews.

The officers, though spared the greatest blows by dint of better food and quarters, were not wholly immune to the afflictions from which their men were dying in such terrible numbers. The first senior officer to die in the strait was the *Fidelity*'s captain, Jeurian van Bockholt. Whenever called upon, Van Bockholt had faithfully done his duty. That he was no ruthless self-seeker was shown by the warm heart his men had borne toward him, and whenever the sick had been evacuated to land, it had been he to whom their care had been entrusted. Yet his active role in the expedition had not disguised the fact that he was gravely ill; ever since they had sailed from Dover he had been afflicted by "a consumption" and had hardly enjoyed a day of good health. Already once before, shortly after their departure from Brava, he had been on the brink of death. And though, by the time of their arrival at Annobon he had rallied sufficiently to participate in the raid on the settlement, he failed to regain his health in full. The long passage across the Atlantic had sapped the little strength that remained in him, and on April 28, only thirty years of age, Van Bockholt passed away peacefully. He was buried with full honors, and by way of exception three shots were fired from each ship.

On March 3, after a long and awkward session of the ships' council, Balthasar de Cordes, the twenty-two-year-old cousin of the admiral, was appointed as the new captain of the *Fidelity*. In spite of his close blood ties to the admiral, the young merchant-son had not been given a senior position in the fleet yet. Nor had he thus far stood out for his conduct as his predecessor had done. And though, formally, it was De Cordes' inexperience that had kept the council from appointing him to such a position at an earlier juncture, to those who were better acquainted with De Cordes' capricious character it was no surprise that it had taken the ships' council so long to invest the youth with the heavy responsibility of running a ship and with the care for those who sailed in her.

Mindful of the poor state of provisions, Van Beuningen set out on May 7 with a number of men in two boats to explore the strait in search of seals. From Green Bay the distant wailing of the mammals could often be heard, but they were hardly ever seen and the few that had chanced up the bay had shied away when the men drew close. Van Beuningen had noticed that the seals would occasionally gather on the islands in the middle of the strait (Charles Islands), opposite Green Bay. Drawing close to the islands, the men in the boats could not make out any of the mammals. Instead, to their surprise, they spotted seven canoes among the rocks, rising and falling with the swell. No life could be seen on the narrow beach but as the party made ready to land, it was suddenly pelted by a hail of stones. Natives, "reddish of color, with long hair down to their shoulders," had appeared on the headland from where they assailed the visitors "with such ferocity that the vice admiral dared not approach the island." The natives, sensing their advantage, quickly descended to the beach and fell into their boats "amid much clamor and shouting." Realizing that the natives were closing in and getting ready to fight, Van Beuningen ordered his men to shoot. Four or five natives were hit and thrown into the water by the impact of the bullets. The rest, startled to see their fellows fall in such sudden numbers, hurriedly rowed away, back toward the islands, where they took flight inland. Van Beuningen, judging it

Potgieter's curiously Caucasian rendering of the strait's inhabitants. One of them holds the weapon which Potgieter describes in detail. The physician also recorded their remarkable habit of transporting fire in their boats.

wiser to leave "these furious and bloodthirsty people," gave orders to leave the island and return to the fleet.[2]

No more natives were sighted for the next few weeks but, on May 26, the Dutch were again caught off guard. As on most other days a number of men had gone ashore in search of food and firewood. Potgieter, who had gone with them, later recalled how some had parted from the rest. From afar he had seen how they had gone into the nearby mountains in the hope of finding something better, when they were attacked by a group of natives who had appeared from the woods, killing three of the men and wounding two others; and he had little doubt that they "would also have killed the two injured, had not Captain de Cordes come to their aid." The physician further recalled how the natives "went altogether naked, with the exception of one, who had an old seal skin tied around his neck that covered his back and shoulders." All of them, he noted, had carried spears of hard wood, which they had hurled at their victims by hand, "very fiercely and straight." Attached at the base to a length of dried gut, the weapon's foremost point was fashioned like a harpoon, with long teeth that caused it to remain firmly lodged in the victim's body. Back on board the *Fidelity*, Potgieter found that in one of the two men the harpoon had gone straight through four layers of clothing, into the chest's cavity, so that he could only remove the projectile by cutting away the surrounding tissue, "and had to push some right through, since they were lodged so deep in the body."

All the while fierce storms continued to claim both human and material offers. On July 8, Dierick de Groot, boatswain's mate on the *Hope*, was tragically lost. He was working in the beakhead, making repairs to the rigging, when he lost his footing and fell into the sea through the lattices. And though the young sailor remained afloat, calling for help, he could not be saved, "since it blew so hard that no one dare enter the boats." Shortly afterwards, the caravel captured at São Tiago was lost. It was driven ashore in a squall and wrecked. To replace it and to keep the men occupied, the ships' council decided to have the men assemble the sixteen-ton pinnace, brought along in sections in the hold of the flagship. On July 16 the four large sections, together with timbers, props, and supports were ferried to the shore, where the vessel was put together in eight days. She was christened *Postillon*, and Gillis Janszoon, junior skipper on the *Faith*, was appointed as her captain.

The expedition had now spent more than three months in Green Bay, and they had gone through the heart of winter. "Many times," Adams recalled, "we had the wind good to goe through the Straights, but our Generall would not." They had been the first Europeans to winter in the strait and the cost in lives was commensurate; 120 men had perished in the constant battle against cold, disease, and hunger. Those still alive had reached the very limits of endurance and were thoroughly demoralized. To bolster their spirits, on August 2, all able men were ordered ashore, where, amidst the deep snow, a sermon was held to thank "God almighty for having shown His mercy," and to pray for "prosperity on the long journey ahead." At the same solemn occasion the bay that had been the scene of such suffering was renamed Cordes Bay.

Three more weeks the expedition stayed in Cordes Bay. Then, on August 23, a moderate wind began to blow from the northeast and orders were given for the fleet to make sail. But the wind did not last and on the next morning, with "sails hanging," anchors were cast in twenty-eight fathoms along the southern shore. Later in the day, when the tidal current began to work in their favor, all six ships managed to pass Carlos III Island, situated in the narrowest section of the strait, halfway into the second leg, and at ten o'clock at night the fleet anchored in a bay on the southern side of the strait.

The following day De Cordes had all able men once more assemble on the shore. There he announced that on the request of his officers he had "resolved to leave a monument in the Strait, of so Glorious a Dutch Fleet, having passed here with such effort, with such trouble, and amid such danger." He had called into life a fraternity consisting of the expedition's "principal heads"—himself, Vice Admiral Gerrit van Beuningen, Captain Sebald de Weert, Captain Dirck Gerritszoon Pomp, Captain Balthasar de Cordes, and Captain Gillis Janszoon. Inspired by the *leo belgicus*, the proud symbol of Dutch independence, it had been named the Brotherhood of the Unfettered Lion, and in the presence of the assembled men, the admiral pro-ceeded to swear in his fellow members. All solemnly vowed that "no troubles, distress, nor fear of death would move them to brook any-thing that might lead to the detriment of the welfare of their coun-try"; that they had "undertaken to risk life and livelihood to harm their arch-enemy wherever possible"; and that they intended "to plant the Dutch Coat of Arms in those provinces from where the King of Spain gathers the riches with which he has sustained his war against the Netherlands." Finally, amidst yet more ostentatious ceremony, the bay was renamed Ridders (Knights) Bay, and to commemorate the occasion, a high pillar bearing a plaque with the names of the six dignitaries was erected at the entrance of the bay.

On August 28, a moderate wind began to blow from the southeast, enabling the fleet to leave Ridders Bay and pass Crooked Reach, the narrowest section of the strait. Here the strait was not more than a gunshot across, offering hardly any room for maneuvering, so that when the wind shifted to the northwest later in the day, they had to drop anchor again, this time in a small inlet, only half a mile down the strait. The inlet was set off from Ridders Bay by a high promontory that jutted out into the strait. In the absence of better winds, De Weert was sent back with a number of his men to uproot the commemorative pillar so that it could be placed on the promontory, for everyone to see. Yet hardly had they rounded the promontory when they "perceived about eighty savages, who sat on land, having with them as much as eight or ten large Dinghies or Canoes." Spotting the boat, the natives called out, beckoning the men to come ashore. De Weert, being with only few men, most of whom were unarmed, wisely ignored the calls of the natives. On his

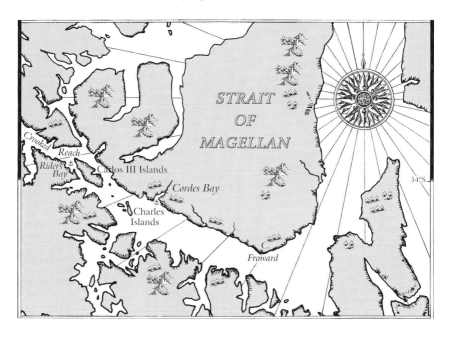

return, a larger party was dispatched, in three boats, but when it arrived where the natives had been, all it found was the "signs of their cruelty." They had exhumed the remains of the dead that had been interred on the bay's shore. The remains of the admiral's physician, Master Jan Janszoon, found floating facedown in the bay's shallows, had been severely disfigured. The grave of the bottler of *The Gospel* had also been desecrated, although his remains could not be found. An even larger expedition was launched to search for the bottler's remains and to punish "this unnatural people." But by nightfall, having searched the bay's many inlets and crevices in vain, the dejected party gave up its search and returned to the ships empty-handed. All they had found was a fragment of the memorial plaque, which had been smashed to pieces.

Prior to the fleet's final departure the captains were issued with new instructions. In case of their dispersal after they had left the strait they were to sail for Santa María—a small island on the Chilean coast, just south of Concepción. At Santa María they were to wait for the others for six weeks. If this time was to elapse without them being able to reunite, each should take in provisions at the said island and go "wherever he could, and wherever seemed best."

Then, on the morning of September 2, 1599, the wind once more veered south-southeast, and two days later, under a starlit sky the Dutch fleet left the western mouth of the strait and entered the Pacific Ocean, one year behind schedule. The ships were in a reasonable state of repair. During their stay in Cordes Bay, much of the rigging had been replaced, whilst extensive repairs had been carried through on the weakened hulls and masts. In worst condition was the *Faith*. Her improvised mast, consisting of eight sections, was too short, causing her to be a poor sailer and to slow down the other ships. Most worrying was the level of provisions, for whilst the crews had been halved, rations were running low all the same. On board *The Gospel* there was left 3,000 pounds of biscuit, 500 pounds of oil, 100 pounds of rice, a few cheeses, and a barrel of

wine. It was only sufficient to last for another five months at best—
a state of affairs much the same on board the other ships.

Over the next days the wind gradually veered to the northeast,
allowing the fleet to keep their course due northwest, "with which,"
according to Adams, "we followed our pretended Voyage toward the
Coast of Peru." But on September 7, the sea turned rough, forcing
the *Love* and *Fidelity* to stow their boats. During the next few hours
the winds kept gathering strength, and before long the first ship was
in trouble. Due to the constant pounding, *The Gospel* lost her
bowsprit. It dragged with it the spritsail topmast, threatening, in
turn, to tear down her foremast too. With no other choice left,
Captain Pomp ordered his men to haul in the sails and fire a signal
shot for assistance. The call for help was first answered by the *Faith*
and *Fidelity*, both of which hove to and followed suit. On board the
Fidelity attempts were made to relaunch the boat, but with no sail
to keep her steady she began to pitch heavily, burying her bowsprit
in the high seas, until she too had lost her spritsail topmast. The
struggling ships were joined by the *Love*, which also took in her sails.
Only on board the *Hope* the operation had apparently gone unnoticed, for she remained under sail and was rapidly running away
from the rest. Presently the other ships were enveloped in a dense
fog, and confusion began to take hold of their crews as they "could
see neither the flagship, nor each other." In this precarious state the
four ships drifted southwards, pitching and rolling uncontrollably
under bare poles amid the towering Pacific seas. All the while the
crew of *The Gospel* were frantically trying to heave in the bowsprit
and secure her foremast in an attempt to keep formation, but within
a day the three tall ships, driven faster southward by their size, had
lost sight of the smaller vessels. They had also partly lost sight of
each other, for at some point the *Love* had disappeared without a
sign, so that by the evening of September 8 only the *Faith* and the
Fidelity remained together.

On September 9, 1599, judging it "ill advised, by drifting in
such manner, to miss the favorable wind," De Weert signaled to set

sail again, hoping to find the other ships ahead. His prayers were partly answered when after three hours' sailing the *Postillon* and *The Gospel* were found under sail toward the leeward. On Pomp's request, carpenters of the *Fidelity* and the *Faith* were ferried over in the *Postillon* to help his crew install a makeshift bowsprit. It was a move De Weert and De Cordes came to regret, for that night, yet another storm tore the small convoy apart, marking the last time the *Postillon* and her crew were ever seen.

VI

FAITH

Well Faithful, thou hast faithfully professed
Unto thy Lord: with him thou shalt be blest;
When faithless ones with all their vain delights
Are crying out under their hellish plights,
Sing Faithful, sing, and let thy name survive,
For though they killed thee, thou art yet alive.

The *Faith* and the *Fidelity* had kept together in the great storm. For six days they weathered it together, all but bare of sails, drifting southwest before fierce and unrelenting northwesterly gales. On September 16, 1599, having reached a southern latitude of 54°15', the wind shifted south-southwest and died down. That day, Nicolaes Ysbrantszoon, the *Faith*'s skipper, was given a seaman's burial among the becalmed waves. It was a serious loss for Captain De Weert; already he had lost most of his officers and now he had "no one to take care of anything, since the said Skipper, in all his affairs, was fastidiousness itself." For several days winds remained southerly, enabling the ships to repair to a more northerly latitude. But on September 19, the wind veered back to the northwest and grew to such a gale that both ships were forced to drift without sail for fear of being capsized. They were also making heavy water. On the *Fidelity* it seemed to enter the ship from every seam, spoiling large quantities of ship's biscuit and rising so high that the men on her 'tween-decks were wading through it at knee height. The *Faith*, meanwhile, was beginning to show serious signs that she was falling apart under the constant strain; a gap wide enough to insert one's hand had opened between her gallery and her hull, and shifts had to be called to work the pumps round the clock.

96

Over the next week the weather improved little, although by September 26 the storm had lost some of its intensity so that both ships were able to carry their topsails. That night they were sailing northeast before a stiff westerly breeze, when the lookout on the *Faith* spotted land on the lee side that ran away toward the east. With too little sail to beat back to open water, De Weert was forced to go about over starboard. There was no time to fire the agreed signal, and to warn the men aboard the *Fidelity*, he ordered his men to make as much noise as possible. The clamor was picked up on the *Fidelity* and, forced on by the unrelenting Roaring Forties, both ships continued southward, following the heavily serrated coast of the Chilean archipelago, all the way back to the strait. At daybreak the lookout spotted Cape Pillar, two pointed islets marking the entrance of the strait. By the time darkness set in the cape had been passed and both ships were running back up the strait. They remained under sail until the morning, when their captains were able to communicate and decided to seek a good anchorage, as they had already progressed some twenty-four miles up the strait. A suitable bay was sighted along the southern shore on the evening of September 28, and that night, having battled against seemingly endless storms for almost a month, the weary crews once more brought their battered vessels to anchor in the Strait of Magellan.

For the next three weeks bad weather confined the two ships to their newly found anchorage, which was soon christened Troubled Roads (Wordsworth Bay), for in spite of the season, one storm followed upon the other. At times, Potgieter noted, the "winds fell with such squalls over the mountains, that no rope held" and the men lived in constant fear of losing one of the anchors. This happened on October 10, when the cable of the *Faith*'s daily anchor broke. The anchor was retrieved but the same happened four days later. Again, the men tried hard to salvage the anchor, but "since it had gone down into a crevice, it was impossible." They had also lost their sheet anchor, which, when it was eventually raised, turned out to have broken under the strain.

The same kind of trouble afflicted the *Fidelity*. In the night of October 17, she reeled from her anchor and was only kept from running ashore by two hastily dropped spare anchors. When they were raised the next morning their cables were all but rent.

A better anchorage was found on October 19, a few miles farther into the strait, where a bay cut deep into its southern shore. Toward the middle of the bay the lead went down to sixty fathoms, forcing both ships to anchor close under the shore. Desperately short of anchors, De Weert was only able to moor his ship by making fast two ropes to some trees on a nearby headland. The ship's two spare anchors had been stowed away deep down amongst the ship's ballast, and to reach them, they would first have to transfer the water barrels to the upper decks.

The operation was begun early in the morning of October 22, and after a long day of hard work most of the unwieldy and heavy barrels had been distributed over the upper decks. Toward the evening the men were finally ready to haul up the massive anchors, when another fierce storm tore over the strait. One of the shoreropes broke, caus-

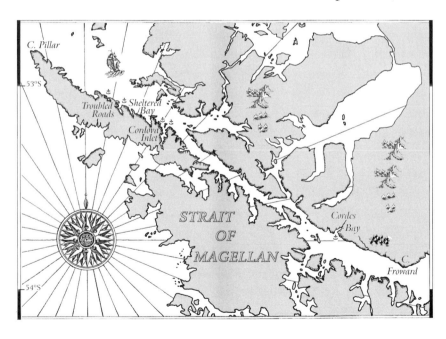

ing the top-heavy vessel to list heavily. To keep the ship at her mooring, men were sent into the boats to lay out the broken sheet anchor, but it failed to bite. Held by only one rope, the ship began to drift toward the shore, threatening to crush into the *Fidelity* on her way. De Weert now ordered his men to broach the water barrels and drop them down the hold, and sent others ashore to pay out another rope. His presence of mind saved the day, and the following morning, the storm having died down, his dead-tired men were finally able to haul up the anchors. Their work did not stop here, for having once more hoisted up the empty barrels, they now had to row them ashore, refill them in a nearby creek, ferry them back to the ship, and lower them down into the hold again.

Amid the constant toil and turmoil, morale on the *Faith* sank to an absolute low. It was close to two months since they had entered the Pacific Ocean. Now, even though it was midsummer, they were again sailing up the strait, and nothing suggested that conditions were improving. Ever since they had first entered the strait, some seven months before, constant privation had whittled away morale and only the thought of progress, however slow, had kept the men going. Now their mood had turned defeatist, and their attitude was one of indolent obstinacy. Only Claes Janszoon, the boatswain, took to heart his captain's admonitions, but he too was "discouraged by the unwillingness of the mates," who "feigned illness in the Captain's presence, and insolently voiced their unwillingness to lift their hands in his absence." Even the few remaining officers had lost their will to go on; they continually petitioned their captain to return home, arguing that provisions were running low and that there were not enough men to handle the ship. But De Weert was not ready to contemplate return yet. Instead, he called in the help of De Cordes, who sent over his skipper, Anthonis Anthoniszoon, with a number of men to help out with the work at hand.

One more month was spent in the relative protection of the bay they had named Sheltered Bay (P. Churruca). Then, on December 2, a stiff northeasterly wind and the outgoing tide promised to carry the ships back to sea. But too much time was lost in maneuvering out of the bay; by the end of the day the wind again backed to the northwest, and the ships were forced yet farther up the strait.

When night fell, topsails were reefed and both ships moved closer to the southern shore to seek another anchorage. Pushed up the narrowing strait by the great Pacific swell, both ships sped along in the dark, skimming past the foot of vast mountains that rose ominously from below the strait's deep waters, while the cold winds that fell down their slopes made play with the little sail that was carried. It was dangerous sailing, and when the first man aboard the *Fidelity* finally saw the danger, they had come within yards of a protruding reef. Only in a frenzied last-ditch effort was her skipper, Anthonis Anthoniszoon, able to steer his ship clear. In the maneuver the boat had come astern and would have sunk had not the sailmaker Sander Sanderszoon, a "nimble youngster," fallen into it to help the men on board take her in. But before they were able to do so the youth was thrown into the black waters and lost in the surge without a sound. Late that night, having progressed twelve miles from Sheltered Bay, the *Faith* and the *Fidelity* entered a vast bay that ran deep into the south side of the strait, where both ships anchored.

At dawn it appeared that, even though both ships had anchored in the same bay (Cordova Inlet), they lay several miles apart. Not at ease at being so far apart, De Weert went over to the *Fidelity* to persuade her captain to bring his ship round to where the *Faith* was. De Cordes, however, refused to leave his moorings. He intended to use the relative calm to repair his damaged and only boat, which would take five or six days. Not willing to leave his own anchorage either, De Weert had his spare boat sent over to the *Fidelity* to be used during the repair. Then, on December 8 they were overtaken by such a storm as they had "never seen before." For two days the storm raged over the strait. When it had died down, De Weert again went over to see how the *Fidelity* had fared and to collect his spare boat. But there was no sign of the ship, nor was there any flotsam on the nearby rocks to suggest that she had foundered. Then, after a two-days'

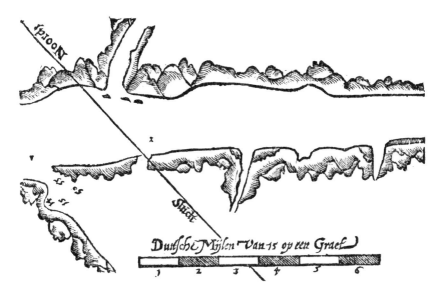

Outgherszoon's chart of the section of the strait just west of Long Reach. The character **v** marks the entrance of Cordova Inlet. The character **x** marks the entrance of Cordova Pass, where De Weert found the *Fidelity* moored to an island.

search she was found moored behind a small island. She had lost her anchor in the first day of the storm, forcing her to remain under sail until the third day, when the winds had calmed and she had been able to make fast to the island. The storm had also interrupted the repair of the boat, and the next morning De Weert returned to his ship without his spare boat but with "a happier heart."

For a week the two ships remained at their separate moorings until, on the evening of December 14, another storm arose from the northwest, severing the hawser of the *Faith*'s sheet anchor. Only two anchors now remained and most of the cables were worn. Not willing to risk his last good cable and unable to make back to sea, De Weert ordered sails to be set and repaired to Cordes Bay. When he passed the island where he had found the *Fidelity* a week before, he had a gun fired, "to which, as far as we could tell, she replied with a likewise shot." The moment passed in an instant, for though the *Faith* was sailing under no more than a reefed jib, she was driven along at a threatening speed. To slow her down De Weert ordered the only remaining boat to be towed along with a kedge anchor for ballast, but presently it too was torn away by a large wave and not seen again. Hurtled along "between two lands without seeing either," De Weert and his men spent a night "in constant fear of mistaking the one inlet for the other, or sailing onto the cliffs." But at daybreak they safely reached Cordes Bay, where they awaited the arrival of the *Fidelity* with high hopes—hopes that seemed to be answered on the evening of December 16, when the *Faith*'s lookout spotted a boat entering the bay from the east.

It was, however, not De Cordes' boat but that of Jacob Claeszoon, vice admiral of the expedition of Olivier van Noort. Invited on board the *Faith*, Claeszoon related how his fleet had left the Netherlands some six weeks after De Weert's fleet had sailed. They had kept almost equal pace, passing Cape Verde in the middle of October and arriving at Cape Lopez on December 25, 1598. There they had spoken to two Dutch merchantmen and had learned that Mahu's fleet had spent a month at the cape. Wasting no time, they had started out on their own passage across the Atlantic the next day, reaching the Brazilian coast on February 3 of the next year. Five days later they had called at Rio de Janeiro to victual, but had lost much time in negotiations with an unforthcoming local governor; when they had tried their luck on the nearby island of St. Sebastian, seven of their men had been killed in an ambush. Then they had battled southwards against continuous storms until, on March 20, in a latitude of 32°15'S., they had decided to sail to the island of Santa Helena to pass the winter. They had failed to find it, but after two more months at sea they had reached Santa Clara, where they had tended to the sick and scuttled one of the four ships. At last, toward the end of November 1599, after four failed attempts, they had entered the strait. They had passed the two narrows in less than two days, but on the Penguin Islands three of their men had been killed by natives. Van Noort had retaliated by killing twenty-five natives.[1]

The next day the *Faith* was visited by Van Noort in person. Seeing the poor state her crew was in and hearing how they had lost their two boats, the admiral promised De Weert that he would give him "reasonable assistance" and that he would have his carpenters make a boat. Two days later Van Noort's fleet joined the *Faith* in Cordes Bay, upon which De Weert was invited aboard the flagship, the *Mauritius*, where Van Noort invited him to join his fleet, which was ready to push on at the earliest opportunity.

That opportunity presented itself on December 20, when a southeast wind slowly blew the four ships up the strait. They reached Carlos III Island two days later. On previous passages, De Weert had noticed the strong current that ran through the narrows on either side of the island. Even in the northern and widest narrow, the current was formidable and the *Faith* had only been able to pass it with a strong quartering wind; this time there only blew a moderate wind and his worst fears materialized when the other ships quickly began to outrun her. She had not been careened since their departure from Annobon; the thick coat of barnacles that now encrusted her hull slowed her down until, in the rush of the narrow, she stopped making any progress at all, so that, while the other ships passed the island and anchored in Ridders Bay, the *Faith* was forced to anchor where she had been halted. Early the next morning, when the tide began to work in her favor, another attempt was made to join the fleet, but this time it was a stiff northwesterly wind that forced the vessel back. A third and fourth attempt proved equally futile, and on the morning of December 25, the wind still being too weak, De Weert and his men looked on in despair as Van Noort's ships set sail, bearing down Crooked Reach and out of sight. A freshening breeze brought renewed hopes but then despair when, in the course of a fifth attempt, it developed into a gale that split the foremast down the core, so that once more they had to repair to Cordes Bay.

Back at square one and without a boat to row ashore, De Weert decided to have his men assemble the longboat the *Faith* carried in her hold. Its two foremost sections were put together on board in order to ferry the remaining sections ashore. This was done on December 29, and in two more days of hard work the boat was completed. When launched, however, she appeared to be far from watertight, and on New Year's Day she was brought back ashore to have her seams recaulked. After another hard day's work she was ready to be launched again, when two boats appeared at the entrance of the bay, this time from the west. They were Van Noort's; the very same storm that had broken the *Faith*'s foremast had driven his fleet back to Ridders Bay. Invited on board the *Faith*, and shown the poor state of her provision the admiral again promised "all possible help," but departed the next morning without having made any specific commitments. Anxious to keep Van Noort to his promise, that same day De Weert had the longboat fitted with sails and dispatched his scribe and ensign with one of his pilots. First they were to sail for Ridders Bay and hand to Van Noort a request for two months of ship's biscuit; then they were to sail on and look for the *Fidelity*. The men returned after a week. They had not found the *Fidelity*. Worse still, Van Noort had flatly refused to honor his earlier commitment, "excusing himself with the long journey ahead, not knowing how long it might take."

It was the final blow to De Weert's hopes for a continuation of the journey. A week before, when they had sailed into Cordes Bay for the second time, his men had again turned mutinous. Even Jan Outgherszoon, his most senior officer, had declared himself in favor of returning home. He had openly criticized De Weert's "unspeakable loyalty to the Shipowners" and derided his determination to reach the South Seas as folly. Once there, the old salt had argued, they would "assuredly perish," for not only were they too weak to land and obtain (by force) what they required, neither had they the power to remain at sea. There, after all, "the King [of Spain] has a great fleet of ships, which would easily surprise us, we only being on our own." With no sign of the *Fidelity*, with a store of biscuit barely enough for three months, and with his men "weak and powerless from hunger," De Weert had been forced to concede that without

104

Van Noort's assistance a continuation of their journey had become an impossible proposition. Now, with Van Noort's refusal to do just that, De Weert had been robbed of his last means to rally his men behind him, and thus he gave in to his men's demands to take in provisions at the Penguin Islands.

The *Faith* reached the Penguin Islands on January 12, 1600, dropping anchor off St. Martha, the smallest of the three islands. Some ten months before, De Weert and Van Beuningen had buried merchant Jan Dirckszoon van Dort on the island. Now, leaving behind Outgherszoon and three men to man the ship, De Weert had all able men ferried ashore to kill as many penguins as possible.

Most of the morning was spent in happy pursuit of the sluggish birds, but toward noon, in the midst of the hunt, the men were alarmed by the report of a rifle. It had come from the direction of the longboat. During the morning the winds had picked up and the three cabin boys who had been left behind to guard the boat had not been able to pull her ashore. By the time the men had reached the scene it was too late. A large wave had lodged her among some outjutting rocks; the sea was too high and the boat was too far out for them to safely reach her. Soon the first planks burst and with each new wave she was losing timber and gaining water. Powerless to intervene, and with no appetite to kill any more penguins, the men looked on as their only means of rescue was being crushed before their eyes. Only when the tide had run out and the water had receded far enough were they able to salvage what remained of her. She was damaged almost beyond repair; both her sides had caved in and her sections were badly warped, causing her to leak profusely through all her seams. Some tools and nails were recovered from the floor of the boat, but there was no wood on the island, whilst Outgherszoon, the only carpenter among the crew, was on board the *Faith*.

The marooned men now had to look for a way to pass the night. Though short, summer nights in the strait were cold, and in their effort to salvage the longboat all had been drenched to the bone.

The island offered no means of shelter and the men spent the night huddled together, roasting penguin meat over a small fire they had made from some of the longboat's timber. The next day they set about to try and repair the battered vessel as best they could. With only a few tools but no materials at their disposal, the men had to improvise. Burst seams were caulked with makeshift oakum, made from match cords and rope, and to fill the largest holes, the fore-deck and after deck were dismantled. She was also stripped of all her fittings. This made the vessel lighter, whilst the extracted nails were used for repairs. Nails ran short nevertheless, so that the cabin boys had to cut nails from wood. By the evening the morale of the men had been somewhat lifted when after a long day of hard work one side of the boat was restored. After one more night in the open and one more day of hard work, the other side was completed too, and with four leather buckets to hose her out she seemed sturdy enough to ferry the men back to the *Faith*.

To everyone's relief, the longboat held, and before long they were well under way to the ship. It was only then that one of them spotted a cave in the slope of the land. Only visible from the water, the cave turned out to be the place where Van Noort's men had landed, for when De Weert ordered his men to row back to inspect it, they found it littered with the putrefying remains of natives. Potgieter, who was again amongst those who had gone ashore, noted how one of the natives wore a cloak of feathers "whereover hung a net, from the lower end of which hung some small bones and stones for adornment," whilst his head, too, was adorned with feathers. He was obviously their chieftain, and had been made to undergo some sort of mock execution, for though he had been shot like the rest, his hands were tied behind his back. Then, as their eyes began to adjust to the darkness of the cave, the men realized that they were not alone. Crouching at the back of the cave sat a woman. Potgieter recalled that her face had been painted and that she wore "a mantle of wild skins, of Penguins as well as other beasts, all nicely sewn together with sinews." Like the other natives he had seen, she was "course in limb and exceedingly tall," though, in contrast with the men, she had "cut her hair very short." De Weert gave her a knife, with which she "seemed very pleased, since she indicated that on the largest island were many more birds." But when she "begged with signs to be brought to the mainland," De Weert, anxious to return to his ship, "left the woman behind, meaning to find occasion to return and bring her where she wanted, the which did not happen."

Though the longboat had safely carried the men back to their ship, the damage was so extensive that Outgherszoon found it impossible to restore her and she had to be abandoned. They had only brought along a limited number of penguins and now they were without any means to go ashore. On January 18, after another lengthy counsel with his few remaining officers, a tired De Weert

The events on St. Martha. To illustrate their costume, Potgieter has brought back to life the Indians' chieftain. In the background, the true state in which the man was found, as well as Sebald de Weert and his men, praying for their delivery.

announced to an elated crew that they were sailing home. In more ways than one the *Faith*'s departure was a forced one. That day yet another fierce west-northwesterly storm drove the ship off her anchor. She began to drift toward a long reef that projected from the southern extremity of the island, and with no time to raise the anchor, De Weert had to order his men to cut the cable. The hard winds forced them to spend two more days in the strait, amid great fears of losing the one remaining anchor. But on the morning of January 21 they rounded Cape Virgin and, bearing east-northeast, started out on the long journey home.

It was only three hundred miles into that journey that, on January 24, in 50°40'S., they sighted three small islands toward the lee side. Large colonies of penguins crowded their rugged shores, but without a boat it was impossible to land. Outgherszoon noted that none of the islands occurred on any of the maps carried on board, and thus they were christened the Sebald Islands.[2]

Locked into the rhythm of the elements, the crew again found its routine and discipline on board returned to some semblance of what it had been, although there were the occasional glitches; such as on February 1, when De Weert had "a Brussels man named Nicolaes Blieck" locked up belowdecks. He had forced the storeroom with a crowbar, and was caught with a bottle of wine and a sack of rice. The next day he was led before the captain, who, in view of the sparsity of victuals, went for the heaviest penalty and sentenced the culprit to death. Curiously, the sentence was taken hardest by his mates, who begged the captain "most humbly for his life." Rightfully suspecting his men's culpability in the offense, and well aware that, with so few, every working hand counted, De Weert once again gave in to their pleas and reduced Blieck's sentence to a thorough lashing. But on February 27 Blieck was charged again. Though he had not been caught red-handed, he was found in a drunken stupor—a state that, given the small daily rations, could only be explained by his recidivism. This time round, the captain stood firm, and on March 1, Blieck was hanged from the foresail yardarm.

The day of Blieck's execution had marked their passage of the tropic of Capricorn. They were now sailing in well-traversed waters, so that De Weert had his men retrieve the cannon, which had been put amongst the ballast to add to the ship's stability. On March 14 they had the sun straight overhead. Two days later the wine rations were stopped; the one barrel that remained had to be reserved for the sick, who were gaining in number by the day. On March 24, in a latitude of 7°N., land was sighted but not toward the east, where it was expected, but toward the north-northwest. It was Cape Mount. They had again strayed off course and had ended up on the Ivory Coast. Outgherszoon's miscalculation was taken "very ill by the captain," but the crew, by now thoroughly sickened by the meager rations of salted penguin meat, believed they had reached the "land of promise." This time they failed to sway their captain, who ordered them to put away from land and run straight for home.

The next five weeks were spent in the Doldrums, but where the winds had left them, the sea came to their aid. A large shoal of fish had begun to follow the ship and the delighted men were able to catch "as much Tuna, Shark and other fish as they could eat." Fearing the absence of both wind and fish, De Weert instructed Outgherszoon to build a vessel with which they could row ashore. All loose timber had been exhausted, but in twelve days the pilot-carpenter grafted a small sturdy boat from some Nordic beams taken from the 'tween-decks. In the event the boat was not needed, for on April 24 a fresh breeze blew back life into the *Faith*'s sails. It was the herald of impending storms that would soon carry away the ship's topsails. But once the storm had spent itself, a fair east-northeasterly wind carried her steadily north, so that by May 21 she had passed Cape Verde and had reached the tropic of Cancer. Here the shoals of fish left her, so that her crew had to fall back on the fish they had salted, but "those who ate of it grew red over their entire body, as if they had been lepers."

On June 12, two sails were seen at dawn. They were English merchantmen. Their commander, an old man, was invited on board

109

to bring them "new tidings from the Fatherland," and perhaps "some assistance and victuals." Tidings the Enlishman brought, and they were more than encouraging. During the two years that they had been away, Prince Maurits had marched his troops into Flanders and driven back the Spanish, all the way down to Ostend. Victuals, however, the English commander could not spare, as he had hardly enough for his own men. One more storm blew the homeward-bound ship from her course, this time toward the French coast, but on July 9 the white cliffs of Dover rose above the horizon. Four days later, on July 13, 1600, the *Faith* and her skeleton crew of thirty-six was sailing back up the Maas. Two years before she had sailed from that same river with three times the number of men.

VII

FIDELITY

How Talkative at first lifts up his plumes!
How bravely doth he speak! how he presumes
To drive down all before him! but so soon
As Faithful talks of heart-work, like the moon
That's past the full, into the wane he goes;
And so will all, but he that heart-work knows.

Following her separation from the *Faith* the *Fidelity* had managed to beat her way out of the strait against the storms for a second time. Again she was repeatedly driven southwards before fierce north-westerly winds and for months on end her crew had to give their all to keep her afloat. But eventually the winds died down and Subaltern Mees Sanderszoon was able to record in his diary how "on the third of march 1600, in a latitude of 43°15' South of the Equinox, we sighted land to which we bore, as we could not stay out at sea any longer for hunger." Eighty more miles they followed the rugged coast northwards, until they found an anchorage in a large bay "which we called Sheep Bay [Bahía de Ancud], after the multitude of sheep which we found there." No sooner had they anchored, than they were met by natives in canoes carrying potatoes, vegetables, and fruits, for which the emaciated men on board "thanked God that we had come to such a good place." That place was Lacui, a narrow peninsula on the north end of the island of Chiloé.

The next day men were sent out in the boat to explore the area and try to obtain from the natives more provisions. They returned toward the evening with sheep, poultry, eggs, honey, flour, fruits, and "apples like those in Holland." There was even bread made of potatoes, which was "very good in taste." Provisions were cheap, too.

Ten sheep had put them back only half a guilder, while most of the other commodities had been traded against no more than some "Mirrors, Needles, Paternosters, blue Eosados, and other Trinkets." The bartering continued over the following days, although enough time was found to ferry ashore and assemble the longboat. On March 8 she was used to tow the *Fidelity* farther up the bay. There, behind a cape christened Philip's Hook after the natives' chieftain, Don Philippo, the *Fidelity* was driven onto the beach to have her encrusted hull cleaned and recaulked. The hard work was completed by March 14, when at noon, the tide being in, she was floated again and readied to put to sea.

De Cordes, however, had no intention of leaving yet. He had abandoned the idea of sailing for Santa María, the fleet's agreed point of rendezvous. Almost six months had passed since the storm had blown the fleet apart and the six-week waiting period had longsince lapsed. In such an event, the instructions read, each should go "wherever seemed best," and to him the island of Chiloé seemed good enough. During the previous days he had spent a lot of time in conversation with a Creole. The man went by the name of Jerónimo, and the things of which Jerónimo spoke stirred the imagination of the young Dutch captain.

Chiloé, it appeared, was occupied territory; in 1558 Spanish forces had come over from the mainland and subjugated the island's inhabitants by force. On the east side of the island they had built a settlement called Castro. The settlement was not very imposing—a few houses and a church, standing on a hill—with a wooden palisade as its only defense. The real obstacle, according to Jerónimo, was the settlement's fifty-strong garrison; soldiers on horseback who plundered Chiloé's gold reserves and crushed each and every attempt of the natives to reclaim their land. Jerónimo was convinced, however, that with the help of the Dutch captain and his men the invaders could be defeated. De Cordes agreed, and with the help of Jerónimo, he and chieftain Don Philippo worked out a plan by which the long-suffering inhabitants of Chiloé would be "liberated from Spanish

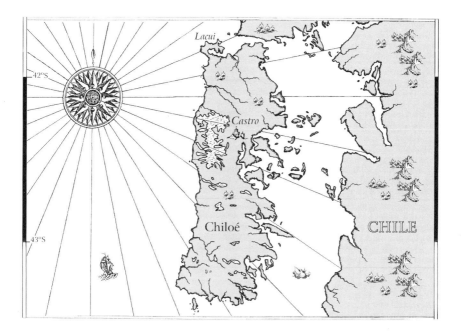

tyranny." De Cordes would fit the longboat with a piece of light artillery and row her to Castro with some twenty-five well-armed men. There he would be joined by Don Philippo, who would lead three hundred of his men overland. Once Castro was taken, so De Cordes vowed, he would "build a Castle there, to secure the place against the Spaniards"—a prospect that, to the natives, "seemed very agreeable, as they showed that they wanted to come and live round our fortress for its defense."

The punitive expedition departed on March 17. By the evening of March 22, after five days of constant rowing, De Cordes and his men were less than a day away from Castro. They continued to row throughout the night until, early in the morning, they reached the settlement's roadstead and could see smoke spiraling into the morning air from behind the palisade. No sooner had they arrived, than De Cordes ordered his men to fire a warning shot and had one of them put ashore with a white vane and a letter in which the captain demanded to be spoken to.

Castro's magistrate, Ruiz de Pliego, was at a total loss as to what to do. Recently the natives had rioted again, and only a few days before, the garrison had left Castro to suppress any signs of a new uprising. Captain Luis Pérez de Vargas had ridden south with twenty of his men; Lieutenant Martin de Iribe had ridden north with another twenty men; only ten soldiers had remained behind to protect the settlers, mainly old men, women, and children. With no time to reach either of his captains, and unable to reach a decision by himself, the intimidated magistrate decided to consult his fellow settlers. These "were all of one opinion that the request of the captain had to be granted." And thus, they dispatched Pedro de Villagoya, "respected citizen of Castro," to negotiate with the Dutch and to "handle the affairs in peace and friendship."

To his considerable relief De Villagoya was met by a "young and amiable Dutch captain" who recounted in vivid detail "the long journey they had made, what misery they had endured, and the terrible losses they had incurred." The Dutchman further avowed that he was "a Catholic," who had come to America with nothing else in mind than to trade. All this failed to impress De Villagoya very much, but then De Cordes revealed that the Indians from Lacui were planning to attack Castro. De Cordes explained that he had pretended to assist the natives, but only to win time to warn Castro's citizens—as he was doing now. They had to act fast, however. Undoubtedly the Indians were already in the vicinity, waiting for signs of hostility. All they needed to do to foil the pending attack was to simulate a skirmish—the onrushing Indians could then be safely eliminated. In return for his collaboration De Cordes required little more than groceries, bread and thirty salted cows, for which he would amply reimburse them.

De Villagoya's surprise at the Dutch captain's "open and friendly disposition" was shared in no small measure by De Cordes' own men, who looked on in growing disbelief while their captain, "faithless in his earlier alliance," agreed to "refrain from assisting the Chileans." Their misgivings were voiced by the *Fidelity*'s skipper,

Anthonis Anthoniszoon, who deplored the "cunning trade" and the "false conditions" on which his captain sought to conduct it. But De Cordes ignored Anthoniszoon's protestations and proceeded to work out with De Villagoya the details of his plan. To make the Indians believe that a skirmish had ensued, both parties were to exchange fire at dawn using blank rounds. To add realism to the pretense, the Spanish would set fire to one of the settlement's houses, on which sign De Cordes and his men would land. Then they would jointly crush the natives.

The whole enactment went as planned—right down to the torching of the house. Only then, as the Dutch raiders set off toward the shore through the cold morning fog did De Cordes reveal to his startled men the true duplicity of his dealings, promising them, in Sanderszoon's words, "that all that we would find within the fortress would be ours" and that he "intended to fulfil his earlier Accord with the Chileans." On his orders, six Spanish soldiers, sent out to meet them at the waterfront, were callously shot at close range. The settlers, seeing their terrible mistake, hurriedly retreated behind the palisade. An exchange of fire followed in which more Spanish soldiers were killed and a Dutch bottler was shot in the leg. De Villagoya, who now realized that he had been deceived by the Dutch captain and that the alliance between the Dutch and the Indians had been for real, informed De Pliego that the Indians might join the invaders at any moment. Seeing no other way out, the magistrate offered to surrender the place if he and his people were allowed to withdraw to the church. The offer was readily accepted by the Dutch, who proceeded to pillage the village at their leisure.

At this junction the Dutch raiders were joined by Don Philippo and his men and presently an almost surreal sequence of events ensued. It started when some of the natives managed to get hold of one of the settlers and slaughtered the hapless man in front of the church—an act that elicited such a desperate response from those within that De Cordes changed his mind and furnished the settlers with "weapons against the Chileans." This, in turn, greatly confused his own men, who with good reason feared to be "overtaken by the Spaniards." Not so De Cordes, however, who reappeared from the church with a gilded plate and a silver chandelier from the altar and ordered his men back to the boats, at which, not only Sanderszoon but also "our Chilean friends, as they met us, were very surprised," yet once again "our Captain deceived them with a facetious lie, saying that we could not hold the fortress for want of gunpowder."

The raiders returned to Lacui on March 25. There, the reunited men feasted as their captain divided the spoils of their exploits. Yet the spoils were modest, and to De Cordes they seemed to underscore rather than constitute the riches of which Jerónimo had spoken.

Meanwhile, the revelry on board the *Fidelity* stood in sharp relief with the events that unfolded on land. Dogged in their determination to evict the settlers, upon the departure of their former allies, the Indians had laid siege to Castro's church. But the settlers, rearmed by the Dutch and aware that they would not be spared, had resisted fiercely and the day had drawn to a close without a decision either way; and the next day the Indians' hopes of a victory were crushed when Spanish soldiers on horseback had suddenly appeared and driven them out of Castro. A large number of them had been killed; the remainder, including Don Philippo, had only managed to escape by hurling themselves into the canoes they had brought along. They returned to Lacui one day after the Dutch, deeply disappointed in their so-called allies, and refusing to sell them any of their provisions. But their suffering had not yet ended; on March 27 a large number of the Indians who had camped on the shore, not far from where the *Fidelity* lay moored, were surprised by another group of Spanish soldiers on horseback and butchered to a man. De Cordes and his men, irked at the natives' refusal to trade, looked on from the *Fidelity* in wry amusement without firing a single shot.

Following the massacre, when two of the Spanish beckoned to be brought aboard, De Cordes did act and sent the boat over to collect them. One of them was lieutenant Martin de Iribe; the soldier he had brought along had been wounded by the natives. Nothing in De Iribe's demeanor suggested that he had heard about the raid on Castro, and he and his man were allowed to remain on board until the latter had been nursed back to health.

On April 2, not long after De Iribe had ridden inland at the head of his squadron, three more Spaniards appeared on the waterside; they had deserted and sought to ally themselves with the Dutch. Castro's magistrate, they said, had hidden large quantities of gold within the settlement, and for a fair share in the proceeds they would direct De Cordes to it. The men were immediately hired by De Cordes, who now faced the daunting task of again having to win over his former ally, Don Philippo, without whose help Castro could not be taken. In the event, the chieftain's hatred of the Spanish proved stronger than his loathing of the Dutch; although it was only "with the greatest of difficulty" that the Dutch captain finally "regained Friendship with the Chileans." This time, however, the chieftain insisted that they sail together, and to meet his demand, De Cordes ordered his men to sail for Castro with the *Fidelity*.

When, on April 13, the *Fidelity* arrived before Castro, few of her crew were surprised to be greeted by gunfire. De Cordes, undaunted by the hostile reception, landed a large group of Indians and had them draw one of the ship's cannon up the slope toward the settlement. It took until early morning of the next day to get the piece into position, when a few shots sufficed to blast a hole in the palisade. But when the natives stormed the breach, they were felled in their dozens by grapeshot. It came from a house at the center of the settlement. In the three weeks that had passed since the previous raid the settlers had turned the house into a small fortress; they had bricked up its windows, leaving only loopholes to shoot from; round the house they had erected a high fence, in which they had mounted two swivel guns. Loaded with musket balls, nails, and other metal shrapnel, both guns were now being applied with deadly effect against the onrushing natives.

Fearing casualties amongst his men, De Cordes quickly changed tactics; he now marched straight for the church, situated on an elevation overlooking the settlement. There he put up a white flag, inviting the Spaniards to come to the church and assuring them that they would not be harmed. And to his men's and Sanderszoon's amazement "the aforesaid Spaniards, 29 in total, came to us in the church," although the soldiers, "who were 24 strong and armed, would not come but rode inland in disarray." On De Cordes' orders, the magistrate, nine old men, and all the women and children were made to go into the house; the nineteen remaining men were taken to the ship, where they were locked into the hold. That night, whilst the settlers anxiously awaited what the next day would bring, De Cordes and his men feasted on the former's hard-earned produce.

An enigma even to his own men, De Cordes remained reticent about the fate of the settlers until the next day, April 15, when he sent for the magistrate and the nine old men and "made all of them lay off their weapons"—and the full horror of his gruesome intent finally sank in. By then it was too late. In a last, desperate attempt, De Pliego begged De Cordes to hold him and the others to ransom. It was to no avail. That day, within the sanctity of their own church, "all were murdered on command of our Captain." Of the nineteen men who had been kept on board, six were kept as hostages. The rest were weighed down with stones and drowned.

Eager to collect his reward, the following day, De Cordes launched an extensive search for the hidden gold but after a day of frantic digging and to the captain's great annoyance none of it was found. The prevailing sentiment amongst his men was again best expressed by Sanderszoon, who in the privacy of his diary berated his captain for not having the Spanish unearth the treasure prior to their execution. This "great folly," he argued with harrowing logic, had been all the more unforgivable, "since the Spanish, their women and children being in our power, would have presented us with the like." They were the regrets of the same subaltern who only five weeks before had thanked God for their own delivery.

Safely ensconced in their newly won stronghold, the Dutch now unleashed a reign of terror on the surrounding area in which the women and the property of the men they had murdered all became fair game. The predatory raids that were launched from the stronghold with menacing frequency were carefully logged by Sanderszoon, first on April 20, when "we brought back from a foray various Chilean women," who, according to an almost apologetic subaltern, "brought us the corn from which we baked bread"; then on the following day, following "another foray," in which "we set fire to many farm houses"; and on April 28, when "we again made a foray and took about 200 Sheep"; and again on May 2, recording a yield of "some Oxen, which we preserved in Salt for our Ship."

The first thing Captain Luis Pérez de Vargas had done following his retreat from Castro was to dispatch two of his men to the mainland. They were to try and reach Osorno, the nearest Spanish stronghold, and bring back reinforcements. Meanwhile, through one of the women sent out by the raiders to collect the corn, he had managed to contact one of the three men who had deserted, who had come to repent his actions when his new cronies had murdered their captives. On April 24, the scheme was exposed and the informant hanged, but the man had lived long enough to inform De Vargas that the Dutch were about to leave Chiloé. And it was with great relief that, toward the end of April, De Vargas heard that General Francisco del Campo had arrived on Chiloé with a large number of reinforcements from the mainland.

The attack was launched before dawn on May 10. A Dutch guard was taken out before he could sound the alarm, but when the Spanish troops made a breach they were surprised by the natives, who had slept along the palisade and now engaged them in man-to-man combat. The Dutchmen initially joined in the fighting, but when the natives began to fall in great numbers, De Cordes ordered his men to withdraw to the fortified house. From there they began to fire indiscriminately into the melee, killing a large number of their allies in the confusion. Realizing that their friends had again deserted them and cared little at whom they were aiming, the natives fled the settlement and disappeared inland.

The fighting had lasted for just over an hour. When it started, the Dutch had been twenty-five strong. Six of them had been killed and, hopelessly outnumbered without his allies, De Cordes now tried to effect a cease-fire in which he and his men would be allowed to retreat to the ship. Del Campo's response was unequivocal; without further ado he ordered his men to set fire to the house. Presently the house was enveloped in flames, and when dense smoke began to billow from its windows, the firing ceased. But when the Spanish breached the fence around the house, the occupants had gone. They had escaped through a hidden door in the fence at the rear of the house. Under cover of the smoke, they had crossed the clearing to the breach in the palisade, through which they now hurled themselves down the slope, toward the safety of the ship. Two of them were shot down before they reached the waterfront. The rest, who had reached the waterfront, tried to follow De Cordes into the boat. Those who fell short and took to the water were hounded down by Spanish on horseback, "so that again six men were killed, and only five of us, besides those who were in the boat, arrived on board, very wounded." And "thus," Sanderszoon concluded matter-of-factly, "came our dominion in this place to an end."

Ever erratic and unpredictable, De Cordes did release his hostages before he sailed from Chiloé. They were put ashore after the *Fidelity* had returned to Lacui. Some recognized it as his one good deed. Yet to Sanderszoon "our captain once more displayed his thoughtless stupidity," since the Spaniards "were not only freely set ashore, but each was given for his defense a Firelock with powder and Lead." Then, on May 26, almost three months after he had made the first entry, Sanderszoon ended his grim record of the whole sordid interlude by noting in his diary how, "we set sail before a southeasterly wind," and how, with fourteen hands lost and one-and-a-half pounds of gold gained, "we parted from the place of Chiloé."

Seven months the *Fidelity* had spent in traversing the Pacific Ocean when, toward the end of December 1600, she made land in a latitude of 1°49'N. By now the ship's original complement of eighty-six had been reduced to only twenty-four. Yet they had reached their destination; they were now sailing the waters of the Molucca Sea, home to the legendary Spice Islands of Makian, Maluku, Motir, Tidore, and Ternate. And it was under Ternate's towering volcano that the *Fidelity* anchored and was met by a boat carrying a white man who greeted the startled men on board in their own tongue.

The man introduced himself as Franck van der Does and explained how, two years before, on May 1, 1598, he had sailed from the Netherlands with the fleet of Jacob van Neck. Two of the fleet's ships, the *Amsterdam* and the *Sticht van Utrecht*, under the command of Vice Admiral Wijbrand van Warwijck, had been the first Dutch ships to reach the Spice Islands when they cast anchor off Ternate on May 22, 1599. Van Warwijck had departed again on August 9, leaving behind Van der Does as factor for the Compagnie van Verre. He invited De Cordes and his officers to visit him at his

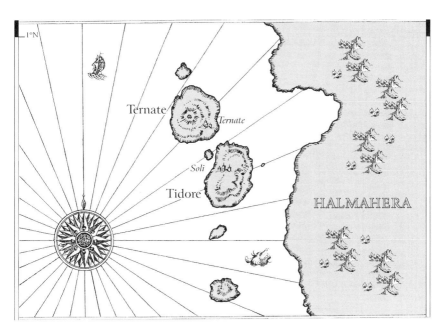

residence as soon as they had somewhat regained their strength. And a few days later, in the course of a sumptuous banquet, the factor set out to his guests the history and intricacies of local power relations.[1]

Of old there had existed between the sultans of Ternate and Tidore a bitter feud; both islands produced great quantities of clove, and ever since the first Javanese and Chinese junks had found their way to the islands, both sultans had competed for their favor. Then, toward the end of the fifteenth century, the first Portuguese had arrived, to be shortly followed by the Spanish. In their drive for territorial expansion both empires had sought to gain the upper hand by forging expedient but shifting alliances with the local sultans. Even after 1529, when the Spanish had forfeited their claims to the Moluccas under the Treaty of Tordesillas, lingering territorial ambitions continued to express themselves in regular border disputes and hostilities between the two islands. Eventually, toward the middle of the sixteenth century, the Portuguese had become the main foreign presence in the region with a stronghold on Ternate. But this, too, changed. In 1570, the sultan of Ternate, the powerful Baäb Oellah, had reduced the stronghold and evicted the Portuguese from his island. From then on, the Portuguese had only maintained two strongholds on Tidore. But their presence on the island continued to be a thorn in the side of Ternate's sultan, even more so in that of Oellah's son, Sahid al din Berkat Sjah, who had come to power when his father was captured by the Portuguese, cut into pieces, and sent to Malacca to be put on display. With the arrival of the Dutch he had gained a new ally in his fight against his eternal enemy; by the same token, the sultan of Tidore had gained another foe. And when De Cordes finally took his leave, Van der Does warned his fellow countryman that he should take heed not to fall into the hands of the Tidoreans, or the Portuguese, who still maintained two fortresses on the island.[2]

De Cordes, however, chose to ignore Van der Does' advice. And on January 3, 1601, the *Fidelity* anchored off the coast of Tidore, near a small settlement called Soli, approximately half a mile from

122

the nearest Portuguese stronghold on the island. She was not met by gunfire and the coastal calm seemed to belie Van der Does' cautious words. Before long, a boat pulled away from the shore and, as it drew near, a man in the front stood up and addressed them in Portuguese. It was the commander of the stronghold, Captain Rui Gonçales de Sequeira, requiring to know the purpose of their visit. De Cordes replied that they had come to trade and had brought "divers wares" for the purpose. Answer came that they could probably trade their wares against cloves, which were abundantly available on the island. Encouraged by De Sequeira's words, De Cordes gave orders to anchor closer under the shore, but his men, weakened by the long journey, were unable to turn the windlass and he had to call on the Portuguese for assistance. By dawn the *Fidelity* was safely moored, but her crew grew wary of the great number of soldiers that had come on board, and on their insistence De Cordes asked the Portuguese to leave again.

To De Cordes, however, it seemed that things were developing with great expedience; they had been on the island for no more than a day and already he had established friendly relations with the Portuguese. He had even been invited to a banquet, to be given in his honor at the local sultan's residency—a privilege he clearly relished, for when he went ashore the next day, he was dressed in a scarlet cape, and took with him an expensively ornamented harquebus, to serve as a present for the sultan. Later in the day he returned in high spirits, announcing, as the skipper Anthonis Anthoniszoon later recalled, that they "might traffic freely" and that the sultan had showed him "enough clove as to constitute half the ship's cargo." He was to conclude a treaty with the sultan the next day.

Two years later, the events of that day, January 5, 1601, were still recalled in vivid detail by the skipper. While the captain had gone ashore to settle his affairs with the sultan, he and a skeleton crew had remained behind to look after the ship; the rest had gone ashore to collect the fresh provisions De Cordes had obtained the previous day.

No sooner had they departed than a Portuguese pilot had arrived, inviting the skipper and carpenter Gerrit Jacobszoon to "sit themselves down on the grass before the ship and enjoy breakfast together." They had accepted the invitation but even as they had dug into the offered food he had felt a nagging fear at the pit of his stomach. Then he had heard a muffled cry from the ship. He had rushed toward the ship, when, looking back from the water's edge, he saw how "the Portuguese cut off the head of the same Gerrit and cast it away along the beach." It had all happened in an instant; when he reached the *Fidelity*, she had been taken by the Portuguese.

Another member of the *Fidelity*'s crew to clearly remember the events of that day was the twenty-nine-year-old gunner Aert Anthoniszoon. He had been among those who had remained on board and had seen how, as soon as the skipper had gone ashore, a boat with Portuguese had arrived alongside the ship. He had complained to the ship's merchant that "the Portuguese should be kept from the ship," but the merchant had replied that "since we had a contract with the Portuguese, they should come aboard." Once on board, the Portuguese had slain all who were on deck. Only he and the two cabin boys, Jan Janszoon and Joris Adriaenszoon, had been able to escape belowdecks. From there they had continued to resist, "shooting into the Portuguese and their boats with guns and muskets," until they too had been forced to surrender. Together with their skipper, they had been brought to the town of Tidore, where they were imprisoned with the Scottish boatswain William Lyon and bottler Andries Janszoon.

The boatswain and bottler had been with those who had gone ashore to victual. They had only just landed when they were alarmed by the report of gunfire from the direction of the ship. They had made it to the boat, but on their way back to the *Fidelity*—where they "feared that things were going badly"—they had been overtaken by one of the sultan's *kora-kora*. Following their surrender, all had been dispatched in the same manner as the carpenter. They themselves had only been spared to help man the ship.

By comparing their experiences the prisoners had also been able to reconstruct the last moment of their captain. The gunner recalled how shortly before the skirmish had ensued, the captain had briefly come back on board; he had gone into the companion to "put on another pair of shoes." It had been at that very juncture that the Portuguese boat had drawn near and that the gunner, on the captain's reappearance, had repeated the concern he had already voiced to the merchant, to which the captain had replied "that he would make the said Portuguese leave the ship." That was the last he had seen of him. As soon as he had disappeared over the bulwarks, the killing had begun. What the gunner had missed had been seen by one of the cabin boys. He had been in the companion to help the captain with his shoes, and it had been from one of its windows that he shortly afterwards saw how the captain "was stabbed by the Portuguese on entering the boat."[3]

Six men De Cordes had spared upon his departure from Chiloé; only six of his men were spared following their arrival in Tidore. Of those six men, only three ever made it back to the Netherlands. Two of them, Anthonis Anthoniszoon and Aert Anthoniszoon, were summoned on November 19, 1603, to appear before the Council of Rotterdam to give testimony of the terrible fate of the *Fidelity* and the final moments of her wretched crew. Joris Adriaenszoon was the last of her men to return home. He had been placed on a Spanish ship and made many journeys between Manila and the Mexican port of Acapulco before he finally returned to Rotterdam in 1614.

VIII

THE GOSPEL

Come hither, you that walk along the way,
See how the pilgrims fare, that go astray!
They catched are in an entangled net,
'Cause they good counsel lightly did forget:
'Tis true, they rescued were, but yet you see
They're scourged to boot: let this your caution be.

The Gospel had lost all contact with the rest of the fleet in the great storm. With the help of the carpenters brought over from the *Fidelity* and the *Faith* her crew had installed a makeshift bowsprit, but fierce northwesterly winds continued to haunt her. She was repeatedly driven southwards, at one stage as far as a latitude of 56°S., but no land was ever sighted. Then, toward the end of September 1599, the weather settled and favorable winds enabled Captain Dirck Pomp to set course for Santa María. For the crew of the small vessel the respite came none too soon. A month before, when they had sailed into the Pacific Ocean, they had still been thirty-six men strong. Now there were only twenty-four, six of whom were gravely ill, leaving barely enough to handle her sail.

Land was first sighted early in November, when *The Gospel* made landfall in the Chiloé Archipelago in a latitude of 44°S. From there Pomp set his course due north, for the island of Santa María. Not much later the first island was sighted. The island, however, lay in a more southern latitude than Santa María. Assuming it to be Mocha, which lay south of Santa María, Pomp passed the island, expecting to soon reach the point of rendezvous. It was a fateful error, but not an error wholly of his own making. In the maps by which he was navigating, the island of Santa María lay in 36°S.—

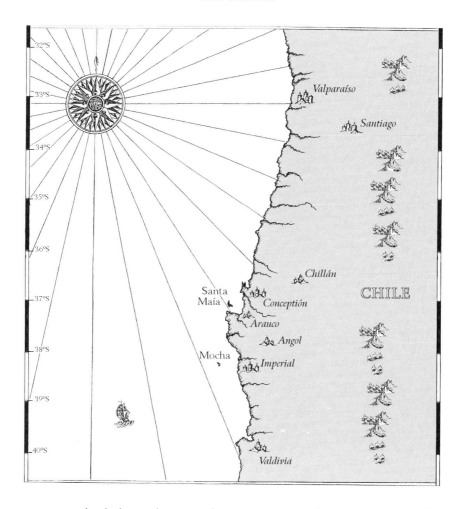

a too northerly latitude. In reality Santa María lay in 37°15'S. The island of Mocha lay in 38°20'S. Having inadvertently left Santa María behind, Pomp continued north along the coast, until it became apparent that he had overrun his destination. Yet, instead of going back, Pomp decided to sail on to try and victual somewhere on their way along the Chilean coast. In a latitude of 34°S., a beach suitable to land a shore party was spotted amongst a fold in the land. Taking their chances in the heavy Pacific swell, the men launched the boat but the surf was too rough and they had to return without one man having been put ashore.

127

They were now well within the Spanish sphere of influence; at any moment they might encounter a Spanish vessel. Although too hungry to be concerned about their safety, they were too small in number and too weak to man the guns and still their hunger by means of raiding. With no other options open, Pomp eventually decided to sail for Valparaíso, which lay only twenty miles northward along the coast. There he would try and convince the local authorities of his peaceful intentions in the hope of thereby obtaining the desperately needed victuals and have the sick tended to.

When *The Gospel* reached Valparaíso on November 17, 1599, only a handful of her crew were still fit enough to perform their duties. From the ship they could see a small group of locals who had gathered on the beach, apparently out of curiosity. They dispersed again when Pomp and six of his men boarded the boat, cast off, and headed toward land. All seemed peaceful as the boat drew close to the beach, then dug into the sand, and Pomp jumped ashore with a white vane, calling out *"cristianos."*[1] Hardly had he uttered the word, when his voice was drowned by the report of gunshots—they had run straight into a Spanish ambush. In the first volley Pomp was shot in the leg; his gunner, Jacob van Purmerlant, was hit in the shoulder. Within moments soldiers came charging toward the shoreline. Pomp, in spite of his wound, managed to clamber back into the boat, while his men struggled to float the craft and steer it through the high surf. For a moment all seemed lost when soldiers on horseback stormed far into the surf. With their long lances they injured the provost, who was helping to push the boat out to sea. Then, in a last, desperate effort the men managed to brave the surf and row away from the shore and the Spanish troops. Utterly exhausted, but without incurring any further casualties, the men finally reached the safety of the ship.

For the moment the men aboard *The Gospel* were safe; no other ships were to be seen in the area, making an immediate Spanish offensive unlikely. It did little to alleviate their desperate situation. Although none of the sustained injuries were life threatening, they nevertheless reduced the already diminished number of able men. Pomp's injury was the worst, making it impossible for him to use his leg. Yet he, too, had been fortunate, as the bullet had gone straight through his leg, leaving a relatively sterile wound. The sick were the worst off. Many of them were more dead than alive, simply waiting for death to release them from their misery. Among them was the skipper, Dirck Gerritszoon, Pomp's half brother, who drew his last breath that same evening.

The next day brought new hope when the lookout spotted a boat approaching from the shore. It was manned with a small number of Spaniards carrying a white flag. Van Purmerlant, who went out in the boat with Pomp to meet them, later recalled that one of the Spaniards spoke first. He asked whether they were English, to which Pomp responded that they were Dutch, "seeking to traffic with them peacefully." Answer came that the Spanish at Santiago "had much war with the inhabitants of the Land" and were "in great distress, having need of many things." Were they, therefore, to "pay the King his Duty" they would be allowed to trade. This being said, the Spaniards were invited aboard, where both parties spent the rest of the day in negotiations.

The Spanish party was led by Captain Jerónimo de Molina, the most senior magistrate of Santiago and a shrewd negotiator. Taking stock of the appalling conditions on board the Dutch ship, De Molina offered Pomp 12,000 ducats for the vessel and its contents, as well as a free escort for him and his men to Buenos Aires, from where they could sail home. It was a tempting offer, and any lingering intents to reject it and continue their journey evaporated when Pomp consulted his men, who all "bemoaned the hardships they had hitherto suffered," and begged their captain not to "lead them to their total doom while friendship was offered to them here"; injured, old, and "worn out by the long journey," the man who three months earlier had so solemnly vowed to risk life and limb to harm his archenemy, decided to relinquish his first ever captaincy—it was his second fateful error, this time wholly of his own making.

129

When the following day *The Gospel* entered the bay of Valparaíso, she was immediately boarded and all who sailed on her were incarcerated. The ship was placed under the command of Captain Diego de Ulloa. On November 24, he was ordered by De Molina to take with him a small detachment of Spanish soldiers and sail the newly acquired vessel to the seaport of Callao. There, he was to present her to Don Luis de Velasco, the Spanish viceroy of Peru, who also presided over the colonies of Chile, Argentina, and Brazil, but resided in the Peruvian capital of Lima, eight miles inland from Callao. On the eve of *The Gospel*'s departure six of the Dutch prisoners were released to handle her sail. They were boatswain Laurens Claeszoon, gunner Jacob van Purmerlant, quartermaster Jacob Bol, ship's carpenter Adriaen Dirckszoon, and the two cabin boys, Pieter Janszoon and Jan Claeszoon.

De Molina's words had not been wholly devoid of the truth. When *The Gospel* arrived before Valparaíso, the Spanish throughout Chile were under siege from the Araucanians, the country's indigenous people. The trouble had started on December 23, 1598, when the newly appointed governor, Martin García Oñez de Loyola, and his escort were ambushed by Arauco near Curalaba. De Loyola had died fighting and so had most of his men, only four of whom escaped to tell the tale. The Araucanians, inspired by their first victory, had risen to a man. Santa Cruz had been the first town to fall, when it was evacuated on March 7. It was followed a month later by Imperial, a seaport just south of the island of Mocha; the town was reduced to ashes, but its garrison, some ninety men strong, had held out by entrenching itself in the residence of the local bishop. Soon all of the Spanish settlements south of Santiago were under siege. Learning of De Loyola's death and the revolt it sparked, De Velasco had appointed his best general, Francisco de Quiñones, as the new governor of Chile with *carte blanche* to quell the revolt. The capable and war-hardened De Quiñones had immediately sailed for the port of Concepción, some twenty miles north of the island of Santa

María, arriving in May 1599. He intended to march for the seaport of Arauco, reinforce its fortress, and from there to try and liberate the besieged men at Imperial. Situated only a few miles south of Concepción, Arauco was of strategic importance in halting the Araucanians in their drive northwards. Yet De Quiñones had only a hundred men at his disposal and his plan came to nothing. Nor could he prevent the loss of the more northern, inland town of Chillán, which fell on September 13. The worst blow to Spanish confidence came in the night of November 24, when the Araucanians took Valdivia, killing over a hundred men and holding four hundred women and children to ransom.

In the very midst of this crisis, on June 22, 1599, Don Luis de Velasco received an urgent letter from Don Gaspar de Acebedo, the viceroy of Mexico. The latter had received word from the Duke of Medina-Sidonia, the governor of Andalucía, that "from the port of Rotterdam, Olivier van Noort, citizen of the said town," had "departed with 6 ships, to sail through the Strait of Magellan so as to arrive at the province of Chile." According to the somewhat mis-informed De Acebedo, Van Noort had hired "two pilots, who had sailed with Francis Drake and Thomas Cavendish when they entered this sea, as well as some sailors who had passed through the strait with Pedro Sarmiento." More accurately, De Acebedo related how Van Noort had sailed with "more than 800 sailors, each with their own musket; and had brought with him a large quantity of harquebuses, swords, spear heads, halberds, horse bits and stirrups," as well as "persons of divers vocations and engineers, to put ashore." De Velasco's initial response was skeptical. He deemed a Dutch attack "very unlikely," since the ships in question had sailed on August 8, 1598, and, in view of the fleet's route, tiding of their arrival on the coast of Chile should already have reached him.

De Velasco was proven wrong in his complacency when, toward the middle of November, the Council of Santiago received a press-ing missive from De Quiñones in Concepción. In the letter, dated November 5, 1599, the governor recounted how a few days earlier one of his captains, Pedro de Recalde, had sailed from Concepción with two ships to reinforce the fortress at Arauco, but how atrocious weather had forced him to take refuge behind the island of Santa María. And it had been on the following day, November 4, that De Recalde had seen how a "large raider" had anchored off the island, and how it "had raised its gun ports and brought out its guns, as if it were awaiting the arrival of other vessels." Ignorant of the ship's provenance, De Quiñones urged the council to take the necessary precautions against "a possible landing of the English in the port of Valparaíso," and to relate the news to Lima as fast as possible. Following De Quiñones' instructions, De Molina had immediately dispatched a messenger to Lima, and that same day, he himself had departed for Valparaíso, where he arrived on November 14, just in time to intercept *The Gospel*.

De Molina's messenger arrived at the viceroy's residency on December 2, to be followed, four days later, by another messenger, carrying a letter by Don Diego Rodríguez de Valdés, the governor of Argentina. In it the governor related how, toward the end of July of the same year, a Dutch ship (*De Silveren Werelt*) had sailed up the Río de la Plata. He had arrested her captain, a certain Cornelis van Heemskerck, who had come ashore with some of his men to seek provisions. Van Heemskerck's interrogation had revealed that his ship had been part of a fleet of four, which was bound for the Strait of Magellan. De Valdés further reported that he had received word from Salvador Correa de Sá, the governor of Brazil, saying that on February 10 of the same year, four Dutch ships had arrived in Rio de Janeiro seeking to victual. De Sá had declined to do so. Instead, he had pursued them to the island of St. Sebastian, where he had ambushed them, killing seven, although de Valdés failed to mention in his letter which fleet it was that De Sá had spoken of.

On the heels of these ominous tidings, news from Callao that, on December 8, Captain Diego de Ulloa had sailed into that port with a Dutch vessel that had been captured at Valparaíso three weeks earlier, was veritable music to the ears of a by now seriously distraught viceroy—especially the news that De Ulloa had brought along six of her original crew. Taking no chances, De Velasco immediately departed for Callao to interrogate the Dutchmen in person and find out what he could about Dutch overseas ambitions. An interpreter was found in the person of one Jan Hendrikszoon, alias Joan Enriquez Conobut, a Dutch sailor who resided at Lima and, so the viceroy's men assured him, a *"persona de confianza."*

The interrogations began on December 11, 1599. Starting with Jan Claeszoon, with his eighteen years the youngest, the men were interrogated one by one in ascending order of rank. The cabin boys were cross-examined in one day; the remainder were subjected to a more thorough grilling, lasting roughly two days for each man. The last to take his turn was quartermaster Jacob Bol, whose interrogation ended on December 21.

The men were forthcoming, at times almost solicitous, in their answers. Gunner Jacob van Purmerlant gave a detailed assessment of the firing power of each ship, as well as an inventory of the arms and ammunition they had carried in their holds. He was also able to at least name their captains as well as some senior officers. He knew that two of the three pilots on the flagship had been Englishmen. One of them, "Master Chat" (Timothy Shatton), had personally told him that he had sailed through the strait before under Thomas Cavendish. The other, a certain Adams, one of two brothers, was "very skillful in the art of navigation." The cabin boys were keen to testify to the observance of religious practice on board the ships. Claeszoon avowed that each ship had its holy patron and that their crews gathered twice a day to say the Church's four holy prayers. Janszoon knew not of the patrons, but confirmed that the Our Father, the Hail Mary, and the Confession were all intoned daily before mess at noon and after mess in the evening. Despite the men's often meandering and at times contradictory statements, in the course of two and a half weeks, De Velasco was able to gain a good impression of the expedition's size, strength, and itinerary.

The expedition's actual *raison d'être*, however, remained tantalizingly elusive. Laurens Claeszoon believed the expedition had been the idea of two merchants from Antwerp, but apart from the names of the two men, he was unable to give any details about the participants in the venture. All knew that Mahu had been one of the shareholders, but not whether De Cordes had been financially involved, nor even whether by profession he was a merchant or a soldier. Especially galling were the men's conflicting statements concerning the destination and purpose of the expedition. The two cabin boys both agreed that the plan had been "to go through the Strait of Magellan." But Claeszoon rejected this out of hand, saying that he and all others with him had expected "to sail round the Cape of Good Hope, to the East Indies, to Java major and minor, the Moluccas and Japan"; had they been told at the outset that the plan was to sail through the Strait of Magellan, so he reasoned, no man would have let himself be enlisted. This was affirmed by Van Purmerlant, who agreed that Japan was the place where they were to trade their wares. Adriaen Dirckszoon did not know about the route nor the purpose of the expedition, although he did feel he had been duped. And while all of them stressed the peaceful intent of the expedition, all were at a loss when confronted with the large quantity of arms that had been described in such detail by the gunner. Van Purmerlant philosophically suggested that it was the "good and evil that could be found throughout the world" that had required them to bring the necessary means of defense. In this he was outdone by Dirckszoon, who held that "nothing in this world is permanent," that "all is subject to change and alteration," and that "words and friendship are never constant"; and thus, since "there is no one whom one can trust," they had been forced to take the necessary precautions. In the event, the questions the testimony of the gunner had raised were most plausibly answered by that of cabin boy Jan Claeszoon, who explained that if they "were not given the required victuals by means of bartering, they would seek to obtain them as best they could, so as not to die of hunger."

These explanations nevertheless failed to convince the viceroy. Going by the outfit of *The Gospel*—a vessel he now knew to be the smallest in the fleet—it was evident that the fleet had been equipped for more than the mere pursuit of trade, even a forced one. His suspicions seemed to be confirmed by her cargo, which included shovels, spades, and axes. His men had also found some Spanish wine barrels and, more ominously, a rent gun—obviously, she had seen some sort of action. Another burning question for which he had failed to obtain a satisfactory answer was why her captain had sailed for Valparaíso, instead of Santa María. The island, after all, had been the fleet's agreed place of rendezvous. It had also been the place where De Quiñones' man had sighted the large raider, awaiting others. That had been at the beginning of November, which in turn seemed to tie in with the time at which his prisoners said they had left the western entrance of the Strait of Magellan.

To have these questions answered, De Velasco enclosed them in a letter to the Council of Santiago, instructing it to put them directly to the ship's captain. This was done on February 10, 1600, when Pomp was subjected to a lengthy interrogation by his captor, Captain Jerónimo de Molina. Pomp made no secret of the hostilities with the Portuguese in São Tiago, although he carefully avoided mentioning how they had sacked the Spanish settlement on Annobon. Like his men, he believed the expedition had been destined for the East Indies with a view to "sell or exchange goods." He, too, claimed he had been ignorant of the route by which that destination was to be reached—up until Cape Lopez, that was; there "the Admiral and the remaining captains had taken council and decided to enter this sea through the strait of Magellan." He himself had spoken out against the plan, since he was more inclined toward those regions where he was at home and of which he had experience, being "around the Cape of Good Hope, up to Portuguese India." But the other members of the ships' council had been of the opinion that "it would be better to enter the South Sea," since "its countries, being rich," would best enable them to sell their merchandise;

with the money earned there they would "sail for the Moluccas to load spices," or "to Japan, where there was much silver." De Molina wanted to know whether Pomp had been aware that "without a license from His Majesty they could not trade, nor make any contracts under the Crown of Castile, and in particular in the Indies, and above all in the South Sea, into which no one could enter through the strait of Magellan without being a pirate, even if by birth he were a Spaniard." Pomp confessed he knew as much, prompting De Molina to demand why they had sent their ships through the Strait of Magellan. To this Pomp retorted that when he had left his country he had been "neither the Admiral nor the freighter of the said ships, nor the captain of any one of them." He had merely been "a simple sailor," who sailed to "support his life and livelihood." To such men, he observed, "matters are never related when secret voyages are made." But he was quite sure "that it had not been the Admiral's principal aim to raid, nor to cause any harm," since they had come loaded with merchandise and "he who desires to deprive others of their possessions only needs to carry men and weapons, as the English and other pirates do." Asked why, then, they had "brought with them an English pilot who had been in the South Sea with Thomas Cavendish, the pirate who had taken much treasure," Pomp replied that "for all regions, the English pilots are more certain of their seas and more experienced than the Dutch."

Pomp's chance to give final consistency to his case came when, in closing, De Molina wanted to know why he had not called at the island of Santa María to wait for his companions in accordance with his instructions, and what reasons had compelled him to come to the port of Valparaíso. Pomp's answer was unequivocal. When he had left the Netherlands he had "never intended to come to these quarters, but to India and the Moluccas, round the Cape of Good Hope." Once the ships' council had decided otherwise, he had "no power to resist the Admiral and the remaining captains." But afterwards, when he had been made captain of a ship and had been separated from the others by a storm—as he had recounted—he had "not wished to reunite with them." This because the others "had chosen to cause detriment and harm in these seas wherever they could." He himself, after all, was "a Catholic Christian," who had resided in Portugal and Castile most of his life and did not want to take the wrong road by causing "detriment to the King our Lord." Instead, he had "taken recourse to all kind of means" to come to Valparaíso, where he could render the cargo and the ship under his command "to the service of His Majesty."

A transcript of Pomp's interrogation reached Lima well in time for the viceroy to incorporate it in his "Comprehensive relation of reports on pirates for the year 1599," which he dispatched to the king of Spain on May 8. De Velasco was not fooled by Pomp's exercise in servility. He informed the king that, as far as he could tell, most of the ships "had come well equipped with ordnance, much powder and shot, and other ammunition." This at least had been the case with the ship that had arrived at Callao and which, "although it was the smallest of them, carried 19 cannon, and also 2 in her hold, as well as all other necessary requirements of warfare." He had therefore sent two well-armed galleons and a pinnace to the coast of Chile to seek out and destroy the raiders; if none were found, they were to "remain on that coast until the 20th of March in case the other raiders of which word had been received might arrive."

The two galleons and the pinnace sailed from Callao on January 1, 1600, under the command of General Don Gabriel de Castilla. Between them, they carried "more than 300 well-armed soldiers, much artillery, ammunition, and victuals." This military force, however, had nothing to do with the Dutch but was intended to relieve De Quiñones, who, when the three ships arrived at Concepción on February 14, immediately marched toward Angol, recaptured it within a day, and then rushed to the aid of his beleaguered men in Imperial, whom he liberated at the end of the same month. Before De Quiñones set off inland, however, he furnished De Castilla with an important piece of information; the raider that his man had sighted off Santa María the previous year had been joined by a second one, although both ships had long since departed.

True to his instructions, De Castilla continued to patrol the Chilean coast until March 21. On that day he himself set sail from Santa María and returned to Callao, where he arrived exactly a month later. Still not at ease, he had left behind the pinnace *Buen Jésus*, instructing her captain, Francisco de Ibarra, to "remain there the whole month of March, and thereafter to reconnoiter all the ports up to Callao so as to learn what happened in these places and bring back word of it."

Bring back word De Ibarra did, when, on May 6, he arrived in Callao—in a boat. Summoned by the viceroy to explain what had happened to his ship, the disheveled and embarrassed captain related how, on the afternoon of March 25, 1600, only four days after De Castilla's departure from Santa María, two Dutch raiders had arrived on the island's roadstead. Outclassed and outnumbered he had tried to outrun them, and for a day and a night he had kept them at bay, but eventually his ship had been overtaken and boarded. The raiders had "belonged to the squadron of Oliver de Nort, the innkeeper." Van Noort had manned the *Buen Jésus* with his own men and taken him and the rest of the crew on board his own ship, the *Mauritius*, where for the next days they had been held prisoner and forced to bear witness to Van Noort's raids on the Chilean main. The raiders had first sailed for the port of Valparaíso, where they set fire to two ships and added another one, the *Dos Picos*, to their fleet. From Valparaíso, they had followed the coast northwards until, on April 1, they had called at Huasco, some three hundred miles farther north. There, the raiders had stayed for five days, replenishing their water supplies. When they left, they had put him and the other prisoners ashore, although they had taken the pilot, Juan de Sandoval, and two slaves with them. During his short stay on board, De Ibarra had learned that the raiders intended "to sail for the ports of Arica, Quilca, Payta, Guayaquill, and Cape San Francisco to take what they could get; and from there to the coast of New Spain, and do the same there; and thenceforth to California to careen and await the ship that would come from the Philippines in the month of November." Yet De Ibarra carefully avoided any mention of his treatment during his stay on the *Mauritius*, nor the reason for his release.[2]

Not so Olivier van Noort, who in his journal entry for March 26, 1600, recorded with considerable glee how the captain and pilot of the Portuguese vessel had fallen at his feet and begged for mercy. Without too much coercion they had told him that they had carried victuals to Arauco and Concepción and had been lying in wait for ships that might come through the Strait of Magellan, of which they were to report to the Spanish ships of war that lay in Lima and Arica. To Van Noort's surprise, the Spaniards also told him that "they had already had word of our advent a Year in advance, with name and surname, so that the entire country was in a state of uproar, and her ships of War were lying in wait for us." It was not the last time that Van Noort would be surprised at the mysterious ways in which news traveled, for, on March 28, he recorded how, during the raid on Valparaíso, he had miraculously "obtained in that place, some letters, written in Dutch, from one Dierck Gerritsz." The letters had related how Pomp's ship, *The Gospel*, had reached Valparaíso in a "desolate state," how she had been seized and sent to Lima, and how he and his men were now held "miserably captive." Also mentioned by Van Noort but carefully omitted by De Ibarra was how, on the latter's release, Van Noort had "paid him great friendship and gifts, so that he in turn would pay ample favor to the prisoner Dirck Gerritsz, in Lima, the which he promised." De Ibarra's promise proved hollow. Van Noort dutifully reported the fate of Pomp and his men to the authorities on his return to the Netherlands on August 27, 1601.[3]

There, meanwhile, the tables had turned in the republic's favor. On July 2, 1600, Prince Maurits had routed the Spanish forces in the Battle of Nieuwpoort among the dunes of the Flemish coast. Some four thousand of the Spanish elite troops had been killed.

Seven hundred others were taken prisoner, among them Admiral Francisco de Mendoça, over whom both parties had soon entered into negotiations to settle the conditions for his release. A preliminary agreement was reached on January 16, 1601, enabling De Mendoça to return to Spain on May 29, 1602. By then, the Dutch emissary Tymon Barenszoon van Ens had already been sent to the Casa de la Contratación in Seville with a long list of Dutchmen "held prisoner in Spain, Portugal, India, and other dominions of the King." On it were the names of Captain Dirck Gerritszoon Pomp and his men, held "miserably captive" in Lima.

Thus it was that De Velasco was forced to let go again the few Dutch pirates that had fallen into his hands. They were to be sent to Porto Bello, where they would be attached to the annual fleet for Lisbon. But not all at once. Writing to the king of Spain, on May 19, 1602, De Velasco explained that "with this fleet I send three Dutchmen, belonging to those who were captured on one of the ships that entered the South Sea and are destined for the Casa de la Contratación." Six others, however, "I will not send, as they are dangerous and extraordinarily intelligent, in particular the pilot and captain." These men he would send "separately, at different times."[4]

One of the first three crewmembers of *The Gospel* to safely reach the Netherlands was Jacob van Purmerlant. On February 27, 1603, shortly after his arrival in Amsterdam, he was called before an assembly of the States of Holland and furnished with thirty guilders and a letter to Petrus Plancius, through whose offices he was to be "examined well in all." This was done on March 17, when the learned scholar recorded in meticulous detail what had happened to the gunner and his fellow sailors in Spanish captivity.

Following their interrogation, Van Purmerlant and the other men had been placed on a galley early in January 1600. They had served on the galley until March 15 of the same year, when five of them, including Van Purmerlant himself, had converted to the Catholic faith and had entered different monasteries. The two who had not converted had found different employ: the carpenter had remained "in the King's service at Callao"; the cabin boy had been retained "in the Court of the Viceroy." For two years Van Purmerlant had pursued monastic life, until the spring of 1602, when, through the offices of the general of the Jacobite Order, he and two of the men who had been brought up from Santiago—Daniel Arnold Maartenszoon and Christiaen Albertszoon—were nominated for release. They were dispatched to Panama, where they had joined a mule caravan carrying "the Silver for the King" across the isthmus to Porto Bello. From there they had embarked in the early summer, arriving at the Spanish port of Cádiz early in December 1602. Eventually they had found their way back to the Netherlands, where they arrived toward the middle of February 1603.

The six "dangerous" men, including Pomp, arrived back in the Netherlands roughly two years later. Pomp, too, had converted to the Catholic faith and entered a monastery after he had been brought to Lima. He had even been allowed to accompany some monks on a journey inland, all the way to the settlement of Cuzco, high up in the Andes and some three hundred miles from Lima. Then, on May 5, 1603, he and the five remaining prisoners had been allowed to leave. One year later they had finally arrived in Lisbon, where on July 1, 1604, emissary Van Ens was able to report the safe release of "six prisoners who have come from Lima," being "Dirck Gerritzen Pomp van Enkhuizen, chief merchant and captain on the ship of Pieter Verhaegen through the Strait of Magellan; Cornelis Lamberts Matelieff, pilot; Pieter Tielmans, carpenter; Jacob Bol; Arent Jansen; Adriaen Pauwelszoon, carpenter."

Back home, Pomp wrote a short report "On the situation of Chile and what power the Spaniards have in that Country." Drawing on what he had heard during the three years he had spent in Chile, he described in harrowing detail the terrible losses the Spanish were suffering at the hands of the land's original inhabitants; and how the women held captive by the Araucanians at Valdivia were being "ransomed for a few Spurs, a Bridle, Stirrup belts, or a Rapier," but that "the King has forbidden it, lest the Chilese would acquire too many Weapons." Especially at Arauco the situation was grim. There the natives had laid siege to a small fortress, driving its fifty or so inhabitants to the brink of starvation. The beleaguered men had eventually been liberated, but not before the natives had vented their anger on the crew of a small ship sent out with provisions and reinforcements, but which had run aground nearby. All thirty men on board had been dragged ashore and butchered—all except the trumpeter, a certain "Laurens, born to Dutch parents in the Danish port of Bergen" and one of the survivors of *The Gospel* who had been pressed into service by the Spaniards.

Not all of Laurens' fellow sailors who eventually made it back home arrived to find domestic bliss; their contemporary chronicler Levinus Hulsius recorded for posterity how, when the "good men came home, three of them found their Wives married to other Men, which caused no little Strife amongst them."

IX

HOPE & LOVE

Out of the way we went, and then we found
What 'twas to tread upon forbidden ground;
And let them that come after us have care,
Lest heedlessness makes them as we to fare,
Lest they for trespassing his prisoners are,
Whose castle's Doubting, and whose name's Despair.

Having lost sight of the *Fidelity* and the *Faith* in the great storm, the *Love* had been driven southwards, reaching a latitude of 54°30'S. So had the *Hope*, for on September 9, 1599, the *Love's* lookout sighted the flagship's three tops. For the next ten days, the two ships managed to stay together, but on the night of September 19, the *Love's* foresail was torn away, and once more she lost sight of the flagship. Finally weather and winds allowed her to set course for the Chilean mainland, and toward the end of the same month, land was sighted at a latitude of 46°S. It was no coincidence that the *Love* made landfall at that latitude. Through an incomprehensible miscommunication, Van Beuningen had misunderstood the fleet's point of rendezvous, believing it had been set at 46°S. instead of 36°S., the equally erroneous latitude of the island of Santa María. They had made landfall near the entrance of a wide bay that offered a good anchorage, fresh water, and beaches where they could land a boat. And thus, hidden amongst the high and protective headland, they awaited the arrival of the other ships.[1]

The bay where the *Love* had anchored ran deep into a vast peninsula that disintegrated into innumerable little islets to the north and faced a wide gulf to the south. To the starved men's delight the natives that inhabited the peninsula turned out to be "good in nature," and during the first days following their arrival bells, knives, and other items were eagerly bartered against sheep and potatoes. The natives seemed content with the trade, but after a week they left the vicinity of the bay and were not seen again. The next weeks were used to assemble the longboat to replace the boat that had been lost in the storm.

For twenty-eight days the *Love* remained at anchor in the bay until, on October 27, Van Beuningen decided to put to sea again and sail for the port of Valdivia. The Bay of Valdivia was reached on November 4, but the hard westerly winds made navigation up the bay impossible. Changing his mind, Van Beuningen now ordered his men to set sail for the island of Mocha, which was reached on the morning of the next day. But here, too, hard winds made it too dangerous to anchor and once again Van Beuningen decided to sail on, this time for the Gulf of Arauco. When, on November 6, the *Love* ran into the wide bay, the weather had settled and not far from Point Lavapié, just south of Santa María, she anchored close to the shore in fifteen fathoms.

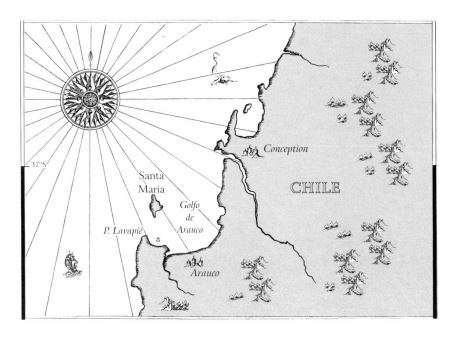

Meanwhile, rations were running dangerously low again. During the four weeks the crew had spent waiting for the other ships, most of the sheep and potatoes they had bought from the natives had been consumed, and apart from the rock-hard ship's biscuit, there was nothing left in the form of nourishment.

But signs were promising. Adams had been on deck as they had rounded Point Lavapié and had seen "many people tossed about the cape." He also recalled how, following their arrival in the bay, a number of men:

> went with our boats hard by the water side, to parle with the people of the lande, but they would not suffer vs to come a lande, shooting great store of arrowes at vs. Neuerthelesse, hauing no victualls in our ship, and hoping to find refreshing by force, wee landed some seuen and twentie or thirtie of our men, and droue the wilde people from the water side, most of our men being hurt with their arrowes. And being on land, we made signes of friendship, and in the end came to parle with signes and tokens of friendship, the which the people in the end did vnderstand. So wee made signes, that our desire was for victualls, shewing them iron, siluer, and cloth, which we would give them in exchange for the same. Wherefore they gaue our folke wine, with potatoes to eate, and drinke with other fruits, and bid our men by signes and tokens to goe aboord, and the next day to come againe, and then they would bring vs store of refreshing: so, being late, our men came aboord, very glad that we had come to a parle with them, hoping that we should get refreshing.

That evening Van Beuningen had the ship's council convene to assess the situation. All agreed that they had taken a great risk the day before, "for there were people in aboundance unknown to us: wilde, therefore not to be trusted," although they had also found that the natives were open to persuasion. The council therefore resolved "to goe to the water side, but not to land more than two or three men at the most." The next day, November 7, Van Beuningen had the newly assembled longboat launched and set out toward the shore with twenty-seven men. Adams, who had again remained behind, looked on from the deck of the *Love* as the captain and his men drew near the shore and "the people of the countrie made signes that they should come a lande." Then he watched how:

> the people not comming neere vnto our boats, our capten, with the rest, resolved to land, contrary to that which was concluded abord our shipp, before their going a lande. At length, three and twentie men landed with muskets, and marched vpwardes towardes foure or fiue houses, and when they were about a musket shot from the boates, more then a thousand Indians, which lay in ambush, immediately fell upon our men with such weapons as they had, and slewe them all to our knowlege. So our boats did long wait to see if any of them did come agen; but being all slaine, our boates returned, which sorrowfull newes of all our mens deaths was very much lamented of vs all.

The blow was hardest for Adams, whose brother, young Thomas, had been amongst the men who had gone ashore.[2]

With Van Beuningen dead, captaincy was transferred to the *Love*'s skipper, Jacob Quaeckernaeck. Still desperately short of victuals, Quaeckernaeck decided to leave the protection of the bay and try and victual on the nearby island of Santa María. They reached the island on November 8, and great was their euphoria when under the shore of the small island they found the *Hope* riding at her anchor. The initial elation at their reunion was soon dampened when, boarding the flagship, Quaeckernaeck and his pilot major found the men on board "in as great distress as we, having lost their General [Simon de Cordes], with seven and twenty of their men, slain at the island of Mocha, from whence they departed the day before we came by."

Quaeckernaeck and Adams' worries were well founded. Out of the one hundred and thirty men that had sailed on the *Hope* only thirty-three remained. The shortage of men was even more acute on board the *Love*, where there were "scarce so many men left as could wind up our anchor"—only twenty-eight in all. To make matters worse, both Van Beuningen and De Cordes had taken their best men ashore "so that all our officers were slain." As on the *Love*, only two officers were left among the crew of the *Hope*: Adams' "good friend Timothy

Shatton [who] was pilot in that ship," and the twenty-year-old son of the admiral, Simon de Cordes Jr., on whose young shoulders now came to rest the heavy responsibility for what remained of the fleet.

To Francisco de Quiñones the news from his captain, Pedro de Recalde, that, on November 4, he had sighted a large raider at anchor off the island of Santa María could not have come at a worse moment. Ever since his appointment as governor of Chile six months earlier, he had tried to quell the Araucanian revolt, but with the limited means at his disposal he had failed to make much progress. Only three weeks before, he had been forced to cede the inland town of Chillán, and even though De Recalde had managed to relieve the strategic port of Arauco, it had done little to halt the Araucanian onslaught. Meanwhile all of the governor's ships were deployed in the transport of victuals and reinforcements between Lima and Concepción. Yet even if he had had the ships, he had not the means to man them for a sea battle with the well-armed raider, which he presumed to be English. All he could do, therefore, was to dispatch a messenger to Santiago urging its council to take the necessary precautions against an English raid on the port of Valparaíso and to relate the news to the viceroy in Lima as fast as possible. To Santa María he sent one of his ablest captains, Antonio Recio de Soto, with instructions to find out the identity and destination of the raider.

As soon as De Soto arrived at the island he set out toward the alien ship to try and obtain the information the governor required. This proved not too easy, for the Spaniard was not allowed on board. Instead, he was asked to return the next day, when he was given two letters from the fleet's commander, one addressed to the governor, and one addressed to the inhabitants of the island. The latter, composed in a poor mixture of Portuguese and Spanish and signed by a certain Admiral De Cordes, explained that they were Dutch traders who had come as "friends, that they were subjects of the King [of Spain], and that therefore they expected to be received well in Chile." It further demanded that "since they had come with peaceful intentions, they should be sent victuals against payment and that they expected someone to visit them and discuss the conditions under which this was to be done." Not in the position to come to any arrangements with foreigners, let alone Dutch, on his own authority, De Soto informed De Cordes that he would submit his letter to the governor in Concepción as soon as possible.

The letter to the governor differed little from the one addressed to the island's inhabitants. Not for a moment, however, did De Quiñones doubt that he was dealing with "the enemy, pirates." Worse still, he now knew that he had more than one enemy ship to deal with. Just before De Soto had departed from Santa María, on November 8, another ship had arrived. More might follow, for the observant Spanish officer had noted that even after the second ship's arrival the lookout in the flagship's highest top had remained at his post. For the governor, the only ray of light amid all these dark bodings was that, oddly, the Araucanian revolt had worked in his favor. Only days after De Recalde had witnessed the arrival of the second raider at Santa María, the Araucanians had appeared in triumph before Concepción. It had been a gruesome yet curiously gratifying sight, for, impaled on the ends of their long spears, they had carried the severed heads that could only have belonged to the pirates. Obviously the raiders had landed and had been mistaken by the Araucanians for Spaniards. Yet even if De Quiñones had wanted to, he himself was unable to meet the pirates with the same boldness. The best strategy, he resolved, was to play along with the game and provide the raiders with the victuals they required. This would at least forestall any open hostilities and, with some luck, enable De Soto to get on board the raiders to gauge their true strength.

The governor's counterplot seemed to work wonderfully well. On his second visit to Santa María, De Soto was indeed invited on board the flagship and warmly welcomed by the young admiral. Moreover, his request to remain on board was granted so that, during the next two days, he was able to get a good impression of their strength. The ships seemed in reasonable condition, but not so their crews. The complement of the flagship was only forty-seven men, a number of them gravely ill. And even though he was not allowed to visit the other ship, from the flagship he could clearly see that she, too, was poorly manned. He had heard from the governor about the slaughter near Point Lavapié and he rightly suspected that they had barred him from the ship "so as not to reveal the small number of men that were in her; since, apart from the men amongst them that had died on the way, the hostile Indians of Arauco had killed more than 26 or 27 of their men that had gone ashore in a boat." Their admiral, meanwhile, continually importuned him for fresh victuals, yet at the same time claimed that they had enough provisions to last for another two years. What De Soto had been shown of their supplies, however, could not have lasted them for more than two months at most—an estimation that was underscored by the great eagerness with which they accepted the sheep, oxen, chickens, and cereals that were eventually brought over from the island on his instructions. On his departure, De Soto was presented with another letter for the governor. In it De Cordes thanked the governor for his assistance and offered himself and his ships "to the service of Your King and of Your Grace." In closing, the commander requested the assistance of a pilot to help them safely bring their two ships laden with costly wares to Concepción as soon as possible.

In spite of his initial skepticism De Quiñones was inclined to give De Cordes the benefit of the doubt. The fervor with which the Dutch admiral offered to serve the Spanish cause was flattering enough in itself, whilst his hatred toward the Araucanians was undoubtably genuine. The gruesome procession outside the town walls of Concepción two weeks before seemed to give sufficient credence to the admiral's bold assertion that "we will fight against the Indian dogs if Your Grace would want our assistance"—sufficient credence, at least, for De Quiñones to dispatch a pilot to Santa María with a letter in which he professed to have "received the delightful news with the greatest pleasure" and was making preparations to bring the two ships "under the King's service with all possible means."

The true reasons for his conviction of the inevitability of De Cordes' collaboration De Quiñones set forth in another letter, which he entrusted to De Soto, who was to deliver it to the viceroy in Peru. It was only fitting that his trusted officer should bear the good tidings. It had been De Soto, after all, from whom the governor had learned that the Dutch pirates "have a shortage of everything, that they have no food and folk, and that, in case they go on, they will without doubt perish," reasons that led him to believe "that they will be in this port within two days."

Despite the reasoned care with which De Quiñones arrived at his conclusion, no Dutch ship ever arrived in Concepción. To enhance their negotiative strength, the Dutch had done what they could to conceal the recent losses they had suffered and to improve the poor condition of the few who remained. Rations had been raised and before De Soto returned from Concepción, half the *Love*'s crew had been transferred to the flagship. To everyone's relief the ploy had worked. Through the offices of De Soto they had obtained the dearly needed victuals, and as soon as the Spaniard had left, those in command of the two remaining ships sat down to consider how and where to they should continue their journey.

The ships' council now consisted of no more than Simon de Cordes, Jacob Quaeckernaeck, and the two English pilots, William Adams and Timothy Shatton. It had been more by necessity than by choice that the pilots had been allowed back on the council, and no sooner had they been readmitted than they clashed with their captains over the most immediate problem: the severe lack of men on both ships. The pilots proposed "to take all things out of one ship, and to burn the other." But that, according to Adams, "the captains that were made new, the one nor the other, would not, so that we could not agree to leave the one or the other." At last it was agreed to divide the men equally between the two ships and continue the journey as best they could. And there lay the next problem. With some thirty men each, they had not the power to follow

Drake's example and raid the ports along the Chilean and Peruvian coast, nor did they stand much chance in an encounter with a Spanish ship. Such an encounter was very likely, as they had learned from De Soto, who had told Adams "how upon that coast of Peru, the king's ships were out seeking us, having knowledge of our being there." They also knew that at least one of their ships had already fallen into enemy hands, since De Soto had also told Adams that "one of our fleet, for hunger, was forced to seeke relief at the enemies hand in Santiago." And thus, on November 27, 1599, "we stood away directly for Japan." They did so advisedly, for "we gathered by reason that the Mollucas, and the most part of the East Indies were hot countries where woollen cloth would not be much accepted, whilst by report of one Dirck Gerritszoon [Pomp], which had been there with the Portugals, woollen cloth was in great estimation in that Island."

During the first part of the crossing winds remained favorable, so that after only two months of sailing Adams was able to record how both ships "passed the line equinoctial with a fair wind," and how, not long after they had crossed the Line, "we fell with certain islands in sixteen degrees of north latitude [Guam Islands], the inhabitants whereof are men-eaters." To some of the Dutch sailors the fear of being starved to death apparently outweighed their fear of being eaten alive, for when the ships "came near the islands, and having a great pinnace with us, eight of our men being in the pinnace, ran from us with the pinnesse, and (as we suppose) were eaten of the wild men, of which people we took one: which afterward the general sent for to come into his ship." Then, toward the middle of February, having come "into the latitude of seven and twenty and eight and twenty degrees, we found very variable winds and stormy weather," which, by February 23, according to the experienced pilot, had developed into "a wonderous storm of wind, as ever I was in." It was into the second day of that storm that disaster struck, and that "we lost our consort, whereof we were very sorry."

The loss seemed especially tragic in view of the long way they had come. Since their departure from Santa María, both ships had covered close to eight thousand nautical miles. It had taken them four months to do so and if Adams' reckonings were correct they could expect to reach land within a matter of weeks. This happened on March 24, when "we saw an island called Una Colona" (Kazan Rettō). The island, which derived its name from its column-like shape, featured on one of Adams' maps, informing the pilot that they were now less than six hundred miles away from Japan.

By now the condition of the *Love*'s crew had reached appalling depths. Even Adams, not a man easily given to despair, lamented "the misery we were in, having no more but nine or ten able men to go or creep upon their knees: our captain, and all the rest, looking every hour to die." Yet with undaunted resolve "we proceeded on our

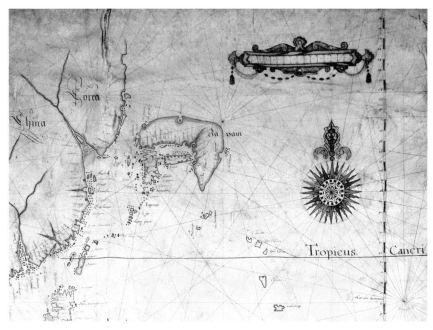

Japan as it appears on one of Doetszoon's plain charts, carried by the *Love*. Cabo des Cestos terminates exactly in a latitude of 30°, the latitude in which Adams sought to make landfall. Una Colona lies just above the tropic of Cancer.

former intention for Japan." Adams, now the most senior officer still able to perform his duties, knew that the Portuguese and Spanish ships mainly sailed on Japan's western ports, which were situated on the most western island of Kyushu. On his maps, Japan's opposite extremity lay some three hundred miles east. Here the main island of Honshu curved south in a long cape called Cabo des Cestos, terminating in a latitude of thirty degrees. With no method to determine his longitude, the only sure way for the pilot to find the cape was to sail due west along a latitude of thirty degrees. But the cape was not found. To increase his chances Adams now changed his course to a more northerly direction, and finally, "in thirty-two degrees and a half, we came in sight of the land, being the nineteenth day of April [1600]."[3]

PART 3

HONORS & REWARDS

rom the aforesaid cape of Cabo de Camico five miles thence to the point of the land, one runneth north north-west alongst the coast, and on the way one finds four or five Ilands and Cliffes, and right across from the aforesaid point, there lie two other Ilands, close to the land, having betwixt them a narrow Straight, and close by, on the north as well as on the south, many small Ilands and Cliffes (large and small). These two Ilands and the small Ilands and cliffes lie east and west from the cape being the end of Tosa, in a height of 33 1/6 degrees. All the coast is high land, with the Ilands lying beside, the depth being 60, 70 fathome near the land. From thence onwards begineth the Straight or narrownesse between the Iland of Tosa and the land of Bungo, and had you occasion to anchor in these quarters, then heed the land of Tosa, where you will find muddy ground. When you have rounded the aforesaid cape with the two Ilands, the land begins to trend westward, all of it being high land, having within, close under the south side, a small Iland; which Inlet you should heed so that the current shal not draw you in. Having passed this Inlet, you shal come to see a small round Iland (to wit, midway of the Channel of the Straight), which you should pass on the east side, and thence alongst the Coast five miles onwards, you shall see another Iland, lying close to the land, the which towards the Sea is beset with many stone Cliffes and Rocks. Beyond this Iland towards the northeast, one mile and a half on the way, lye two other Ilands together. Beyond these two Ilands, another mile and a half onwards, lyes another long Iland being plain or a field on top, stretching north west and southeast, the south eastern end being the highest. Inside these Ilands towards the west lyeth the Inlet of Usqui, where resides the King of Bungo.

—— Jan Huyghen van Linschoten, *Reysgheschrift*, 1594

Japan at the turn of the sixteenth century was a fragmented country on the verge of unification. For more than a century it had been in a state of endemic turmoil, known to the Japanese as the "period of the warring states." That period had begun in 1467 when, with the outbreak of the Ōnin War, the capital Kyoto was utterly reduced to ashes. Even as the smoke cleared, the wave of anarchy that had been set in motion swept the countryside, so that by the end of the fifteenth century the country had disintegrated into more than two hundred separate fiefdoms.

The continuous strife in which low overthrew high bred a new generation of leaders, the powerful warlords, or *daimyō*. They were bold men, ruthless in their pragmatism, but also innovative by necessity, as they had to find new ways to increase their military strength in their perpetual struggle for territorial expansion. For the greatest and most gifted amongst them that struggle was not a pursuit in itself but one that must ultimately lead to Japan's reunification.

The first and most cruel of these great unifiers was Oda Nobunaga, a young chieftain of uncertain pedigree. It was he who took the first step toward unification when he crushed the forces of the most prominent contenders and established an overlordship centered around Kyoto, where he installed a puppet general, or *shōgun*, to give legitimacy to his military dictatorship. Nobunaga's death at the hands of one of his senior vassals in 1582 gave rise to perhaps the greatest and certainly most erratic of unifiers, Toyotomi Hideyoshi. A humble soldier by birth, Hideyoshi had risen from amongst Nobunaga's ranks and added to those he inherited most of the country's remaining domains in two massive campaigns for which he mobilized some two hundred thousand troops. Yet Hideyoshi's accomplishments were not merely martial. Under his rule extensive land surveys were undertaken. These in turn were used to determine tax levies. Land size, tax levies, and samurai income were all expressed in rice yields. Its unit was the *koku*, roughly five bushels of rice, enough to support one man for a year. To enable the safe levy of taxes and to reduce the risk of armed rebellion, a nationwide sword hunt deprived all but the samurai class of weapons, while the latter were firmly bound in allegiance to the lords. Finally, to ensure that he would be succeeded by his son, Hideyori, he called into life a Council of Regency, consisting of the five leading daimyo. They were to bear the responsibility for the drafting of high policy. To oversee the execution of the council's policies, and to curb the power of the regents—each a territorial magnate in his own right—he further installed five commissioners. Yet in spite of Hideyoshi's precautionary intent, it was the council's head, the patient and farsighted Tokugawa Ieyasu who on the former's death in 1599, was best poised to eventually reap the full benefits of all these innovations.

Ieyasu's ascendancy did not go down well with all of those in power; several of the other four regents, formerly aligned to the house of Toyotomi, were eager to take on the unappointed successor. Indeed, one of them, Uesugi Kagekatsu, was already openly defying Ieyasu's drive for centralized control. Upon Hideyoshi's death, he had withdrawn to his stronghold, Wakamatsu castle in Aizu, a hundred miles north of Edo, where he had begun raising a large army. Yet it was one of the five commissioners, the master of intrigue and onetime favorite of Hideyoshi, Ishida Mitsunari, who was to cast the historical die when, at the end of the sixteenth century, he rallied a coalition of Japan's western warlords against the eastern forces of Tokugawa Ieyasu. Soon these two forces were to be pitted against each other in a decisive battle the victor of which would preside over Japan's total unification.

It was in 1543, at the very outset of this drive toward unification, that the Portuguese became the first Europeans to set foot on Japanese soil, when they reached Tanegashima on

Japan's most southern island of Kyushu in a Chinese junk. In a country at war, the Western firearms that were carried by the carracks that followed in their wake were warmly welcomed. So were the large quantities of Chinese silk they brought over from Macao, for it was not long after the first Portuguese carrack had arrived in Chinese waters that the Middle Kingdom had broken off all official relations with its eastern tributary. To blame were the fearsome *wakō*, the Japanese pirates. Protected by Japan's western warlords, they freely roamed the China Sea, wreaking widespread havoc and destruction all along the mainland. Even after Hideyoshi had subdued the island of Kyushu and had sought to legalize overseas trade by issuing patents franked with his vermilion seal, the *wakō* continued to be a menace. By then, the few Japanese red-seal ships that did carry some silk from mainland ports had long lost the race against the *Goa Dourado*, the Great Ship from Golden Goa, which on its last leg from Macao to Nagasaki carried up to eighty tons of the coveted fiber.

A pivotal role in the commercial dealings between the Portuguese and the Japanese merchants was played by the Jesuits. Like the merchants, they, too, had arrived in Japan with the first Portuguese ships. Amidst war and famine, their promise of a better world found fertile soil; within a few years they had found a devoted following; by the middle of the century even a number of the western daimyo had been baptized. It was on their request that the Jesuits first began to act as bullion brokers with the Chinese merchants in Macao. Their financial acumen and command of the Japanese and Chinese languages drew them in deeper; before long they had become indispensable intermediaries in the Portuguese traffic between the two alienated countries. Though deeply embarrassed by the marriage between God and Mammon over which they presided, perennially burdened by their Mission's spiraling costs, the Jesuits could do little else than partake in this worldly trade.

In as far as it impinged on the Iberian trade, Japan's rulers condoned the Jesuits' urge to proselytize as a necessary evil. Ironically, of all three unifiers, it was Oda Nobunaga who proved to be most sympathetic toward the Jesuits—a sympathy that was fired by their mutual hatred of Buddhist sects. Unhampered by government interference, the Jesuits were able to proselytize freely, so that by the time of Nobunaga's death they had won some 150,000 Japanese souls. Even under the first years of Hideyoshi's erratic reign the Jesuits were able to continue their work, and soon the number of converts reached a peak of 200,000. Then disaster struck, when, on June 25, 1587, Hideyoshi issued an edict in which all the Jesuits' hard-earned privileges were revoked. Japan, it stated, was the land of the Gods, and stirring up the populace to commit outrages was deserving of severe punishment. All padres, therefore, were to leave Japan within twenty days. Unwilling to quit the country, the missionaries fled to Kyushu. There, protected by the Christian warlords, they continued their work in secret, hoping to weather the storm by lying low. Over the next months, much of what they had achieved was undone. Japanese converts were ordered to either recant, go into exile, or commit suicide. Jesuit properties in Osaka, Hakata, and Sakai were confiscated, and starting in the capital, one by one the *nanbanji*, the "temples of the southern barbarians," were destroyed.

Yet the storm abated and in the relative calm that followed, the Iberian contest for the Japanese soul was to erupt in full force. In spite of a papal bull, issued by Pope Gregory XIII on January 23, 1585, forbidding any religious order except the Jesuits access to Japan on pain of excommunication, already before the last decade of the sixteenth century a number of Spanish friars had found their way to the island country. Their real chance to break the Jesuit monopoly came in 1591, when Hideyoshi sent an envoy to Manila in an effort to establish trade relations between his country and the Philippines. The two Spanish pseudo-embassies that followed were both led by Franciscan friars. To the horror of the Jesuits the friars were cordially received by Hideyoshi, who allowed them to remain in Japan in the hope of thus attracting the Manila traders. Encouraged by their friendly reception and largely ignorant of what had gone before, the Franciscans did exactly that for which the Jesuits had been punished; they began to openly celebrate Mass in the shogun's capital. Then, on February 5, 1597, the inevitable happened, when in the very image of Golgotha, twenty-six Franciscan friars were crucified on the slope of Nishisaka Hill overlooking Nagasaki. The punishment was only exacted after each of them had been mutilated and made to walk to their ends, all the way from Kyoto, through the center of every town and hamlet on the way, so as to serve as an example for all those who entertained any thoughts of following in their footsteps. Their sentencing and the way in which it was exacted spoke volumes about Japanese fears of Iberian designs against their country, for the friars had only incurred the tyrant's wrath after a Spanish galleon from Manila had been wrecked on Japan's coast shortly before. In all Spanish overseas conquests, the galleon's indiscreet captain had boasted, it was the missionaries who had paved the way for the conquistadors by first converting the impressionable indigenous people and thus inuring them to the Christian benevolence of Spanish rule.

To their eternal dismay, time and again, the Iberian missionaries had to concede that it was Mammon and not Him whose name they professed who had come to their aid. The Iberian role in the silk trade proved so important that, even though he had decreed that all foreign missionaries leave his country, Hideyoshi never took any active measures to ensure that they did so. No more foreign missionaries died during the last years of his reign, and even though Ieyasu viewed the activities of the missionaries with the same suspicion as his predecessor, he too preferred to endure their presence rather than do without the trade in which they partook. And thus, while their immediate problems were domestic in scope, it was the external conditions that forced each of the three great unifiers to turn their gaze abroad in order to address them and, in doing so, face yet more. For it was the sea that linked Japan to the vital wellspring of Southeast Asian commerce; it was the sea that had brought to Japanese shores the Western ways of warfare; yet it was the sea, too, by which the great Christian empire was subjugating ever widening parts of Asia.

X

THE ARRIVAL

O world of wonders! (I can say no less)
That I should be preserved in that distress
That I have met with here! O blessed be
That hand that from it hath delivered me!

The *Love* had made Japanese landfall, but only few of her crew were aware of the historical occasion. Since their departure from Santa María they had been at sea for four months and twenty-two days. Apart from those who had fled in the pinnace, two others had died, so that only twenty-four men were still alive. Besides Adams no more than six could stand on their feet, and the pilot knew that with each day that they remained at sea more men would die. They were now sailing up a wide channel that ran northwest between two highly serrated headlands. And it was toward the western end of the channel, where the two islands almost touched by two narrow peninsulas, that the pilot of the battered vessel decided to put about and seek a safe anchorage in a wide bay that ran deep into the southern shore. That anchorage was found on April 20, 1600, when the *Love* lowered her sails near a wide, white beach, not far from a hamlet on the northern shore of the bay.[1]

No sooner had the few able men managed to anchor, when their ship was surrounded by a large number of small craft that had been launched from the shore. They were manned by what, judging by their simple manner and scant clothing, seemed to be local fishermen. Unable to communicate with the natives and with no strength to offer any resistance, the few able men on board had to stand by feebly as, one after the other, the nimble Japanese began to clamber aboard and remove each and every item that was not too heavy or too large to be supported by their fragile vessels. Adams was nevertheless relieved to find that the fishermen, who were unarmed, "offered us no hurt," even though they "stole all things they could steal." The next morning another, larger vessel approached, this time from across the bay, farther inland. It was a Japanese junk. She had obviously been dispatched by some local ruler, for when she drew near, she turned out to be manned by a large number of soldiers. They were led by a handful of officials, who stood out from the rest by their grave demeanor and imposing garments. Presently all came on board the *Love* and whilst the soldiers watched over her crew, the officials proceeded to painstakingly inspect the ship and her contents. Toward noon, the officials left, while the soldiers remained behind. Two more days the *Love* remained anchored under the bay's northern shore. During that time three more of her crew died. The remainder clung on to life with what energy they had, all the while scrutinized by their stoic guards. Then, on April 22, the junk returned with a large fleet of smaller vessels and the ship was towed to a large port at the head of the bay.[2]

The *Love* was clearly not the first foreign vessel to visit the port. A number of Chinese junks were moored in the harbor, and as the men were led through the town's cramped alleys, they soon found that the town had its own foreign quarters, mainly inhabited, it seemed, by Asians from the mainland, although among the crowd they had also seen a number of Portuguese merchants.

To the men's great relief they were put up in a large and comfortable house and given everything they needed in the form of food and refreshments. All of them were in a deplorable state. More than half, including Captain Quaeckernaeck, were on the brink of death. And though all were tended to with much care by their Japanese hosts, for some, the degree of their exhaustion and the advanced stage of their afflictions left little hope for their recovery; three more men died within the first week of their arrival, so that by the end of the month, only eighteen men out of the *Love*'s original complement of one hundred and ten were left. Quaeckernaeck, too, pulled through, but only just.

The other survivors were William Adams, Melchior van Santvoort, Jan Joosten van Lodensteyn, Jan Cousynen, Gisbert de Coning, Jan van Oudewater, Jan Abelszoon, Jan Tol, Jan Roos, Pieter Janszoon, Pieter Blanckert, Michiel Physzoon, Thomas Corneliszoon, Jacob Swager, Jan Corneliszoon, Elbert Woutersen, and Jacob and Willem.[3]

It was during the first few, uncertain days that the house was visited by a group of Japanese officials. They were accompanied by a Portuguese, who introduced himself as Padre João Rodríguez, the procurator of the Jesuit Mission in Japan. Rodríguez informed Adams that they were in the province of Bungo on the northeastern shore of the island of Kyushu. The hamlet where the *Love* had anchored was called Sashū, and she had been towed to the port of Usuki. It had been on behalf of the lord of Usuki, Ōta Shigemasa, that he had come down from his residency in Funai, the capital of Bungo, in order to interview the pilot.[4]

Adams, who had a reasonable command of the Portuguese language, faithfully answered the questions that were put to him.

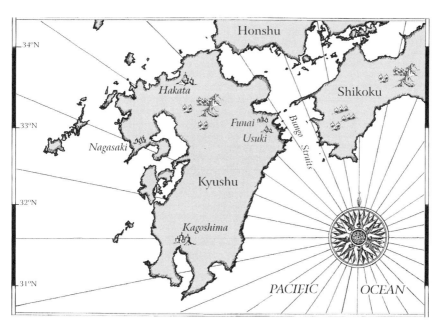

He explained that they had left Holland with five ships, that they had passed through the Strait of Magellan, that from there they had intended to sail for the Sunda Islands, but that a great storm had blown them apart. Equally truthful was his assertion that it had taken them four months to cross the Pacific. For obvious reasons, however, he carefully avoided any mention of their encounters with the Portuguese on São Tiago and Annobon, and the losses the latter had suffered in the process. Instead, he tried to make the Japanese believe that, after the two ships had passed the tropic of Cancer, their crews had been struck by a highly contagious disease, which had claimed 155 lives. Yet in spite of his efforts, in the course of the interview, it became abundantly clear to Adams that having to make his case through the mouth of an Iberian was "not to our good, our mortal enemies being our Trunchmen"—a view in which he was strengthened in the course of the following days, during which he learned that the padre:

> reported of us that we were pirates, and were not in the way of merchandising. Which report caused the governors and common people to think evil of us: In such a manner that we looked always when we should be set upon crosses; which is the execution in this land for theeuery and some other crimes.

For two of the *Love*'s weakened crew, Gisbert de Coning and Jan van Oudewater, the threat of being crucified alive was too much to bear. They chose to join forces with the Portuguese, having been assured by the padre that in doing so their lives would be spared. These "traitors," Adams later fulminated, "sought all manner of ways to get the [ship's] goods into their hands, and made known unto them all things that had passed in our voyage." Both men disappeared from the house shortly after Rodríguez' visit.[5]

It had not been on Ōta Shigemasa's request that João Rodríguez had come down from Funai. It so happened that on the very day the *Love* had anchored just off Sashū, the procurator was visiting the area. Hearing of the arrival of a foreign ship, he had immediately sensed that something was awry—it was still early in the year, well before the southwest monsoon began to blow, and Portuguese and Spanish vessels came over from the mainland or the Philippines. No other European ships had ever been sighted off Japan's shores and he had logically assumed "that it might be a ship, which went from Mexico to the Philippines, but had been blown off its course by a storm." He had sent out two of his men in one of the fishermen's boats to see whether her crew was in need of anything, but they had turned back midway with the disturbing news that she was Dutch. He had returned to Funai, but as soon as he learned that the ship had been towed away by Ōta's junks, he had departed for Usuki to inform the port's ruler of the danger the aliens posed and to seek his permission to submit the heretics to an interview. Armed with what he had coaxed out of the pilot he had returned to Funai, from where he dispatched a messenger to Alessandro Valignano, the Mission's Padre Visitor who currently resided in Nagasaki.[6]

On hearing the troubling news, Valignano instantly sat down to write to Terazawa Hirotaka, Nagasaki's governor and the Council of Regency's highest representative on the island. Crucially, Terazawa was also a onetime convert to the Catholic faith. Valignano presented the arrival of the "Lutheran Pirates" as a grave threat to Japanese interests, arguing that the Dutch were the "enemies of the Portuguese and all Christians." Appealing directly to any residual Christian sentiments in the governor, Valignano stressed the need to have the heretics dealt with, either by having them expelled from Japan forthwith or by having them crucified—the only rightful penalty for those who lived by piracy.

Unknown to the Jesuit, by the time Terazawa read Valignano's letter he had already received several missives from Ōta in which the latter reported the arrival of a Dutch vessel, that he had secured its contents, and was now awaiting further instructions. Aware of the political and economical ramifications of the arrival of a non-Iberian vessel in Japanese waters, Terazawa had immediately sent a messenger to the Council of Regency in Osaka. Then, a few days after he had received Valignano's letter, he departed for Usuki to verify the Jesuit's assertions in person. Upon his arrival he had the ship and its contents impounded and, with the help of the local Jesuits, had his men draw up a careful inventory of what remained of the cargo, which turned out to consist of:

> eleven great chests with coarse woollen cloths, a box with four hundred branches of coral and as many of amber, a great chest of glass beads of divers colors, some mirrors and spectacles, many children's pipes, two thousand *cruzados* in *reals*, nineteen large bronze pieces of ordnance and other small ones, five hundred muskets, and five thousand balls of cast-iron, three hundred chain-shot, 50 quintals of powder, three great chests of coats of mail, three-fourths having breastplates and pectorals of steel, three hundred and fifty-five darts, a great quantity of nails, iron, hammers, scythes and mattocks, and various other kinds of implements.

With such a cargo, the Jesuits on their part concluded, "it would seem they were coming to conquer and inhabit."

Their views were mainly shared by Ōta. It was true that much of the ship's content had been taken away by the locals, but what remained gave little credence to Adams' claim that they were merely "in the way of merchandising," leading Ōta to the conclusion that Quaeckernaeck and his men were "not of good title" since they "did not carry goods in such quantity or of the same quality as brought by the other ships that came to Japan." Nor had they "come well dressed, and splendid with the pomp of servants and attendants, as the other merchants were accustomed to come, but only as soldiers and sailors, and besides with much ordnance and arms."

No such conclusions had as yet been drawn by the governor; nor the Council of Regency, for on the first day of May, four large junks entered Usuki harbor. On board was an envoy from the council's head, Tokugawa Ieyasu, with instructions to bring the captain of the Dutch ship to Osaka for questioning. Quaeckernaeck, however, was

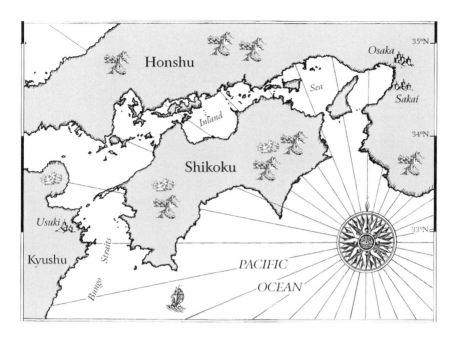

still gravely ill, so that it fell on Adams, the second-most senior officer, to represent him. Allowed one man to attend him, the next morning, Adams departed with the ship's merchant, Jan Joosten van Lodensteyn. Several days were spent on the Inland Sea, separating the main island of Honshu from the island of Shikoku. They sailed its full two-hundred-mile length before they arrived at the seaport of Sakai, where both men were lodged until May 12. On that day Adams was taken apart and made to re-embark alone. He was then ferried round to Osaka, where he was led ashore and brought to the northern wing of a vast castle.[7]

Upon his arrival in the castle, Adams was met by two officials, who led the pilot into a large matted room, where all three of them sat down cross-legged. At length, upon some signal, the two men rose and led Adams to another room. In it, seated on a slight elevation, sat Tokugawa Ieyasu, resting one arm leisurely on a lacquered armrest, and raising the other, beckoning the pilot to enter.

The regent omitted all forms of ceremony and immediately began to question Adams by means of signs, some of which the pilot understood and some he did not. Yet despite the limitations of their exchange, and to Adams' considerable relief, the regent "viewed me well, and seemed to be wonderfull favorable." It had clearly been with a view to form such an impression independently, without the aid of an interpreter, that Ieyasu had chosen to subject Adams to this mode of questioning; for presently the two men were joined by a Portuguese interpreter through which the regent asked Adams "of what land I was, and what moved us to come to his land, being so far off." Having brought with him some of the sea charts on board the *Love*, Adams "showed unto him the name of our country," and explained "that our land had long sought out the East Indies, and desired friendship with all kings and potentates in way of merchandise, having in our land diverse commodities, which these lands had not: and also to buy such merchandise in this land, which our country had not." Ieyasu did not pursue the matter any further but now wanted to know "whether our country had warres." Adams acknowledged that the Netherlands was at war with Spain and Portugal, but stressed that it was "in peace with all other nations." Asked in what did he believe, he replied "in God, that made heaven and earth."

The rest of the day was spent in much the same fashion. And thus, whilst Adams marveled at the opulence of his new surroundings, a "wonderful costly house guilded with gold in abundance," the regent continued to bombard the pilot with questions in his seemingly insatiable curiosity:

> He asked me diverse other questions of things of religion, and many other things: As what way we came to the country. Hauing a chart of the whole world, I shewed him, through the Straight of Magellan. At which he wondred, and thought me to lie. Thus from one thing to another, I abode with him till mid-night. And Hauing asked mee, what merchandize we had in our shippe, I shewed him all. In the end, he being ready to depart, I desired that we might haue trade of merchandize, as the Portugals and Spanyards had. To which he made me an answer: but what it was I did not understand. So he commanded me to be carried to prison.

Two long days passed before Adams was again led before Ieyasu. Again the regent grilled the pilot on the purpose of the Dutch expedition, and again Adams replied as he had done two days before. The regent also returned to his questions concerning the countries with which the Netherlands was at war, demanding to know why this was so. Yet the steadfast consistency with which the pilot answered all questions seemed to satisfy the regent, for even though Adams was taken back to prison, this time, he was given better lodgings than before.

Although their treatment had improved, both Adams and Van Lodensteyn were left completely in the dark as to the fate that awaited them, nor were they given any news about what had happened to their ship and the rest of the crew. For the pilot, the uncertainty about their immediate future was aggravated by his nagging conviction that the Jesuits continued to conspire against them—a fear that again proved to be well founded. As Adams later learned, whilst he was in prison, "the Jesuits and Portuguese gave many evidences against me and the rest to the Emperor, that we were thieves and robbers of all nations, and were we suffered to live, it should be against the profit of his Highness, and the land." As they had done in Usuki, the Portuguese demanded that the heretics should be immediately tried or expelled so that "the rest of our nation without doubt should fear and not come here any more." And thus, whilst the pilot and the merchant remained imprisoned, their enemies sought to make the most of their advantage, "making access to the Emperor, and procuring friends to hasten my death."

Ieyasu was far from putting Adams or any of the *Love*'s other crewmembers on the cross. So far, the Dutch had done his country no harm and the pilot's revelation that the Netherlands was at war with Spain and Portugal threw an illuminating light on the zeal with which the Jesuits sought to incite him and his countrymen against them. It also went a long way in explaining the large quantity of armor the Dutch ship carried in its hold.

And it was the ship's cargo, rather than her crew, that concerned the regent at this juncture. Coming as it did around the time he was beginning to receive the first reports of Uesugi's movements, the missive from Terazawa that a large foreign ship had arrived in Usuki, her holds stacked with the coveted Western implements of war, could not have come at a more opportune moment for the regent. Having the ship's chief officer come to Osaka had not only helped him to gain a better insight into the designs and motives of those who had sent her hither; it had also conveniently allowed him to do with their ship as he pleased. And thus, with the same junk that had sailed for Usuki to collect the pilot, he had dispatched a messenger to Terazawa, instructing the governor that, as soon as the foreign crew had sufficiently recovered, they should be made to bring their ship round to Sakai together with what was left of her cargo. This was done not long after the pilot and his attendant had departed. On the ship's arrival in Sakai toward the middle of May, Ieyasu had immediately traveled down from Osaka to inspect her and her cargo. He had ordered the woolen cloth and all else that remained of the merchandise to be sold. Yet her vast cargo of arms and ordnance he had confiscated forthwith.[8]

Events were now succeeding each other in rapid succession. That same month Ieyasu had summoned Uesugi to come down to Osaka to explain his conduct. As he had expected, the latter had blatantly ignored the summons and continued to build up his forces around Wakamatsu castle. Meanwhile, Ishida Mitsunari was on the verge of doing the same in the western provinces—provinces where he could reckon on the support of a number of powerful warlords. By the middle of June it had become clear that the time of reckoning had come and Ieyasu set about devising a plan to outwit those who conspired against him. Within the next few weeks he would go up to Edo. There he would raise an army of some fifty thousand men at the head of which he would march north to quash the incipient rebellion. By moving against Uesugi (only a minor foe) he would cause Ishida to reveal his true colors, and then he would move against him. For the campaign against Uesugi and for those that would inevitably follow, he could make good use of the arms that had been found in the hold of the Dutch ship. Her cannon, too, could be put to good use. The most practical solution would be to unload them at the port of Uraga, from where they could be transported overland to Edo castle, which he intended to make his new power base. Already the castle was undergoing reconstruction, and to kill two birds with one and the same stone, he would have the ship load timber on her way hither.

Forty-one days Adams and Van Lodensteyn had spent in prison when, on June 22, Adams was once again led before Ieyasu. Once again the pilot was subjected to a thorough interrogation by the regent, at the end of which he was asked:

> whether I were desirous to go to the ship to see my countrymen. I answered very gladly: the which he bade me do. And this was the first news that I had, that the ship and company were come to the city. So that with a rejoicing heart I took a boat, and went to our ship, where I found the captain and the rest, recovered of their sickness; and when I came aboard with weeping eyes was received: for it was given them to understand that I was executed long since.

Adams and Van Lodensteyn's initial elation at their reunion with their fellow sailors was dampened when they learned that the *Love* had been fully stripped of her contents. The blow was particularly hard for Van Lodensteyn. Given the circumstances, he could hardly be held accountable for the fate of the cargo, but as the ship's only surviving merchant he would nevertheless be the one who would have to report the considerable loss to the *bewindhebbers* if ever he was to return home. For Adams the loss was less pronounced but frustrating enough. Except for the maps that he had taken with him to Osaka, all his nautical instruments and records had been taken away, "so that the clothes which I took with me on my back I only had." The two men were not the only ones to have lost out, for "from the

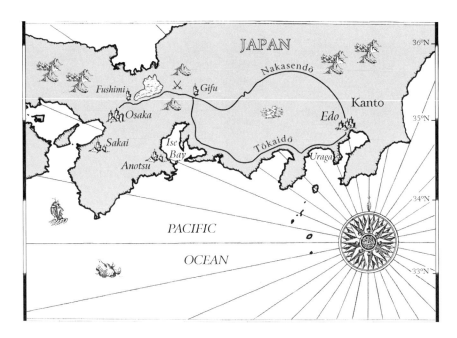

capten and the company, generally, what was good or worth the taking, was carried away." All, however, were well recompensed for their loss; on Ieyasu's personal orders a grant of 50,000 *real* was "delivered in the hands of one that was made our governor, who kept them in his hands to distribute them unto us as wee had neede."

The *Love* remained on Sakai's roadstead for another month, during which part of the grant was used for major repairs and the purchase of victuals. Then, on July 23, orders came that they were to bring the ship round to the Kanto region, farther east along the coast. First, however, they were to call at the port of Anotsu, in the Bay of Ise, where they were to load timber, which they were to carry all the way up to the port of Uraga, on the tip of the Miura Peninsula, guarding the mouth of Edo Bay. Once there, the timber would be transferred to smaller vessels and carried to Edo. For reasons unexplained, the ship's cannon and a large quantity of rounds and powder had been left on board. It was clear that they were not intended for the ship's defense, for they were safely stowed away in her hold, only to be unloaded at their last port of call.

The events of that year, the fifth year of Keichō (felicitous longevity), took their course very much as Ieyasu had foreseen. No sooner had he ridden north to engage Uesugi's forces, than Ishida had shown his hand by raising an army and laying siege to Fushimi castle, Ieyasu's official residency, just south of Kyoto. Though staunchly defended by one of Ieyasu's vassals, the castle fell on September 8, after ten days of frantic fighting. Meanwhile, Ishida had begun championing the cause of Toyotomi Hideyori, Hideyoshi's rightful successor, a shrewd move with which he was winning the support of a large number of western warlords. He had already raised some eighty thousand troops, at the head of which he was now marching eastwards, toward the Kanto region, on the assumption that Ieyasu would be pinned down by Uesugi up north.

Brilliant strategist that he was, Ieyasu had anticipated the move. To keep Uesugi in check, he had persuaded a number of northern daimyo to attack the rebel warlord from the north. This left both his hands free to deal with Ishida's advance from the west. Already by September 11, he had returned to Edo castle from where, in all tranquility, he directed both the minor campaign against Uesugi and the major campaign against Ishida. To meet Ishida's forces, he had divided his own forces in three. His son, Hidetada, was to lead a force of thirty thousand men along the Nakasendō, the main inland route. At the same time, his most trusted commanders would lead another large force along the Tōkaidō, skirting Japan's east coast. Both forces were to unite just south of Gifu, where the two main roads converged. Not until October 7 did Ieyasu himself stir from Edo castle. By then the conduct of his commanders had convinced him of their unswerving loyalty. On his orders, they had crossed the Kiso River and taken Gifu castle, where they were awaiting his arrival. This happened on October 17, when Ieyasu rode into Gifu at the head of thirty thousand troops.

All that now separated the western and eastern forces were two mountain ranges: the Ibuki mountains ranging down from the north; the Yōrō mountains up from the south. Both ranges met at the small post town of Sekigahara, the gateway between western and eastern Japan. And it was on the plains of Sekigahara, some ten miles east of Lake Biwa, that, on October 21, 1600, the eastern and western forces finally clashed. For most of the morning the outcome of the battle hung in the balance. At noon the advantage seemed to be with the western forces, but then, one of its flanks changed sides and began to attack their former allies. Surprised and outnumbered, the western forces began to crumble, and when Ishida fled the scene the battle was over.

Like all great leaders, Ieyasu proved magnanimous in victory. Drawing on the strength of his immense prestige he began to make sweeping changes in the allocation of land amongst the daimyo. Those who had been most loyal were elevated to the status of *fudai*, or house daimyo. These were allocated fiefdoms close to the center of power, which was moved to Edo. Those who had sided with Ishida were forced to move to the country's periphery or saw their fiefdoms greatly reduced in size. These became the *tozama*, or outside daimyo. Their continued loyalty was ensured through a system of alternate attendance, requiring them to establish residencies in the capital and regularly attend formal occasions in Edo castle. Every other year they were allowed to return and tend to their fiefdoms, leaving their wives and children behind to serve as hostages. To give shape to his newly found regime, Ieyasu restored the Bakufu, the ancient institute of governance that had succumbed under civil war. Ieyasu's ascendancy was sealed in 1603, when the emperor pronounced him Sei-i Tai-shogun, the Barbarian-Subjugating Generalissimo.

The crew of the *Love* had played their part, too. Following their departure from Sakai, they had safely reached Anotsu, where, in accordance with their instructions, they had loaded timber. But on the second leg of their journey they had encountered several storms and they had only arrived in Uraga toward the end of August, much later than anticipated. Upon their arrival the timber had been transferred to smaller crafts, whilst the guns and ammunition had been put ashore. Then the men that were most fit had been ordered to disembark. Together with the guns they had been taken to Edo and quartered on the precincts of a vast castle, where they discovered how the timber that had been carried by the *Love* was being used in the construction of a northern wing. Only then did they learn that they were to be attached to a vast army in order to operate the guns that had been taken from their own ship. They had departed on September 1, traveling north until they had reached a place called Aizu, where they had laid siege of Wakamatsu castle. Then, at the news of Ieyasu's victory, Uesugi had surrendered, and the Dutch gunners had returned to their ship.[9]

The *Love* made several more journeys between Japan's eastern ports on behalf of Ieyasu, and before long her crew had spent the better part of two years in Japan. At length, driven partly by his responsibility toward the *bewindhebbers*, partly by his men's desire to sail home, Quaeckernaeck set about to seek permission to leave Japan. Making use of the close bond that had developed between his pilot and the shogun, he prevailed on Ieyasu to let them "get our ship clear, and to seek our best means to come where the Hollanders had their trade." In the process a large part of the grant was returned to Ieyasu in the form of costly gifts, yet neither the gifts nor the pilot's supplications were to any avail, and they were made to understand "that we should not have our ship, but to abide in Japan." It was around that time that Quaeckernaeck and Adams had to contend with a number of men among the crew, who "would not abide any longer in the ship, but every one would be a commander." Faced with the prospect of having to spend the rest of their lives in the island country, they began to rebel against their superiors and encouraged the rest of the crew to demand that each should receive his share of what was left of the grant. Unable to persuade his men otherwise, Quaeckernaeck finally gave in to their demands and "the part of every one being divided, every one took his way."

XI

THE FRUITION

Thus far did I come loaden with my sin,
Nor could aught ease the grief that I was in,
Till I came hither. What a place is this!
Must here be the beginning of my bliss?
Must here the burden fall from off my back?
Must here the strings that bound it to me, crack?

Following their breakup the crew of the *Love* began to settle in their new abode as best they could. The senior members among the ship's crew used the limited influence they had gained to make a living for themselves. For others, such as boatswain's mate Jan Cousynen, caulker Jacob Swager, and ship's carpenter Pieter Janszoon, who knew only the crafts they had learned, it was difficult to find their niche in the bewildering feudal complexity of Japanese society. After their share of what had been left of the grant had run out, they were forced to subsist on the stipend of two pounds of rice a day and twelve ducats a year—a stipend that had been granted by Tokugawa Ieyasu to each of the survivors, irrespective of their position, as a reward for the services rendered.

Some went into trade. Most successful amongst them were Jan Joosten van Lodensteyn and Melchior van Santvoort.[1] Both men married Japanese, Christian women and used their share of the grant to set themselves up as merchants. Even though both enjoyed a considerable degree of freedom, initially, neither of them was allowed to trade by themselves but were forced to do so through the offices of a Japanese host and essentially acted as intermediaries in the Asian-Iberian trade. For Van Lodensteyn, drawing as he did on his experience as ship's merchant, trading came naturally. He settled in the foreign quarters of Edo, where he began to trade in silk, porcelain, gold, ivory, paints, spices, and most of the other commodities that reached Japan on Chinese and Portuguese vessels. During the first decade his business prospered, at one point employing as many as four Japanese assistants, each of whom could act on Van Lodensteyn's behalf. Yet, coarse in his manners and often late in his payments, the Dutch trader made enemies with the same ease with which he traded, and following an incident in which he incurred the wrath of none other than the emperor himself, his demise became inevitable. That demise was hastened by an earthquake that destroyed the large storehouse he had built on the outskirts of Edo. For Van Santvoort, who had been the *Love*'s scribe, trade in an alien country posed an impressive challenge, but his sound character soon won him a favorable reputation among Japanese officials. He used his part of the grant to buy a property in Sakai. Soon the establishment was regularly visited by purveyors to the imperial court, who came to sample the costly foreign silks. Amongst his wide clientele were also Osaka's countless artisans. They required woolen cloth such as had been carried by the *Love*, but already introduced to Japan by the Portuguese during the middle of the sixteenth century. Highly durable and waterproof, the sturdy fabric had found widespread application in the manufacture of military garments, an industry that had reached its very peak at the time of the *Love*'s arrival.

Pieter Blanckert, Michiel Physzoon, Thomas Corneliszoon, Jan Tol, and Jan Roos had found employment most easily. They were the men who had been chosen to operate the *Love*'s guns in the campaign against Uesugi Kagekatsu. The onus had brought its rewards. Once they had entered the service of Ieyasu, they had not merely acted as gunners but had also been called upon to instruct a number of the regent's men in the art of gunnery. Given the importance of this new and revolutionary art, the men's newly won position had been one of considerable esteem. For the lowly sailors, perpetually at the beck and call of others, their new job as instructor had been made all the more agreeable by the deference with which their students had accepted their authority. Back on board the *Love*, a number of them had bucked at taking orders and refused to continue in their subordinate role as simple sailor. Simple they might be, yet they were intelligent enough to know that on shore their expertise was in high demand. And so it was, for no sooner had they departed with their share of the grant, than they were hired by Matsura Shigenobu, the daimyo of Hirado, to instruct his men in the "Dutch art" of gunnery. Since it concerned the latest military technology, all was surrounded with the utmost secrecy. Not all of the Japanese students, however, were able to observe discretion. Writing to a close friend, one of the Japanese gunners could not refrain from boasting that "I have now learned and been told everything about the use of cannons and it is no matter to be thought of lightly."

Of all the men who outlived their ordeal on the *Love*, the English pilot fared best. During his early years in Japan, Adams, too, spent many an hour instructing Ieyasu's soldiers in the use of European weaponry.[2] Following the country's pacification, he tried his hand at commerce, but his heart was not in it and he was not as successful as the Dutch. Like Quaeckernaeck he preferred to spend his time aboard the *Love*. Assisted by a Japanese crew, the Dutch captain and English pilot kept plying between Japan's countless ports to carry goods on behalf of the shogun, until, in the autumn of 1603, on their way to Uraga, they were overtaken by a typhoon. Not far from the port, the *Love* was beached and though the crew were saved the ship was irretrievably lost.[3]

Ieyasu, appreciative of the *Love*'s contribution, by now knew that Adams had spent his youth as an apprentice shipbuilder, and asked the pilot to build him a new ship. Fearing that the end result might not please his benefactor, Adams at first declined, objecting that he was "no carpenter, and had no knowledge thereof." But the shogun insisted, and early in the following year the pilot set about to organize the construction of the first Western-style vessel on Japanese soil. A launching site was prepared on the banks of the Itō-ō River, not far from the port of Itō, on the east side of Izu Peninsula. There, with the help of the *Love*'s carpenter, Pieter Janszoon, and a small army of Japanese craftsmen, the keel was laid of a Dutch-style pinnace, calculated to have a displacement of some eighty tons on completion. The ship was launched within a year and rigged in the European way. The results of Adams' and Janszoon's labors so much pleased the shogun that he had the men build another vessel. This ship, christened the *Sea Adventure*, had twice the displacement of her predecessor and was seaworthy enough for transpacific voyages.[4]

With shogunal approval, the pilot spent many of the following years aboard his ships, making several voyages up and down Japan's eastern coasts to explore and chart their situation as far north as a latitude of 36°. At Ieyasu's court, his considerable knowledge of

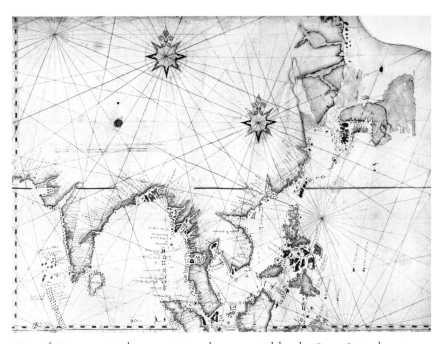

One of Doetszoon's three surviving charts carried by the *Love*. It is almost certain that the corrected coastlines of eastern Japan and the Asian mainland were drawn by Adams, using the observations he made on his many voyages.

Western sciences earned him the title of *komon*, or adviser, in which capacity he instructed Ieyasu in the fundamentals of geometry and mathematics. He even advised the Japanese ruler in his handling of foreign affairs, which, according to the pilot, pleased the shogun to such an extent that "what I said he would not contrary. At which my former enemies did wonder; and at this time must intreat me to do them a friendship, which to both Spaniards and Portingals have I done: recompensing them good for evil."

The many rendered services and the exceptional rapport with the shogun that resulted caused the English pilot's star to steadily rise on the Eastern firmament. Eventually, Adams was raised to the status of shogunal retainer, a *hatamoto*, or bannerman, and allotted an estate measuring between 220 and 250 *koku*. In the Japanese feudal scheme of things, in which bannermen might possess fiefdoms with yields exceeding 3,000 *koku*, Adams' estate was of little significance, yet it was the first Japanese land hitherto bestowed an individual European. The small fiefdom, which Adams likened to an English lordship, was worked by some eighty to ninety men that, in

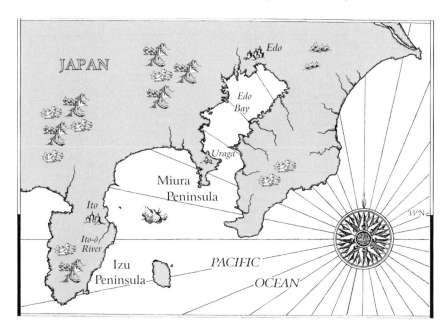

his own words, "be as my slaves or servants." Like most of his bannermen, Ieyasu required Adams to reside within the Kanto region,
close to the capital, yet the shogun had not bestowed the fiefdom on
his adviser without the latter's original vocation in mind. Called
Hemi, after the name of the village that lay on its outskirts, Adams'
fiefdom was situated only a few miles away from the port of Uraga,
right at the heart of the Miura Peninsula. It was the peninsula that
was to lend the English pilot the name by which he became most
widely known along the island country's eastern coasts—Miura
Anjin, the pilot from Miura.[5]

Though married back in England, like most of the *Love*'s other
survivors, Adams too had taken a Japanese wife. He married a young
woman by the name of Magome Oyuki. She was the daughter of
Magome Kageyu, the proprietor of a packhorse station at Denmachō,
not far from Nihonbashi, Edo's famous bridge, where the country's
main traffic arteries met. Amongst the countless stations that strad-
dled Japan's five main roads her father's station was the largest, and
thus, even though her family did not belong to the samurai class,
Oyuki's position in life was not unbefitting the social status of a
bannerman, and was probably as far as a Japanese match for a for-
eigner in feudal Japan went. She bore Adams two children, both of
whom Adams gave Christian names; a boy, who was named Joseph,
and a girl, who was named Suzanna.

The marital bliss of his newfound life did not cause Adams to
forget his old one. His concern over his English family, "my poor
wife: in a manner a widow, and my two children fatherless," ampli-
fied by the awareness that technically he had become a bigamist,
gave the God-fearing sailor the "greatest grief of heart and conscience." He had repeatedly petitioned the shogun to let him "go out
of this land, desiring to see my poor wife and children according to
conscience and nature," but on each and every occasion the shogun
had flatly dismissed his request, telling the pilot that he should
"byde in his land." Thus Adams remained a prisoner of fate, unable
to leave the country, and unable to send word to his loved ones,

since the only other Europeans to visit Japan were the Iberians—and they were at war with England.

Unknown to the *Love*'s survivors, word of their fate had reached home. And it was again through one of Admiral Olivier van Noort's serendipitous encounters that word of the survivors of Mahu's fateful expedition reached the Netherlands.

Following his encounter with De Ibarra's *Buen Jésus* and the raid on Valparaíso, Van Noort had progressed north along the South American west coast. On April 25, 1601, he had reached the height of Lima, when further interrogation of the pilot, Juan de Sandoval, whom he had kept on board, brought to light that De Ibarra had set a trap. When the latter had learned that he was to be put ashore at Huasco, he had instructed De Sandoval to pilot Van Noort's ships to Cape San Francisco, at 0°45'N. De Ibarra himself would try and reach Lima to warn the viceroy sufficiently in time to intercept the Dutch raiders. Hearing of the plot and not keen on a confrontation with De Velasco's ships, Van Noort had deemed it judicious to abandon any further raiding on the Spanish main. Dispatching the pilot by setting him overboard on suspicions of mutiny, he had set sail across the Pacific to try his luck in the Philippines, reaching Manila Bay on November 24, 1601. For several weeks his two remaining ships had blocked the bay's entrance before the port's authorities had felt obliged to send down two ships of war. The battle that ensued lasted for most of the day and ended in a draw. The smaller of Van Noort's ships, a pinnace under the command of Lambert Biesman, had to engage with a foe seven times her size and was eventually forced to surrender. And though Van Noort's own ship, the *Mauritius*, had sunk her assailant, with five of his fifty-odd men killed and over half of them injured, he had seen no other way than to resume the voyage, and set course for the island of Borneo.

On January 3, 1602, upon her arrival under the coast of Borneo, the *Mauritius* encountered a Japanese junk. The vessel, which had come from Nagasaki and was destined for Manila, had been blown off its course by a storm and had been forced to seek shelter. The majority of her crew were Japanese sailors, the only non-Japanese members being the pilot, a Chinese from Macao, and her captain, an old Portuguese salt from Port a Port. Both were invited aboard the *Mauritius* by the Dutch admiral.

The Portuguese captain, who went by the name of Emanuel Luiz, had spent most of his sailing years plying between Manila, Malacca, and Macao. He had lived in the last two ports, but had recently moved to Japan, where he had settled in the port of Nagasaki on the Japanese island of Kyushu. He had sailed from Nagasaki two months earlier. Prior to his departure, however, he had made a journey along Japan's east coast, and it had been on that journey that he had spoken to the crew of a large Dutch ship, riding at four anchors in a good harbor near the port of Anotsu. From them he had learned that they had crossed over from Chile with two ships, one of which had been lost, and that they had arrived at a place called Bungo. Their passage had been "very miserable," so that when they arrived, they had been only twenty-five strong. Since then eleven more had died, but the fourteen of them who had remained alive "were free to go wherever they pleased and had been allowed to build a small Ship to sail where they pleased."[6]

The Portuguese captain did not recall the name of the vessel but estimated that she must have measured 250 tons. This, in turn, led Van Noort to believe that his guest had spoken to the *Hope*, which he knew to be the flagship of the company of Pieter van der Haegen. Hoping to contribute to the well-being of his compatriots, Van Noort did the same as he had done with the captain of the *Buen Jésus*. After he had bought from the Portuguese captain "some hams and other victuals," and "paid him to his contentment" Van Noort asked the captain "to do the Hollanders all possible favor on his return to Japan." This Luiz promised to do, asking Van Noort "to furnish him with a Flag of our country, with a passport, which was given to him in the name of his Excellency."

Inevitably, word of the encounters between Japanese and European vessels also reached the ears of Ieyasu. Through his vast network of informants, he had learned that the Dutch presence in the Far East was going from strength to strength. In the year after the Dutch had arrived in Japan, two Dutch ships had reached Patani, on the east coast of the Malay Peninsula, where they had founded a trading post. This was not surprising. Patani was a major port for chinaware and silk, and as such a chief gateway to the Chinese market. Over the following years more Dutch ships had come: six in 1602, another two in the year that followed, and in 1604 another Dutch fleet had cast anchor on the settlement's roadstead. Meanwhile word had come in that Dutch ships had also been sighted off the Chinese coast. From the intelligence gathered by his spies, from the nervous dismissals by the Portuguese and Spanish missionaries, and from what he had learned from the English pilot, it became increasingly clear to the shogun that before long he would have to deal with more than just the Iberian presence. Sooner rather than later other Dutch merchantmen, armed to the teeth like the ship on which the English pilot had arrived, would appear before Japan's poorly defended ports and seek to trade—with or without his approval.

Not that Ieyasu was opposed to the arrival of competitors on his country's shores. The towering expenses of the vast military campaigns of 1600 had severely drained his treasury and in order to replenish it he relied heavily on the profitable seaborne trade with the Asian continent. In the absence of direct trade relations between Japan and China, the Portuguese had filled the existing vacuum nicely, whilst the weapons they had brought along had been an added bonus. But there were drawbacks, the chief one being that in their mutual dealings, the Japanese and Portuguese merchants relied heavily on the offices of the Jesuits. To complicate matters, the Jesuits were also held in great esteem by the Portuguese merchants and sailors, and every attempt to suppress their odious teachings had had an immediate effect on the number of Portuguese ships that called at Japanese ports. Lately that number had dwindled anyhow, for with the advance of the Dutch in Southeast Asian waters, the visits of the Great Ship from Goa had become ever more sparse.

The crippling effect of the Dutch advance on the Iberian trade and the degree in which that trade depended on the offices of the Jesuits could not have been brought home more forcefully to Ieyasu than early in 1604, when he was visited by João Rodríguez. As the man responsible for the financial management of the Jesuit Mission in Japan, Rodríguez was deeply troubled by the small number of Portuguese ships that had called at Japanese ports over the last few years. That decline, he reminded Ieyasu, had been the combined result of increased intolerance among local Japanese rulers toward the Mission's activities on the one hand and the increasing menace of Dutch raiders on the other. As an intermediary of sorts, he himself was trying hard to assist the shogun in his efforts to breathe new life into the Iberian trade. Yet since the Mission itself depended on the very same trade for its livelihood, with each year that the Portuguese galleons had failed to come, so the financial resources of the Mission had dwindled. By now they were in such dire straits that without substantial financial support from the shogun they would have to dismantle the Mission and leave the country. Needless to say that with their departure the Jesuits' stimulative role in the silk trade would come to an unfortunate end.

Rodríguez' point was taken, and Ieyasu promised financial support to the Mission. With respect to the Dutch "menace," however, the shogun begged to differ. It had become clear to him that it would only be in Japan's interest to placate the Dutch. Their arrival, after all, was bound to result in a healthy rivalry between the two European nations—a rivalry that could only have a positive effect on the price of their commodities. Moreover, as he had learned from Adams and as he had observed in the pilot's fellow crewmembers, Dutch traders were perfectly able to conduct their affairs without the help of the Jesuit padres. When, therefore, not long after he had been visited by Rodríguez, he was once more approached by Adams to let him go so that he could "be a means that both the English and Hollanders

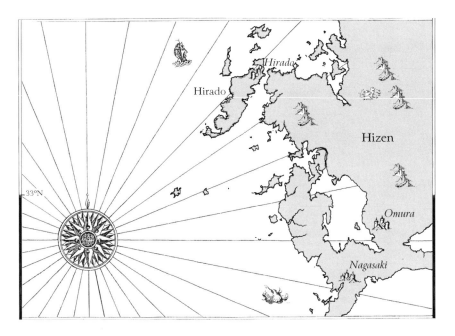

should come and traffic here," the shogun yielded to the pilot's sup-plications, although it was not Adams whom he allowed to go, but Jacob Quaeckernaeck and Melchior van Santvoort, who were allowed to try and reach the Dutch settlement in Patani.

Nor was it without reason that the port from which Quaeckernaeck and Van Santvoort eventually sailed was that of Hirado. Originally a squalid and rundown robber's den from where the *wakō*, the fear-some Japanese pirates, sailed to raid the Chinese main, Hirado had grown into a bustling port of commerce once the Portuguese galleons had found their way to the island halfway through the sixteenth cen-tury. It had been the then lord of Hirado, Matsura Takanobu, who had been the driving force behind the blossoming trade. Keen to attract more foreign ships to the port and apparently favorably inclined toward the Jesuits and their learning, Matsura soon man-aged to draw the Portuguese away from the other southern ports of Kagoshima, Hakata, and Funai, and in less than a decade Hirado became the Iberians' main port of call in Japan. During the first years not more than one Portuguese ship called at the port annually, but soon the number doubled, and in 1561 no less than five ships were moored in the small but sheltered roadstead of Hirado bay. By then close to a hundred Portuguese merchants had settled in Hirado. The resident Jesuits had been allowed to build a church, where they held masses for a parish that included some five hundred Japanese converts, amongst them a considerable number of high birth. And it was with the latter's conversion and the Jesuits' attempts to use their influence to their own advantage that trouble had begun.

To Matsura's great annoyance, one of the Jesuits' converts was none other than his own brother. The latter had become so infused with the Jesuits' teachings that he set out to destroy the countless effigies and idols that littered the local landscape. This in turn had led to reprisals from the Japanese monks, who set fire to a cross in Hirado's Christian cemetery. Serious rioting followed. A Buddhist temple was burned down and a number of people injured, and only after Matsura had expelled the Jesuits from his fiefdom did the unrests abate. This had been in 1559, but the magnetic pull with which the Jesuits attracted Portuguese trade soon caused Matsura to reconsider, and within two years he allowed the Jesuits back into his fiefdom. In 1565 they were even allowed to build a new church. It had all been to no avail. During the following year the execution of four Christians suspected of spying for Ōmura Sumitada, the Christian daimyo of the neighboring fiefdom of Hizen, had resulted in yet another riot and a complete cessation of Portuguese trade. This time Matsura was not able to restore trade relations, for the merchants that had been scared away by the unrests had found a new port to sell their wares: the nearby port of Nagasaki, opened to the Portuguese in 1568 by Ōmura Sumitada.

Nor did Matsura Shigenobu, who succeeded Takanobu in 1584, manage to lure the Portuguese back to Hirado. Exasperated by the Jesuits, vexed by the Portuguese monopoly on foreign trade, and resentful of the central role that Nagasaki had come to play in it, Shigenobu was more eager than ever to restore his port to the glory it had known during his father's early reign. And thus, when early in 1605, he learned from his Dutch instructors that Ieyasu had allowed their captain to sail for Patani in order to attract Dutch trade to Japan, he immediately sent word to Edo that he would provide the Dutch with a Japanese vessel at his own expense. In April of the same year Shigenobu received official permission and without delay work was begun on a vessel large enough to carry the two Dutchmen to Patani. The incurred costs Matsura considered as an investment in the future Dutch trade at his port.[7]

Sailing with the the northeast monsoon, Quaeckernaeck and Van Santvoort departed from Hirado in the autumn of 1605. With him Quaeckernaeck carried a small bundle of papers, mostly letters by the other survivors of the *Love*, written to their relatives back home. Most important, however, was a Japanese document. This document, a few handwritten lines, ratified with the shogun's red seal of state, was the passport that allowed Dutch merchantmen to call at any Japanese port of their liking.[8] The voyage was fortuitous, and on December 2, of the same year in which they had sailed from Hirado, both men arrived safely in Patani.

Upon their arrival in Patani, Quaeckernaeck and Van Santvoort were met by Ferdinand Michielszoon, the head of the Dutch factory. Michielszoon had sailed as chief merchant on the largest Dutch fleet that had thus far sailed for the Far East. That fleet, consisting of fourteen sails, had sailed from the Texel on June 17, 1602, under the command of Admiral Wijbrand van Warwijck. Having reached Bantam on April 29 of the following year, two of its ships, the *Erasmus* and the *Nassau*, under the command of Claes Jansz. van Dijck, had sailed for the Chinese coast and arrived on Macao's roadstead on July 31, 1603. There they had happened on the Great Ship from Goa, ready to start on its last leg to the Japanese port of Nagasaki. Caught totally by surprise, the Portuguese captain and his crew had fled ashore, leaving their ship and her cargo of silk (valued at fl. 1,4 million) and a large quantity of gold to the ecstatic Dutch raiders. The next year Van Warwijck himself had sailed for Macao with a view of forcefully opening up trade with the Chinese. But strong winds had blown him off his course, and his final attempt to trade through the Chinese settlers on the Pescadores Islands had failed equally. It had been on his return voyage to Bantam that Van Warwijck had called at Patani and had appointed Michielszoon to take charge of the Dutch factory.[9]

The Dutch foothold in Asia, Michielszoon informed his guests, remained precarious. As yet the Portuguese continued to dominate the South China Sea and the Dutch had their hands full in driving them out of the East Indian archipelago. As a result, he had no means to send any ships to Japan. Nor did he at present expect the arrival of a Dutch ship on which Quaeckernaeck could sail for the Netherlands in order to deliver the shogun's trade license to Prince Maurits. He could not even offer the two men employment, since the factory was already stretched beyond its financial means. All he could do was to offer his guests a roof over their heads until they could find an opportunity to sail.

Half a year Quaeckernaeck had to wait for an opportunity to sail home. Then, toward the end of July 1606, news reached Patani that a Dutch fleet of nine sails had arrived on the other side of the penin-sula, where it had laid siege to Malacca. To his great delight the cap-tain learned that this fleet was under the command of his very own cousin, Cornelis Matelieff de Jonge. Taking with him his men's let-ters and the shogun's license, Quaeckernaeck immediately set out to join the fleet. He traveled overland to Johore, at the tip of the peninsula, where he arrived toward the middle of August. Here he visited Dasa Zabrang, the local raja and the rightful ruler of Malacca, who had been ousted by the Portuguese and had been quick to ally himself with the Dutch—three months earlier Zabrang had committed a large number of his men to assist in the siege. On August 18, the scene of battle seemed to have moved out to sea where, according to Zabrang's men, the Dutch had been engaged by a large Portuguese fleet. The next day the wind dropped and early that morning Zabrang and Quaeckernaeck set off with six of the raja's *kora-kora* toward Matelieff's flagship, the *Oranje*, to learn how the battle was going.

Matelieff warmly welcomed his long-lost cousin. In the long exchange that followed, the admiral related how he had sailed from the Netherlands the previous year with instructions to capture the strategic port of Malacca, the last Portuguese stronghold on the peninsula. Since the beginning of May he had held the port under siege, but in spite of Zabrang's reinforcements, the arrival of two more Dutch ships in July, and the superiority of his artillery, he had thus far failed to evict the Portuguese from their stronghold. That failure, he acknowledged, was largely due to the genius of the stronghold's commander, the redoubtable André Furtado de Mendoça, and the exceptional valor of his merely 150-strong garrison. The thousand troops that Matelieff had pitted against this diminutive force had thus far had their hands full in repelling its heroic sorties, especially the town's handful of Japanese warriors who were fighting alongside the Portuguese troops. Almost two hundred men had so far been lost, whilst over 500,000 great shot had been hurled into the fortress to little effect. An eventual Dutch victory by way of starvation had gone up in smoke when five days earlier scouts had spotted sixteen Portuguese sails off Cape Rachado, some thirty miles northwest of Malacca. Troops and artillery had again been re-embarked in preparation of a sea battle, which had indeed ensued the previous day. Though far from victorious, the Dutch had done better at sea than on land: although both sides had lost two ships, the Dutch, with only 150 dead, had suffered only a third of their enemy's casualties.

Amongst the Dutch casualties had been one of Matelieff's chief officers, the captain of the *Erasmus*, and since his fleet was getting ready again for action, the admiral offered his cousin the ship's captaincy. He assured his cousin that the letters of the *Love*'s crew would be sent home at the earliest opportunity. The trade license from the

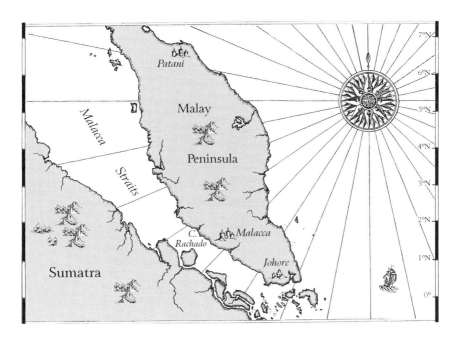

Japanese ruler he would take back to the Netherlands himself, whilst he would instruct his chief merchant, Victor Sprinckel, who was to found a factory in Macao, to send a ship to Japan at the earliest opportunity. First, however, the Portuguese had to be routed. Quaeckernaeck was quickly won over by his illustrious cousin, and within the same day took up his post on the ship that by a curious irony carried the original name of the *Love*.

The next few days, however, saw little action; only sporadically and at great distance did the two fleets exchange fire. The standoff continued until August 23, when a lack of gunpowder forced Matelieff to divert his fleet to Johore. Unhampered by the Dutch, the admiral of the Portuguese fleet, Don Martim Affonso, landed in triumph to relieve Malacca's starving citizens. Having had his ships careened and their magazines restocked with powder, Matelieff departed from Johore on October 10, when he learned that his adversary had divided his fleet into two squadrons of seven ships. One squadron, under the command of Dom Alvaro de Menezes, had sailed north, out of the Strait of Malacca. The other, under the command of the admiral himself, had anchored off Cape Rachado. Seizing his chance, Matelieff immediately conducted his fleet back up the strait, reaching the cape on October 22.

The ensuing battle, which lasted well into the night, ended in a resounding victory for the Dutch. The Portuguese vice admiral's ship, the *São Nicolau*, was boarded by three ships, and her crew, twelve men aside, slaughtered to a man. Their fate was shared by the crew of another Portuguese ship, the *Todos os Santos*. The *São Simão*, under the command of Captain André Pessoa, one of the heroes of the defense of Malacca, had meanwhile boarded the *Amsterdam*. After a long struggle she was beaten off. The next morning she was found drifting with only twenty men in her alive. The *Erasmus* and the *Mauritius* engaged and eventually captured the *Santa Cruz*. The battle was over when the Portuguese admiral had his remaining four ships run ashore and set alight to keep the Dutch from seizing them.

Portuguese casualties had been horrendous, but many Dutch had died, too. Amongst them was the captain of the first Dutch ship to have reached Japan. Quaeckernaeck's last moments were recorded for posterity by Jacques L'Hermite de Jonge, a young scribe on board the *Erasmus*. Writing home to his father, the young scribe told his father of the battle and described how "in the fury, our skipper, Jacob Quaeckernaeck, was shot straight through the head with a musket bullet, upon which he fell over dead without uttering a word; so that it seems that this man has had to dwell in these countries for so long only to die so senselessly here."

XII

THE CONCLUSION

Here I have seen things rare, and profitable;
Things pleasant, dreadful, things to make me stable
In what I have begun in hand:
Then let me think on them, and understand
Wherefore they showed me was, and let me be
Thankful, O good Interpreter, to Thee.

Quaeckernaeck's death had not been in vain. The Dutch interest in the profitable trade in silver and silk between China and Japan, first raised by Dirck Gerritszoon Pomp's account, and rekindled in the summer of 1601 when Olivier van Noort brought back news that one ship out of Mahu's fleet had reached Japan and that her crew was employed by its ruler, reached fever pitch in 1606, when word arrived from the Dutch factory in Patani that the Japanese ruler had dispatched her captain with a license to trade—within a year, it would lead to renewed efforts to try and reach the island country.

For *bewindhebbers* Johan van der Veken and Pieter van der Haegen, Van Noort's tidings had held no such hopes. For them, the news that the *Love* had been confiscated by Japan's ruler to carry wood, coming as it did with news of the Spanish capture of *The Gospel* and the imprisonment of her crew, signaled the end of their enterprise. A year before, the *Faith* had returned with only a third of her original crew. Most of what was left of the cargo had perished and what was still marketable was nowhere near enough to recoup the incurred losses. Any lingering hopes of a miraculous recovery in the image of Drake, Cavendish, or even De Houtman, were finally and irrevocably crushed with the return of the few survivors of the *Fidelity* toward the end of 1603. The harrowing account of her captain's dismal conduct and her crew's gruesome end were a fitting epitaph to what was to become one of the most disastrous expeditions in Dutch merchant maritime history.

The failure of the expedition seriously affected the fortunes of both Van der Haegen and Van der Veken. Inevitably, the greatest part of the loss was borne by Van der Veken, who lost fl. 250,000 of the fl. 267,000 he had invested; yet, able to fall back on his vast capital resources and friends in high places (who exonerated him from liability for the loss of the four 24-pounders and the loan from the States of Holland), he managed to stay afloat and live up to his maxim: *Stabilis fortuna merenti*. And though Van der Haegen's stake in the venture had been much smaller, to him its failure was a far greater blow. When he had paid off his debts, he was all but bankrupted. Yet his brush with lady fortune did not affect his entrepreneurial spirit. He even managed to organize a similar, more successful expedition to the Indies a few years later. But the demise of his business partner in that enterprise, the colorful Balthazar de Moucheron, was to drag him down too. Van der Haegen spent his last years counterfeiting money—a highly lucrative albeit illegal trade. Hounded by creditors and prosecutors, he only escaped his inevitable fate by passing away before they caught up with him.

Not all those who joined in the race for the East had shared Van der Veken and Van der Haegen's misfortune. Indeed, many of the expeditions that had sailed in the wake of De Houtman had met with similar or even greater success, so that by the turn of the century no fewer than eight different companies were participating in the Rich Trades. The resulting rivalry caused such oscillations in the market that their merchants, worried about the plummeting prices of the East Indian commodities, approached the States of Holland and Zeeland to intervene. After lengthy negotiations and considerable pressure from Johan van Oldenbarneveldt, in the spring of 1602, all *bewindhebbers* agreed to unite forces. Their companies were merged into the first true multinational, the United East India Company (Vereenigde Oost-Indische

Compagnie). A state-backed, joint-stock company, the VOC was federated into chambers that ran their capital and operations individually, yet observed the overall policies dictated by a board of directors, the Heren Zeventien. And it was these illustrious seventeen gentlemen who made the first efforts to acquire a stake in the Sino-Japanese silk trade.[1]

Wijbrant van Warwijck's expedition was not only the first to sail under the banner of the VOC, it was also the first to sail with instructions to try and establish trade relations with the Chinese and, if possible, the Japanese. Van Warwijck failed on both accounts, but where he dropped the torch, it was picked up by Cornelis Matelieff de Jonge.

Following the battle at Cape Rachado, Matelieff did eventually sail for China with four of his ships, arriving on Macao's roadstead on July 25, 1607. But the local Chinese authorities were so unforthcoming that, on August 16, the Dutch admiral decided to sail up the delta of the Pearl River to obtain in Canton what he had failed to obtain in Macao. Only then, after he had sent a scout ahead with a Chinese junk to reconnoiter the river upstream, did the Dutch admiral realize the price he had paid for his failure to destroy the Portuguese fleet before it had been split up: upriver they were awaited by six Portuguese ships that had arrived from Malacca ten days earlier. To his growing dismay, Matelieff further learned from the Chinese captain of the junk that these were the first Portuguese vessels to reach Macao in two years. In that period the colony had been reduced to such penury that it had been on the very point of evacuation. What had made the event particularly auspicious for the Portuguese was that one of the six ships turned out to be the Great Ship from Goa. Her arrival, weighed down as she was with a cargo sufficient to sustain two years of trade, had heralded the financial rescue of the settlement. Meanwhile, the Portuguese fleet's commander, Captain-Major André Pessoa, had apparently also got wind of Matelieff's arrival, for his ships had set sail and were now slowly cruising downriver. Matelieff, with only three ships and a yacht at his disposal, could do little else than to concede defeat and leave.

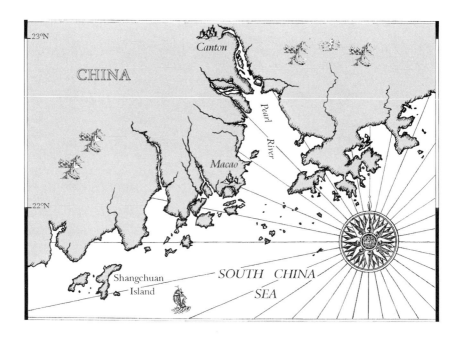

The closest Matelieff came to a direct Japanese encounter was on September 14, 1607, when, shortly after his departure, he called at Shangchuan island, some sixty miles west of Macao. There, just off the shore, rode three large junks, manned by the fearsome *wakō*. They had come from Cambodia and were on their way to Hirado. Though pirates, Matelieff treated them with courtesy, even inviting aboard their chieftain, who presented him with a Japanese sword and a suit of armor and expressed his desire that the Dutch regard them as friends. Matelieff promised as much, asking the chieftain to convey his words to the lord of Hirado. As the Dutch admiral recorded the encounter in his journal, his thoughts inevitably went back to the events at Malacca the year before, when he had buried his cousin, one of the first Dutchmen to have visited the mysterious country that brought forth such fierce and fearless men:

> All these Japanese crews were robust men and had a marked appearance of being pirates, as in fact they were. They are of a firm and resolute nature, for when they see that the Chinese have the upper hand

of them, they slit their own bellies in order to avoid falling alive into the hands of those pitiless enemies, who would make them endure unspeakable torments, even going as far as to slice up their limbs one after another. They said that they knew of Jaep Quaeck, and that there were still in Japan eight or ten Dutchmen who were building ships for the Emperor, and that these were shortly expected to arrive in Patani.

Following his encounter with the *wakō*, Matelieff set course for Bantam, but not with all of his ships. Acting on the chieftain's information, he sent the *Mauritius* to Patani, instructing his chief merchant, Victor Sprinckel, to take charge of the Dutch factory and await the arrival of the "Emperor's ship" from Japan.

Whilst these encounters were taking place in the South China Sea, back in the Netherlands the Heren Zeventien persisted in their efforts to reach Japan; meeting on February 2, 1606, they resolved to request Prince Maurits "to write a letter to the King of Japan" and that "such persons will be sent by his Excellency as are appointed by Admiral Paulus van Caerden." One of the men chosen by Van Caerden to represent the prince was none other than the now sixty-two-year-old Dirck Gerritszoon Pomp, who had returned from Spanish imprisonment only the year before. Van Caerden sailed on April 20 of the same year. Numerous events, including an unsuccessful siege of a Portuguese fort on the East African coast, kept his ships under way until January 6, 1608, when they finally cast anchor in Bantam's roadstead. They did so next to those of Matelieff, which were loading spices before sailing home. From there, Van Caerden sailed on to the Spice Islands, arriving at Ternate toward the middle of May. It was as far as the voyage went. Over the following months much of the expedition's resources were spent on the establishment of a stronghold on the nearby island of Makian. Then the fleet disintegrated when first two of its ships were wrecked on the island's reefs and two others had to sail home to avoid sinking through rot and woodworm. And when Van Caerden was captured by the Spanish, all hope of reaching China, let alone Japan, was abandoned. For Dirck Gerritszoon Pomp the curtain had fallen long since. During the two-year-long voyage he had become all but blind. At Bantam he had been transferred to Matelieff's ship with six other men destined to be carried home. The old hand never saw Enkhuizen again; he died mid-journey, his body worn and wasted by half a century at sea.

The *wakō* chieftain's reports had been true enough. When Sprinckel arrived in Patani aboard the *Mauritius* on November 8, 1607, to take charge of the Dutch factory, he indeed found moored on the port's roadstead a ship from Japan. It was, however, not a ship built by the *Love*'s survivors, nor was it the "Emperor's ship," but a Japanese junk, and the one Dutchman on board was Melchior van Santvoort. Before Quaeckernaeck had departed for Johore, Van Santvoort had returned to Hirado with the southwest monsoon. Back in Japan, he had obtained another red-seal passport, again so as to sail for Patani, but this time for purely commercial reasons. Matsura's junk was laden with cereals that the Dutch merchant was to trade against the commodities on offer in Patani.

For the new head of the Dutch factory, Van Santvoort's arrival presented a good opportunity to resolve unfinished business. It had been Sprinckel, after all, who had been instructed by Admiral Matelieff to reciprocate the commercial overtures of the Japanese ruler as soon as the factory had been established in Macao. With Matelieff's failure to reach Macao and with no ships to spare, Sprinckel had resigned himself to a serious delay in establishing Dutch trade with Japan. Though the arrival of the Japanese junk had not changed these prospects, at least Van Santvoort's arrival gave the factor a means to share them with the Japanese ruler. And on February 6, 1608, just before Van Santvoort left for Japan, the factor sat down to write two long explanatory letters. On his arrival in Japan, Van Santvoort was to hand both letters to Adams, along with a present for the shogun consisting of a small collection of Dutch porcelain, crystal mugs, French wineglasses, as well as some samples of Dutch cloth.

One of the letters was addressed to William Adams in person. In it, Sprinckel thanked the pilot profusely for the services rendered. He related how Quaeckernaeck had joined Matelieff's fleet off Malacca, how he had informed the admiral of their travails in Japan, and how he had fallen in the battle at Cape Rachado. For the reason of their delay in reaching Japan, Sprinckel referred Adams to his second letter, which was addressed to the shogun, and advising Adams to read it several times to ensure that its content would be fully understood by the Japanese ruler. In that letter the factor confirmed the receipt of the trade license, expressed his deep gratitude on behalf of Prince Maurits, and set out to explain how the latter had sought to reciprocate the shogun's generous gesture:

> His majesty shall be advised how in the 12th month of the year 1605, eleven ships sailed from our fatherland for the East Indies under the command of Admiral Cornelis Matelieff de Jonge, amongst which were 4, namely, the flagship Oranje, the Middelburgh, the Mauritius & Erasmus, which were destined to sail to the kingdom of China with great quantities of money and goods so as to seek trade as do the Portuguese and other nations; and that I myself was destined to stay there in case that trade might have been acquired; and from where for the first time a ship would have sailed for Japan with silk and goods according to my instructions.

Not the Portuguese but bad weather and Chinese prevarication, according to Sprinckel, had forced Matelieff to leave Macao. The factor did, however, allow the Portuguese to play their part in the battle at Cape Rachado, which he described in glorious detail. As a result of that battle and the long time they had spent at sea, their ships had been so riddled with shot and woodworm that they had been forced to return home without delay. These "lawful and natural causes," Sprinckel claimed, had thus far stalled the Dutch trade in China and Japan. He expected that it would take at least two or two and a half more years before the next Dutch ship would reach Japan. In closing, the factor again apologized for the delay and expressed his fervent hope that in the meantime "his majesty shall not slack-

en his love and affection toward us, even though we do not doubt
that the Portuguese (our mortal enemies) will not rest to persuade
his majesty otherwise by every kind of cunning and deceit, yea the
greatest of lies."

Though less than genuine in his extenuations, in his expectations
Sprinckel had been sincere enough. On December 20, 1607, yet
another fleet, this time thirteen sails under the command of admiral Pieter Willemsz. Verhoeff and Vice Admiral Francois Wittert,
had left Holland for the Far East. It was the second-largest fleet to
have sailed thus far, and its leaders were clearly made to understand
what was expected of them:

> Considering that these countries and the East India Company attach
> the greatest importance to the Chinese silk-trade and the Moluccan
> spice-trade, thus hereby the admiral, vice-admiral, Ships' Council,
> chief merchants, supercargoes, skippers and all officers of some influ-
> ence, are commended to the aforesaid trade in particular and to use all
> possible means to acquire and procure that commerce.

Verhoeff's secret instructions, equally dictated by the Heren
Zeventien, left no doubt as to the way in which this objective was to
be achieved. On his way to the East Indian archipelago, the admiral
was to take every opportunity to annoy the enemy, taking special care
to intercept and attack the Portuguese fleet that was to sail from
Lisbon later that year. Once in the East Indies, he was to do what
lay in his power to drive all Spanish and Portuguese vessels from
Tidore, Ternate, or wherever they might be encountered. Once the
Moluccas were rid of the last Iberian vestiges, he was to conduct part
of his fleet to the Philippines and crush any remaining Spanish resistance and, if possible, intercept the richly laden galleon from
Acapulco. The countless junks that swarmed the East Asian seas,
however, were to be treated with courtesy; their merchants were to be
plied and pampered so as to warm them to the Dutch presence,
although Japan itself was not yet specifically mentioned.

All that was to change on February 11, 1609, when, en route from Johore to Bantam, Verhoeff's fleet was joined by the *Goede Hoop*, which carried new instructions from the Heren Zeventien, drafted in response to a rapprochement between the Netherlands and Spain. In anticipation of a truce in which the mutual status quo would be honored, it had become crucial to quickly win the Spice Islands and to acquire or consolidate contracts with friendly local kings and princes wherever possible. On his arrival in Bantam the admiral furthermore learned that this year's Great Ship from Goa was carrying the richest cargo in years. And thus, on February 19, in a hastily convened session of the fleet's ships' council, Verhoeff drew up a new plan of action. He himself was to sail half of the fleet to Banda, Ternate, and Tidore to try and win the islands for the Netherlands. Meanwhile Vice Admiral Wittert was to sail the rest of the fleet to Macassar and do likewise. A yacht, the *Delft*, was to be sent back to Johore with new instructions for the *Roode Leeuw met Pylen* and the *Griffioen*. The latter had remained behind to cruise the Strait of Malacca and look out for the Portuguese fleet

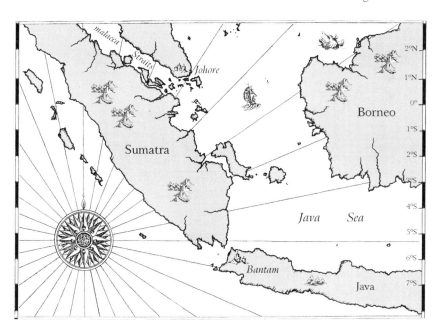

from Lisbon, which was expected to arrive from Goa with the next southwest monsoon. Both were to sail immediately for Patani and load a token cargo of silk and pepper. This makeshift cargo was to be complemented by immediately sailing for the Strait of Formosa and there to await and take the Great Ship from Goa. Enriched with her cargo they were to sail for Japan with the same monsoon and try to force the Portuguese out of the Japanese market.

It took until May 4 before the *Delft* arrived in Johore. On the same day the ships' council, consisting of Captain Jan Walichszoon and chief merchant Abraham van den Broeck from the *Roode Leeuw met Pylen*, and Captain Cornelis Corneliszoon t'Hart and chief merchant Nicolaes Puyck from the *Griffioen*, decided to sail for Patani as soon as winds would allow. This happened within a week, and on May 27 both ships safely reached Patani. Within a few days they had acquired a modest cargo of silk, pepper, and some lead, and on the last day of the month both ships set sail for Formosa. Being the faster of the two, the *Griffioen* was the first to reach the strait, but the only sail encountered was that of a large Japanese junk. One of her crew spoke Portuguese. She was on her way from Cambodia to Nagasaki with hides and wood. According to her captain, the Dutch had erred in their timing. He told them that the Great Ship from Goa never left Macao this early in the year. With his permission, the interpreter was taken on board, and on June 26, after some more days of waiting, course was set for the island of Hirado.

The *Griffioen* reached Japan on June 28, 1609. Four more days she spent under the unfamiliar coast, until, on July 2, with the help of local sailors, she safely arrived in the port of Hirado. There she was joined by the *Roode Leeuw met Pylen*, which had found her way to the port with the help of a Japanese pilot taken on board near Nagasaki. She had arrived the previous evening and had anchored behind a cape, not far from Hirado. Later in the day, the tide being in, both ships were met by a large fleet of boats, each manned with a dozen oarsmen, which towed the two ships into the narrow harbor. The next day the boats returned, now escorting a barge, carrying three officials, who were invited on board the *Griffioen*. The officials informed the hastily assembled ships' council that they had come on behalf of their lord, Matsura Shigenobu. He had gone up to Edo on his annual visit to the shogun, Ieyasu's son, Tokugawa Hidetada, who had succeeded his father in 1605. They expected their lord to return within five or six weeks, yet should the Dutch want to set up trade in Hirado, they were required to first visit Tokugawa Ieyasu, who currently resided in Fuchū, halfway up the Tōkaidō toward Edo. Though retired, in practice, the old shogun still held the reigns of power, especially where it concerned Japan's foreign relations.

On July 4, the members of the ships' council went ashore for the first time. They had been invited to Matsura's residency, which stood on an elevation overlooking the harbor. Here they were received with much hospitality by the officials who had visited them the day before. Speaking through the interpreter, their hosts assured them that the lord of Hirado would be greatly pleased by the sight of their ships in his harbor and that he would provide them with whatever they required. Messengers had already been dispatched to inform their lord, as well as the governor in Nagasaki, that the Dutch had arrived. At noon the men returned to their ships, where the rest of the day was used in writing letters to the shogun and the *Love*'s survivors. Two days after the letters had been handed to Matsura's men, a junk sailed up the narrow bay. On board was Melchior van Santvoort. Following his departure from Patani the year before, he had first sailed for Siam to drop one of Sprinckel's agents. The incurred delay had forced him to spend the winter in Cambodia. From there he had eventually sailed for Japan, arriving in Hirado with the same monsoon as they had, though several months earlier. Upon his arrival he had handed Sprinckel's letters and the gift to Adams, who had immediately departed for Fuchū.

Van Santvoort had been in Nagasaki on business, when he was approached by the port's new governor, Hasegawa Fujihiro. Having learned that Dutch vessels had arrived in Hirado, the latter had asked Van Santvoort to accompany two of his deputies on their way there to invite the Dutch to pay him a visit at his residence in Nagasaki. On Van Santvoort's advice, the ships' council decided to send Jaques Specks, one of the junior merchants, to return with Van Santvoort to Nagasaki and explain to the governor the scope and purpose of their visit.

The two men arrived in Nagasaki on July 9. There, to Specks' great chagrin, they found moored in the port's spacious harbor the *Nossa Senhora da Graça*, the Great Ship from Goa they had sought to catch in vain. His chagrin grew when they learned that she was the richest Portuguese ship to have arrived in Japan for many years. And they had barely missed her, for she had arrived only a few days before they had. Going ashore, both men were conveyed to palanquins and brought to the governor's residence, where they were put up for the night.

That evening, over a lush banquet given in their honor, the governor inquired whence they had come, whether they were satisfied with their harbor, what they were carrying, and what was the purpose of their visit so that he could correctly inform the shogun. The men replied that their harbor was satisfactory and that they had come to seek his majesty's friendship and free trade on behalf of their own king and country. As a sample of the wares in which they sought to trade, they had brought the shogun a present consisting of two cases of raw silk, one hundred and thirty bars of lead, and two golden decanters with a value of fl. 240. Five days later, the two men returned to Hirado, both thoroughly satisfied with their excursion to Nagasaki and the "very great friendship and presentations received and offered in that place."

In spite of appearances, it was not Hasegawa's fondness for the Dutch that had induced him to display such solicitude. True it was that in his capacity of governor he had a duty to inform the shogun. True it was, too, that in that same capacity he was entitled to value and procure for the shogun the choicest samples of silk. But, as the Jesuits in Nagasaki well knew, much of what was bought in the name of the shogun was sold locally to line the pockets of the governor and his cronies; and in order to preserve and perpetuate this profitable scheme Hasegawa had to placate both Ieyasu and the Portuguese. Looking after the needs of the shogun naturally was Hasegawa's prime task—a task in which he regularly relied on the offices of his sister O-Natsu, Ieyasu's favorite concubine. Keeping on good terms with the Portuguese had proven more difficult. They regularly refused Japanese guards on board their ships. Then there were the widely fluctuating prices of their commodities, which had frequently upset the Japanese merchants. In 1604, similar problems had led to an acrimonious dispute between the Portuguese merchants and the then governor, Terazawa Hirotaka, a dispute that had only been settled through the intervention of Padre João Rodríguez and the dismissal of Terazawa. To avoid future price disputes, the Council of Regency had introduced the *ito-wappu*, or "silk-yarn allotment" system. Known to the Portuguese as the *pancada*, it enabled the representatives of the merchant communities of Kyoto, Sakai, and Nagasaki to buy up the Great Ship's cargo of raw silk in bulk, at fixed prices.

Given the many difficulties with which his relationship with the Portuguese was fraught, to Hasegawa the arrival of the Dutch presented an interestingly new perspective. Yet from what he had so far learned from Van Santvoort, the Dutch were still forced to procure their silk through Patani: obviously they were not in the position to take on the Portuguese monopoly of the silk trade yet. Moreover, the Dutch had chosen Hirado as their port of call, so that, feigning and fickle though he was, for the time being, the governor chose to side with those who had chosen Nagasaki as their port of call.

It so happened that the captain of the Portuguese vessel that currently rode on Nagasaki's roadstead was Captain-Major André Pessoa—and he had his own agenda. After he had chased Matelieff's squadron down

the Pearl River, Pessoa had parted with his squadron and, mindful of
the presence of a larger Dutch fleet in Chinese waters, put into Macao
on the *Nossa Senhora da Graça* for the winter. He had intended to sail
toward the end of July, but a missive from Bantam had warned him of
the arrival of yet another Dutch fleet, whose admiral had issued specific
instructions to two of his ships to intercept the Great Ship from Goa.
Since no Portuguese ship had sailed for Japan in the previous year, the
Nossa Senhora da Graça now carried the overdue supplies of two years
for the Japanese market, making it all the more crucial that she reach
Japan unharmed. Losing no time, he had departed on May 10 in the
hope of thus outrunning the Dutch. In the event, he might as well have
waited. A typhoon had driven his ship way south and only through a
providential mist had he been able to escape the patrolling raiders.
Having outwitted his rivals at sea Pessoa now sought to do the same
on Japanese soil. Here he knew he had the upper hand, for the vast
riches that he had safely delivered in Nagasaki would not only safe-
guard the unstinting cooperation of the port's governor, they would
undoubtedly make his case against the Dutch before the shogun,
whom he hoped to visit soon, all the more palatable.

In his first assumption the Captain-Major had been right
enough. Hasegawa had obsequiously complied with all his requests.
He had pledged to keep him posted about all Dutch activities and
do whatever he could to help him get the better of them. To do so
it was vital that Pessoa see the shogun before they did, and here,
too, Hasegawa's cooperation proved instrumental. During the banquet the governor had generously offered to ferry the Dutch embassy
all the way to Osaka on one of his barges—a barge that would arrive
sufficiently "in time" for Pessoa to make a good head start and
reach Fuchū well before the Dutch.

The governor's barge arrived in Hirado on July 24. Three days later,
the first official Dutch embassy, consisting of Jacob van den Broeck,
Nicolaes Puyck, and Melchior van Santvoort, set off on its long
journey to visit the Japanese ruler. Puyck, who kept a diary through-

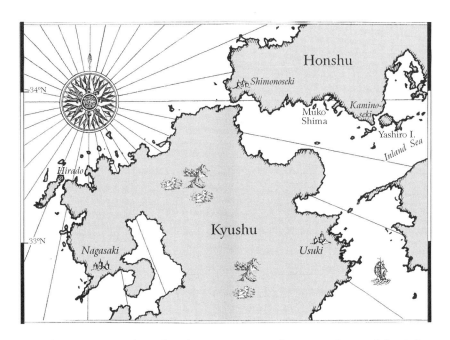

out the journey, thought the country to be "very beautiful." The land was "high and mountainous," "very populous and fertile," and on the water he "saw small sails everywhere."

It was two days after they had departed that one of the small sails drew up alongside the governor's barge. To the surprise of the Dutch, it carried a messenger from Matsura, who conveyed the delight his master had taken in hearing of their arrival and informed them that his lordship had meanwhile embarked from Osaka, expecting to meet them on the water midway. Later in the day they were met by another boat, this time with gifts of salted salmon and Japanese rice wine. Having returned Matsura's compliments with two lengths of silk, they continued their journey, passing through the narrow Strait of Shimonoseki at night, until, at noon, they anchored in the shelter of Mukōshima, a small island off Honshu's southern shore, some sixty miles east of the strait, to await a favorable wind that would carry them up the Inland Sea.

Near the end of the following day the wind gradually veered west, enabling the barge to round Kaminoseki on Honshu's southeastern cape. From there course was set northeast, up the Inland Sea. At dusk, they were met by yet another of Matsura's boats and were informed that not far from where they were, just off Yashiro Island, the daimyo lay anchored with three of his barges. Anchoring close by, the Dutch envoys went aboard one of the barges, where they were welcomed by an ebullient Matsura. Puyck was struck by the youthfulness of the sixty-five-year-old daimyo, who appeared "gay in spirit" and "very curious to hear or see all things foreign." The happy exchange lasted till well into the night, when, accompanied by one of Matsura's retainers and furnished with a letter of recommendation to the shogun, the guests returned to their own barge.

Four more days were spent on the sheltered waters of the Inland Sea until, on August 4, the small company sailed up the Yodo River, on whose estuary lay the vast metropolis of Osaka. Here marine traffic grew so dense that during the few miles before they arrived at their destination, Puyck counted some five hundred vessels, large and small.

The vast, sprawling commercial metropolis of Osaka was unlike anything the Dutchmen had ever seen before, yet, in one respect, it resembled the commercial capital of the ambassadors' home country, for Osaka, too, had its moats. As in Amsterdam, the moats that lay along Osaka's main traffic arteries were filled with countless crafts, all carrying goods of commerce directly to the equally vast number of shops and workshops that lined the unpaved but tidy streets. None of the buildings were more than two stories high and all were built of wood and clay. Their façades were mostly open, only shielded from wind and weather by a short curtain so as to allow the passerby a direct view of their interiors, where shop owners and artisans alike openly plied their trades. Here and there the façade was broken by the pleasant contours of a temple or shrine, set apart from the street's commercial bustle by a small courtyard. Far more numerous were the many hostels, promising the weary traveling salesmen all the delights of Osaka's nocturnal pleasures. And it was at one of these that the small craft to which the embassy had been transferred drew up along the side of the moat and that her passengers were welcomed by two more of the *Love*'s survivors, Jan Joosten van Lodensteyn and Pieter Janszoon.

The men had only one day to enjoy each other's company and exchange their experiences, for both Van Lodensteyn and Janszoon were about to depart for Nagasaki on business, so that, on the evening of August 5, having spent only one night and one day in the Japanese capital of commerce, the envoys re-embarked to continue their journey upriver. The following evening, they reached the castle town of Fushimi, where the men finally left the barge and lodged for the night in one of the Tōkaidō's many stations, while the horses by which they were to continue their journey overland were readied for the next day.

Once on the road, the rested men soon came to miss the cool comfort of traveling over water. It was now high summer in Japan, and only the early hours of morning and the shade of the pine trees that lined the road offered the Westerners some relief from the sweltering heat. In spite of the taxing climate and the discomfort of travel, the two-hundred-mile journey along the Tōkaidō offered a rare opportunity to take in the country's stunning scenery and experience the road's endless hustle and bustle, crowded as it was with soldiers, merchants, couriers, pedlars, pilgrims, and countrymen, all hurrying to and fro between its many post towns. At each of these the horses were exchanged so that, in spite of the heat, the Dutch embassy made good progress, putting behind it an average of thirty-five miles a day, so that it reached Fuchū on August 13, 1609.[2]

Upon their arrival in Fuchū, the embassy met two more members of the *Love*'s crew, Pieter Blanckert and Thomas Corneliszoon. Shortly after their departure from Osaka they had encountered two other survivors, so that by now they had met half of the *Love*'s remaining crew. Most were now living in Uraga, had taken Japanese wives, and spoke the language. Puyck observed that even though they "had obtained permission of his majesty to return home with our arrival," and though "we had offered them free passage," all of them "remained in that place of their own free will." The two men were able to inform the embassy that three days before the commander of the Portuguese carrack that Specks and Van Santvoort had seen in Nagasaki had arrived in Fuchū. It appeared that he was also seeking an audience with the shogun, but in spite of his insistence, he had been made to wait until the Dutch had taken their turn.

On the same day of their arrival, the Dutch envoys were required to see Gotō Shōzaburō, Master of the Mint. Like Adams, Gotō was one of a number of gifted men with whom Ieyasu had surrounded himself since he had delegated the formal affairs of state to his son and withdrawn to his present abode. Long before the Battle of Sekigahara, Gotō had acted as contractor for Ieyasu's armies and had been the brain behind his currency policies. Gotō received the men with great courtesy. Accepting their gift of three lengths of

Tokugawa Ieyasu's passport presented to the Dutch embassy, briefly stating that "Whenever Dutch ships come to Japan, they shall be refused by no one, at whatever port they may arrive. So in future, shall this commandment be observed, and they be able to come and go as they please, without any reserve whatsoever."

212

satin, he informed his guests that he would notify the shogun of their arrival and would convey to him what it was that they sought to obtain. Next the embassy was invited to the residency of Honda Masazumi, head of the Council of Regency and Ieyasu's most trusted vassal. Well disposed to Westerners and a close friend of Adams, Honda frequently acted as Ieyasu's foreign minister. It was in that capacity that he personally authorized all applications for red-seal passports, including the one that had enabled Quaeckernaeck and Van Santvoort to sail for Patani. Honda accepted the letter of recommendation from Matsura, but would not take any of the offered gifts. Instead, he bade his guests welcome and promised to advance their cause with the shogun, who would see them the next day.

When the men were led into the presence of the shogun the next day, any doubts about the outcome of their mission were soon dispelled. Ieyasu showed himself "very pleased" with the gifts of raw silk and even the bars of lead were accepted with grace. Particularly gratifying to the Japanese ruler seemed a letter from the Dutch prince— a token of respect to which the Spanish king had never felt compelled to stoop. It was not without effect. And it was not without a fair degree of pride that Puyck observed that the potentate not only "offered free traffic," but "promised to reimburse our expenses" and even to "assist us in case we were in need of money."

On August 20 the embassy was again called into Ieyasu's presence. Two days earlier Pessoa had also received an audience, but the captain-major had clearly failed in his efforts to turn the Japanese ruler against the Dutch envoys, as the shogun displayed the same goodwill toward them as he had done six days earlier. He presented the envoys with a beautifully ornamented Japanese sword, a written reply to the prince, and the coveted passport with the red imprint of his great seal of state. Three other passports enabled the Dutch "to build a house of a size convenient to ourselves, and to bring our wares and merchandise therein and to sell them as best we can." To their added delight they were "in no way restricted as the Portuguese are, who have watchmen in their ships by night and day, whilst a fixed price is set upon their merchandise and they cannot sell it for a penny more, all of which they deeply regret."[3]

It was on their return to Hirado that the Dutch embassy finally met the man who had been so instrumental in their fortune. On September 4, one day after the governor's barge had set forth from Sakai, as it was approaching the eastern narrow between Honshu and the island of Shikoku, it was met by one of the shogun's ships. On board was William Adams. The exchange that followed, taking place as it did on the becalmed evening waters of the Inland Sea, brief and fleeting though it seemed, yet conveyed the deep bond that had tied the fate of the English pilot so inextricably to the destinies of these distant nations. Adams was the first to speak, explaining that he had come from Hirado, where he had been sent with letters from the shogun. He had been instructed by Matsura to convey his friendship to them and inform them that the daimyo had granted them a plot of land to build a factory. In parting, the Dutch envoys urged Adams to again recommend their case to the emperor when he came before him, and to treat favorably those whom they would leave behind to run the Dutch factory. Adams promised to do so, vowing himself to be "a friend of the Netherlands and to regard it as his fatherland."

When the embassy returned to Hirado on September 13, 1609, it learned that Adams had visited their ships in the company of Hasegawa Fujihiro four weeks earlier, on August 19; the governor had heard from Adams that Ieyasu intended to grant the Dutch a license to trade with Japan, and he had come down from Nagasaki in person to pay his respects. He had urged the Dutch to strictly comply with Japanese regulations and, above all, to avoid the kind of trouble the Iberians had caused. On the governor's departure, Adams had remained behind to help the Dutch procure accommodations for a Dutch factory.

Matsura had been very forthcoming; he had furnished them with a spacious house and a piece of land right next to the harbor. Acting on Adams' advice, the ships' council had prepared a large number of gifts for all Japanese dignitaries and officials with whom they had dealings. In keeping with Japanese custom, the gifts had been carefully selected for their size and value to reflect their recipients' position. The governor they had sent a gift consisting of an elaborately ornamented Dutch harquebus, fifteen bars of lead, fifteen lengths of scarlet, as well as some large flasks filled with olive oil, Spanish wine, and brandy, whilst his interpreter and senior servant had been given a length of damask each. Similar presents had been sent to Gotō Shōzaburō and Honda Masazumi. For the lord of Hirado, who continued to display a great interest in Western armament (and required all foreign vessels that entered Hirado to discharge at least one piece of ordnance), they had prepared a special present: he and his son each received a small piece of artillery, complete with powder and accessories. His servants and the four guards who had been posted on the *Roode Leeuw met Pylen* and the *Griffioen* were thanked with a gesture of fl. 14.20 each. The expenditure for all these gifts totaled the considerable sum of fl. 888.60.

On September 20, the ships' council convened once more, this time to deliberate on the organization of the factory. It was agreed that the first Dutch factor in Japan should be their junior merchant, Jaques Specks, who was to be assisted by three merchants, Hans Verstrepen, Laurens Adriaenszoon, and Nicolaes Pieterszoon, and a young lad for errands, Crijn Corneliszoon. To help them penetrate the Japanese market, Melchior van Santvoort would act as the East India Company's agent in Sakai, a service for which he would be paid fifty guilders a month, the equivalent of a captain's salary. One more of the *Love*'s survivors was employed on behalf of the Dutch factory. This was boatswain's mate Jan Cousynen, one of the two men the embassy had met on the Tōkaidō following their departure from Osaka. Given his good command of Japanese, Cousynen was hired as an interpreter for a fee of twenty guilders a month. Specks and his men quartered in rooms above the factory, where, looked after by a Japanese host and a small army of cooks and assistants, they would be able to live in considerable comfort. The only shortcoming in the support of their well-being was that they lacked professional medical care. Shortly after their arrival in Japan, the physician on the *Griffioen* had been stabbed in a brawl with one of his fellow crewmembers. Both men had died of their wounds, so that only one physician remained, and since his presence was deemed to be more urgently required on board the ships, it was decided that the factory's staff would have to make do with no more than a chest of medical supplies and a medical dictionary.

A more immediate concern was the amount of merchandise; all they had to tide them over until the next Dutch ship would reach Hirado was what remained of the token cargo shipped at Patani: fl. 15,231 worth of raw silk, 203 bars of lead, 12,000 pounds of pepper, and some 300 Spanish *reals*. The contribution these items presented to the advancement of Dutch-Japanese commerce was modest at best, and without any certainty about when the next Dutch ship would reach Hirado, the ships' council was keenly aware that, in order to maintain their precarious foothold in Japan, much depended on the goodwill of the Japanese authorities—a goodwill, in turn, that very much depended on their good relationship with the English pilot. And thus, on the eve of their departure from Japan, on October 2, 1609, the ships' council issued Specks with careful instructions. In all matters he was to comply with the wishes of the lord of Hirado and the governor of Nagasaki. Above all, however, he was to entertain good relations with Adams and regularly send him gifts to "sustain him in his devotion."

It was during the long journey home that the valuable lessons learned during their three months' stay in Japan were succinctly recapitulated by Puyck in a memo to the Heren Zeventien. Many, he argued, were the hurdles that stood in the way of a blossoming trade between the Dutch Republic and the Empire of Japan, yet for all these hurdles to be taken successfully it was of paramount importance that "attention be paid to the pilot of the ship of Jacob Quaeckernaeck, who resides in Japan, for he is a man of standing and has great prestige and intimacy with the Emperor."

Epilogue

More than a year had passed when on June 1, 1611, the *Oranje* and the *Brack*, anchored on Hirado's roadstead with a cargo of silk, lead, steel, spices, ivory, and even some Dutch cheese, although, except by the factory's staff, the latter met with little enthusiasm. The two ships were followed by the *Roode Leeuw met Pylen*, which returned to Hirado in 1612 in the company of the *Hasewindt*, carrying a cargo with a total value of fl. 26,187, and adding Dutch linen wear and cloth to the factory's range of commodities. Two years the Dutch factory had to bridge before, in August 1614, two more ships, the *Jacarta* and the *Enkhuizen*, entered Hirado bay. Over the following years, the trickle of ships gradually increased, until, in the summer of 1617, six Dutch vessels were moored in Hirado's narrow harbor.[1]

By then the Dutch were not the only Europeans with a factory in Hirado. On June 11, 1613, the *Clove* became the first English ship to be towed into Hirado's harbor. Invested with the title of Her Majesty's Envoy Extraordinary and Minister Plenipotentiary to Japan, her captain, John Saris, had sailed from the Downs two years earlier with the mission to establish trade relations with Japan. With Adams' help Saris soon achieved his objective. On November 26 of the same year, the East India Company, too, had its own factory in Hirado. Its staff consisted of eight men, headed by Cape merchant Richard Cocks. Yet, in spite of Adams' assistance, the English factory faced overwhelming odds.

When Saris sailed from Hirado on December 5, 1613, the chief commodities that Cocks had at his disposal were broadcloth, and some woolen and cotton piece goods. The limited Japanese demand

217

for such European goods, however, was already satisfied by the Dutch, who undersold their wares and thus "glut the place before the coming of ours." Even after English ships began to arrive with the goods that did matter—"steel and lead among metals; silk among materials"—the English faced an uphill struggle in their competition with the Dutch, who operated along the commercial avenues that had been explored by Melchior van Santvoort and Jan Joosten van Lodensteyn over the previous decade. To offset the Dutch advantage, the English posted agents in Edo, Kyoto, Osaka, and Sakai, but on Ieyasu's death, on April 17, 1616, when the foreigners were forced to limit their activities to Hirado, English prospects became bleaker and bleaker. Finally, on April 25, 1623, the Council of Defense of the East India Company in Batavia reluctantly decided to dismantle the English factory in Hirado. For a full decade Cocks had kept the English factory in Hirado alive, without ever making any profit.

Meanwhile, the Iberians had their own problems to deal with. During Hideyoshi and Ieyasu's reigns, Japanese dependence on the Iberian merchants for the supply of silk had checked any urge to move wholesale against the missionaries. With the arrival of Dutch and then English traders, such impediments had been removed and Christian persecution had returned with a vengeance. In 1611, the year in which the first Dutch ships arrived with a cargo of silk, the Tokugawa Bakufu issued its first anti-Christian edict. Two more edicts, issued in 1613 and 1614, branded Christianity as an evil sect and called for the expulsion of all foreign missionaries. Under these laws a number of Japanese evangelists were executed, yet as long as Ieyasu lived, not one foreign missionary who defied his decrees was put to death. Ieyasu's broad-minded policy, however, was not pursued by his successor. Only five months after Ieyasu's death, the Council of Regency issued an edict ordering all daimyos to see to it that none of their subjects adopt the Christian faith. Many Japanese Christians, priests and converts alike, were to die for their refusal to abjure the faith. For the first time, foreign missionaries were amongst the persecuted. In early spring 1617, a Jesuit, a Franciscan, a Dominican, and an Augustinian friar were decapitated at Omura—one head for each denomination. The killings reached a grueling climax on August 10, 1622, when fifty-five Christians were executed on Nishisaka Hill, the very same hill where twenty-six Franciscan friars had found their end a quarter of a century before. Nine of the twenty-five men who were burned at the stake were foreigners. When Japanese justice had taken its course, the remains of the martyrs were cast into a wide pit filled with timbers and left burning for two days. Then their ashes were put into bags, loaded onto boats, and carried far out to sea, where they were scattered on the waves, so as never to return to Japanese soil again. Afterwards, the participating fishermen were forced to strip naked and cleanse themselves and their boats of the last vestiges of Christianity.[2]

The Dutch, too, were obliged to write their own particular chapter in the bloody annals of Christian persecution in Japan, albeit in the blood of others. In February 1638, the then factor, Nicolaes Couckebacker, responded to an urgent "request" from the Bakufu to take under fire Hara castle on the Shimabara Peninsula. The year before, the formerly abandoned castle had become the last stand of some twenty thousand rebels. The original insurgents were mainly peasants who had risen against the merciless cruelty with which their lord had levied his taxes. As the revolt gathered momentum, they had been joined by other malcontents, including a few hundred lordless samurai; and when they were joined by a vast number of persecuted Christians from the islands of Amakusa, across the water, their struggle had taken on the zest of a religious war. For the Dutch, the security of their commercial interests prevailed over any moral qualms. On February 21, Couckebacker put out of Hirado port on the *Rijp* and during the next three weeks he looked on as his men fired more than 370 rounds into the castle from the ship and an improvised shore battery, inflicting heavy casualties amongst the already starved rebels. Four weeks later, in a massive assault on the stronghold by some forty thousand of the

Bakufu's troops, all the rebels, including old men, women, and children, were slaughtered.

The Shimabara Rebellion sounded the death knell of the century old Portuguese trade with the island country. The first Dutchman to sense the end of the Iberian presence was Couckebacker's successor, François Caron. During Caron's visit to the shogun's court in June 1639, he was asked so often and urgently whether the Dutch East India Company was in a position to replace the Portuguese in case they were banned from Japan that he came away elated. And sure enough, when Captain-Major Vasco Palha de Almeida put into Nagasaki with two Portuguese carracks toward the end of the following month, neither he nor any of his men were allowed ashore. Nor were they allowed to disembark any of the goods they carried, not even in payment of outstanding loans with Japanese merchants. Instead, De Almeida was presented with an edict by the Council of Regency. Dated July 5, 1639, the edict stated that henceforth no Portuguese were allowed to enter any Japanese port. Those who did would be put to death, while their ships would be burned. De Almeida was ordered to sail with the first fair wind and hand a copy of the edict to the authorities in Macao. So he did. But, commerce with Japan being the chief source of their prosperity, the authorities in Macao persisted, and one year later, almost to the day, another Portuguese ship, carrying an embassy of four Macao dignitaries, arrived in Nagasaki harbor. No sooner had she anchored than she was surrounded by Japanese vessels and divested of her rudder and sails. All who sailed in her were incarcerated. They remained imprisoned until August 2, 1640, when the envoys were led before two Bakufu delegates and told that they and their suite of fifty-seven men were to die. The following morning, all who had been sentenced to death were offered a last chance to save their lives by renouncing Christianity. All refused; and on August 4, 1640, they were led to Nishisaka Hill and decapitated. Their ship was burned. Only the lowest of the crew were spared. They were put on a Chinese junk "so that the bruit of this example may reach Macao."

As Caron had anticipated, Iberian adversity brought Dutch prosperity. Already in the year that the Shimabara Rebellion was suppressed, eleven Dutch ships had entered Hirado Bay, carrying a cargo with a total value of close to four million guilders; and before the year was out Couckebacker had laid the foundation stone of a new factory. Two years later, the annual number of ships that called at Hirado had risen to thirteen, while the total value of imports rose to an all-time peak of more than six million guilders. In that year the completion of the new factory was commemorated in an inscription on one of the building's crossbeams. Yet by a cruel twist of irony it was that very inscription that marked the end of the Dutch presence in Hirado, for in the sturdy wood were carved the ciphers "ad 1640"—the date of completion according to the Christian Era. On November 9, 1640, Caron was instructed to tear down his factory, stone by stone, in the exact opposite order in which they had been laid. Caron complied and that same day two hundred Dutch sailors set about to dismantle the Dutch factory. Six months later, the Dutch were ordered to remove themselves to Nagasaki. There they were lodged on the small, artificial island of Deshima, off the port's eastern shore, built four years earlier to accommodate the Portuguese merchants. Again the Dutch complied, and on February 10, 1641, the *Castricum*, the last Dutch ship to call at Hirado, raised her anchor and silently slipped out of its narrow bay. And thus, whilst Matsura saw his port once again sink back into oblivion, the Dutch began their long imprisonment in their gilded cage, an imprisonment that would last for more than two centuries.

Notes

Introduction

1   Outgherszoon's work, comprising twenty-two folio pages, was published in Amsterdam in 1600 by Zacharias Heyns under the title: *Nieuwe Volmaeckte Beschryvinghe der vervaerlijcker Strate Magellani, waer in van mijl tot mijl, van Baye to Baye, tot met der Schippers ende Stuurlieden d'opdoeningen vlytighlijck verthoont, ende de streckingen beschreven worden, door Jan Outghersz. van Enchuysen, die de selve Strate (Stuerman zijnde op' 't ship 't Geloove genaemt) hen ende weder gezeylt, ende over de 9 maenden daer in gheleghen heeft.* Outgherszoon's work was not translated, nor was it ever reprinted. The 1606 Amsterdam edition of Gerhardus Mercator's atlas for which Outgherszoon's work was used, was published by Jodocus Hondius. See F. C. Wieder, *De reis van Mahu en de Cordes door de Straat van Magalhaes naar Zuid-Amerika en Japan 1598–1600* (hereafter *De reis*) part 2, 73–76; part 3, 158.

2   The full title of Zacharias Heyns' work is *Wijdtloopigh verhael van 't gene de vijf Schepen (die int jaer 1598 tot Rotterdam toegherust werden, om door de Straet Magellana haren handel te drijven), wedervaren is, tot den 7 September 1599 toe, op welcken dagh capiteijn Sebald de Weert, met twee schepen door onweder vande Vlote versteken werd. Ende voort wat groot gevaer en elende hy by de vier maenden daer naer inde Strate gheleghen heeft, tot dat hy ten lesten heel reddeloos sonder schuyt oft boot, maer een ancker behouden hebbende, door hooghdringhende noot weder naer huys heeft moeten keeren, meest beschreven door M Barent Jansz. Cirurgijn.* The original work comprised sixty-eight folio pages and was illustrated with nine copper engravings and one woodblock print, all taken from Potgieter's drawings. Following its publication by Zacharias Heyns in 1600, it was reprinted in an unabridged edition in 1617. It reappeared in an abridged version in *Begin ende voortgang* in 1644, 1645, and 1646. In 1648 and 1650 it was published by Joost Hartgers. The last edition in the Dutch language saw the light in 1663, this time published by Saeghman. A faithful German translation by the famous Frankfurt publisher Jan Theodoor de Bry was issued in 1601 (*Grand Voyages*, vol. 9, part 2). Based on the German translation was a Latin version, issued by the same publisher in 1602. *De reis*, part 3, 153–158.

I : The Outset

1   The Texel is the anchorage off Texel, the largest of the Dutch islands.

2   The names of the two ships are not known.

3   Of the *Mauritius* and the *Hollandia*, with 460 tons each the largest vessels in the convoy, the former carried six of the heavy 24-pounders and fourteen 18-pounders, while the latter carried seven 24-pounders and thirteen 18-pounders. The 260 ton *Amsterdam* carried six 24-pounders and ten 18-pounders, and the 50 ton pinnace *Het Duyfken* was armed with two 24-pounders and six 18-pounders.

4   These were the Betsimisaraka, a people of Melanesian descent that had settled on the east coast of Madagascar, who were accustomed to the Portuguese ships that had frequented the island since the early 16th century. They were not the only ones to suffer from the arrival of the Dutch on Madagascar. During their stay on the southern side of the island, the Dutch had had several encounters with the local people to obtain victuals. The first furtive encounters had been relatively peaceful. Impressed with the strings of beads the aliens carried, the natives had willingly disposed of their few cattle. Most coveted were simple tin spoons, which the tribesmen wore in their earlobes—an adornment preferred above even silver spoons. For the Dutch, however, the few livestock that were acquired in this way did not long meet the considerable demands of the fleet's hungry crews. Desperate to obtain sufficient fresh victuals, the land parties sent ashore had gone about their task with ever increasing rigor, inclined simply to take and bargain *fait accompli*. The natives, apprehensive of the intentions of the aliens, became more and more unapproachable, and before long, the remaining sporadic encounters turned hostile. Three men who had been sent inland in search of food were pursued by a group of tribesmen and only managed to escape with their lives by relinquishing all their belongings down to their last garments. Then followed the first casualty when, caught in an ambush, midshipman Franck van der Does opened fire, killing one of his assailants. At the next encounter more natives died. A number of prisoners were taken, too—a man, two women, and four children. The women were released with their siblings, but the shackled man drowned in an attempt to swim ashore. The two remaining boys were kept to be taken back to Holland as curiosities and given the names Laurens and Madagascar. The gruesome climax came when following another Dutch "visit" to one of the inland villages, the natives killed one of the men on guard at the Dutch encampment. The Dutch retaliated by razing the village to the ground. Only one villager was

caught, and after he was expediently identified as one of the perpetrators, the hapless man was tied to a pole, buried to his waist, and "justice was administered" by a firing squad of twelve man. See J. W. *IJzerman in De eerste shipvaart der Nederlanders naar Oost-Indië onder Cornelis de Houtman, 1595–1597*, parts 1, 2, and 3, Linschoten Vereniging *Werken*, vol. 7, 25, and 32, The Hague, 1915–1929, 9–30, 8–13, and 6–14.

5   De Houtman was the first to choose open water when, on March 15, he set sail with two ships for the East—only to meet his death at the port of Aceh, poisoned and dispatched by the sultan's men. His fleet was followed by that of Ten Haeff, who sailed with three ships on the 25th of the following month. The largest fleet, consisting of eight ships under the command of Jacob van Neck, left for the East on May 1. The last expedition to leave Holland in 1598 was that of Olivier van Noort, the first Dutchman to circumnavigate the globe.

II : THE CONTEXT

1   Plancius practiced what he preached. In one instance, he was preaching at Meenen, when he and his parish were attacked by a mob of anti-Orange Wallonian Malcontents. Plancius escaped by swimming across the river Leie, but failed to rescue his library, which was publicly burned at Ieperen. J. Keuning, *Pertrus Plancius: Theoloog en Geograaf*, Amsterdam, 1949, 4.

2   After its last appearance in 1598, in an edited edition by the publisher Lenert Rans, Plancius' map gradually fell into obscurity, until almost three centuries later, it resurfaced at an exhibition in Madrid, submitted by the Colegio del Corpus Cristi monastery in Valencia, where it still is today.

3   Plancius' early view of the polar region consisted of a curious, almost contradictory blend of scientific observation and medieval lore. Thus, while he dismissed lingering fears amongst old salts that the strength of the magnetic north would cause nails to be drawn out of ships' hulls, in his biblical map he inhabits the area by pygmies only three feet in stature. Less superstitious, but equally spurious, is his vision of a vast Arctic continent, divided into four islands by narrow straits through which the world's oceans are drawn irrevocably north to terminate in an all-consuming polar vortex. In his first world map of 1592, Plancius had not yet fully abandoned the idea of an Arctic continent, although, by then, he had seriously come to doubt the veracity of his assumptions. As if to accommodate the possibility of an open passage (and possibly to conform to Waghenaar's descriptions of the region in the *Thresoor der Zeevaerdt*), Novaya Zemlya is separated from the polar continent by water.

In his map for Van Linschoten's *Itinerario* (the year of the first expedition), the four islands are still intact, although they now extend far less southward. See *Reizen van Jan Huygen van Linschoten naar het Noorden (1594–1595)*, Linschoten Vereniging *Werken*, vol. 8, The Hague, 1914, xvii–xvxix, lxxxiv.

4   A considerable part of these investments was carried by sub-investors, yet it is clear that already by the second venture Plancius had to his disposal considerable sums of money. No records exist to reveal what gains were made through these investments, yet here again the rate by which his stake has increased over the two latter expeditions speaks for itself. For the financial details of the second expedition, see J. Keuning, *De Tweede shipvaart der Nederlanders naar Oost-Indië onder Jacob Cornelisz. van Neck en Wybrant Warwijck (1598–1600)*, part 1, Linschoten Vereniging *Werken*, vol. 42, The Hague, 1938, xlvi. For details about the third expedition, see J. K. J. de Jonge, *De Opkomst van het Nederlandsch Gezag in Oost-Indië (1595–1610)*, part 4, The Hague, 1862, 102.

5   Very little is known about Olivier Brunel. Born in Brussels, it was probably at an early age that Brunel traveled to Kola (Murmansk) to make his fortune. Sometime after 1557, whilst under way to Kholmogorui, he was arrested by the Russian authorities on suspicions of spying, taken to Moscow, and imprisoned. For several years Brunel languished in prison, until he was released through the offices of the merchants Jakof and Anikieff Stroganoff. In their service, Brunel made a number of commercial voyages, as far afield as Astrakhan on the Caspian Sea and Khasan on the Sea of Japan. It was on one of these journeys that he traveled north, to the living grounds of the Nenets, and followed the course of the River Ob. Between 1570 and 1575, still in the service of the Stroganoffs, he traveled by boat to the Netherlands via Kola. He arrived in Dordrecht and from there traveled on to Antwerp and Paris, where he traded the wares he had brought with him. From then on, he regularly traveled between northern Russia and the Netherlands, but also east of the Urals. In 1576, he boarded a Russian coaster (*Lodija*) and by way of the Yugor Strait again reached the River Ob. The following year he was back in the Netherlands, where he met the Dutch entrepreneur Jan van de Walle, with whom he traveled overland to Kola to expand the latter's trade with the northern port. It was probably on one of his visits to the Antwerp bourse that Brunel and De Moucheron met and that the two adventurers by nature decided to launch a Dutch expedition to the regions Brunel had visited on board the Russian coaster. See S. P. L'honoré Nabe's *Reizen van Jan Huygen van Linschoten naar het noorden (1594–1595)*, Linschoten Vereniging *Werken*, vol. 8, The Hague, 1914. xlii–li.

226

III : THE OUTFIT

1   Following the convention of the time, formally, the *bewindhebbers* were at the same time the chief authority and principal shareholder (*hoofdpartici-panten*) in the venture. In reality, however, a large part of the financial burden was carried by a vast number of ordinary shareholders (*participanten*). They enjoyed a commensurate share in the profit but had no say in the company policies, nor in the way in which its funds were managed. Shares were recorded under the name of the *bewindhebbers*, and often changed hands. Thus, a certain Nicolaes de Colenaer put in fl. 600 under the name of Van der Haegen only to sell his share to Wouter Willekens a year later. More eager to exchange his share for hard currency was Hans de Buck, who sold his shares worth fl. 300 within only four months of the fleet's departure. Others, such as Daniel van der Meulen, made more substantial investments. This merchant in cloth and onetime extra-ordinary ambassador to the king of Denmark put down his stake at fl. 2,200, although he, too, sold on most of his shares to other speculators. Wieder, *De reis*, part 1, 105.

2   Although in general there was a surplus of sailors for ships trading in European waters, the reverse was true for ships with more exotic destinations. Even though expeditions to the East had not yet acquired the notorious reputation of the later East and West Indiamen, from their experience on Spanish and Portuguese vessels, many sailors were well aware of the perils that beset those on ships bound for distant seas and tropical destinations, nor had it escaped the seafaring community at large that De Houtman had only returned with a third of his original crew. It was this grim realization, more than anything else, that repelled those whose talents held out hopes for a better station in life, while attracting those whose only hope was to relieve their immediate destitution. See Boxer, *The Dutch Seaborne Empire 1600–1800*, London, 1965, 9–21.

3   There is some reason to believe that Adams may have been a member of Willem Barents' third expedition in search of the Northwest Passage, in 1596, and sailed under Captain Jan Rijp, although the evidence is very poor. The main evidence is provided by the Portuguese historian Diego de Couto, who drew on Portuguese sources that had spoken to Adams following his arrival in Japan, and who is quoted at length in William F. Sinclair's *The Travels of Pedro Teixeira; With His "Kings of Harmuz" and Extracts from His "Kings of Persia,"* Hakluyt Society *Works*, series 2, vol. 9, London, 1902, lxxvi. For a thorough treatment of the other available evidence, see Rundall's introduction to *Narratives of Voyages toward the North-West, in Search of a Passage to Cathay and India. 1496 to 1631*, series 1, vol. 5, xi–xx.

IV : The Crossing

1   Not all aboard the Dutch fleet were as understanding of the decision not to reclaim the Dutch vessel from the English. The leaders of the expedition, undoubtedly, were more aware of the possible consequences of trade with the enemy. Under the Anglo-Dutch treaty the Dutch had committed themselves to a seizure of trade on enemy ports. Yet as an indispensable source of revenue, trade, be it with foe or friend, was vital to the survival of the United Netherlands, and thus, the mercantile section of the treaty had been a dead letter from day one. Nevertheless, the treaty was still in force, and under it the hundreds of Dutch merchantmen that continued to sail to the Iberian Peninsula were technically reduced to smugglers, giving the Dutch port authorities the right to impound all ships carrying Iberian commodities, although, in practice, this right was rarely exercised. With a smaller stake in European naval trade and thus less to lose, the English displayed greater alacrity in keeping to the letter of the treaty. Consequently, apart from the considerable risk of having their vessels impounded by Spanish authorities and, occasionally, by the Dutch port authorities, Dutch skippers faced the additional risk of being raided by one of the many English privateers that swarmed the Iberian peninsula. At the time of the Nonsuch treaty, these privateers had been kept in check by a queen still hopeful of a peace settlement with Spain. But following the Armada they were given free rein to "annoy" the enemy and those who traded with them. The putative reason given by the English privateers for their conduct left little room for argument, yet the seizure of a Dutch merchantman, loaded with precious cereals from the Baltic, conveniently served to satisfy the domestic needs for food commodities at a time when England was frequently plagued by shortages.

2   Sailing in a pre-chronometer age, navigators of the 16th century had no certain means to determine longitude at sea. The only way in which this could be done was by the laborious and notoriously unreliable method of "dead reckoning," by which the position of a vessel at any moment was found by applying to the last well-determined position the run that was made since, using the ship's course and the distance indicated by a crude log (a piece of wood made fast to a long line knotted at regular intervals), which was timed by a diminutive sandglass.

3   In 1580, on his way back to Spain after his own successful passage of the Strait of Magellan, Pedro Sarmiento de Gambóa visited Ribeira Grande and described it as follows: "This city of Santiago de la Ribera, which was founded 110 years ago, has a bad situation and a worse port; but the place

was selected on account of the supply of water. It contains a few more than 450 houses of stone, the best being that of the Bishop, who is named Bartholomé Leyton. There are three forts commanding the anchorage, each with ten good bronze pieces of artillery, and good gunners. They told us that there were 20,000 negroes in the island, and a considerable trade with them. The custom house officers said that the customs were worth more than 10,000 ducats to the King annually. The other settlement is called 'Playa,' at the distance of four leagues. The island does not produce wheat, but they raise cattle and sheep. There is little water in the higher parts, except in the ravines, where there are some sugar mills; and maize cultivation, which they call 'millo,' besides fruits." See Clements R. Markham, ed., *Narratives of the Voyages of Pedro Sarmiento de Gamboa to the Straits of Magellan*, Hakluyt Society *Works*, series 1, vol. 91, London, 1894, 187–188.

4 When Drake visited São Tiago in 1585, five years after he had raided Nuno de Silva's ship off Ribeira Grande, he not only sacked Ribeira Grande and Praia, but also added to his fleet a caravel from Ribeira Grande's shipyard, numerous cannon and barrels of gunpowder, topped off with a huge supply of victuals, including bread, flower, oil, and wine, as well as potatoes, oranges, lemons, cocoa beans, figs, and dates. Moreover, all this was done within the space of only ten days, although, admittedly, he had done so using double the number of men in Mahu's fleet. See Harry Kelsey, *Sir Francis Drake: The Queen's Pirate*, New Haven, 1998, 95–98, 253–256.

5 In fact, the eleven men had not been lost. They had been separated from the fleet, but had managed to reach the African coast, albeit considerably later than the main fleet. Having searched in vain for the fleet, they had ended up at Cape Lopez. Here they abandoned the caravel and signed on on two merchantmen belonging to De Moucheron, which were bound for the West Indies and arrived at La Española in June 1599. See *De reis*, part 1, 168.

6 The Dutch explorer Pieter van den Broecke, who visited Annobon sixteen years later, found it to be "abundant in refreshments of all sorts, such as apples, limes, lemons, melons, pineapples, cassia, corn, beans, ginger, and other fruits. In the way of livestock and cattle, there were oxen and cows, sheep, goats, pigs, fowl, doves, and parrots." Enough reason for Van den Broecke, too, to "thank God" when he reached the roadstead of Annobon. Van den Broecke was "very well received" by the then governor of the island, Manuel Ferrera Velozo—a hospitality that was remarkable given that, in the wake of De Cordes, the islanders suffered repeatedly at the hands of Dutch expeditions, notably those under the command of Olivier van Noort in 1599

and Joris van Spilbergen in 1601. K. Ratelband, *Reizen naar West-Afrika van Pieter van den Broecke 1605–1614*, The Hague, 1950, 81–83.

V : The Passage

1   The first to mention the trees was Barent Jansz. Potgieter, who had observed how the island in the bay was "covered with green trees, like the laurel, yet exceeding in height, always green, the barks or peelings being as bitter as Pepper." See *De reis*, part 1, 186. Potgieter's observations were somewhat contradicted by De Weert, who later recalled that the tree "not only grew on the islands in the bay…but throughout the strait." Nor had it "any semblance with the laurel, as some may have said, although the scent of the leaves is like the scent of bay-leaves, but they are wider and greener, yet the tree remains green (as indeed do most of the other trees, which grow in the strait) and it sprouted at the top, and at times is so wide that it approaches a girth equal to two or three human bodies." It did not, however, "bear any fruit, as far as we could observe, even though in full we spent some nine months in the strait, in which interval, by necessity, if it had not been barren, one should have observed either flowers or the fruit, be it ripe or not." "Brief van Sebald de Weert aan Johannes de Laet Sr., vader van Johannes, den bekenden bewindhebber en geschiedschrijver der West-Indische Compagnie, 20 April 1601," *De reis*, part 1, 133.

2   The "savages" Van Beuningen and his men encountered on the Charles Islands belonged to one of the three native tribes that inhabited the Patagonian peninsula. Their territories were roughly dissected by the strait—the Yaghans in the south, the Onas in the east, and the Alacaluf in the north. Of the three tribes, the Alacaluf inhabited the largest area, running along the northern periphery of the strait, up along the west coast, and all the way to the Gulf of Trinidad. These natives had lived here since time immemorial, subsisting on the sparse produce of the land and on what they caught in the thousand inlets of the vast Chilean archipelago. The Dutch were not the first to encounter the Indians. Although Magellan was the first to pass through the strait, he did not sight any Indians, although at night he did see fires on the southern shore of the strait, leading him to call the land south of the strait Tierra del Fuego. That the "Patagonians," as the Indians were mistakenly called, were not a hostile people is conveyed by the first recorded encounter between the Indians and Europeans, which occurred in January 1526, when the expedition of García Jofre de Loaysa entered the strait for its first, unsuccessful attempt (the strait was only passed several months later). The encounter was recorded for posterity in remarkable detail

by Captain Andres de Urdaneta, who arrived in Santiago Bay (on the northern shore of the strait, between the two narrows) on the *Anunciada*. See Clements Markham, *Early Spanish Voyages to the Strait of Magellan*, Hakluyt Society *Works*, series 2, vol. 28, London, 1911, 45. The Indians were also sighted by the next Europeans to visit the region, the fateful Portuguese expedition under the command of Simon de Alcazava, who was killed by his own men. See Martin Gusinde, *Die Feuerland Indianer: Ergebnisse meiner vier Forschungsreisen in den Jahren 1918 bis 1924*, Mödling bei Wien, part 3, vol. 1, 1974, 24. Drake's expedition, too, had encountered the Indians, and Francis Fletcher, the chaplain on board the admiral's ship, was to give a remarkably undiluted description of their habits. See William Sandys, ed., *The World Encompassed by Sir Francis Drake; Being His Next Voyage to that to Nombre de Dios*, Hakluyt Society *Works*, series 1, vol. 16, London, 1854, 74–75. Due to the protracted period over which Pedro Sarmiento de Gambóa surveyed the region, his encounters with natives were more frequent and intimate, and the personal account of his findings abound in detailed descriptions of the Indians and their customs. See Clements R. Markham, *Narratives of the Voyages of Pedro Sarmiento de Gamboa*, 45, 62-63, 66, 69, 108–109, 111, 118–119, 146–147.

VI : FAITH

1   Van Noort's journal sadly confirms the gruesome nature of the encounter. It describes how on December 25, 1599, on the smallest of the Penguin Islands, "we saw people, to whom we rowed out armed in two Boats, but arriving at the foot of the Island, we saw the Inhabitants up high, signalling to us that we should go away, throwing down Penguins from above, and as we approached, they shot with Arrows; and before arriving on the Island, we saw that they were forty in number, at which we shot, though [they] walked away and hid themselves; [then] we made out a Cave in the slope of the land, which could not be entered from above and steep from below, in which a large number of people were gathered and [who] for a long time defended themselves by shooting, so that three or four of us were hurt, and although we approached them by force, they would not surrender, until we shot the men; then we came upon some Women and Children, who lay on top of each other, the Parents on the Children to rescue them, that they might not be shot; many were dead and hurt, [and] we took three male slaves and two girls, whom we took on board, after which we learned (through one who learned the language) the situation of the land, which was as follows. This race is called Enoo, inhabiting a land the which they call Cossi, but this small island is called Talcke, the other large one is called Castemme, on which are many

Penguins, with which they chiefly nourish themselves and which is their food; of the skins they make their coats, the which they carry round their body and are otherwise naked, living in holes made in the earth. To our knowledge they had come from the main Land to this Island, for we saw yet many men on the point of the land, which is not more than a mile from there, to fetch Penguins for their food. There are on the mainland many Ostriches which they call Tacke, and which they catch and eat; there are also other Animals, which they call Cassoni, we suspect that these are Deer or Roebucks. This people are many Races together, of which we suspect there are many, keeping their dwellings separately; for they knew of four other Races, to wit: Kemenetes occupy a place called Karay. Kennekas occupy Karamay. Karaike occupy a place that is called Morine. All these are people of stature like the Enoo, whom we had caught, of the size of a common man in our country, otherwise they are broadly built with a high Chest, paint their faces and foreheads with diverse Paints. The Men had tied their Privies with a thread, and the Women had in front of it a piece of Penguin skin, the hair that hangs across the foreheads of the men, is cut short with the Women. They all go naked, having only a Penguin or other bird Skin round their bodies, which they call Oripoggre, and the Penguins Compogre, which are sewn together so well, as if it had been done by a Furrier. There is yet another Race Landwards called Tirimenen, which occupies a Land called Coin. These are tall People like Giants, being ten or eleven feet tall, who come to War against these other Races, accusing them of being Ostrich eaters, through which it seems that they consume better food or nourishment than the others, but we suspect that they are all Man-eaters." *Olivier van Noort*, 35–36.

2   The three most northerly islands of the Falkland Islands group, now called the Jason Islands. Sebald de Weert was wrong about the islands. Since 1527, these islands had already been marked on numerous maps, usually under the name of Sanson Islands. See *De reis*, part 1, 238, part 2, 43, 74.

VII : Fidelity

1   The *Amsterdam* and the *Sticht van Utrecht*, under the command of Vice Admiral Wijbrand van Warwijck, were part of the expedition of Admiral Jacob van Neck and were the first Dutch ships to reach the Moluccan archipelago. They had arrived on the eastern side of the island on May 22, 1599. It took almost a month before they were able to commence trade with the sultan and load a modest quantity of clove. See J. Keuning, *De tweede schipvaart der Nederlanders naar Oost-Indië onder Jacob Cornelisz. van Neck en Wybrant Warwijck 1598–1600*, part 3, Linschoten Vereniging *Werken*, vol. 46, The Hague, 1924, 104–135.

2   Van der Does' cautions are reminiscent of those given by Baäb Oellah to Francis Drake when the latter visited the island at the end of 1579. The sultan warned Drake that he should not go to the Portuguese island of Tidore. Drake chose to heed the warning and accepted the sultan's invitations, upon which the sultan let him know that "he would sequester the commodities and traffic of his whole island from others, especially from his enemies the Portuguese (from whom he had nothing but by the sword), and reserve it to the intercourse of our nation, if we would embrace it." The sultan's overtures were reciprocated by Drake, who sent a velvet cloak to the sultan and promised to return in greater force. He never did; although it is probable that he intended to honor his commitment, and that the purpose of the Fenton expedition was to establish an English factory on Ternate. See Kelsey, *Sir Francis Drake*, 198–200. Although Drake might have forgotten about the island, the islanders did not forget him. Admiral Jacob van Heemskerck, speaking to one of the sultan of Ternate's men on his visit to Ambon, found himself "amongst others, questioned about an English captain, who some 20 years ago had arrived well loaded at Ternate and had ran onto a cliff, and to get the ship free again, had put two pieces of artillery on the side of the ship, after which the two pieces were dropped by walking the men from star- to larboard, and with the movement the ship was propelled off the cliff and anchored before Ternate. The captain gave the king a velvet robe and a golden ring, which is worn on the hand and on which one can whistle [*sic*], which the king keeps in great esteem. The king presented to give him in return a ship full of cloves, and when the ship was fully loaded with the same, [Drake] thanked the king and promised to return another year with 3 or four ships to help the king to drive the Portuguese from the Moluccas, and since I suspected that it had been captain Dareck, I gave him answer that the captain of whom he spoke was dead; to which he said that he was sorry and that he had reckoned the same must have happened, since he did not doubt that the captain would otherwise have come as he had promised." See J. Keuning, *De Tweede Schipvaart*, part 3, xliv, 193.

3   The wretched end of De Cordes also came to the ears of Jacob van Neck, when, in June 1601, he visited Ternate on his second expedition to the East Indies. Shortly after his arrival at Ternate, Van Neck met the sultan and his men and "understood from them that the Portuguese, who have their residence in Tidore, had very treacherously boarded a ship, which had come from the South Sea and was one of the ships of Admiral Mahu. They had received its captain with great friendship and got him so far as to come ashore with some of his cleverest men to help tie up a buffalo, which they had promised him for refreshment. When he afterwards intended to go aboard again, they

had killed him in the boat and thrown him in the water like a dog." H. A. van Foreest and A. de Booy, *De vierde schipvaart der Nederlanders naar Oost-Indië onder Jacob Wilkens an Jacob van Neck, 1599–1604*, part 1, Linschoten Vereniging *Werken*, vol. 82, The Hague, 1980, 183–184.

VIII : THE GOSPEL

1   In Spain, only Roman Catholic Christians called themselves *cristianos*.

2   Acting on De Ibarra's information, the viceroy dispatched four ships under the command of his brother Juan de Velasco to intercept and destroy Van Noort's fleet. De Velasco sailed from Callao on May 8, 1600, but his fleet was caught in a storm in which his ship and all who sailed in her were lost.

3   Through Pomp's letter Van Noort also heard how Pomp had overrun Santa María. Van Noort immediately recognized that Pomp had been bound to overrun the island, "since in the Maps and Writings of Petrus Plancius it lies at 36 degrees south of the Line, and we found the same to lie at 37 deg. 15 min.; for had we not had the Writings of the English Captain Melis we would have missed it ourselves." The "Writings of the English Captain Melis" Van Noort refers to would almost certainly have corresponded with the findings of Thomas Fuller, skipper of the *Desire* under Thomas Cavendish, who situated the island between 37°14' and 15'S. J. W. IJzerman, *De reis om de wereld door Olivier van Noort, 1598–1601*, part 1, Linschoten Vereniging *Werken*, vol. 27, The Hague, 1926, 60.

4   One of the "dangerous" men to be employed by the viceroy was Laurens Claeszoon. In 1603 the Dutch boatswain was placed on another expedition to the Strait of Magellan, this time in search of foreign raiders, again under the command of Don Gabriel de Castilla. Leaving Lima early in the year, the expedition reached a southern latitude of 64°, where it "had much snow," returning to the Chilean coast in April of the same year. During the next year he was placed on the fleet of the bishop of Quito, Don Fray Luis López de Soles, destined for the Galápagos Islands, from where, according to Claeszoon, "those from Peru fetch much Timber for Ships and Houses; and there are many Sheep, Goats, Fowls, plenty of Fish, good Water, sound Masts, but heavy, [as they are] very tough," and "there was a kind of Hemp, called Caboulie, of which they make Ship's Rigging." With the bishop's retinue he had also traveled inland. From the bishop's residence, in Quito, they had traveled some 50 (Spanish) Miles northeast over the Andes in order to reach Pasto, and for which "one has to cross three difficult rivers." And from

there farther north to Popayán, "which is 36 Miles," and down again to the coast, on the Río de Bonaventura, "where the barques lie" and which "is very wide" and "runs into the bay of Gorgona." Claeszoon's last voyage under Spanish command took him all the way to Panama, and "from Panama to the Capital of Veragua, called Signora de Guida," which "lies on the Río de los Ostiones," where he had seen how "in the year 1607, 14 ships were on the stocks." From there, the forty-year-old boatswain was finally allowed to sail home, where his accounts of his travels were recorded by Plancius and later incorporated into the "Instructions and Journals of the Brazilian and East-India Voyages, since 21 April 1623 to 28 August 1681." See J. W. IJzerman, *Dirck Gerritsz. Pomp, alias Dirck Gerritsz. China: De eerste Nederlander die China en Japan bezocht 1544–1604*, Linschoten Vereniging *Werken*, vol. 9, The Hague, 1915, 159–161.

IX : HOPE & LOVE

1　The bay in which the *Love* anchored (Bahia Maria on Doetszoon's chart) is almost certainly Fiordo Burns, a narrow bay that runs deep into an island-like projection of the Peninsula de Taitao, creating two smaller peninsulas, Penla Skyring on the north and Penla Duende on the south. The gulf to the south of Peninsula de Taitao is Golfo de Penas.

2　The reason for Van Beuningen's hostile reception was discovered by the Dutch only five months later when, during his interrogation of the pilot of the *Buen Jésus*, Olivier van Noort learned that "two ships of the company of Verhaegen had been at the island of S. Maria, and on which Symon de Cordes was General, of whom they said he had been slain to death on the mainland with 23 of his men by the Indians; to wit, opposite S. Maria lies a point called Lavapie, onto which they went, meaning to obtain some victuals there through a false Spaniard who was with the Indians and lured them ashore with the pretence of friendship, and were surprised and slain to death, 23 in all, including General de Cordes [Van Beuningen]. The Indians, not knowing that they were Hollanders, thought that they had victoried against the Spanish, arrived in great triumph before Concepción, carrying on their lances the heads [of Van Beuningen and his men], with which they vexed the Spaniards (who have their Government in Conceptión)." See *De reis om de wereld door Olivier van Noort, 1598–1601*, part 1, Linschoten Vereniging *Werken*, vol. 27, The Hague, 1926, 61.

3　In his letter "To my unknowne frinds and countri-men" Adams describes how "we proceeded on our former intention for Japon, and in the height of

thirtie degrees, sought the northermost [?] Cape of the forenamed Iland."
Whether the word "northermost" is a slip of the pen by Adams or by the person who transcribed his letter is unclear, yet it is almost certain that Adams is referring to what was believed to be Japan's easternmost cape, i.e., Cabo des Cestos. This would be logical from a navigational point of view, since the cape in question would be the first landfall and, significantly, farthest removed from the ports frquented by the Portuguese, which Adams knew to be Japan's western ports, mainly situated on the island of Kyushu. It is also borne out by the charts by which Adams was sailing, for on Doetszoon's chart the most southern extremity of Cabo des Cestos lies exactly at 30°. See Thomas Rundall, *Memorials of the Empire of Japan in the 16th and 17th Centuries*, Hakluyt Society *Works*, series 1, vol. 8, London, 1850, 23.

X : The Arrival

1   Having sailed northwest, they had sailed straight up the Bungo Suidō, a wide channel separating the most southern island of Kyushu from the eastern island of Shikoku. It was not the pilot's calculations that were to blame. As Adams was to find later, the cape he had sought "lieth false in all cards, and maps, and globes; for the Cape lieth in thirty-five degrees 1/2, which is a great difference." See Rundall, *Memorials*, 23.

2   The arrival of the *Love* in Japan is mentioned in only one of the surviving Japanese records of the period. The *Nagasaki komonjo* mentions that "[i]n the 5th year of Keichō [1600], a large vessel arrived at Sakai-ura, which on inquiry was found to be a Dutch ship come to trade. She was ordered to proceed to Edo. On her voyage there, she was overtaken by a gale at Uraga and wrecked. The crew proceeded to Edo by land, where they resided for some time, having no vessel in which to return to their native land. Among the crew were two men, called Yayosu [Jan Joosten van Lodensteyn] and William Adams." See Okada Akio, *Miura anjin*, Tokyo, 1984, 302–313.

3   The surnames of the last two men are not known. Adams puts the number of those who were still alive on arrival at twenty-four ("sicke and whole"), and mentions the subsequent death of six others, leaving eighteen. See Rundall, *Memorials*, 24. Although Adams is not always consistent in his figures, it is reasonable to assume this figure is correct. Almost all other sources, however, put the figure at twenty-five. According to the Jesuit chronicler Fernão Guerreiro the *Love* "brought only five and twenty men alive, and these sick and prostrated by the cold and hunger that they suffered on such a long voyage, of whom two died on arrival." According to Diego de Couto "there were

alive but five and twenty." For both sources, see William F. Sinclair, *The Travels of Pedro Teixeira; With his "Kings of Harmuz" and Extracts from His "Kings of Persia,"* Hakluyt Society *Works*, series 2, vol. 9, London, 1902, lxxix. Their reports partially tie in with that of Emanuel Luiz, the Portuguese captain of the Japanese junk encountered by Van Noort. Luiz, who spoke to the *Love* on its way from Sakai to Edo, puts the initial number at twenty-five, and mentions that only fourteen of her crew were still alive when he spoke to them in Anotsu. See IJzerman, *Olivier van Noort*, 129–130.

4   João Rodríguez was a man of exceptional drive and ability. Born in 1561, in the Portuguese town of Sernancelhe, Rodríguez had come out to the East at the age of fifteen. Following his arrival in Japan, he had entered the service of Ōtomo Yoshishige, the daimyo of Bungo, who was known for the warm heart he bore toward the Christian faith. Yet it was not only for his religiosity that Rodríguez was hired by the daimyo. Bold and highly intelligent, Rodríguez proved an excellent soldier. He saw action in several of the daimyo's military campaigns, including a disastrous campaign in 1578, against the neighboring province of Higo, in which Ōtomo was routed by the daimyo of Satsuma. The following year Ōtomo had converted to the Christian faith—a conversion that coincided with the arrival in Bungo of Alessandro Valignano, who had come to Japan with the aim of establishing an educational system based on the Christian teachings. It was with Ōtomo's help that the first Jesuit Collegio was established in Funai, the capital of Bungo, situated some fifty miles up the coast from Usuki. Rodríguez had been one of the first students to enroll in the Collegio, studying Latin and philosophy, until he was ordained in 1587. Over the next few years he had deepened his study, especially that of the Japanese language and literature, which he pursued under the superintendence of his old Japanese master. His efforts were rewarded in 1590, when Valignano took him along on his visit to Toyotomi Hideyoshi. The latter was so impressed with the Jesuit's command of the Japanese language that, on Valignano's departure, he insisted Rodríguez remain behind as the official court interpreter. In this function the Jesuit became known as João Rodríguez Tçuzzu, after the old Japanese term *tsūzu*, or "interpreter". In 1591 he was appointed procurator of the Japan Mission, a position which he occupied until his expulsion in 1626. It is for his seminal works on the Japanese language, however, that João Rodríguez Tçuzzu is still remembered today. See Boxer's *Portuguese Merchants and Missionaries in Feudal Japan, 1543–1640*, Aldershot, 1986, vi, 338–369.

5   Nothing is known of Oudewater's fate after he left the house. The little that is known about Gisbert de Coning has been handed down to us by Richard

Wickham, who employed De Coning at an annual salary of £20 for the English at their factory in Hirado and who described him as "a Fleming whome Capt' Adams knoweth, & of his company, between whom there is no great friendshipp. Neverthelesse he hath shewen himself redy to doe me any service here or elsewhere. He is of late growen very poore by reason his house at Urimgava [Uraga], with all that ever he had, was there consumed by fire. He is desirous to seeke his living in honest fashion for that he is married here at Uringawa, where his wife and children remayne." Anthony Farrington, *The English Factory in Japan, 1613–1623*, 2 vols., London, 1991, 192.

6   Terazawa Hirotaka was the first man to occupy the powerful position of Nagasaki *bugyō*. He was appointed to the position shortly after the district had been subdued by Toyotomi Hideyoshi's massive campaign of 1592.

7   John Saris (see Epilogue), the second Englishman to visit Osaka after Adams, described the town and its castle as follows: "We found Osaka to be a very great town, as great as London within the walls, with many faire timber bridges of a great hight, serving to pass over a river there as wide as the Thames at London. Some fair houses we found there, but not many. It is one of the chief sea-ports of all Japan; having a castle in it, marvellously large and strong, with very deep trenches about it, and many bridges, with gates plated with iron. The castle is built all of free-stone, with bulwarks and battlements, with loope holes for small shot and arrows, and divers passages for to cast stones upon the assailants. The walls are the least six or seven yards thick, all (as I said) of free-stone, without any filling in the inward part with trumpery, as they reported unto me. The stones are great, of an excellent quarry, and are cut so exactly to fit the place where they are laid, that no mortar is used, but only earth cast between to fill up void crevices if any be." In Thomas Rundall, *Memorials*, 60–61.

8   There are a number of revealing but ultimately inconsistent contemporary references to the fate of the cargo carried by the *Love*. First of all, there are Adams' letters. Although Adams nowhere specifically mentions what happened to the ship's cargo, from his letters it is clear that between the time he last saw the ship in Usuki and the time of his reunion with the ship in Sakai, the *Love* had been fully stripped of what had been left by the natives upon its arrival. In his own words: "From the ship all things were taken out: so that the clothes which I took with me on my back I only had." Whereas upon his departure from Usuki he had still been able to take "a chart of the whole world," now "[a]ll my instruments and books were taken. Not only I lost what I had in the ship, but from the captain and the company, generally,

what was good or worth the taking, was carried away." See Thomas Rundall, *Memorials*, 26. Then there is the letter by Jacques L'Hermite de Jonge to his father, written from the *Erasmus*. Drawing on Quaeckernaeck's account, De Jonge recalls that "the Ship [the *Love*], which was weighed down to the ground with artillery, ammunition, and other goods, the King of Japan took for himself; and the rest they consumed for their own upkeep." See *Begin ende voortgangh vande Oost-Indische Compagnie*, 145–187. As usual, the Japanese records are tantalizingly vague. The *Nagasaki komonjo*, although it mentions that "in the 5th year of Keichō, a large vessel arrived at Sakai," it does not refer to the cargo at all. The *Tōdaiki* at least mentions "a great quantity of armor and large guns, the armor being largely from the waist up"; yet, whilst it is the only known document to mention Ieyasu's inspection of the vessel, apart from revealing that Ieyasu "ordered the scarlet woolen cloth to be sold," it does not give any concrete clues as to what happened to the guns and armour after their arrival in Sakai. See Okada Akio, *Miura anjin*, 1984, Tokyo, 32–33. The Iberian records, by contrast, are the most specific. Fernão Guerreiro carefully describes how Ieyasu "at once sent a captain of his to Bungo to have the ship brought to Meaco or to Sacay, where he took possession of her as a wreck, according to the laws of Japaõ." See Fernão Guerreiro, *Relãçao annual das coias que fizeram os Padres da Companhia de Iesus nas suas missões de Iapão, China, nos anos de 1600 a 1609*, vol. 1, 1600–1603, Coimbra, 1930, 107–108. Diego de Couto is less specific about the ship's cargo and simply holds that Ieyasu, "after he had ordered the ship to be emptied, sent her to the kingdoms of Canto to load timber." See Diego de Couto, *Da Ásia década XII*, Lisbon, 1788, 447–454.

9   Regrettably, no firsthand account of these events by any of the *Love*'s survivors has survived. From the records that have survived, however, it is clear that a number of them were mobilized by Ieyasu in his campaign against Uesugi Kagekatsu. Fernão Guerreiro mentions how, following the *Love*'s arrival in Sakai, Ieyasu "sent her to a port of his kingdoms of Quantō, with the Hollanders that came in her, and eighteen or twenty pieces of ordnance; and all the rest that she carried he retained, the greater part of which was arms and a large quantity of powder." See Fernão Guerreiro, *Relãçao annual*, part 1, 107–108. Diego de Couto is even more specific about the way Ieyasu employed her crew and claims that "the Hollanders that were most in health he [Ieyasu] sent to serve as bombardiers in a war that he ordered to be undertaken against a rebel lord who was called Cangeatica [Kagekatsu]." Diego de Couto, *Da Ásia década XII*, 447–454. Adams, in his letter "to my unknowne frinds and countri-men," makes no specific references to the military use of

the ship's cargo or her crew. This is quite understandable: both the shipowners and the Dutch government, after all, had invested their money in the weaponry so that it might be used to annoy the Spanish or Portuguese—not to help settle a domestic Japanese conflict. Different, of course, it was with his letter to his wife. Significantly, it is this letter which is broken off at the very point where Adams is about to relate the events after his release from prison. According to Purchas (vol. 1, book 3, 132) this was done "by malice of the bearers." If this is true, then the latter part of Adams' letter may have been suppressed either by the Dutch or the English. See Thomas Rundall, *Memorials*, 33–40.

XI : THE FRUITION

1 During his stay in Japan, Captain John Saris (see Epilogue) met both Van Lodensteyn and Van Santvoort. His diary entries speak volumes about the characters of both men: "The 11th [July 1613] there came to vizite me one Melser van Jonford, a Fleming, and one of those which came in the shipp with Mr. Addams into this counterye....I did offer him intertenament, finding him verye stayde and vnderstanding, boath in the language as allso in traficke, or to bring him into England yf he so pleased, but he refused boath, being better affected to this course of life, houlding it farr more contenting then yf he weare in his owne counterye." Ten days later, "John Yozen the Fleming, which came from Syam and is said to haue bought the wood aforesaid of Sr Lucas, Came to vizite me, and lefte with me a letter for Mr. Addams. He said he would proue the wood was sould to him, to paye two for one at his retorne to Siam, but the matter resteth tell Mr. Addams doth come, whose letters will make the truth manyfaste. The ould King came while this Fleming was with me. He tould me he was of no accompt and verye much indetted in the counterye." See Ernest M. Satow, *The Voyage of Captain John Saris to Japan, 1613*, Hakluyt Society *Works*, series 2, vol. 5, London, 1900, 102–103, 105–106.

2 In the contemporary record *Aichū ryūon kiryaku* Adams' qualities as a weapon instructor are appraised as follows: "he had a remarkable talent in the art of gunnery and instructed a great number of soldiers in this art; which caused him to be highly esteemed by the Tōshō Daijingu-sama [Tokugawa Ieyasu]." See Okada Akio, *Miura anjin*, Tokyo, 316.

3 Though the *Love* herself was wrecked, her wooden figurehead in the image of Erasmus was salvaged. For several centuries it was kept in the Ryūkōin temple in the village of Azuma (Tochigi prefecture), where it became the

subject of local folklore until, early in the 20th century, it was rediscovered and transferred to the Tokyo National Museum, where it has remained on display to the present day. See Okada Akio, *Miura anjin*, Tokyo, 34–38.

4   In 1610, following the wreckage of the Spanish ship *San Francisco* on the Japanese coast, the *Sea Adventure* was lent to Don Rodrigo Vivero de Velasco. De Velasco, the governor of the Philippines, had been aboard the *San Francisco*, which was under way from the Philippines to Mexico. The governor was treated with great hospitality and was offered Adams' ship to continue his voyage. De Velasco accepted the offer and rechristened the vessel the *Santa Ana*. He so much liked her that upon his arrival in Mexico, he refused to send her back but, instead, had her value estimated and the sum (according to Dutch sources, paid in kind) sent with the next ship that sailed for Japan. See *De reis*, part 3, 23.

5   In 1616 Captain Richard Cocks, the Cape Merchant of the Hirado factory, visited Adams' estate and noted the following in his diary: "This [Hemi] is a Lordship geuen to Capt. Adames pr. the old Emperour, to hym and his for eaver, and confermed to his sonne, called Joseph. There is above 100 farms, or howshols, vpon it, besides others vnder them, all which are his vassals, and he hath power of life and death over them: they being his slaues; and he having an absolute authoretic over them as any tono (or king) in Japan hath over his vassales." See Thomas Rundall, *Memorials*, 86.

6   Together with the port of Hakatanotsu and Bonotsu, the old port of Anotsu (present-day Tsu) was one of the three main ports in the western half of the main island. Van Noort spells the name of the port as "Atonsu"—a harmless mistake in itself, but one that, in combination with the port's subsequent change of name, has led to a considerable amount of confusion. Wieder, for instance, unable to find a port by that name, presumes it to be the bay of Tosa on the south side of the island of Shikoku. Given the time of the encounter—some three or four months before Van Noort's encounter with the Japanese junk, i.e., the autumn of 1600—this is very unlikely, since, by that time, the *Love* had at least already been brought round to Sakai. See *De reis*, 16. Even Okada is at a loss and eventually arrives at Uraga through a sophisticated but ultimately unnecessary formula (a=u, t=r, o=a, z=g). See Okada, *Miura anjin*, 313.

7   On September 23, 1611, two years after the Dutch had founded their factory in Hirado, Specks recorded in his journal how he had presented Matsura with a costly present "in respect of the damages and costs that his

Exelency has hitherto suffered on behalf of our Nation, having some 8 years ago expressly built and equipped a junk at his own expense, with which Jacob Quaeckernaeck and Melchior van Santvoort were brought to Patane, and obtained from his Imperial Excelency, permission [for them] to leave [Japan] and to relate the events and situation to our people [in Patani]; which had cost his Excelency more than 1,500 Catty of silver or 1,875 Reals of eight, yet had brought him not one penny of profit." See *Begin ende voortgangh vande Oost-Indische Compagnie*, 97.

8   During the Edo period there were essentially two types of passports. One was the *kokuinjō*. This document carried a black seal (*kokuin*), which could only be issued on the authority of a daimyo. The most authoritative passport, however, was a *shuinjō*, since this document carried the red seal (*shuin*) of the shogun himself.

9   The first Dutch factory in Patani had been founded in 1601. In that year, on November 7, Admiral Jacob van Neck had called at the port on his return from Macao during his second expedition to the East. He, too, had been frustrated in his attempt to get foot on the ground in Macao. Seventeen of his men, sent out to reconnoiter the place, had been intercepted by the Portuguese and beheaded as pirates. In the absence of direct trade relations with the Chinese, Van Neck had stayed on in Patani to build a Dutch factory. He had appointed his chief merchant, Daniël van der Leck, as factor, who was to promote Dutch commercial interests in the region with the help of seven assistants. Before Van Neck departed on August 23, 1602, two other Dutch fleets had arrived, and by the end of 1602, as many as three Dutch factories, employing some twenty-six men, saw to the commercial needs of the various Dutch companies. Van der Leck had stayed on in his post as chief factor right up until Van Warwijck's return from China, when he was relieved by Michielszoon. By then the three factories had been merged into one on behalf of the United East India Company. H. Terpstra, *De factory der Oostindische Compagnie te Patani*, The Hague, 1938, 1–17.

XII : THE CONCLUSION

1   Prior to the establishment of the VOC, a number of expeditions like that under the command of Mahu and De Cordes had considered Japan as a possible destination. The expedition of four ships that left Amsterdam in December 1599 under the command of Jacob Wilkens and Jacob van Neck was one of them. So was the first expedition under Jacob van Neck, which sailed in 1600, as well as the expedition under the command of Jacob van

Heemskerck, which sailed in 1601. Yet even though all of these expeditions sailed with instructions that allowed their commanders to eventually sail for Japan, reaching and establishing trade with the island country never was the main objective, and none of the expeditions ever came close to the realization of such plans. See *De reis*, part 3, 38.

2   Puyck's travel account has for the first time been reproduced in a non-Japanese language in Van Opstall's study about Verhoeff's expedition, even though a far more comprehensive reconstruction is given by Kanai Madoka. Regrettably, Puyck's awkward rendering of Japanese place-names leaves much to ask for and some of the places he visited have to be inferred. Nevertheless, a reasonably probable itinerary of the first Dutch embassy can be reconstructed. For clarity, place-names are given in the order in which they are situated along the route by which the embassy traveled (starting from Hirado), rather than the exact order in which the embassy passed each place on its way to and on its return from the shogun: Hirado (Firando), Nagoya (Naugoia), Hakata (Fayatte), Enoshima (Emosma), Jinoshima (Jonohoae), Wakamatsu (Wabramate), Ora (Orio), Kurozaki (Core), Kokura (Popolercu), Shimonoseki (Simmesacke), Mukōshima (Maqougossima), Murozumi (Merosanij), Kaminoseki (Kammesacke), Okikamuroshima (Vanoto), Kurahashi (Couranga), Kamagari (Amangij), Takasaki (Takisacke), Tadanoumi (Tadanomij), Mihara (Moye), Tomo (Thome), Shimotsui (Singay), Ushimado (Ulsamado), Murotsu (Madijo), Muroyama (Orajamme), Himeji (Famape), Akashi (Akanen), Dembō (Demgoe), Sakai (Sacay), Osaka (Osacke), Hirakata (Figatta), Fushimi (Fisonij), Miyako (Mayoque), Ōtsu (Oost), Kusatsu (Consatij), Ishibe (Esibe), Minakuchi (Mimatsz), Tsuchiyama (Soetsiau), Seki (Sacka), Sekinochizō (Sebijseho), Kameyama (Coumamme), Yokkaichi (Jokotij), Kuwana (Cuano), Miya (Meay), Narumi (Narmij), Chiryū (T'sio), Okazaki (Osacke), Fujikawa (Fongijdamme), Akasaka (Asacke), Yoshida (Yosmey), Futagawa (Stangwa), Shirasuka (Foretsche), Arai (Akai), Maisaka (Mayacke), Hamamatsu (Gamotij), Mitsuke (Maskenocko), Fukuroi (Thosera), Kakegawa (Kakamma), Nissaka (Nisacke), Kanaya (Kama), Shimada (Sumada), Fujieda (Faedseda), Okabe (Jahij), Mariko (Mardij), Fuchū (Sarigu). M. E. van Opstall, *De reis van de vloot van Pieter Willemsz. Verhoeff naar Azië 1607–1612*, part 2, Linschoten Vereniging *Werken*, vol. 74, The Hague, 1972, 345–355. Kanai Madoka, *Nichiran kōshōshi no kenkyū*, Kyoto, 1986, 99–107.

3   The last words are not those of Puyck but of Hendrick van Raay, a junior merchant who, on the return journey of the two ships, was left behind in

Patani "to purchase there all kind of Chinese wares profitable in Japan and obtainable there for a good price." Van Raay had not been part of the embassy, but since the ships that had visited Japan did not immediately return home, he was entrusted with Ieyasu's passports and letter to the Dutch prince, which he dispatched to the Heren Zeventien by way of the *Pauw* on November 8, 1610. In the appended "Narrative of the Journey to Japan in 1609," Van Raay gleefully recalls the Portuguese outrage at the Dutch privileges—"all of which annoys them intensely, and the more so because their envoys reached the Emperor's court five days before ours, but were not received. However much they reviled us saying that we were pirates and not merchants at all, and a thousand other insults, it did not help them, but they had to wait until ours were first heard and had received their answer from the Emperor, and then were likewise received." C. R. Boxer, *Portuguese Merchants and Missionaries in Feudal Japan*, I, 77.

EPILOGUE

1   The exact number of Dutch vessels (including yachts and junks) that called at Hirado between 1609 and 1640 is as follows: 1609, 2; 1611, 2; 1612, 2; 1614, 2; 1615, 5; 1616, 4; 1617, 6; 1618, 3; 1619, 9; 1620, 5; 1621, 26; 1622, 24; 1623, 7; 1624, 2; 1625, 5; 1626, 6; 1627, 7; 1628, 4; 1629, 5; 1630, 5; 1631, 5; 1632, 5; 1633, 3; 1634, 8; 1635, 8; 1636, 11; 1637, 12; 1638, 11; 1639, 13; 1640, 13. For ship names, details about tonnage, and dates of arrival and departure, see W. Z. Mulder, *Hollanders in Hirado 1597–1641*, The Hague, 1975, 263–301.

2   Japanese and European sources vary widely on the total number of Christians that fell victim to Japanese persecution after 1614. Some Japanese sources claim the number lies at 280,000, but, as Boxer points out, this figure is based on a misreading of Arai Hakuseki's *Seiyō kibun*, in which he includes apostates as well as martyrs. The true figure is more likely to lie somewhere between 6,000 and 7,000. See C.R. Boxer, *The Christian Century in Japan 1549–1650*, Los Angeles, 1967, 360–361.

Sources

Chief Dutch Sources

Frederick C. Wieder, *De reis van Mahu en de Cordes door de Straat van Magalhães naar Zuid-Amerika en Japan 1598–1600* (hereafter *De reis*) parts 1, 2, and 3, Linschoten Vereniging *Werken*, vols. 21, 22, The Hague, 1924. J. W. IJzerman, *Dirck Gerritsz. Pomp, alias Dirck Gerritsz. China: de eerste Nederlander die China en Japan bezocht 1544–1604*, Linschoten Vereniging *Werken*, vol. 9, The Hague, 1915. J. W. IJzerman, *De reis om de wereld door Olivier van Noort 1598–1601*, parts 1 and 2, Linschoten Vereniging *Werken*, vols. 27, 28, The Hague, 1926. H. Kern, *Itinerario: voyage ofte Schipvaert van Jan Huygen van Linschoten naer oost ofte Portugaels Indiën 1579–1592*, parts 1, 2, 3, 4, and 5, Linschoten Vereniging *Werken*, vols. 2, 39 and 43, The Hague, 1910–1939. A second reprint of the *Itinerario* is in H. Terpstra, *Itinerario: voyage ofte schipvaert van Jan Huygen van Linschoten naer oost ofte Portugaels Indiën 1579–1592*, parts 1 through 3, Linschoten Vereniging *Werken*, vols. 57, 58, and 60, The Hague, 1955. G. P. Rouffaer and J. W. IJzerman in *De eerste shipvaart der Nederlanders naar Oost-Indië onder Cornelis de Houtman, 1595–1597*, parts 1, 2, and 3, Linschoten Vereniging *Werken*, vols. 7, 25, and 32, The Hague, 1915–1929. J. Keuning, *De tweede schipvaart der Nederlanders naar Oost-Indië onder Jacob Cornelisz. van Neck en Wybrant Warwijck 1598–1600*, parts 1, 2, and 3, Linschoten Vereniging *Werken*, vols. 44, 45, and 46, The Hague, 1924. A. de Booy, *De derde reis van de V.O.C. naar Oost-Indië onder het beleid van Admiraal Paulus van Caerden uitgezeild in 1606*, parts 1 and 2, Linschoten Vereniging *Werken*, vols. 70 and 71, The Hague, 1968. H. A. van Foreest and A. de Booy, eds., *De vierde schipvaart der Nederlanders naar Oost-Indië onder Jacob Wilkens en Jacob van Neck (1599–1604)*, part 1 and 2, Linschoten Vereniging *Werken*, vol. 82 and 83, The Hague, 1980. M. E. van Opstall, *De reis van de vloot van Pieter Willemsz. Verhoeff naar Azië 1607–1612*, parts 1 and 2, Linschoten Vereniging *Werken*, vols. 73 and 74, The Hague, 1972. Hendrik Ottsen, *Journaal van de reis naar Zuid-Amerika 1598–1601*, Linschoten Vereniging *Werken*, vol. 16, The Hague, 1918. J. K. J. de Jonge, *De opkomst van het Nederlandsch gezag in Oost-Indië (1595–1610)*, parts 1 through 5, The Hague, 1862. H. Terpstra, *De factory der Oostindische Compagnie te Patani*, The Hague, 1938. J. Keuning, *Petrus Plancius: theoloog en geograaf 1552–1622*, Amsterdam.

CHIEF ENGLISH SOURCES

Arthur Coke Burnell and P. A. Tiele, eds. *The Voyage of John Huyghen van Linschoten to the East Indies: From the Old English Translation of 1598*, Hakluyt Society *Works*, series 1, vols. 70 and 71, London, 1850. Edward Heawood, *A History of Geographical Discovery in the Seventeenth and Eighteenth Centuries*, New York, 1969. William Corr, *Adams the Pilot: The Life and Times of Captain William Adams, 1564–1620*, Folkestone, 1995. Richard Blaker, *The Needle-Watcher*, Tokyo, 1986. Thomas Rundall, *Memorials of the Empire of Japan in the 16th and 17th Centuries*, Hakluyt Society *Works*, series 1, vol. 8, London, 1850. Edward Maunde Thompson, *Diary of Richard Cocks: Cape Merchant in the English Factory in Japan, 1615–1622*, Hakluyt Society *Works*, series 1, vols. 66, 67, London, 1883. N. Murakami and K. Murakawa, *Letters Written by the English Residents in Japan*, Tokyo, 1900. Tadashi Makino, *The Blue-Eyed Samurai: William Adams*, Ito, 1983. C. R. Boxer, *Jan Compagnie in Japan, 1600–1817: Anglo-Dutch Rivalry in Japan and Formosa*, Oxford, 1968. W. Z. Mulder, *Hollanders in Hirado, 1597–1641*, The Hague, 1975. R. Boxer, *Portuguese Merchants and Missionaries in Feudal Japan, 1543–1640*, Aldershot, 1986. Michael Cooper, *They Came to Japan: An Anthology of European Reports on Japan, 1543–1640*, Los Angeles, 1965. Michael Cooper, *Rodrigues the Interpreter: An Early Jesuit in Japan and China*, New York, 1974. Derek Massarella, *A World Elsewhere: Europe's Encounter with Japan in the Sixteenth and Seventeenth Centuries*, New Haven, 1990. Dr. Antonio de Morga, *History of the Philippine Islands: From Their discovery by Magellan in 1521 to the Beginning of the XVII Century; with Descriptions of Japan, China and Adjacent Countries*, New York, 1970.

CHIEF JAPANESE SOURCES

Makino Tadashi, *Miura anjin no sokuseki*, Tokyo, 1997. Tateishi Yu, *Ieyasu to wiriamu adamusu*, Tokyo, 1996. Philip Rogers and Koda Norimasa, *Nihon ni kita saisho no Igirisujin*, Tokyo, 1993. Makino Tadashi, *Aoi me no samurai*, Ito, 1984; Okada Akio, *Miura anjin*, Tokyo, 1984. Minagawa Saburō, *Keiseki no higashi Indo kaisha to William Adams*, Tokyo, 1983. Kikuno Matsuo, *William Adams no kōkaishi to shōkan*, Tokyo, 1977. Minagawa Saburō, *William Adams kenkyū rekishiteki tenbō to ningen Adams*, Tokyo, 1977. Ishi Ichirō, *Umi no samurai*, Tokyo, 1973. Koda Shigetomo, *Miura anjin*, Mita, 1936. Kato Sango, *Miura no anjin*, Tokyo, 1917. Iwazaki Yoshirō and Egashira Iwao, *Miura anjin to Hirado Eikoku shōkan*, Tokyo, 1960. Suganuma Teifū, *Hirado bōekishi*, Tokyo, 1892. Toyama Mikio, *Matsura-shi to Hirado bōeki*, Tokyo, 1967. Kanai Madoka, *Nichiran kōshōshi no kenkyū*, Kyoto, 1986. Huber Chieslich and Ōta Yoshiko, *Kirishitan*, Tokyo, 1999. Iwao Seiichi, *Nihon no rekishi: sakoku*, Tokyo, 1974.

CHIEF GERMAN SOURCES

Arthur Wichmann, *Dirck Gerritsz.: Ein Beitrag zur Entdeckungsgeschichte des 16ten und 17ten Jahrhunderts*, Groningen, 1899. J. C. Adelung, *Vollständiger Geschichte des Schiffahrten nach den noch größtentheils unbekannten Südländern*, Hanover, 1767. L. Hulsius, *Achte Schiffahrt oder kurtze Beschreibung etlicher Reisen, so die Holländer und Seeländer in die Ost-Indien von anno 1599 bis zum anno 1604 gethan*, Frankfurt am Main, 1608. O. Nachod, *Die Beziehungen der Niederländisch-Ostindischen Kompagnie zu Japan im 17ten Jahrhundert*, Leipzig, 1897. Martin Gusinde, *Die Feuerland Indianer: Ergebnisse meiner vier Forshungsreisen in den Jahren 1918 bis 1924, unternommen im auftrage des Ministerio de Instrucción Pública de Chile: die Halakwulup: vom Leben und Denken der Wassernomaden in west-Patagonien*, part 3, vol. 1, Mödling bei Wien, 1974.

PART 1 : DREAMS & ASPIRATIONS

A supreme, yet somewhat colored account in the English language of Spanish repression, the ensuing Dutch revolt, and the eventual establishment of the United Netherlands is given in Pieter Geyl's *History of the Dutch-Speaking Peoples, 1555–1648*, London, 2001. A more balanced and equally authoritative treatment of the subject is given by Jonathan I. Israel in his magisterial *The Dutch Republic: Its Rise, Greatness, and Fall, 1477–1806*, Oxford, 1998. For a careful study of the Leicestrian years see F. G. Oosterhoff, *Leicester and the Netherlands 1586–1587*, Utrecht, 1988. A Dutch work dealing with the first one and a half decade of Dutch involvement in the Rich Trades with the East Indies is Johan van der Woude's *Coen koopman van Heeren Zeventien: geschiedenis van den Hollanschen handel in Indië (1598–1614)*, Amsterdam, 1948.

I : THE OUTSET

A thorough treatment of the first Dutch expeditions to the north is in S. P. L'honoré Naber, *Reizen van Willem Barents, Jacob van Heemskerck, Jan Cornelisz. Rijp en anderen naar het noorden, 1594–1597*, parts 1 and 2, Linschoten Vereniging *Werken*, vols. 14 and 15, The Hague, 1917. Although not mentioned here, Van Linschoten's participation in the first two northern expeditions and his personal account is dealt with in S. P. L'honoré Naber's *Reizen van Jan Huygen van Linschoten naar het noorden (1594–1595)*, Linschoten Vereniging *Werken*, vol. 8, The Hague, 1914. Gerrit de Veer's account of all three voyages was translated into English by William Philip in 1609 and has since been edited by Charles T. Beke, and published as *A true Description of three Voyages by the*

Northeast toward Cathay and China, Undertaken by the Dutch in the Years 1594, 1595, and 1596, by Gerrit de Veer, Hakluyt Society *Works*, series 1, vol. 13, London, 1853. C. P. Burger pays particular attention to the germination of the plan for a Dutch northern expedition in his article "De Deurvaert by Noorden om naar Cathay ende China," in *Het boek*, part 18, The Hague, 1929, 209–256, 273–280. The journals kept by Willem Lodewijckszoon and other participants in the first Dutch expedition to the East Indies was first brought together by G. P. Rouffaer and J. W. IJzerman in *De eerste shipvaart der Nederlanders naar Oost-Indië onder Cornelis de Houtman, 1595–1597*, parts 1, 2, and 3, Linschoten Vereniging *Werken*, vols. 7, 25, and 32, The Hague, 1915–1929. A general treatment of the expedition is given by J. C. Mollema, *De eerste schipvaart der Hollanders naar Oost-Indië, 1595–1597*, The Hague, 1935.

II : THE CONTEXT

Van Linschoten's letter to his parents is reproduced in J. W. IJzerman, *Dirck Gerritsz. Pomp, alias Dirck Gerritsz. China*, Linschoten Vereniging *Werken*, vol. 9, The Hague, 1915, 8–13. John Saris' praise of the *Itinerario* is quoted in Ernest Mason Satow, *The Voyage of Captain John Saris to Japan, 1613*, Hakluyt Society *Works*, series 2, vol. 5, London, 1900, 188. Petrus Plancius' scientific contribution to the early expeditions is described at length in J. Keuning, *Petrus Plancius: theoloog en geograaf 1552–1622*, Amsterdam, 1946, 67–138. Plancius' request of 1594 to the States General for a patent on his sea chart with waxing latitudes is quoted in Keuning, *Pertrus Plancius*, 90. Thomas Hood's puzzlement at the principle of Mercator's maps with waxing latitudes is quoted in E. G. R. Taylor, *The Haven Finding Art: A History of Navigation from Odysseus to Captain Cook*, London 1958, 222. Albert Haeyen's struggle with the same is quoted in Keuning's *Pertrus Plancius*, 91. Plancius' instructions for the first and second expeditions in search of the Northeast Passage are reproduced in Gerrit de Veer's *Reizen van Willem Barents, Jacob van Heemskerck, Jan Cornelisz. Rijp en anderen naar het noorden 1594–1597*, part 2, Linschoten Vereniging *Werken*, vol. 15, The Hague 1917, 194 and 218. His instructions for the third expedition have not survived, even though the aforesaid work does contain extracts from the journal Willem Barents kept during that expedition. Plancius' revised memorandum for the navigation of the Southwest Passage has been reproduced in full in J. K. J. de Jonge's *De opkomst van het Nederlands gezag in Oost-Indië*, part 2, 185–201; see also Keuning, *Pertrus Plancius*, 100–107, 120–135, 139–142. Details on Plancius' financial involvement in various expeditions are given in the same work, 139; see also J. Keuning, *De tweede schipvaart der Nederlanders naar Oost-Indië onder Jacob Cornelisz. van Neck en Wybrant Warwijck 1598–1600*, part 3, Linschoten Vereniging *Werken*, vol. 46, The Hague, 1924, xlvi–xlix.

III : The Outfit

The request by Van der Haegen and Van der Veken to the States of Holland is reproduced in *De reis*, part 1, 105. The personal background of the participants and the degree of their financial involvement in the venture are dealt with in the same volume, 3–18. So are the backgrounds of the fleet's commanders and officers, 69–99. For the little that is known about Jacques Mahu, see E. van Meteren, *Memorien der Belgische ofte Nederlandsche historie*, Delft, 1599, 407; and J. F. le Petit, *La grande chronique de Hollande*, part 2, Dordrecht, 1601, 699. Adams' early life is described in William Corr's, *Adams the Pilot: The Life and Times of Captain William Adams, 1564–1620*, Folkestone, 1995, 12–17. For an example of Drake's secretiveness, see Harry Kelsey, *Sir Francis Drake: The Queen's Pirate*, New Haven, 1998, 125. The original Dutch translation of Nuno da Silva's description of the Strait of Magellan is in J. W. IJzerman, *Itinerario*, part 5, 296–297. An English, but incomplete, translation of Van Linschoten's *Reysgheschrift* appeared in England in 1598. It was from this work that Hakluyt took Da Silva's account for his second and enlarged edition of his *Principal Navigations*, ed. 1600, III, 742–748. The early English translation, which has been quoted here, is in Zelia Nuttal, *New Light on Drake: A Collection of Documents Relating to his Voyage of Circumnavigation 1577–1580*, London, 1914, 258–259. The States General's view on the expedition's value ("Register der Resolutien van de Staten-Generaal der Verenigde Nederlanden van het Jaar 1597") is quoted in Wieder, *De reis*, part 1, 107. The great quantity of shipped armaments and military equipment is listed in *De reis*, part 1, 30–31. This data is largely based on the statements by Jacob Dirckszoon van Purmerlant during his interrogation by De Velasco; see *Dirck China*, 60–61. For details about the military aspect of Van Noort's expedition, see J. W. IJzerman, *Olivier van Noort*, part 1, Linschoten Vereniging *Werken*, vol. 27, The Hague, 1926, 34–35, 47–50. The route by which news of Van Noort's boastings finally reached the governor of Peru are recorded in J. W. IJzerman, *Dirck China*, 54, 124–125.

PART 2 : TRIALS & TRIBULATIONS

For a vivid description of the working-life on board 16th and 17th century Dutch merchantmen, see Herman Ketting, *Leven, werk en rebellie aan boord van Oost Indiëvaarders*, Amsterdam, 2002. A detailed treatment of penalties aboard Dutch merchants is given in J. R. Bruijn and E. S. van Eyck van Helsinga, eds., *Muiterij: oproer en berechting op schepen van de VOC*, Haarlem, 1980. See also C.R. Boxer's *The Tragic History of the Sea, 1589–1622*, Cambridge, 1959, 73–93; and, *The Dutch Seaborne Empire, 1600–1800*, London, 1965, 9–21.

IV : THE CROSSING

The encounter with the English squadron off Cape S. Vincente is briefly mentioned by Dirck Pomp during his interrogation in Santiago and described at length by the six crewmembers of *The Gospel* during their interrogation in Callao; see IJzerman, *Dirck China*, 31, 72–75. The events in the Cape Verde Islands are based on Barent Janszoon Potgieter's version of events as described by him in the *Wijdtloopigh verhael van 't gene de vijf schepen (die int jaer 1598 tot Rotterdam toegherust werden, om door de Straet Magellana haren handel te drijven), wedervaren is, tot den 7 September 1599*; see *De reis*, part 1, 151–164. Some details about the negotiations between Mahu and the local governor, and the role played by Dirck Pomp are described at length by Pomp during his interrogation by De Molina in Santiago; see IJzerman, *Dirck China*, 32–33. Adams' account of the dispute between pilots and captains at Praia is only mentioned by him in his letter to his wife; see Rundall, *Memorials of Imperial Japan*, 33. The stay at Cape Lopez and De Weert's visit to the native village is described by Potgieter; see *De reis*, part 1, 168–176. It is also mentioned in some detail by Pomp and his men during their interrogations in Chile and Peru; see IJzerman's *Dirck China*, 33, 68–77. The only source for the events on Annobon is Potgieter's account; see *De reis*, part 1, 176–180. The loss of the *Faith*'s main mast during the crossing of the Atlantic is recorded by Potgieter; see *De reis*, part 1, 180; as is the effect of the reduction in men's rations on board the *Faith*, 181. Adams' description of the same effect on board the *Hope* is in Rundall, *Memorials*, 34. The ominous change in the color of the sea near Río de la Plata is also described by Potgieter; see *De reis*, part 1, 181–182; as are the effects of the mysterious illness that afflicted the men on the *Fidelity*, part 1, 182.

V : THE PASSAGE

The loss and efforts to salvage the *Faith*'s anchor are recorded by Potgieter; see *De reis*, part 1, 184. Jan Outgherszoon's description of the difficult passage of the Second Narrow is taken from his *Nieuwe, volmaeckte beschryvinghe der vervaerlijcker Strate Magellani, waar in van mijl tot mijl, van Baye tot Baye, tot nut der Schippers ende Stuerlieden d'opdoeningen vlytighlijck verthoont, ende streckingen beschreven worden, door Iaj Outghersz. van Enchuysen*; see *De reis*, part 2, 58. The burial of Jan Dircksz. van Dort on the smallest of the Penguin Islands (Santa Martha) is recorded by Potgieter; see *De reis*, part 1, 184. De Cordes' decision not to sail on but take in victuals shortly after their departure from the Penguin Islands is recorded by Adams both in his letter to his wife and in his letter to his "unknowne frinds and countri-men"; see Rundall, *Memorials*, 19, 34. The rounding of Cape Froward is recorded by Potgieter; see *De reis*, part 1,

186. The most detailed description of Cordes Bay and the hardships suffered during the four months spent amidst its protection is given by Potgieter, *De reis*, 186–193. The hardships suffered during the wintering in Cordes Bay and the scramble for food are dwelt on by Dirck Pomp's men during their interrogation by De Velasco; see *Dirck China*, 77–78. Given the purpose of his work, Outgherszoon's description is mainly limited to the bay's physical characteristics, although he does mention the presence of wood, mussels, and fresh water; see *De reis*, part 2, 63. Adams is least specific about the bay, only mentioning in his letter to his wife that it was situated on the north side of the strait, four leagues from Elizabeth Bay. See Rundall, *Memorials*, 34. The execution of Jacob Willemszoon is mentioned by Potgieter; see *De reis*, part 1, 189, as well as by Jacob Dirckszoon and Adriaen Dirckszoon, although their statements are not altogether consistent; see *Dirck China*, 78. Jeurian van Bockholt's death is recorded by Potgieter; see *De reis*, part 1, 189. The native ambush is also described by Potgieter; see *De reis*, part 1, 190–192. It is also mentioned by Dirck Pomp during his interrogation; see *Dirck China*, 33. The farcical ceremony on the banks of Ridder's Bay is described by Potgieter; see *De reis*, part 1, 194. The poor state of provisions is described in considerable detail by Pomp's men during their interrogation; see *Dirck China*, 80. The loss of *The Gospel*'s bowsprit is mentioned by Potgieter; see *De reis*, part 1, 197–198, and by carpenter Adriaen Dirckszoon, who was ferried over from the *Faith* to assist; see *Dirck China*, 79.

VI : FAITH

The death of skipper Nicolaes Ysbrantszoon is recorded by Potgieter; see *De reis*, 198–199. So is the death of Sander Sanderszoon, 211. The arduous stay in the various bays on the south side of the strait's western entrance is described both in the accounts of Potgieter and that of Outgherszoon, although the latter is mainly limited to nautical aspects; see *De reis*, part 1, 201–218, and part 2, 65–68; see also J. C. Adelung, *Vollständiger Geschichte des Schiffahrten nach den noch größtentheils unbekanten Südländern*, 176. The incipient mutiny aboard the *Faith* is described by Potgieter; see *De reis*, part 1, 205–209. The encounter between De Weert and Van Noort is described both by Potgieter, *De reis*, part 1, 219–229, and by Van Noort himself in his journal *Beschryvinghe vande voyagie om den geheelen werelt cloot ghedaen door Olivier van Noort van Utrecht*; see *Olivier van Noort*, part 1, 41–44, 171–172. Van Noort's journal also mentions the encounter with one of Mahu's men at Cape Lopez, 8–9. For Van Noort's version of the earlier massacre on the Penguin Islands; see *Olivier van Noort*, part 1 34–35. The *Faith*'s failure to pass the narrow at Carlos III Island is described by Potgieter, as well as Van Noort; see *De reis*, 221–222, and *Olivier van Noort*, 43–44. De Weert and his men's forced stay on St. Martha and the encounter with the Indian woman is described at length by Potgieter; see *De reis*, part 1, 228–236. For another perspective on the confrontation between the Europeans and the indigenous people of the Patagonian peninsula; see Martin Gusinde, *Die Feuerland Indianer: Ergebnisse meiner vier Forschungsreisen in den Jahren 1918 bis 1924*, vol. 3, part 1, Mödling bei Wien, 1974, 24. Nicolaes Blieck's execution is also recorded by Potgieter, *De reis*, part 1, 238–239. So is the encounter with the English merchantmen, 243. The return of the *Faith* is recorded by the contemporary E. M. van Meteren in his *Historie der Nederlanden*, The Hague, 1614, vol. 23, 466.

VII : FIDELITY

Mees Sanderszoon's account of the *Fidelity*'s stay in the Chiloé Archipelago and his day-by-day account of the raid and occupation of Castro is in *De reis*, 285–299. Other Dutch references to the interlude are in I. de Laet's *Nieuwe wereldt ofte beschrijvinghe van West-Indien*, Leiden, 1625, 369–370; and Arnoldus Montanus' *De nieuwe en onbekende Wereld of beschrijving van Amerika en 't Zuidland*, Amsterdam, 570. A Spanish, though highly contracted version of events is in Crescente Errázuriz, *Seis años de la historia de Chile 1598–1605*, part 1, Santiago de Chile, 1881, 281–301. The Dutch translation of the aforesaid passages is in *De reis*, 266–285. A brief reference to the negotiations between De Cordes and Ruiz de Pliego is made in Claudio Gay's *Historia física y política de Chile*, Paris, 282–283. For a detailed and highly insightful description of the Spanish and Portuguese contest for domination in the Moluccas and the status quo at the time of the *Fidelity*'s arrival in the archipelago see J. Keuning, *De tweede schipvaart der Nederlanders naar Oost-Indië onder Jacob Cornelisz. van Neck en Wybrant Warwijck 1598–1600*, part 3, Linschoten Vereniging *Werken*, vol. 46, The Hague, 1924, xxvi–xxxviii. The same work contains a detailed account of Wijbrand van Warwijck and Jacob van Heemskerck's arrival at Ternate and their reception by the island's sultan, 104–135. The *Fidelity*'s arrival at Ternate and Franck van der Does' warning to De Cordes are recorded by L. Hulsius in his *Achte schiffart*, 46. Also see Arthur Wichmann's *Dirck Gerritsz.*, 43–44, 62. The statements of skipper Anthonis Anthoniszoon and gunner Aert Anthoniszoon to the Council of Rotterdam, given on November 19, 1603, concerning the events following the *Fidelity*'s arrival at Tidore, are reproduced in *De reis*, 304–309; see also J. K. J. de Jonge, *De opkomst van het Nederlandsch gezag in Oost-Indië*, part 2, 479, or Nachod, *Die Beziehungen der Niederländisch-Ostindischen Kompagnie zu Japan*, 96. The account of the *Fidelity*'s last survivor, Joris Adriaenszoon, is recorded by Admiral Matelieff in his "Instructions and Journals of the Brazilian and East Indian voyages since April 21, 1623 to August 1681," which is also reproduced in *De reis*, 311–312.

VIII : THE GOSPEL

For a general history of Chile at the end of the 16th century; see John A. Crow, *The Epic of Latin America*, Los Angeles, 1992, 329–344. Jacob Dirckszoon van Purmerlant's account of Pomp's initial contacts with Jerónimo de Molina is in *Dirck China*, 92–93. The same work also contains: a detailed account of De Velasco's interrogation of the six crewmembers, 54–90; a transcript of De Molina's interrogation of Dirck Pomp, 28–41; and De Velasco's "Comprehensive Relation of Reports on Pirates" to the king of Spain, 124–157. De Quiñones' missive of November 5, 1599, to Santiago's council is reproduced in Errázuriz, *Historia de Chile*, part 1, 123, and only briefly referred to in *Dirck China*, 49. The account by Don Diego Rodríguez de Valdés of Van Heemskerck's arrival at Río de la Plata, and his report of what he had heard from Salvador Correa de Sá, the governor of Rio de Janeiro, is quoted in full in Hendrik Ottsen, *Journaal van de reis naar Zuid-Amerika 1598–1601*, Linschoten Vereniging *Werken*, vol. 16, 121–165. De Ibarra's account of Van Noort's raid on Valparaíso, as recorded by De Velasco in his report to the king of Spain, is in *Dirck China*, 140–150. Van Noort's account of the interrogation of Francisco de Ibarra and Juan de Sandoval and the interception and gist of Dirck Pomp's letters are in *Olivier van Noort*, part 1, 58–66, 177. De Velasco's letter to the king of Spain concerning the dispatch of *The Gospel*'s crew is reproduced in full in *Dirck China*, 157–158, as are Plancius' report of Van Purmerlant's statement, 91–94, and Dirck China's report "On the Situation of Chile and what power the Spaniards have in that Country," 98–104. The fate of the returning men is recorded in Levinus Hulsius, *Achte Schiffahrt: Kurze Beschreibungen, was sich mit den Holländern und Seeländern, in den Ost Indien, 1599–1603 zugetragen*, Frankfurt, 1605, 57.

IX : HOPE & LOVE

The only known source for the *Love*'s first landing on the Chilean mainland (Península de Taitao) after leaving the Strait of Magellan is William Adams' letters, chiefly his letter to his wife; see Rundall, *Memorials*, 19, 35. The landing and killing of Van Beuningen and his men is also described by Adams in both of his letters; see Rundall, *Memorials*, 21–22, 35–36. The gruesome fate of the remains of Van Beuningen (though mistakenly identified as Simon de Cordes) and his men at the hands of the Araucanians (Mapuche) as recounted to Olivier van Noort by the captain of the *Buen Jésus*, Francisco de Ibarra, is in IJzerman's *Olivier van Noort*, 61. Also see Errázuriz, *Historia de Chile*, part 1, 156–158. All that is known about the real fate of Admiral Simon de Cordes is again only provided by Adams in his two letters home from Japan; see Rundall, *Memorials*, 22, 36. The Spanish account of the negotiations between Simon de Cordes Jr. and Antonio

Recio de Soto are in Errázuriz, *Historia de Chile*, 123–128, 156–163. The Dutch version of events, though presented in English, is in Adams' letter to his wife; see Rundall, *Memorials*, 36. A condensed version of the same events is given in *Dirck China*, 48–53. Antonio Recio de Soto's report to the viceroy in Peru of the *Hope* and *Love*'s arrival at Santa María is recorded by the latter in his report to the king of Spain; see *Dirck China*, 134–137. Van Noort's own account of what he had learned from Francisco de Ibarra is in IJzerman's *Olivier van Noort*, 61–63. De Quiñones's spurious report to the viceroy of November 25, 1599, is recorded in Errázuriz, *Historia*, part 1, 163; see also *Dirck China*, 52–53, 136. Adams' account of the decision of the ships' council to follow Dirck Gerritszoon Pomp's advice and sail for Japan, the loss of the *Hope*, and the *Love*'s arrival in Japan are mentioned in both his letters; see Rundall, *Memorials*, 23, 37–38.

PART 3 : HONORS & REWARDS

For a comprehensive and authoritative treatment of Japanese history in the English language; see *The Cambridge History of Japan*, Cambridge, 6 vols., 1999. A considerably earlier but just as authoritative work is James Murdoch's *A History of Japan*, 3 vols., Kobe, 1903, as well as George Sansom's epic *A History of Japan*, also in 3 volumes, Tokyo, 1974. Another major work is Marius B. Jansen's *The Making of Modern Japan*, Cambridge, 2000. The Christian period in Japan is treated at great length and in wonderful detail in R. Boxer's *The Christian Century in Japan, 1540–1650*, Los Angeles, 1967. His equally thorough work *The Great Ship from Amacon: Annals of Macao and the Old Japan Trade*, Lisbon, 1959, gives a magisterial account of the pivotal role played by the Portuguese in the Sino-Japanese silk trade.

X : THE ARRIVAL

The *Love*'s arrival in the bay of Usuki and the treatment of her crew by Ōta's men are related by Adams in both his letters; see Rundall, *Memorials*, 23–24, 38. The Jesuits' account of her arrival is in Diego de Couto, *Da Ásia década XII*, Lisbon, 1788, 447–454. An English translation of the same passage in De Couto's work is in William F. Sinclair's *The Travels of Pedro Teixeira; with his "Kings of Harmuz" and Extracts from His Kings of Persia*, Hakluyt Society *Works*, series 2, vol. 9, London, 1902, lxxvi–lxxxii. A Dutch translation is given in *De reis*, part 3, 129–137. A reference to the interrogation of Adams and the other sailors by Rodríguez is given in Fernão Guerreiro's *Relāçao annual das coias que fizeram os padres da Companhia de Iesus nas suas missões de Iapão, China, nos anos de 1600 a 1609*, part 1, 107–108. A condensed transcript of the same passage is in S. J. François Solier, *Histoire ecclésiatique des isles et royaumes du Japon*, Paris, 1629, part 2, 168–169. Rodríguez' letter to Alessandro Valignano is quoted by Valignano in a report dispatched from Nagasaki on December 20, 1600; see L. Delplace, *Le Catholicisme au Japon*, vol. 2, Brusselles, 1910, 80–81 The tenor of Valignano's letter to Terazawa and his subsequent receipt of a letter from Ōta Shigemasa is given in De Couto, *Da Ásia*, 448. So is the detailed inventory of the *Love*'s cargo, 448–449. The conclusions drawn by Ōta Shigemasa, referred to as *tono* (lord), is in Fernão Guerreiro, *Relāçao annual*, 107. Adams' encounter with Ieyasu is described by himself at length in both his letters; Rundall, *Memorials*, 24–25, 39–40. Jesuit intelligence about the fate of the *Love*'s cargo after the ship's arrival in Japan is mentioned in De Couto's *Da Ásia*, 452; and in Guerreiro's *Relāçao annual*, 108. The same subject is dealt with at length by Okada Akiō in his superb work *Miura anjin*, 31–34. The delay due to bad weather during the *Love*'s voyage from Sakai to Uraga is mentioned by Adams in his first letter; Rundall, *Memorials*, 27. The account of the mutiny amongst the *Love*'s crew is in Adams' first letter; Rundall, *Memorials*, 27.

XI : THE FRUITION

The description of the activities of Jan Joosten van Lodensteyn and Melchior van Santvoort is largely based on their own correspondence; see *De reis*, part 3, 87–119; see also Ernest M. Satow, *The Voyage of Captain John Saris to Japan*, series 2, vol. 5, 102–103, 105–106. Adams' stint as a weapons instructor is recorded in the contemporary Japanese record *Aichū ryūon kiryaku*, quoted in Okada, *Miura anjin*, 316. The only surviving record to mention the wreckage of the *Love* is the *Nagasaki komonjo*, which mentions that "on her way there [Edo], she [the *Love*] was overtaken by a gale at Uraga and wrecked." See *De reis*, part 3, 146. Adams' construction of the two Western-style ships on behalf of Ieyasu is mentioned by Adams in his first letter home; Rundall, *Memorials*, 28. The ships and their method of launching are also described in the contemporary Japanese historical record *Keichō kenbu-shū*, quoted in Okada, *Miura anjin*, 34. Adams' estate in Hemi is mentioned both by himself in his first letter home, Rundall, *Memorials*, 30, and in a number of contemporary Japanese records, such as the *Aichū ryūon kiryaku*, which puts it at 220 *koku* and the *Genroku somo kunisato*, which puts it at 250 *koku*, both quoted in Okada, *Miura anjin*, 68. Details about Adams' marriage (which are disputed by Okada) are in Kato Sango, *Miura no anjin*, Tokyo, 1917, 172–173. Van Noort's encounter with the Japanese junk off Borneo and her captain's news of the *Love* and her crew's fate is in IJzerman, *Olivier van Noort*, part 1, 129. The foreign trade on Hirado and the stimulative role of the Matsura clan in it is described in Toyama Mikio's *Matsura shi to Hirado bōeki*, Tokyo, 1987, 137–192. Matelieff de Jonge's siege of Malacca and the subsequent sea battle with the Portuguese fleet off Cape Rachado is beautifully described by C. R. Boxer in his *Portuguese Merchants and Missionaries in Feudal Japan, 1543–1640*, I, 20–29. Quaeckernaeck and Van Santvoort's arrival in Patani is mentioned by Victor Sprinckel in his letter to Adams, which is reproduced in *De reis*, part 3, 85–86. Jacques L'Hermite de Jonge's letter to his father (in which he describes in detail Quaeckernaeck's arrival on Matelieff's flagship, his subsequent appointment, and tragic end) is printed in *Begin ende Voortgangh vande Oost-Indische Compagnie*, Amsterdam, 1644–1646, 145–187, and also reproduced in *De reis*, part 3, 121–123.

XII : The Conclusion

The effect of the expedition's failure on the fortunes of Van der Veken and Van der Haegen is detailed in *De reis*, part 1, 6–8. Matelieff's encounter at Macao with the remainder of the Portuguese fleet, his encounter with the Japanese pirates, and his personal account of events are given in Boxer's *Portuguese Merchants and Missionaries*, I, 29–33. The exploits of Paulus van Caerden's expedition are recorded in detail in A. de Booy's *De derde reis van de V.O.C. naar Oost-Indië onder het beleid van Admiraal Paulus van Caerden uitgezeild in 1606*, parts 1 and 2, The Hague, 1968. Dirck Gerritsz. Pomp's last voyage home on Matelieff's ship, the *Oranje*, is recorded in the same work, part 1, 32, part 2, 137. Melchior van Santvoort's second visit to Patani is recorded in *De reis*, part 3, 38–39; see also H. Terpstra, *De factory der Oostindische Compagnie te Patani*, 31, 48, 50. Victor Sprinckel's letters to Tokugawa Ieyasu and to William Adams are both reproduced in *De reis*, part 3, 81–86. Admiral Verhoeff's original instructions are reproduced in Margaretha Elisabeth van Opstall's *De reis van de vloot van Pieter Willemsz. Verhoeff naar Azië 1607–1612*, part 1, 182–190. The arrival of the *Goede Hoope* with new instructions following Verhoeff's departure from Johore is recorded in the journal of Verhoeff's expedition, kept by Johan de Moelre and Jacques Lefebvre, which is also reproduced in Opstall's work, part 1, 255; as are Verhoeff's subsequent missive to the ships' council of the *Roode Leeuw met Pylen* and the *Griffioen*, part 2, 327–33; Verhoeff's instructions, 182–190; and the surviving journal of the *Griffioen*, 332–344. Pessoa's arrival in Nagasaki on the *Nossa Senhora da Graça* and his conspiring with Hasegawa to outwit the Dutch are described by Boxer in *The Christian Century*, 271–275. Nicolaes Puyck's account of his embassy to Tokugawa Ieyasu, and the latter's memo to the Heren Zeventien are both in Opstall's *De reis van de Vloot van Pieter Willemsz. Verhoeff naar Azië 1607–1612*, part 2, 345–363 and 355–363.

INDEX